C000070124

SNOW BOYS

SIMON DOYLE

SNOW BOYS

SDPRESS
LONGFORD

SD Press

3 5 7 9 10 8 6 4 2

Copyright © Simon Doyle, 2023

The right of Simon Doyle to be identified as the author of this Work
has been asserted by him in accordance with the Copyright, Designs
and Patents Act 1988

All rights reserved

First published in 2023 by
SD Press
Unit 1A Heatherview Business Park, Athlone Road SSC8117
Longford, Co Longford N39KD82, Ireland

Paperback ISBN 978 1 9163838 6 9
Hardcover ISBN 978 1 9163838 5 2

This publication may not be used, reproduced, stored or transmitted in
any way, in whole or in part, without the express written permission
of the author. Nor may it be otherwise circulated in any form of binding
or cover other than that in which it has been published and without a
similar condition imposed on subsequent users or purchasers

All characters in this publication are fictitious and any similarity
to real persons, alive or dead, is coincidental

Cover layout by SD Press
Cover art by peters_paintpalette

A CIP catalogue record of this book
is available from the British Library and the
Library of Trinity College Dublin

Typeset in Caslon Pro by SD Press

For all the geeks who dared to dream.

And for my American friends who put up
with my British-English spellings.

ALSO BY SIMON DOYLE

Runaway Train
Runaway Skies
Runaway Ridge

CHAPTER 1

DEAN

Ireland has only two seasons. Winter and not-winter.

The difference between the two is about six degrees Celsius. Which isn't a lot. But it makes all the difference when I'm trying to decide which coat to wear to school today. Mum used to say, "It only rained twice this week. First for three days, then for four days."

It was true. Since mid-September, the rain hadn't stopped. I was sick of arriving at school looking like a wrung-out sponge. My hair, which you could politely call dirty-blond, would turn to ocean-brown when it got wet, and it clung to my forehead in clumps and dripped rainwater onto my black-rimmed glasses that kept slipping down my nose.

This morning, the rain was at a level eight on a scale of T-shirt to Noah's Ark. The trees on the street outside were bending under the weight of the storm, and the bus stop was at the end of the block. I put on my heavy parka that zipped up from mid-thigh to throat and pulled the fur-lined hood over my head.

"Breakfast," Mum said when I came downstairs. She was standing at the hallway mirror, tying her hair into a knot at the back of her head. She was lucky. She just had to get as far as the car in the driveway.

"I'll be late."

"Then take an apple, Dean. You need to stop eating your lunch on the bus."

"I eat it on the bus because it's too tasty to wait until lunch-time," I smiled.

"Remind me to give you oatmeal and water tomorrow."

"Yum."

I opened the front door and held it against the invasive push of the wind. November was that time between crisp leaves and the thick, burnt skies of winter.

By the time I got to the bus stop, you could have mistaken me for a skinned squirrel. My parka glistened like violet flesh and the faux fur around the hood had wilted into knots.

Huddled with Ashley under a very pink umbrella, Tony pointed and laughed. I met them the day we moved to Paskill, Cork last year. They'd been sitting on the wall at the end of the street watching as we hauled boxes in from the back of a moving van.

"Welcome to Roadkill," Ashley said when, in a moment of unusual bravery, I waved at them. I wasn't brave around people very often. It hadn't been raining that day. It was not-winter. T-shirt weather.

"Population: four jocks, one emo, two geeks and—where do you fall on the social spectrum?" Tony said.

"I don't fit on the social spectrum."

Ashley and Tony looked at each other and then, as one, said, "Join the club."

So ~~Paskill~~ Roadkill, Cork now had a population of four

jocks, one emo, two geeks and three misfits.

Mum invited them in for pizza that day, knowing I never would. I told you I wasn't very brave, right? And although I still felt out of place and out of sorts, at least I now had two friends to be out of sorts with.

The wind caught Ashley's umbrella and one of the spokes rapped Tony on the head. "Karma," I said, pulling my hood tighter around my face against the icy rain. We stepped back from the edge of the path as a passing car sprayed puddle water into the air.

The bus was warm and damp when it arrived, and Tony and Ashley played Tic Tac Toe in the window fog. They weren't a couple. Tony said he was aroflux and Ashley refused to identify herself with any preference. "We should put all labels in a box and burn it," she said a few weeks after we met.

"But without labels," I said, "how am I going to know who's gay?" Here's the thing. I'd come out to them during study group only because Tony was quite vocal about being aromantic. Sexuality didn't seem to matter to them.

Ashley snorted. "They're called dating apps."

They made coming out seem like no big deal, even though it was. I knew I was gay since I was eleven, but I could never say it out loud. Saying it made it real, and the reality was that being gay in a small town in the extreme southern butt of Ireland was a terrifying and lonely prospect. Being fifteen had its own woes; there was no need to add to that with a special brand of queerness. And I wasn't sure how my parents would take the news.

But Tony's outspoken manner and Ashley's righteous condemnation for all forms of categorisation from sexuality to breakfast cereals ("There's no such thing as kids' cereal. Calling it that won't stop adults from eating that chocolatey goodness.") gave me the strength to label myself before anyone else could, if only to my closest friends. I pulled them into the closet with me and they helped me keep my secret. It was better that way.

As the bus pulled into the school grounds and a sheet of lightning brightened the dark November morning, Ashley asked to copy Tony's homework for one of the few classes they shared, and then she kissed us both on the cheek before saying, "See you at study group later?" Her class rotation differed from ours and her lunch break was thirty minutes after mine and Tony's so we only shared fifteen minutes together. Which was hardly enough time to catch up on all of Tony's gossip. Tony had a lot of gossip.

We slouched off to class, glad to be out of the storm but suffering the ill effects of a sweaty bus ride. Tony's shoes squelched as he walked down the corridor and one of the younger kids laughed until he scowled at him. Tony didn't care about anything. That's one of the things that drew me to them. Tony was so upbeat he could turn the end of the world into a good day. Ashley wouldn't call it the end of the world, of course—that would be labelling it—but she, too, would put a positive spin on it. "No more trig." Maths was her Achilles' heel. "Maths can go screw itself with a sharpened pencil," she said, more than once.

I didn't know what she found so difficult about maths. It was structured. It was ordered. You knew where you were with maths. Unlike English or philosophy where there was no right answer, maths had your back. It said: this is the correct answer, and it cannot be changed. You do not mess with Pythagoras.

Maths was linear, just like I considered my brain to be. One comes before two comes before three, and it was never out of sequence. The world could crumble to ash but as long as one plus one equalled two, I would survive.

Catch a load of this prodigy, sitting at the front of maths class trying to explain constancy to the teacher who either didn't understand how my mind worked or didn't understand maths. When I was ten, my maths teacher marked an answer wrong on a paper despite it being correct.

"You worked it out wrong."

"I still got it right. My working-out is correct."

"But it's not the way it should be done."

I took a piece of chalk and recreated the sum on the board, explaining my reasoning, and how I arrived at the answer, but the teacher was unmoved.

"That's not the way I taught you."

"But my way is faster. And more accurate."

"You got nineteen out of twenty, Dean. You still got an A."

"But my answer is correct."

"Do you want me to give you twenty out of twenty?"

"No, sir," I had said, pushing my glasses up the bridge of my nose with a chalk-coated knuckle. "I want you to accept that my reasoning is correct."

"I didn't teach it that way."

But that wasn't the point. I let it go. After that, I tried to conform my mathematical reasoning to the school curriculum, even though I knew they had an immature understanding of mathematics.

Numbers might be constant, but teachers weren't.

Another constant was school society. Tony and Ashley

hadn't been kidding when they said Paskill had a population of jocks, emos and geeks. It didn't matter what class I was in. I could see the clear division of the pecking order from day one. Sports jocks ruled the stratosphere. You could tell them from the thickness of their thighs and their brains. They said stuff that made me feel smarter just by being around them.

There was one exception. Ben Hunter.

Ben was the tallest boy in class. He was already sixteen. He played on the school rugby and basketball teams, and he played football on the grass behind the cafeteria at lunchtime even though Clannloch Community School didn't have a football team. Schools in Ireland were either rugby schools or footie schools. They couldn't be both. I was sure that was a rule written down by Douglas Hyde, the first president of Ireland. It made total sense.

But Ben Hunter could string a sentence together, and his knuckles didn't graze the dirty tiled floors of the school corridors when he walked. Not that I had ever had much of a conversation with him. Misfits don't mix well with jocks. You'd sooner put a cat in doggie daycare and expect better results.

Ben was the envy of every kid in school. His girlfriend, Erin, was his most ardent supporter. She sat on the sidelines of every game with homemade placards and foam fingers. And rumour had it that she was taking the pill. As if that was anything to boast about. Ireland didn't really have cheerleaders the way American high school movies did, but Erin McNally was Ben Hunter's one-person cheer team.

Gimme a B.

Gimme a break.

Ben sat at the back of the class with the other jocks, except in History where he sat up front. The history teacher was also the basketball coach. History was my second favourite class, so I put myself in the front row between Alex Janey and Ben Hunter. Not because Ben made me feel faint, even though he did, but if I wasn't in the front row, the teacher wouldn't look at me. When talk of three-pointers got out of hand, I tried my best to bring the conversation back to the Irish civil war or the potato famine.

Alex Janey said, "Did your spuds bounce back inside your body when they dropped?"

And Ben snickered.

And the teacher said, "Talking about bouncing balls, Janey, you need to watch your dribbling. You can't get caught out against West Meath next week."

Alex Janey's face went red. And I looked back at my textbook instead of anywhere else.

At the end of the day, when the downpour had been reduced to a level five—not quite wetsuit weather but waders are advised—I slinked out of class with the final bell and waited by the exit for my friends. Study group wasn't a real thing. It meant we could go to Grainger's Coffee Stop on Main Street and enjoy some time together before we had to go home. At the start of our transition year, when Ashley took different classes, it was her way of keeping the gang together. Transition year in Ireland is where you start to study fewer academic classes and *transition* into life. Like what we'd already been studying was useless?

Our order was always the same. Caramel macchiato for her, chai frappe for Tony, and a flat white for me to match my extraordinary personality. I'd occasionally add a sugar packet just to spice things up.

Today, listening to Tony talk about food technology class as if making flan was the greatest thing ever, my thoughts turned to Christmas. It was just over a month away and Mum was already talking about booking a restaurant for Christmas dinner instead of cooking it herself. She said that every year, but we never did. I figured it was just something she said that got her through the trauma of the run-up to Christmas.

"Secret Santa's coming up soon," Ashley said.

"Are we actually doing that? I thought Mr Dobbins was just joking."

"Dobbins doesn't joke about Secret Santa," Tony said. "I heard if you don't participate, you flunk English."

"There's a five-Euro limit," Ashley said. "It's not like it's going to break you."

"What do you buy for some random jock that you know nothing about?" I asked.

"Who cares? Buy them a chew toy. Nobody's going to know who it came from. That's why it's called Secret Santa."

"But the point of Secret Santa is for everyone to guess who bought what. And I don't want to be associated with that kind of aggression."

"You're just scared of getting involved with your classmates," Ashley said. She curled her finger in her empty glass to pick up some of the macchiato residue. "I don't know what you're so scared of. Maybe you'll buy a gift for some boy, and he'll fall in love with you. Maybe Secret Santa is your origin story."

"My origin story?"

"Every hero has one," Tony said. "Spider-Man got bitten by

a spider. Batman had a healthy bank balance and dead parents."

"Spoiler alert," Ashley said. "But he's right. Maybe Secret Santa is yours. This town isn't that small. Someone out there must want a nerdy maths kid with glasses that are too big for his face and a smile that could melt butter."

I pushed my glasses back up my nose and said, "Piss off."

But I laughed. Despite myself.

It wasn't likely.

When our drinks were empty, I refused the offer of a lift from Ashley's older sister who worked at the coffee shop and said I'd walk home alone. Sometimes I just needed the space. The rain had been reduced to a light drizzle.

The sun went down around four-thirty this late in the year and the streetlights glowed bright white in the rippling puddles. I slouched through the streets with my hood up and stopped for a while to watch the workmen put up the town's Christmas lights. They weren't lit; strings of dead bulbs blotting the black night. Men with hard hats erecting pre-Christmas joy.

The beep-beep of a vehicle reversing.

The flashing colours of Happy Christmas signs in shop windows.

Christmas, for most people, meant togetherness. For me, it meant being alone. Sure, I'd spend it with my parents. But I'd watch them kiss under the mistletoe and lie on the couch as they watched romantic Christmas movies where the boy always gets the girl, and I'd understand how empty my life was.

I'd be alone this Christmas, just like every Christmas before.

I had no need for mistletoe.

And mistletoe knew it.

CHAPTER 2

BEN

When I closed my bedroom door to blot out the sound of my warring parents, I punched the wall and threw myself on the bed. The sting in my knuckles wasn't strong enough to take away the darkness in my chest that burned hot and bright.

It never was.

I stared up at the hairline fracture on the ceiling that travelled across the yellowing plaster. The glow-in-the-dark stars I'd put there as a child no longer glowed in the dark. At night, with the light out and the curtains drawn, the ceiling was a void where once there was a galaxy of opportunity.

Downstairs, Mum raised her voice and Dad was crying again, his words muffled by closed doors and angry tears. There'd be an empty brandy bottle on the kitchen table. Brandy always made him bawl.

In the morning, the bottle would be stowed under the sink, or in a cardboard box in the garage, waiting to go out on the garden wall with the recycling beside a dozen other bottles, looking like it belonged there.

And if one should accidentally fall . . .

I rolled over and grabbed my earbuds. I put on some death

metal. It wasn't something I normally listened to, but when Mum and Dad were going at it, it was the only thing that drowned them out. Screaming overcomes screaming.

I couldn't remember the last time we'd had a normal evening at home. Dad was coming back from work later every day. Mum spent longer at the salon where she worked front-of-house, claiming she had to sweep up a bazillion strands of hair because the cleaner quit and nobody else would do it.

And three times a week, there'd be forty Euros on the kitchen counter, trapped under the rusted coffee canister, and a note that said some variation of working late. Won't be home before nine. Order pizza. Kill your father and don't tell me where you buried his body.

Dad bumped into things even when he wasn't drunk. It's like he just wasn't looking where he was going half the time. "Who put that there?" he'd say, tripping over the shoes he'd discarded twenty minutes before, angry at an inanimate object. Or he'd curse with vehemence when his toe found the sharp corner of the coffee table. It seemed like my very name became a swear word along with the others. "For God's sake, Ben," and, "Dammit all to hell, Ben."

"Where's my keys?" Dad would say, with his keys in his hand.

"Dad's going insane," I told Mum a few months ago.

"He's always been like that," she said, stubbing her cigarette out on the glass ashtray she stole from work and lighting a new one. "He tripped coming up the aisle and your granddad and the priest had to help him into a chair for a few minutes before the wedding could go ahead."

She laughed, but it was her tired laugh. Like she was sick of explaining away her husband's awkwardness.

"Your Nana, God rest her, she took one look at him and said, 'Are you sure you want to marry such a klutz?'"

Downstairs, something smashed. I heard it over the screeching in my ears from the music that I didn't want to listen to but had no other choice.

When my phone lit up, I was half relieved to have someone to talk to and half annoyed at the interruption.

> **errrinx**
> I have to use petrecor in a sentence and
> I don't remember what it means.

That was Erin. Not only did she not know the meaning of the word, she couldn't spell it either.

I paused the music, listening to the air outside the bedroom door. There was silence. For a change.

> **benhuntss07**
> It's petrichor. It's the earthy smell after
> rain.

> **errrinx**
> You're a genius. You know everything.

I didn't know everything, but Erin never listened when I told her that. I didn't know how planes stayed in the air without falling out of the sky.

Or how people worked.

Erin McNally had been my best friend since we were thrown together in primary school. She stood behind me in the queue to use the teacher's desk-mounted pencil sharpener and said, "I like your hair."

I'd dressed as the Hulk the day before for a kid's birthday party—I can't remember who anymore—and there was still some green washout dye in patches behind my ears.

We never dated. That'd be like dating your sister. But no one believed me when I said we were just friends. In the early days, before puberty added a couple of feet to my height and a couple of airbags under her shirt, our parents let us have sleepovers as though it was the most natural thing. And it was. We played dress-up and Cops & Robbers. We slept top-to-toe in the same bed, and all the grownups said how cute it was.

But it wasn't like that. I liked boys. I always have.

I came out to my parents once, when I was fourteen. "I think I'm into boys."

Dad narrowed his eyes and Mum said, "No you're not."

"I'm serious."

They didn't buy it.

"Don't let Erin hear you joking like that."

The living room had been fogged by a cloud of cigarette smoke and the nail polish on Mum's toenails was chipped as she stretched her legs out on the couch. Dad was on his knees in front of the coffee table, trying to pour sambuca shots without spilling it everywhere. Which he did anyway. Days like those were a million years ago now.

They were okay, when they weren't arguing. Years ago, I might come downstairs for a late-night snack, and they'd be lying on the couch together watching an old Adam Sandler movie and whispering with quiet smiles lighting up their faces and hands caressing each other.

These days, if they weren't arguing, they weren't in the

13

same room.

The silence below stretched out. One of them, probably Dad, will have gone for a walk to cool down. I'd hear him come home again sometime during the night. I put my phone on Do Not Disturb and got undressed.

It was raining outside but my room was cloyingly warm for mid-November. I slipped out of my boxers and thought about one of the boys from school.

But Erin texted again; the one friend who could bypass my Do Not Disturb. I really should change that. I glanced at the partial message on the lockscreen. *Gemma Ademola is having a party next weekend and she wants to . . .*

I flipped the phone over, leaving her unread, and tried to sleep in the lingering, oppressive heat of my parents' anger under the simpering darkness of my bedroom.

The silence in my room was swollen and bruised. Even the relentless rain had stopped battering the windowpane. Mum's weeping came to me like a snake from the gap under the door, sharp tongue touching my cooling skin. I pulled the quilt over my legs.

Dad came home after two in the morning.

There was no more crying.

When my alarm woke me, my eyes were glued together. Sleep wasn't coming easy anymore. Not for months. I showered and skipped breakfast when Dad said he had to get to the office early. The car ride was punctuated by the rattle of the exhaust that needed to be repaired and when Dad pulled up at the school gates, I said, "See you," and Dad nodded. We were at that awkward stage now.

I got out of the car. And when I did, I turned my back on

him and dragged a smile over my face.

Smiling was easy. It said, I'm good. Go on, ask me how I am. I'll tell you I'm perfect, thanks, and how are you?

I pulled the hood over my head. I saw Dean O'Donnell going through the front doors with his friends, but I didn't wave. We didn't have anything in common except our class schedule.

And then Erin waved.

I cracked my smile wider to show how ordinarily fine I was.

I'd come out to Erin two years ago, too. The day after I'd told my parents.

"You're not gay," she said.

"How do you know?"

"Because you love Ariana Grande, and you play rugby."

As if the two were mutually exclusive. "Gay guys don't like music or sport?"

"Maybe you're bi."

"I'm not bi."

"Gemma Ademola's brother was in a knife fight last night," Erin said.

I didn't know if that connected to my coming out or if she was just changing the subject. "Is Gemma Ademola's brother gay?"

"He was nearly killed," she said.

I understood why my parents didn't want to believe me. They wanted grandchildren. They weren't homophobic, as far as I could tell, although we'd never openly spoken about the subject. Why Erin didn't believe me, I wasn't sure.

I sat at the back of maths class between Erin and Alex Janey and stared at the back of Dean O'Donnell's head. Dean moved to Clannloch Community School last spring, a short, reedy boy with thin lips and a straight nose. The opposite of me. I was tall and my nose had been broken twice from playing rugby. We spoke once, sometime during Dean's first week in school.

I was standing behind him in the lunch queue and accidentally nudged him with my tray. The sharp scowl that Dean threw me over his shoulder made me laugh.

And blush a little.

"What?" Dean said.

"What?"

"What're you laughing at?"

I shrugged and stopped laughing. His cute face tied my tongue. "Where are you from?"

"Blarney."

"Where the stone is?"

Dean's lips flattened further. "It's famous for more than just the Blarney Stone."

"Is it?"

"It's even got a McDonald's."

"You're in the big smoke now, Dean." I liked saying his name. Dean. It sounded like a dimple. "I'm Ben, by the way."

Dean said, "Just watch where you're putting your tray, Ben."

And I wasn't even mad. I couldn't be. I wanted to pick Dean up and squeeze him tight.

Since then, that was the longest we'd ever spoken. These days, we barely acknowledged each other in the school halls. I was almost certain that Tony and Ashley, Dean's friends, had warned him against talking to the sports kids.

When the bell went at the end of class, I realised I'd been

staring at the back of Dean's head the whole time. I liked the little tails of hair that curled there, like fingers that touched Dean's pale skin the way I longed to.

But if nobody believed I was gay, I'd never get to touch a man.

In the hall between classes, I chatted to Alex Janey and a few other boys from the basketball team, but I wasn't paying attention to their words. I yawned, wondering if I could duck into the space under the assembly stage and grab some sleep, and when I went to the men's room to splash water on my face, Dean was standing at one of the urinals.

I wanted to turn around and leave, but my brain froze. I went to the row of sinks and ran the cold water. Dean didn't look over.

When he stood beside me to wash his hands, I gave him a small nod and he twisted his lips into what was probably a perfunctory smile, joyless and brief, macabre in the warped mirror. I held my hands under the freezing water as Dean warmed his fingers under the spitting air of the weak hand dryer. And when he was gone, I splashed water on my face and kept my eyes closed, pressing my knuckles into my eyes. The cold water woke me up, but my brain was still too noisy. One of these days, I'd get a full night's sleep and feel almost human in the morning.

And starting the week in maths class didn't help. Alex Janey said maths was invented by the devil to torment mankind.

By the time I got home, Mum and Dad were still out. The note in the kitchen said, *Get pizza. I'll be back before nine.*

I texted Erin who was there within twenty minutes. She came with vodka and her homework.

We took the pizza up to my room and drank the vodka straight from the bottle. The sting of it was as weak as my knuckles had been on the wall, but at least it dulled my brain. I had no intention of ending up like my parents, but a few sips might help me sleep.

I pulled out my textbooks and Erin leaned across them for another slice. A string of coagulating cheese died between the pages of Irish civil history.

I closed the book. "What's the point?"

"The point of what?"

"Anything," I said. "School," I added.

She nudged my thigh with her foot. "Because you're clever, Ben. And one day you'll get the hell out of Cork."

"And go where?"

"Anywhere you want."

"Anywhere is a lonely place," I said, and I wasn't exactly sure what I meant.

"When are you ever lonely?"

I looked at her narrow face and false lashes. "Do you even know me, Erin?"

"Are your parents still getting you down? You should talk to them."

"Yeah. 'Hey, Mum, Dad—cool it with the fighting, you're pissing me off.'"

"Exactly," Erin said.

I took another swig from the bottle and held it out to her.

"Talk to them," she said. "It's not good, all those raised voices and broken promises. I don't know how you're even managing to stay focused at school."

"I'm not."

She passed the bottle back. "Anywhere is looking far more appealing now, isn't it?"

I screwed the cap back on the bottle and kicked it under the bed out of the way. I was feeling a slight buzz and didn't want it to get any worse. I had practice in the morning.

"I can't even ask someone out on a date. What makes you think I'm brave enough to get out of Cork?"

Erin wrapped her arms around one of the pillows and yawned. "You can have anyone you want. You just have to believe."

I had to nudge her awake ten minutes later.

When I crawled into bed that night, Mum and Dad were at it again.

I could hear their bitter words downstairs.

And the ceiling above my head was still dark.

CHAPTER 3

DEAN

I stared at the blank lines on the sheet of paper tacked up outside the Music room. I wasn't in a band or a music group. I wasn't even sure if I could sing outside of my bedroom with earbuds in and my mind oblivious to the outside world. But I wasn't participating in any extracurriculars this year and Mum had been on my case since the start of term. "Learn the flute for all I care, just do something. It'll be good for you."

"I don't like the flute."

Mum had leaned into me on the couch and pressed her lips against my temple, pushing my glasses aside the way she always does. "So learn Latin or play chess."

I pulled away from her. "Why do you automatically go to the geeky subjects? What about rugby or woodwork?"

"Do you want to play rugby?"

"That's not the point. You shouldn't go around assuming I'm a geek."

She poked my skinny ribs through my thick hoodie. "Why don't you teach maths to other kids? That'll be fun."

"You do know the meaning of the word fun, don't you?"

"Fine. But it'd be worthwhile. And it'd look great on your

record."

Teaching algebra to thirteen- and fourteen-year-olds wasn't what I'd consider fun or worthwhile. I understood maths, but I didn't think I'd be able to explain it to anyone else.

And now the sheet outside the music room said, *Your School Choir Needs You.*

The city hall was to play host to a number of school choirs on Christmas Eve in aid of the Irish Red Cross.

Christmas Eve. As if I wouldn't have anything better to do with my free time.

That was a lie. I'd be home alone on Christmas Eve while other kids went to parties and got drunk and threw up and made out. In that order.

I looked up at the sheet of paper again. There were four names on it. The empty lines below the scrawled signatures were both promises and threats, spaces where I could exist or not. If only I could make the choice.

A pen had been Sellotaped to a piece of string that was tacked in place beside the sheet. *Your School Choir Needs You.*

I was about to reach for the pen when I felt a nudge at my back.

"Can you even sing?" Ashley asked.

I turned, embarrassed. Tony studied the sign-up sheet like a myopic mole, his finger tracing the names that had been scratched there. "Is that Gemma Ademola's name?"

Ashley said, "I've heard her sing. She's good. When's the audition?"

"It's not a strict audition," I told her. "They're having a group session where everyone sings together, and I guess they'll pick whoever sounds decent. It's not like you have to stand in front of judges and hope you don't die on stage."

"Can you even sing?" Ashley asked again.

I shrugged. I thought I could. But people only hear what they want to. And I wasn't about to ask them for their opinion. "Mum wants me to do some after-school club. Just to get me out of the house longer, I guess. But I'm probably not going to do it, anyway. I'm not good enough."

"Too late," Tony said.

I heard the pen clatter against the wall. Tony had written my name in capital letters on the sheet, with a five-sided star at either end.

"Shit, man, cross it out. I'm not getting up there to sing in front of anybody."

"Why not? I've done you a favour. You'd have kicked yourself if you passed it up."

I reached for the dangling pen, but Ashley grabbed it before me. "When's the audition?"

"Tomorrow."

"So sleep on it. When you get to school tomorrow, if you've changed your mind, you can take your name off the list."

I shook my head. "It was a stupid idea. I don't have the balls to sing in public."

"Maybe they'll descend between now and tomorrow."

"I hate you two."

Tony smiled. "We know."

Friends are just enemies that you trust.

I could feel the scratch of my name on the sign-up sheet like it had been carved into my throat. Part of me wanted to slip out of class and cross out my embarrassment, but it would make Mum happy that I was even trying out, and it would show willingness at school, something my teachers were already saying I lacked.

I didn't really lack willingness. I was willing to be alone, to go through life without taking risks. I was willing to hide. Hiding was better than participating. When you participate, there's a risk of failure. Failure that can be avoided when you keep your mouth shut and say nothing.

Maybe I could hide in the back row of the choir.

Thick raindrops performed a dance routine on the windows while our English teacher droned on about William Golding. I wasn't sure the rain would ever stop. At the back of the class, Alex Janey made a pig noise in reference to Golding's *Lord of the Flies*, and Ben Hunter laughed.

"That's enough," Mr Dobbins said, "or I'll exclude the pair of you from Secret Santa this year."

Their laughter continued behind their fists. Alex Janey had one of those snickering laughs that made him sound like a cartoon character, and the more he snorted, the more Ben's face went purple.

Mr Dobbins wouldn't exclude them from Secret Santa. From what I could tell, it was obligatory.

By lunchtime, I'd forgotten about the choir and my big bold name decorated with stars. And by the time I got home, the only thing I could remember of the day was Ben Hunter's face as he tried not to laugh at whatever dumb thing Alex had done. Ben had one of those faces that was square and blocky but symmetrical. A face to be studied.

Maybe I should have joined the rugby team when I'd suggested it to Mum. At least I'd get to see Ben Hunter in a pair of shorts. Or in the shower block. Naked.

"What're you doing?"

I looked up, guilty. I'd taken my schoolbooks out of my bag and put them on the desk in my room but I hadn't opened them. Mum was standing in the doorway.

"You should knock."

"I did," Mum said. "Dinner's ready."

"I'll be down in a minute." I read the back of my chemistry textbook just to take my mind off Ben Hunter's naked body, covered in soap suds in all the wrong places.

The next day, I tried not to think about the choir auditions after school. I turned in my history paper, even though Coach spent most of the class talking about basketball and Alex Janey and Ben Hunter were playing table football with a balled-up piece of paper and their fingers.

"You ready?" Ashley asked when the final bell sounded.

"No."

"You'll be fine. Do you want me to come with you?"

"To do what? Hold my hand?"

"Would it help?"

"Get out of here," I said.

Outside the music room, I looked at the sheet. There were still only five names on it. Mine and the four before me.

I could hear Mr Elliot inside, talking. The door was ajar, and somebody was tinkering badly on the piano. Obviously not Mr Elliot.

I took a deep breath. And before I entered the room, I heard the distinctive squeak of sports shoes on the polished floor.

Ben Hunter came down the corridor in his basketball uniform, yellow and baggy, sweat on his face and neck and a basketball in his hands.

"Think fast," he said, throwing the ball.

It bounced between us, and I caught it on its upward thrust. I almost fumbled it. I passed it back, trying not to look at Ben's legs. Basketball shorts weren't as tiny as rugby shorts.

Ben stowed the ball under his elbow and looked at the music room door. "You're in the choir?"

"It's just an audition. For the Christmas thing."

"I hear Gemma Ademola's trying out for it."

"Yeah."

"She's good."

"I've heard."

We both studied the sign-up sheet and I wished Tony hadn't put stars beside my name like I was some screaming bigshot.

Ben tapped the sheet with his finger. "Good luck."

"You, too."

"Me, too, what?"

I cleared my throat. "Your basketball game. Good luck."

"It's over. We won."

I smiled. My words had run dry and I needed my voice for the audition. I wanted a glass of water. I wanted to lick the sweat off Ben Hunter's neck.

Ben dribbled the ball up the corridor and I watched him go. He wasn't so much of a jerk when he was on his own. Before turning the corner, he shot the ball against the far wall, caught it, cheered for himself, and then he was gone.

Mr Elliot said, "Are you coming in?" He had the sign-up sheet in his hand.

I nodded. My throat was tight.

Inside, Mr Elliot said, "All right. I was hoping for a better turnout, but I guess this is it." He looked at the sheet of paper.

"Existing choir, please take your places. Two rows. New people, just find a spot between the others and try to blend in."

I stood in the back row and took a song book when it was handed to me.

"Let's try something fun to begin with. Song one in your books is *Wake Me Up*. I'm sure you all know it."

I hadn't been expecting Avicii. I thought I was trying out for some Christmas carols, but I knew the song and as the music played from Mr Elliot's computer, I was able to sing along, if only with a reserved voice.

The choir was good. Not amazing, but good.

Gemma Ademola, in the front row, was belting out the lyrics like she was at the 3Arena in Dublin, and Mr Elliot stood at the back of the room, listening. Halfway through the song, he stopped the music, gave us instructions—some he told to sing a little quieter, some he asked to speak up.

We started again.

It sounded better this time.

"Perfect. Let's take it down a notch, shall we? I want to skip to song three in your books."

I checked the sheet. *True Colors* by Cyndi Lauper. I didn't know it.

When the soft music issued out of the speakers, I tried to follow along with the choir who had obviously practiced the song before. They were singing too fast for me, and I had to just mouth the words by the end.

"That was abysmal," Mr Elliot said, but he was laughing. He sat at the piano. "Can I have my newbies front and centre, please? Don't worry, I'm not going to ask you to perform on your own. Yet."

I stood in front of the choir with the four other auditionees, forming a third row. Gemma Ademola was the only one who radiated confidence.

Mr Elliot said, "How many of you know music? For example, this," he played a note, "is a C. Can you hum it?"

We tried.

"And again." He played the same note.

We hummed in unison this time.

"And again," Mr Elliot said, but he played a different note.

We tried to hum the higher note.

"Well done," Mr Elliot said. He had us hum a few more notes before sending us back to join the choir.

This time, as we sang, he moved among us, listening. He moved Gemma over to the left of the choir without stopping the song. Then he took one of the others and moved him to the back row.

I tried to ignore him when he stood in front of me. I glanced down at the music sheet and then trained my eyes on the far wall, singing as much as I could before looking at the words again.

Mr Elliot nodded and moved on to one of the other auditionees. He didn't move me to another spot.

When the song was done, Mr Elliot told the existing choir to go home, and he had the rest of us stand in a row. We practiced scales for twenty minutes until I knew I'd be humming them in my sleep.

At the end, Mr Elliot said, "I was hoping to have to cut some of you because I take great pleasure in tearing down the hopes and dreams of impressionable students." He paused, grinning. We didn't laugh. "Dean," he said, holding up the sign-up sheet. "With two stars."

"I didn't write that."

"You didn't sign up?"

"I mean, I did, but I didn't draw the stars."

"I see," Mr Elliot said. "Are you a countertenor?"

"Am I?" I shrugged. I didn't know what a countertenor was.

"He's very good," one of the others said and I blushed.

"He is." Mr Elliot sat behind his desk. "Welcome to the choir. We'll be practicing three times a week between now and Christmas Eve."

One of the smaller guys said, "I have a dentist appointment on Wednesday."

"Anyone else?" the music teacher asked.

"That'd be a busy dentist's room if we all went," I said.

As we were leaving, Mr Elliot asked me to stay behind. When we were alone, he opened the door wide—it was school policy—and then he returned to the piano. "I don't want you to feel shy or embarrassed on your own, but can you follow along with these notes?" He played three keys on the piano, and then another three when I had hummed them.

"Okay," he said.

When he didn't say anything else, I asked, "Is that it?"

Mr Elliot nodded, a slow and pensive motion. He turned and wrote something on a piece of paper. "I want you to learn these Christmas carols as fast as you can. Can you do that?"

I studied the list. "I guess."

"Don't guess, Mr O'Donnell—do. I want you performing a solo on Christmas Eve."

I laughed. But Mr Elliot was serious.

"I can't."

"Sure you can. You just open your mouth and let the words come out."

"It'll be vomit, that's what'll come out. Trust me."

"Nonsense. You'll be great. See you on Wednesday."

I stood at the bus stop, my hood up, the list of songs still in my hand. I could already taste bile at the back of my mouth. I wanted to lie down on the road in front of the bus and ask the driver to run over my face. This would be the last time I signed up for any extracurricular activities.

Ever.

— CHAPTER 4 —

BEN

I'd had my arm across Erin's shoulders or around her waist so often that I didn't realise I was doing it most of the time. Being tactile with her came as naturally as breathing. We'd been joined at the hip for so long that her touch was my touch. Standing in the hall outside class, sitting in the library or at the cinema, we were a jumble of limbs that would look intimate to an outsider.

So when Alex Janey slumped into the red plastic chair at the table opposite us in the school cafeteria and said, "Get a room," I pulled my arm off her shoulder and scraped my chair aside. My coming out may have been rejected by my parents and Erin, but I'd never be able to share my truth at school if I was always draped over her body.

But having her near me felt safe, normal. We thought so much alike that it was hard to tell who said what. And she was my lifeline at home when Mum was drunk and Dad was slamming around in the garage or the kitchen, getting angry over nothing. He shouted at me this morning when he spilled coffee across his paperwork on the kitchen table. I hadn't even been in the room at the time.

Erin would come in the back door while my parents were in the living room. We'd lie on the bed and talk. She had her own issues to deal with. As far as I could tell, the only normal family was an abnormal one.

She's the one that held me when I was sad or angry. And for that, I loved her more than my own family. I'd punched the wooden post of my headboard once until my knuckles bled and Erin wrapped my hand in a wet towel. I'd been fourteen and Dad's anger was getting out of hand. He'd lash out with his words, thumping the heel of his fist into something to punctuate his point. And I'd retreat to my room out of the way, slamming my bedroom door quietly. That night, Dad's outburst had been about a missed basket. "For God's sake, Ben, you were wide open. What happened?" His voice was high, his face red. I didn't know where the anger came from. A couple of months before, Dad would have laughed it off. "No worries. You'll make it next time. It's no big deal."

But now it was a big deal.

Erin had come to my room in her pyjamas, black silk, etched in unicorns. I wanted to laugh. But my own anger was still rising. And as I talked it over with her, telling her how Dad had made me feel, the tightness in my chest was thicker, and the sting of pain at the centre of my skull edged closer. That's when I'd punched the sharp edge of the headboard and skinned my knuckles enough that blood oozed from the shallow wounds.

Erin had slipped out to the bathroom, soaked a towel and wrapped my hand with it. When I'd calmed down, she said, "Where is he now?"

I shrugged.

Erin said she'd be right back. I heard her creeping downstairs in her slippers, and she was back a few minutes later with the almost-empty bottle of brandy Dad had been drinking.

"Let's see what makes him so happy," she said.

It was the first time we'd ever had a drink. It burned. And it was disgusting, but we drank it anyway. She didn't tell me how she got the bottle or where my dad was, and I didn't ask. I didn't want to know.

But I felt better. Alcohol, or her soothing voice, or both, I wasn't sure, but something made me laugh again.

In the cafeteria, Alex Janey said, "I'm not doing this dumb Secret Santa thing. Dobbins can go to hell if he thinks I'm flunking English because of it."

Erin said, "It'll be fun."

"It shouldn't be allowed. I'm just thinking of the poor kids who can't afford it."

"Five Euros?" Erin scoffed.

But I had to agree with Alex. "It might not be a lot to most people, but five Euros could be everything to some kid." I had firsthand experience of that.

Erin leaned across the table to Alex. "Do you need a lend?"

"I'm just saying, that's all."

When we got to Mr Dobbins' English class, the teacher was wearing a Santa hat. "It's beginning to look a lot like Christmas," he sang as we took our seats at the back of the room.

In the front row, Dean O'Donnell sat closest to the door like he was the getaway driver of a school heist.

When I'd seen him standing outside the music room yesterday, I almost turned to go back the other way. But passing the music room was the most direct way to the changing rooms and I couldn't go home in my basketball shirt or I'd freeze. And this time, I'd managed more than just a useless nod. We'd actually had a conversation. Yay for words.

Mr Dobbins held a cardboard box that he'd wrapped in Christmas paper. He shook the contents and rummaged in it with his fat fist. "Thirty-two names," he said. "All typed out on the same paper so nobody can cheat."

Some of the students groaned.

"Remember, Christmas isn't a day, it's a season," Dobbins said. "I want everybody's gifts in by December fifteenth."

"What if I don't have five Euros to participate, sir?"

Mr Dobbins shook the box again. "Five Euro is a maximum, Janey. You can spend fifty cents if you want to."

"How much is a condom, sir?" somebody asked. Everyone laughed.

"They're free from the family planning clinic." He stood in front of Dean O'Donnell near the door. "You all know the rules. Pick a name, don't tell anyone, and spend up to five Euros on a gift you think they'll like. Gag gifts are fine, so long as they're not unkind. And if you pick your own name, put it back and pick again." He held the box out. "Get in there, Mr O'Donnell. Give it a good rummage."

Dean put his hand in the box. I couldn't see his face well enough to judge his reaction to the name he pulled.

As Mr Dobbins moved across the front row, he said, "There are no swaps allowed. If you swap, Santa will see. You've been in this room together all term. I expect you know each other well enough by now. Dig deep, Miss Carrow, you won't break a nail."

When Alex Janey pulled a piece of paper from the box, he unfolded it and said, "Who?"

Mr Dobbins said, "If you don't know any of your classmates by now, Janey, I feel sorry for your future prospects. Come on, Mr Hunter, there's only a few left. Who's it going to be?" He rattled the almost empty box in front of me.

I closed my eyes. I reached inside, fingers groping the empty space, seeking out the folded squares of paper. I touched one, rejected it, found another. But then I decided to go back for the first one.

Maybe it was luck. Or fate.

I unfolded the paper and turned from Alex Janey's prying eyes.

It said, DEAN O'DONNELL.

And I scrunched the paper in my hand to hide it.

"Who'd you get?" Alex asked.

"Quiet, Mr Janey," Dobbins said. He'd moved on to Erin.

"It had better be me," Alex whispered in a lower voice.

When everyone had taken a name and the box was empty, Mr Dobbins said, "Right. *Lord of the Flies.* Chapter five. Janey, start reading from the top."

Alex Janey's voice droned as he read from the book.

But I couldn't concentrate. The odds of pulling Dean's name from the box were practically impossible. If I'd rigged the draw myself, I still wouldn't have believed it. I looked at the back of Dean's head and wondered what I could get him. And then I wondered who had my name. Was it Dean? That'd be a coincidence too far. The world doesn't work that way. But I didn't care who drew my name. I'd picked Dean O'Donnell's, and that's all that mattered.

On Friday, after the basketball game where I fumbled the ball just as much as I held it, Erin waited for me outside the changing room and we got the bus into town, chugging down the steep hill from the school grounds. I didn't want to tell her whose name I'd picked, but I had to. I was hoping she'd help me find a suitable gift. She'd got one of the popular girls, so she was happy. "I'll just get her that Rita Ora nail polish she's always wearing. That's within the budget."

"What should I get for Dean?"

"I don't know. Get him a gift card for Austin's Game Shack."

"Why there?"

"Because he looks like a geek. He probably plays the Xbox every night and screams into a headset at some twelve-year-old German kids. I don't know."

I wasn't convinced. I didn't think of Dean as a gamer. Brainy, yes, but not a gamer. "What about a Christmas carol CD?"

"Firstly," she said, as we got off the bus, "why? And secondly, nobody buys CDs anymore."

"Your mum does."

"That's the lamest Your Mamma joke I've ever heard."

"You know she's got, like, two million CDs. Anyway. He's in that Christmas choir thing, isn't he?"

"Is he?"

I shrugged. "Gemma Ademola's in it, I think," I said, to cover my tracks.

We walked through the mall. Erin had picked up the purple nail polish she was looking for within a few minutes of arriving. And an hour later, I still had no idea what to buy.

"I told you, just get him a gift card."

"That's lame."

"Fine. What about this mug?" We were in one of those bargain stores that seemed to sell everything you never needed.

I read the slogan on the side of the mug. "'Life is better with a horse, a hat, and a strong cup of joe.' I don't even know what that means."

"So? Neither will he. It's just a stupid gift, Ben. Come on, my feet are sore. Pick something already."

I closed my eyes, spun on my heels, and pointed. I'd let fate take care of it. But my finger touched a kid's toy gun that lit up and made space laser noises. And it was outside the budget.

"I'll give you the extra three Euro," Erin said.

"That's not the point."

She shook her head. "I'm going to wait at the food court. Will you just pick something fast? I'm starving."

She left me alone and I paced the aisles. Nothing interesting leaped out at me. I was about to give up when, on my way out of the store, I spotted a revolving rack of enamel lapel pins. Kitschy slogans—*Warning: May spontaneously break into dance*, or *I speak fluent sarcasm with a side of wit*—and badly painted animals that were either dogs or bears, I couldn't tell.

And then I saw a rainbow with a cloud at either end and a Leprechaun sitting on the top. It was just a rainbow. It was perfect and awful all at once. It said: I think you're cute and by the way I'm gay. Or maybe it said: I'm just a rainbow and Ben overthinks everything so you should ignore him.

Outside the store, I saw Erin coming back down the escalator. I grabbed the rainbow, handed it to the girl at the counter who put in a presentation box, and I paid an extra twenty-five cents for a small paper bag. The girl Sellotaped it shut just as Erin came back in.

"Got something?"

"Yeah," I said, slipping the small package into my pocket.

"There are no free tables at the food court. It's like every kid from here to Limerick is up there, chowing down on rice noodles."

We left the mall and walked down to Grainger's Coffee Stop. And when I got home later, I dropped my gym bag by the washing machine and was going upstairs when I heard Dad's voice. It wasn't directed at me, and it was too quiet to make out the words, but he sounded angry again. I went back to the kitchen and stuffed my basketball gear into the machine. The detergent was running low so I added it to the list on the fridge, and then I locked myself in my bedroom.

I tore the tape off the top of the paper bag and shook the small box into my hand. I took the pin out, flipped it over and studied it. It was just a rainbow. I was overthinking it. Again.

I pinned it to my sweatshirt and looked at myself in the mirror.

It wasn't just a rainbow. It was a *Pride* rainbow.

I wore it to the dinner table. Dad didn't even look up and Mum spent the whole time talking about the customers from the salon. But at least they were home for a change.

I positioned myself so that the rainbow pin was on display as I said, "We have this Secret Santa assignment at school."

Mum nodded.

"We have to buy something for under five Euros. We drew names from a box. I pulled the name of this kid, Dean. Dean O'Donnell." I still like saying his name.

Dad said, "Where's the salt?"

Mum said, "If I get any more hairspray in my nose, I swear. Those girls don't have a clue. They walk around that salon like they own the place."

I went back to my room. I took the pin off and dropped it into the paper bag. I could see the mark it left behind on my sweatshirt.

Everything leaves a mark.

Especially your parents.

CHAPTER 5

DEAN

Ashley groaned as Tony did a celebratory dance. Sunday afternoon bowling had become a tradition not because we enjoyed bowling, but because there was nothing else to do. We were too old for karting and too young for bars.

I liked the darkness of the bowling alley. The dim overhead lights that offset the neon glow of the lane strips. I didn't have the greatest aim, but today I'd played my best in weeks. Tony was leading, of course. Tony always did. But it was unusual for Ashley to be trailing so far behind.

The overhead music was poppy and basic.

"We should join a bowling league," Tony said. He was sitting on three strikes and two spares.

Ashley said, "If you turn up to school tomorrow in a bowling shirt, I'll disown you."

"Bowling shirts are cool."

"Bowling shirts are definitely cool," I said, "if you're a fifty-five-year-old divorced dad with a beer belly."

"Just your type," Tony said, punching my shoulder. "You're up."

I took down two pins with my first shot and then threw a

gutter ball. I wasn't sure if it was an accident or if I meant to throw badly. I was twenty-six points ahead of Ashley and she was sulking.

"We should see a movie when we're done here."

The cinema was next door, connected to the bowling alley by a noisy room filled with claw machines, arcade shooters and two air hockey tables.

Seeing a movie was risky. School kids might avoid ten-pin bowling, but films were universally adored. Cinemas were full of first dates and hormones.

"Besides," Tony said as if somebody had already objected, "unless you want to see that animated dog movie, there's nothing on."

"*My Neighbor Totoro* is showing," I said.

"That was last week. And it's on Netflix, isn't it?"

"It's better on the big screen," Ashley said.

Tony picked up a bowling ball. "I don't know why we're still discussing it; it's not even showing." And as if to punctuate his point and end the conversation, he threw another strike and danced again.

When we were finished bowling, I spent eleven Euros on a skill machine, trying to win a Nintendo Switch, but I left with nothing. We walked further into town, in the direction of Grainger's, huddling against the buildings when the rain got too heavy, but Ashley said she was starving so we stopped at a fast-food chain. We got chicken shawarma to share—I'd spent most of my money in the arcade.

Tony nabbed a table in the busy restaurant as a young couple were standing up, before they'd even left, and although I hate sitting with my back to the room, Tony and Ashley had already slipped into the seats against the wall.

The food was hot and tasteless but it kept Ashley happy and the three of us got along better when she was happy. She always clung to Tony's side on Thursdays when he had food tech. The smell of his cakes or lasagne or whatever dish he'd made that week would fill the school bus so much that every kid who got off the bus before Tony took a deep breath to keep the scent with them for longer. Tony would crack the lid off the container just enough to waft the smell around even more. He was evil that way.

Picking at the chicken from the open wrap, Ashley said, "When are you going to make that red velvet cake again? It was gorgeous."

"Was it?" Tony asked. "I didn't get to taste it. You ate the lot."

We laughed because it was true.

And then Ashley ducked her head low and sipped from her drink.

"Uh-oh," Tony said.

I could tell from both of their reactions that they'd seen someone they didn't want to see. And I could hardly turn around and make it obvious. "Who is it?" I asked.

But an arm wrapped around my neck in a loose chokehold and whoever it was knuckled the top of my head. My glasses slipped as I struggled free from their grip.

"All right, losers?" Alex Janey said.

I could smell beer on his breath as he laughed.

He wasn't choking me. It was more like a buddy-grip. Like we were besties. I leaned away from him when he released me. Half of the basketball team was behind him and I looked for

Ben Hunter but didn't see him. I tried not to catch Alex's eyes.

"What do you want?" Ashley said. She had a knack for talking to people like they were naughty six-year-olds. I swear it'd get her in trouble one day.

"That's no way to treat a friend, is it?" His words were slurred. He leaned over me to pick up a chip and dipped it in the ketchup that Tony had squeezed onto the side of the plate.

Ashley pulled the plate towards her before he could go back in for another one.

Alex had an open can of beer under his coat.

I tried to look casual, like having him standing so close behind me was normal, and I took a sip from my drink. Alex looked down at me. "All right?" he said.

I raised my chin in acknowledgement, too afraid to open my mouth in case my voice broke and revealed how immature I felt.

Alex called over one of the boys from the basketball team and slapped my shoulder. "This here is the brainiest kid in our school. Go ahead. Ask him what pi is."

The tall guy with jet black hair said, "What's pi?"

"Tell him," Alex Janey said.

I couldn't open my mouth.

"Tell him." Alex slapped my shoulder again. It was playful but firm.

I gripped my drink, wondering if I threw it in his face, would it blind him long enough for the three of us to get out of there. Instead, I said, "Pie is a savoury dessert encased in pastry."

I could see Alex trying to focus on me, as if he couldn't quite figure out my explanation. And then he laughed.

He smacked my shoulder. Again.

The black-haired kid said, "I don't get it." He walked back to the others in his group.

Alex Janey indicated the can under his coat. "You want me to pour some in your little boy drink?"

"Nah, I don't like that brand," I said.

"Who'd you get for Secret Santa?"

My mouth ran dry. I'd sadly pulled Alex's name but if I told him that, he'd insist on telling me what to get him.

But Ashley said, "It's a secret. The clue's in the name."

Alex swigged from the can, brazenly close to one of the staff members who was cleaning a nearby table. He tucked it back into his coat. I didn't know where Ben was or why he was missing from the drunken basketball outing, but part of me was glad he wasn't there.

To Ashley, Alex said, "Do you shag both of them or do you just watch while they do each other?"

"Either way," Ashley said, "we're all getting more action than you are. How does that make you feel?"

Alex Janey sucked his teeth, which told us he had no response, and when the boys from the team called to him, he followed them outside and Tony slumped back in his seat like his spine had just been stripped out.

"Well, you were no use," Ashley told him.

"Your words were better than mine."

She handed him her fork. "Take this and go to the toilet. You can use it to pull your scrotum out of your stomach."

Tony raised his eyebrows in mock disbelief, and then we laughed. Her words really were better than anyone else's.

When I got home, Mum was putting up the Christmas

decorations and Dad was in the garage trying to unravel the lights. He'd give up after a while and leave it for me to do, but for now, he was cursing with contentment at the knots.

The tree, a seven-foot sapling, had been planted in a metal bucket as if it would survive the season to be replanted in January, but I wasn't hopeful. Mum was hanging more decorations than it had branches.

"I was going to wait until you got home, but it was getting late," she said. "Did you get something for that boy at school?"

"Yeah." Pulling Alex Janey's name would be my undoing. I could think of no worse person to draw.

Mum handed me a box of baubles. "Start at the top and fill in the gaps."

"What gaps? There are none."

"Where's your Christmas spirit?" She clapped my already painful shoulder and disappeared into the kitchen. I could smell gingerbread. So much for bypassing Christmas this year.

The floor was covered in pine needles when we were done, but the house was suitably festive.

Dad handed me the ball of outdoor lights. "Good luck," he said.

And as I sat at the kitchen table threading a string of bulbs through twists and turns, I couldn't feel less Christmassy if I tried.

We'd been in Cork for almost a year and I still hadn't settled. I felt like a dog thrust into a shelter and left there to fend for itself. The new house was fine, but the wall between my bedroom and my parents' room was too thin. I heard everything.

I'd found new friends—great friends—and I was doing all right at school, but something was missing.

Something was always missing.

When I packed the wrapped gift for Alex Janey into my school bag and slipped into bed for the night, I faced the wall and pressed my nose against the cool wallpaper. Without my glasses on, the swirls on the paper blurred into a mess, just like my life.

Downstairs, I heard one of the Christmas ornaments spit out a tinny rendition of *Jingle Bells*, followed by Mum's laughter. She loved Christmas, despite never wanting to cook a turkey. But Dad said if she didn't cook turkey for Christmas, what the heck would he get to carve on Christmas Day?

Mum said he could carve out the water feature in the garden that he'd promised the year before.

I knew my parents were still in love, the way they absently touched each other in the kitchen or cuddled up on the couch together after dinner. It was sickening and it was sweet.

And I was lonely.

When the weekend crashed into Monday like a shopping trolley into my shins, I stood at the bus stop with Christmas carols swirling around in my head. Mr Elliot hadn't told me which song I'd be performing alone on the stage on Christmas Eve, and of the six carols on the list, *O Come All Ye Faithful* was my least favourite. Even though that was the one song mellowing out my brain with its rousing chords and harmonising backing vocals.

Tony and Ashley didn't mention the incident with Alex Janey, and the bus rattled up the hill towards Clannloch Community School in time for registration.

English was not one of my favourite classes. I didn't get words the way I got numbers.

Gemma Ademola gave me a wave as she disappeared into her first class, and Tony gave me a nudge. "She's totally into you."

"She is not."

"Did you see her waving at anybody else?"

"We're in choir together," I said. "Besides, you're aro-ace. How the hell would you know who she's into?"

Tony shook his head. "There are four types of waves. One, you know them but don't like them." He gave a dismissive flick of his hand. "Two, you don't mind them, but you'd rather not stop and talk. It looks like this. Then there's the friend you haven't spoken to all weekend." His arm waved frantically.

"And the fourth?" Ashley asked.

Tony winked. "You just saw Gemma Ademola do it. The 'I want your babies' wave."

"There's no such thing."

"When they're singing *Away in a Manger* together, you'll remember this conversation."

The bell rang, saving me from the awkward topic. Gemma Ademola wasn't into me. She was probably sucking up because of my solo.

By the time we got to English class, one of the few classes that Ashley shared with Tony and I, Mr Dobbins was his usual cheerful self. "Settle down. Take your seats. If you've already bought your Secret Santa gift, put it in this box." The box on his table was large and covered in wrapping paper.

Ben came in with Alex Janey in toe. He nodded at me as if it was something he always did, and Alex pretended to trip like I'd stuck my foot out. "Hey."

"That's enough, Mr Janey," the teacher said.

I put my present for Alex in the box on Mr Dobbins' desk. I didn't have a clue what to get him over the weekend, but Ashley suggested something to do with football.

Tony had agreed. "Everybody loves football."

"We don't," I pointed out. "And besides, he's on the basketball team with Ben."

"So?"

"So, shouldn't I get him a basketball or something?"

"If he's on the team, why does he need an extra ball?" Ashley asked.

Tony said, "Maybe he's only got one ball and needs a spare."

In the end, I bought him some cheap Cork FC items. It didn't matter what he liked or wanted. It was just a silly Secret Santa gift.

When I got back to my seat, half of the class had lined up behind me to put their gifts in the box.

Alex said, "We should do the gift exchange now, sir."

"What's the matter with you, Janey? It's November," Mr Dobbins said. He made us read from *Lord of the Flies*. And it was boring.

When we were writing down our homework assignment from the board, my pen blotted on the paper and smudged. I reached into my schoolbag for my pencil case to find a new pen, and my fingers brushed against something hard and cold. I took a quick look around the classroom, making sure Mr Dobbins' back was turned as he continued to write on the board. Then I pulled the object out.

I held it under the desk so that nobody else would see, and I shuffled down in my chair to inspect it. It was small and jagged and wrapped in Christmas paper.

I wondered—just for a second—if somebody had accidentally dropped it into my bag instead of the box that still sat on the teacher's desk, but when I turned it over, the stick-on gift tag said, *To Dean.*

I looked at Tony beside me, catching his attention. I held the little gift so that he could see it. His eyebrows knitted into a question. It hadn't come from him.

Glancing around the room again, I tore at the paper, pulling a corner of it. Whoever had wrapped it had twisted the paper around it several times.

When I freed the small object, it was wrapped in tissue paper. I unfolded it and a piece of paper drifted to the floor at my feet. I clamped my foot over it before anyone could see it and looked at the thing in my hand.

It was an enamel pin—a rainbow with a leprechaun over it. But it wasn't the kind of rainbow your grandma would point out in the sky. It was a pride rainbow. Gay and proud.

And because my name had been on the tag, it was meant for me. Was I being taunted?

I closed my fist around it, and then I knocked my pen onto the floor. I stooped and picked it up, along with the piece of paper.

I unfurled it. The handwriting was blocky and written in capitals. *Because I'm too chicken to be your Secret Santa. Merry Christmas.*

I looked up again, scanning the classroom. But nobody was looking at me.

I pushed the pin and the paper into my trouser pocket, and I felt it there for the rest of the period. Whoever it was from, they weren't looking to be discovered.

I picked another pen from my pencil case, but my hand was tingling, and I couldn't focus on the homework assignment anymore. Instead, I found myself drawing tiny rainbows in the corner of my notebook.

We had a fifteen-minute break before Irish class and I stood with my friends by the side of the building near the faded hopscotch lines and the painted footprints that pointed towards the bins.

"Was it one of you?" I asked them.

Ashley turned the small rainbow pin over in her hand, looking for signs of a dedication or prior ownership. "It's just a pin. Whoever it was probably just picked the first thing they found. They always have display stands right inside the door of shops. You're overthinking it."

"But why give it to me now? Why not put it in the box with everything else?"

"It's a sign," Tony said. "A clue."

"A clue to what?" I asked, lowering my voice. "My sexuality?"

"Obviously. But I think it's a sign *from* somebody, too."

"What do you mean?"

Tony said, "You know how I told you Gemma Ademola has a thing for you?"

"Now you're saying her wave wasn't an emphatic declaration of undying love?"

"Oh, it was. No doubt. But now it's clear she's not the only one who's got the hots for you."

"'The hots'?" Ashley laughed. "Listen to Mr Nineteen-Fifties over here."

But I wasn't in the mood to join in. Regardless of whether somebody was sending me a sign about their own sexuality, it was clear they knew about mine.

And that was terrifying.

CHAPTER 6

BEN

It was the dumbest thing I could have done. Ever. There was no contest. Killing a man and then turning myself in would have been far less stupid.

I deliberately missed the bus, hovering inside the school gate until the mob of teenagers clambered on and the red and yellow bus disappeared around the corner. I stood at the gate in the damp air for fifteen minutes before walking down the steep hill towards town. The fierce wind coming from the River Lee numbed my cheeks but I liked it. It helped take my mind off the stupid thing I did.

Buying a Pride rainbow wasn't the dumb part. Dropping it into Dean O'Donnell's bag and hoping he wouldn't be repulsed was the issue. I didn't see his reaction but I knew he'd opened it in class.

And that was probably a good thing. If I'd seen a look of disgust on his face or a scowl of condemnation, I'd have packed up my books and left the room. As it was, I had to get through the rest of the day knowing Dean had the tiny little rainbow in his pocket and was probably grossed out. It was a good thing I had double PE after lunch and the sweat on my face looked as though it was from the rugby match and not my fear of being found out.

I might have come out to my parents and Erin over a year ago—whether they believed me or not—but willingly handing over a small, colourful object that said, *This is me; I am gay for you*, was opening the situation up to a whole new level of awkwardness at school.

And I wasn't ready for that.

When I got home, the house was in darkness. There was no note on the kitchen counter, no cash for a pizza. It meant one thing: Mum was drunk. She didn't work Mondays, and Dad used to work from home that day. But with the aggression swelling between them like a colossal thunderhead for months, Dad worked from the office as much as he could. On her days off, Mum went to the local pub with her coworkers. What started off as a lunchtime libation turned into a mixology marathon.

I opened the fridge, closed it, rooted in the pantry, and took a box of crackers to my room. I dropped my bag on the desk and slumped into the chair, kicking my shoes off without untying the laces. I had to read the next chapter of *Lord of the Flies*, but the idea made my brain hurt. William Golding was wrong. Kids don't need to be stranded on a desert island in order to turn into savages. They just needed to go to school.

I cranked up some music and tried not to think about Dean's slender fingers, his long arms and thin face. But every time I closed my eyes, Dean was staring at me and biting his lower lip and running his hand up his inner thigh and—

The front door slammed. "Ben?"

Shit. Mum was home.

I scrambled to my feet and opened the bedroom door.

"Are you in?"

"No," I whispered, but then I shouted, "I'm doing homework."

If Dean was my homework, I'd get straight A's.

"I bought a tree," she said. I could hear the alcohol in the rasp of her voice.

"I've got homework."

"But I bought a Christmas tree. Come down."

I looked at my book bag. William Golding was rocketing up my list of priorities. But I went downstairs, scratching the back of my head and staring at the Christmas tree she'd brought home. It was barely five feet tall, lopsided and bald on one side.

"Where did you get it from? A dumpster?"

"A bit of tinsel and some baubles, that's all it needs."

"Was it the last one they had?"

"It's all we can afford this year. Do you hate it?"

And yet she could afford to drink a dozen gin and tonics. I tried to smile. I knew things were tight, but I didn't think it was that bad yet. I shrugged. "No, it's nice."

She threw her arm around my neck. "Do you love me?"

"Mum. Get off."

She kissed my cheek. Drunk Mum needed affirmations. "Do you love me?"

"All right, I love you. Now can I go back to my room? I have homework."

"We have a tree to decorate. Do your homework later."

"Mum, I'm in my transition year. This is important."

That's when Dad came home. He took one look at the

53

pathetic Christmas tree and went to the kitchen without a word. I took the opportunity to dash upstairs out of the way.

I could hear the argument even before I closed my bedroom door.

"You're drunk."

"It's Christmas."

"It looks like you pulled that twig out of a beaver's dam on the way home."

"Why've you always got to be so belligerent?"

The back door slammed. Dad was in the garden shed and I could still hear them arguing. If the shouts and screams ever stopped abruptly, the neighbours would probably call the police, and the first place they'd look for a dead body was in that damn shed.

Shout after scream. If they hated each other so much they should get divorced. I'd rather have two homes at opposite ends of the world than live in a warzone. Bombs were dropping all the time, and half of them were unexploded when they landed. It just took one misstep across the minefield to set off another argument. I had no idea Dad knew so many cuss words. And Mum was no better. It wasn't all Dad's fault. Sometimes, she'd egg him on, goading him into a new argument before they'd finished the last one.

I made a fist and thumped the butt of it against my desk. William Golding bounced.

Mum was still screaming, and Dad was roaring, and I opened my bedroom door just to slam it hard. Sometimes the noise of it interrupted their dispute. Sometimes it only fuelled their fire.

I texted Erin. *SOS 15 minutes.*

SOS meant "meet me at Grainger's Coffee Stop". It's where all the kids hung out when they were too old for the community centre down on Crawley Road.

I crept downstairs and slipped out of the house without my parents noticing. Going AWOL gave me a sense of accomplishment.

Fifteen minutes later, I was sitting in the dark corner of Grainger's on a worn leather couch, waiting for Erin.

When the bell above the door chimed, I looked up and saw Dean O'Donnell coming in with his friends. I tucked my head down and studied the cake menu. That's all I needed. They were laughing. Tony, the gangly kid, said something that was obviously hilarious, and my skin tingled at the sound of Dean's vibrant laughter. They stood at the counter and Ashley gave their order, and either they didn't see me tucked into the corner on my own, or they refused to acknowledge me.

But then Erin came in and called my name and everyone looked over. I nodded and my head drooped along with my spirits. I pointed at the coffee table in front of me; I'd already bought her a drink.

Dean and his friends slinked off to the far corner.

"Spill," Erin said, unwrapping the thick scarf from around her neck and dropping onto the couch beside me, her shoulder leaning into me for comfort. "What happened this time?"

I drank, licking coffee foam from my upper lip, and said, "She bought a Christmas tree."

"That's awesome. Did you decorate it?"

"If we put two baubles on it, it'd be overwhelmed."

"That bad, eh? How'd your dad react?"

"Have a guess."

She grumbled and stamped her feet. She'd seen it all before. Dad's anger was getting worse and, at first, he'd wait until Erin left their house before raising his voice at whatever mindless issue had inconvenienced him, but in the last month, he'd stormed into my room twice, shouting about how loud the music was or about making sure the bedroom door was damn-well open when I damn-well had a girl over.

Erin had let her hair fall across her face to hide her embarrassment and I tried to say Dad should be more worried if I had a boy over, but it wasn't the time, and if I aggravated him, I might suffer worse. Dad wasn't physically violent. Not yet.

But I wasn't about to take that chance.

"If you need to stay at mine tonight, I'm sure my mum won't mind," Erin said, holding her coffee cup in both hands and blowing on it.

"I don't have a change of clothes with me. Anyway, she's already drunk, and it won't take Dad long to catch up. They'll be passed out before I get home, I hope."

"You sure?"

"Let's talk about something else," I said.

"Like what?"

"Anything. I don't even care," I said, and I glanced across the coffee shop at Dean's table. I couldn't tell what Dean was drinking—or thinking.

I was hoping she wouldn't ask me what I bought for Dean O'Donnell. She hadn't mentioned it since Friday, and I'd spent the weekend trying not to get under my parents' feet. I was hanging out with Alex Janey and the team on Saturday night under the pretence of having basketball practice. In reality, all we did was sit in Alex's car and listen to music while we talked trash. None of us were old enough to drive yet—you had to be seventeen—but Alex's parents had bought him the car as an incentive to do well in school. It never left the driveway.

I glanced across the coffee shop again. Dean was leaning in to say something to Ashley while Tony was talking on his phone. When he stood up, I thought they were leaving, but he pulled his wallet from his pocket and walked to the counter.

I had one chance.

"You want another coffee?" I asked Erin. I was on my feet before she answered.

I slipped into the queue behind Dean. I could smell him, something sweet that was more than shampoo but less than cologne.

"Hey."

Dean looked over his shoulder. "Hey."

We stood there. Forming a queue. Two strangers, unconnected.

I thought of, and rejected, four different sentences before saying, "How's the choir practice?"

"It's okay."

I nodded. Having nothing to talk about wasn't easy—or having everything to say but no words to say it.

The girl behind the counter said, "Next, please."

Dean stepped up and placed his order.

I said, "This whole Secret Santa thing is exciting, isn't it?"

He shrugged. "Win any more basketball games?"

He was changing the subject. "Yeah," I said, making it sound nonchalant. "I win all my games. That's what I do."

"Oh yeah?"

The server said, "One chai frappe, a flat white and a caramel

57

macchiato."

"That's me," Dean said. "See you."

"Yeah."

Conversations are hard. And the smell of Dean lingered. I would remember that scent in bed later.

I wondered which drink was for Dean as I gave my own order.

"I texted my mum. She's fine if you want to stay over. She specified that you have to sleep on the sofa, though," Erin laughed.

"Lock up your daughters, Ben Hunter's in town," I said.

"You know she's still planning our wedding."

"If I haven't found a man by the time I'm thirty, and you haven't replaced me with somebody new, she may just get her wish."

"Not even."

When we'd finished our second drinks, I didn't want to go home, but couldn't take any more coffee. Erin reiterated her offer of staying at hers, but all my things were at home and if my parents were already angry, staying out would only make it worse.

I tried to catch Dean's eye on the way out, but the glare of the overhead lights caught on his glasses and I couldn't be certain if he'd seen my wave or not.

If there were any stars above us, they were out of sight, masked by the cloud cover and the city smog. A siren wailed across the horizon like an angry child. A car honked as it sped by.

I pulled my collar up against the wind and my pace was slow as I inched home, hopeful that my parents would be passed out on the couch or in bed, but certain that they'd still be awake and screaming at each other.

When I got home, I stood on the pavement outside and listened. Silence.

The living room was deserted.

I pushed the kitchen door open.

And there was blood on the floor.

"Mum?"

The blood trailed in splotches across the grey and white linoleum.

Dad sat at the kitchen table, his back to me. I could see the crease of his shirt as he breathed.

"Where's Mum?" I said, my throat tight. "Dad? Where's Mum?"

Dad turned. He held a tea towel to his face, bright stains of blood discolouring the absorbent fabric.

"I'm upstairs," Mum called. "Don't panic."

And Dad said, "It's all right. Go on up to bed."

"What happened?"

Dad looked away from me. "Go upstairs, son."

It wasn't even nine o'clock. In her room, Mum was sitting on the edge of her bed.

"Mum?"

She shook her head. "Don't worry about it, Ben. It was an accident."

"What did he do?"

"Nothing happened. Just leave it, okay?" She stood up and eased the bedroom door closed.

I went to my room.

Downstairs, Dad had started to cry.

CHAPTER 7

DEAN

I couldn't sleep. I sighed and huffed and rolled over. The darkness of my room was cracked down the middle from the light of a lamppost that shone through the narrow gap in my curtains. The shadows of my NECA figures—the cheaper ones that I'd taken out of their packaging—cast a legion of men in the faint strip of light. I wasn't an action-figure collector in the traditional sense. Dad had started buying them for me when I was ten, back when keeping something in its original packaging sounded like a ludicrous idea. At fifteen, I no longer saw them as toys but as collectibles.

Something else in its original packaging was the rainbow pin I'd received that morning. I could feel the colourful glow of it even as it was buried at the bottom of my bag.

I'd almost lost it in Grainger's Coffee Stop after school when I pulled my books out and the small item skittered across the table and onto the floor. Tony had picked it up and handed it back without a word, and I dropped it into the depths of my schoolbag where it could hide.

This was typical me. I'd get something stuck in my head and no amount of thinking about other things would shift it. I wasn't aware of any other fifteen-year-old who lost sleep over such trivial things. Tony and Ashley would be wrapped up warm in their quilts and snoring, dreaming of whatever a normal kid would be dreaming about. But me? I was blinking at the warm light of the streetlamp and worrying about a tiny enamel rainbow. The smaller a thing was, the bigger its impact on life. An earthquake wouldn't have this much sway over my mind.

I heaved my tired body out of bed. In the dim light, I reached for my bag and fumbled inside, looking for the tiny package. The torn wrapping paper had been folded over to conceal its contents, and when I pulled the rainbow out, I held it up in the sliver of light, adjusting the curtain for a better look.

It was just a rainbow, but it was testament to an identity I wasn't comfortable sharing yet. I could never wear it, not without suffering some awkward questions.

I sat on the edge of my bed and studied it, leaning forward so that it would catch the light, turning it on its end so that it sparkled green and red and yellow. I pinned it to the T-shirt I'd been sleeping in and stood in front of the full-length mirror that was on the back of my door.

I faced myself in the darkness and turned. You could tell what it was even at night, a perfect rainbow. A statement.

I took it off and held the rainbow up to the crack of light again. The fingerprints on it were almost certainly my own. I wasn't sure I'd ever find out who gave it to me. But as I crawled back into bed, I mentally scanned my English classroom. If it was a declaration of love like Tony suggested, that ruled out any of the girls. It obviously wasn't Tony, so that reduced the odds. But there were thirteen other boys in the class to be considered. Not that any one of them jumped out at me as a potential suspect.

I yawned. Detective Dean would have to kick into gear tomorrow.

My problem was the inability to believe that anybody could be into me. It was more likely a joke, a straight jock playing a cruel trick. Somebody like Alex Janey. But the odds of Alex and I being each other's Secret Santa had a probability of 496 to 1. I calculated it.

I groaned. Maths wasn't something I wanted to keep me awake at night, but here I was, playing out equations in the air with my finger. The rainbow pin was clasped in my other hand, and I could feel the warmth of it as it drew in the heat of my skin. I put the pin on my bedside cabinet next to my phone. With any luck, I'd wake up tomorrow and it wouldn't be there.

But when my alarm made my phone vibrate, the enamel pin was still there, shining at me like a beacon of queerdom. And I had a few texts in the group chat.

> **Tony**
> What were we supposed to do for Spanish? I forget.
> **Ashley**
> Escribe sobre un deseo de Navidad.
> **Tony**
> I don't even know what that means.
> **Ashley**
> Philistine. Dean, let him copy your homework on the bus.

As I showered, I thought about Ben Hunter. Ben hadn't

occurred to me during my sleepless night. He'd talked to me in the line at the coffee shop like it was the most natural thing for us to have a conversation. Casual chit-chat with anyone in Ben's league wasn't something that happened to me often, not unless they were asking me to move out of the way or do their maths homework for them. I never thought of myself as a geek, but the jocks certainly did.

Ben had mentioned the Secret Santa thing at Grainger's. And it only struck me now that that was peculiar. Why would Ben be excited about it?

I wondered, as I tucked my shirt into my school trousers, at the possibility that Ben was my Secret Santa. Maybe his interest at Grainger's wasn't indifferent. Or maybe I was reading too much into a casual encounter at a coffee shop where most of the kids in school hung out after class.

Calculate them odds.

But the thing with trying to be a detective at school when you sit in the front row is that all the other kids are behind your back. You can't study them to draw conclusions when you're facing the board. Sherlock Holmes wouldn't have been sitting at the front of class, he'd be standing in the blood at the back, staring at the murder weapon.

In geography, when I looked towards the back of the room where the world map was, I looked for Ben's broad face. He had his head down, writing in his notebook, and I spent too long studying his tanned forehead, the thick bridge of his nose, the shape of his ears under his brown hair. When Ben looked up, my eyes flicked to the world map and I mouthed *Portugal* as if I couldn't remember where it was.

Good save.

Between classes, I followed Ben along the hall, a safe distance behind, and I watched how he interacted with the basketball team, all fist bumps and belching. Erin McNally clung to his side for the most part, and when Ben went into the men's room, I considered going in after him, but I was too afraid of catching him with his pants down and not being able to take my eyes off him.

I stood in the hallway, flicking through TikTok on my phone like I was searching for something important, and then I turned around to study the anti-bullying poster on the wall when Ben came out.

And Ashley said, "What're you doing?"

I span on my heels. "Nothing. What're you doing?"

"I'm on my way to class. Like you should be."

"Where are you heading?"

"History. You?"

"Art."

Ben was gone and I didn't know which class he had now. The next class we shared was English, after lunch, with Mr Dobbins, that offending teacher who was the cause of all my worries.

When we got to the end of the corridor, she gave me a nod and hightailed it upstairs. The bell was ringing.

I didn't catch another glimpse of Ben until English. Even in the cafeteria at lunchtime, sitting by the windows with Tony, I scanned the collection of tables but couldn't see him. Alex Janey was also missing. They were probably playing football on the pitch outside, or down in the gym shooting hoops.

I'd put the rainbow pin at the bottom of my bag because I didn't want to leave it at home and have my parents find it.

And even though it weighed very little, I could feel it among my books, screaming at gravity to release it from its strangling hold.

In English, Mr Dobbins had everyone move their desk aside and put their chairs in a circle. The Secret Santa box had been stowed on top of the shelves in the corner behind his desk, awaiting the gift exchange before Christmas.

As I sat, I looked around the circle of faces, stopping on Ben's comfortable smile. We locked eyes, but I couldn't hold it. I looked at my hands, at the floor, at Mr Dobbins.

Dobbins said, "Right. I'm tired of you guys reading William Golding as if you were dead inside. So today, we're going to act it out." There was a collective groan followed by an uncomfortable laugh.

"This isn't drama," Alex Janey said.

"Your whole life is a drama, Janey. You can be Ralph."

"Does that mean Philip Gamble has to be Piggy?"

"Hey," Philip Gamble said.

"That's enough. On your feet, Mr Janey, you're going to enjoy this if it kills me."

Janey said, "Don't die, sir. That'd make me sad."

Ben and the others laughed. I kept my eyes on the floor. My book bag was between my feet. I was standing at one end of a rainbow. But I couldn't see who was on the other side.

Alex Janey's acting skills were over the top. Even when, in character, he was having a heartfelt conversation with Piggy— which wasn't performed by Philip Gamble—he delivered his lines like an angry sasquatch with a toothache.

If there was anyone in the class that I didn't want to be my Secret Santa, it was Alex. I let my eyes wander over to Ben's shoes instead, black and scuffed, the laces twisted into double knots, the little plastic ends missing and the laces frayed like my nerves.

Ben's foot was tapping like he was listening to music, or he was feeling impatient.

And by the end of class, I still hadn't figured out who had given me the awkward gift, and whether it had been given with interest or spite.

But the more I thought about it, the more I decided it couldn't be a joke. Jokes have a punchline. My Secret Santa would have revealed himself by now, pointing and laughing at the uncomfortable gay boy. It had been more than twenty-four hours and nobody—other than Ben—had even looked at me.

When I got to choir practice after school, Mr Elliot warmed us up with scales and then we jumped into a rendition of *Silent Night*. It was sad and boring until Mr Elliot dropped in a drum beat and a bass line behind his piano playing. "We'd be better with a live orchestra, but the computer will have to do," he said.

He still hadn't told me which song he wanted me to sing on my own, and I realised I should have been more worried about that than I was about the rainbow pin. The nerves hit me in the stomach during the second half of *Carol of the Bells*.

Mr Elliot had his back to us at the piano, but he said, "Sing up, Dean, I can't hear you."

At the end of practice, I sat near the drum kit with my schoolbag clasped in my arms, and I waited for the others to leave the room. When we were alone, I said, "I don't think I can do the solo, sir."

"Sure you can."

"It's making my stomach sick, sir."

"That's just nerves. I'd be scared if you weren't nervous."

"I'll forget the words and—look—my hands are sweaty just thinking about it."

"You're great at maths, aren't you?" Mr Elliot said.

"What's that got to do with anything?"

"How many minutes is the average carol song?"

I shrugged. "Three?"

"Three minutes. And how many minutes are in one day—just one day?"

I worked it out. "One thousand, four hundred and forty."

"Do you see what I'm saying?"

"No." But I did.

Mr Elliot said, "Nerves are a precursor to the truth. But here's the thing, Dean. Nobody can see your nerves when you wear them on the inside. You think I don't get nervous, coming in here every day and teaching music to a bunch of kids who don't want to learn? It terrifies me."

"Then why do you do it?"

"Because," he said, walking around his desk and opening a drawer, "once in a few hundred years, I get to hear a voice as special as the one you'd rather keep to yourself." He held out a piece of paper. "Here."

I took it. It was the lyrics to *O Holy Night.*

"Everybody knows the song. But let's show them how the Irish can take anything and make it better. We'll take a first pass at it on Friday."

"Sir, I can't do it."

"Nerves, Dean. Shape your nerves, don't let them shape you. Remember, what's on the inside isn't seen unless you let it be known. You're better than your nerves."

I sat on the back row of the public bus on my way home. I slouched into the seat and propped my knees against the seat-back in front of me. I rooted at the bottom of my bag for the small rainbow pin and, looking up to make sure no one was watching, I held it between my finger and thumb.

What's on the inside isn't seen, Mr Elliot had said. I had more than nerves on the inside. I had secrets.

I unzipped the breast of my coat and pierced the fabric with the pin on the inside. It was hidden. But it was there. I could feel the cold enamel against my thin shirt.

I might not be able to tell anyone beyond my closest friends that I was gay. But I still had a rainbow on the inside.

CHAPTER 8

BEN

I ate breakfast in silence with my dad. Someone had cleaned up the spatters of blood on the floor from the night before and Mum was still in bed nursing whatever hangover she'd inflicted on herself. Dad's tie was at an awkward angle, mirroring my own.

My cereal was turning to mush.

Dad checked his watch as he stuffed some papers into his laptop case. "Get a move on."

"I'll get the bus."

"Get in the car, Ben, I don't have all day."

"Mum gave me some cash for the bus," I lied. "I'm meeting Erin at the bus stop."

Dad said, "Did you do your homework?" as if he gave a crap. But he didn't wait for an answer.

When the front door clicked shut, I pushed my frosted flakes away. The floor was clean, but I could see where the blood had been, a faint trace. With a blacklight, maybe I'd see years of stains, a story splashed across the walls like a cave painting. I didn't think Dad was violent, but do kids even know what happens after they go to bed?

But it was Dad's nose that had been bleeding. If Mum had punched him, he probably deserved it.

Mum came downstairs as I was pulling on my jacket. "Is your dad gone?"

She looked haggard, her hair a mess and her oversized nightshirt crumpled. It said *ALL I WANNA DO IS SLEEP.* She looked like she needed it.

I nodded and stooped to pick up my bag.

Mum said, "Get me a glass of water, will you? I'm going back to bed."

I let the water run cold before filling a glass and when I sat on the edge of her bed, she looked small and childlike. I'd brought her a couple of painkillers and she gulped the water like she hadn't tasted anything so sweet in all her life.

"I don't deserve you," she said.

"I know." I tried to smile.

"Everything will be okay, Benny." I hated when she called me that. "You'll see."

"Do you want the curtains open?"

"God no," she said, shielding her eyes as if I'd already thrown them wide. She shuffled down the bed and lay on her side, away from me.

I reached out and rubbed her back. "Get some sleep."

"He's not a bad man. He's just going through some stuff."

We all were. I said, "I know."

I closed the bedroom door, leaving her in darkness, and when I grabbed my bag and went outside, Erin was waiting for me on the doorstep.

"We've missed the bus," she said.

"We'll get the next one."

We walked towards town, along concrete streets as grey as the sky. The wind was cold enough to skin you alive. At the next bus stop, we carried on to the next. And we kept walking after that, too.

"How were they?" she asked.

I'd sent her a message last night telling her I'd be getting the bus, but I didn't mention the blood. It wasn't something you could say out loud.

"The usual."

"They need counselling."

"Do you want to be the one to suggest it?"

"Maybe I will." She held her hair out of her face as we turned a corner and the wind pushed against us.

I could sense the words she refused to say. You're not alone. I'm here for you. But best friends don't say those things. Not with words. She side-kicked my ass.

I punched her back, playfully.

We stopped at a corner shop for a couple of warm sausage rolls and she laughed at me when I got pastry flakes on my tie.

"We should ditch school for the day. Hang out at the mall."

I balled the paper from breakfast and dropped it into a bin. "Who are you and what have you done with Erin?"

"I'm trying to cheer you up."

"By suggesting something that we haven't done since we were twelve?"

"I still can't believe we weren't caught. Your mum totally saw us."

"Never play hooky on a Monday," I said. "Anyway, I've got practice at lunchtime. I can't skip."

By the time we got to school, Erin's hands were red and she

held them above a radiator that was only lukewarm.

Alex Janey gave me a raised chin. People don't say hello anymore. "You know how it's my birthday in January?" he said. "I'm thinking of camping on Myrtleville Beach. One night, no parents. What do you think?"

Erin said, "I think you're crazy."

"I wasn't asking you. Boys only."

"You can keep your little gay club because I'm not coming anyway." She walked away, and I felt the sting of her words.

I looked at Alex whose face was wide and hopeful. "You want to spend a night on the coast in a couple of flimsy tents in January? It'll be freezing."

"My brother will get us a load of beer. You won't give a crap about the cold when you're drunk. And I've already told the lads. They're all up for it."

"Who's up for it?"

"Everyone."

Alex Janey never did anything without approval from his friends. He was one of those guys that would go through life on top because people believed he belonged there.

"It's January, though," I said.

"But it's my sixteenth."

"There'd better be a lot of alcohol."

Alex smiled. "And a shitload of girls."

I butted the open heel of my hand against Janey's forehead and ran from him. "You couldn't score in a brothel."

"No running," a teacher shouted.

I turned. Alex was chasing me.

I weaved.

And I slammed into Dean O'Donnell. We went down

72

—hard—sliding into the wall together like a pair of Wrestle Mania lovers. I felt Dean's breath on my face as it was forced out of his body from the impact.

"Shit. Sorry. Are you okay?"

Dean opened his mouth but it looked like he was too shocked to speak.

Half the kids in the hallway were laughing.

Dean's friends were trying to pick him up off the floor.

And at that moment, I realised nobody was trying to help me up. Erin had already left and Alex Janey was laughing harder than anyone else. I didn't know why that made me feel like crap.

As Dean limped away with his friends, walking off the sudden violation of space, I said, "Catch you next time."

Ashley flicked her hair over her shoulder. "Next time, you'd better bust your nose, or I'll do it for you."

"I said sorry," I called after them. It was typical; I had to fall into him to prove I was falling for him. I could still feel Dean's breath on my face.

"Nice layup," Alex Janey said. He made a dunking motion with his hands.

Sitting on my ass on the floor, I moved so that my back was against the wall. I didn't want to stand up. I'd just stay there, on the ground. Alone and lonely.

But the bell rang.

"You coming?" Janey asked.

I groaned and picked myself off the floor. I couldn't get Dean out of my mind. Dean and the rainbow pin.

I didn't think anyone else was stewing over the stupid Secret Santa exercise. People would get a crappy present and they'd laugh about it and it would probably end up in the bin when they got home. And now I had to figure out what to buy Dean to replace the gift I'd given him early. I followed Alex Janey down the hall and into geography. I was pretty sure Dean was in science on a Wednesday morning, not that I'd studied his class schedule or anything. I pictured Dean in a white lab coat, leaning over a beaker that was bubbling on top of a Bunsen burner.

And I wanted to rip that lab coat off him.

I slumped into a chair at the back of class and kept my book bag on my lap to hide my emotions.

Alex Janey folded his arms and slouched over his desk with his head down. It was all right for guys like him, who flit from girl to girl, never committing, never settling for more than a few weeks. If it wasn't all bravado, he had been with more than half of the girls in our class since last year. He said he'd never kiss and tell, but in the locker room, he said it in a way that meant he definitely did those things that the other boys were suggesting.

I saw through it because I did the same thing myself in the past. Alex was probably still a virgin just like me. You say everything without saying anything. That's how you get a reputation.

I'd never lied about my sexuality, and I hadn't told anyone I was dating Erin. People just assumed. And because I wasn't talking about us as a couple, people read more into it. You could be a virgin and still be considered a stud; you just had to stop talking about sex like you'd only just discovered it.

Say less, be more. That was life.

I tried to concentrate on what the teacher was saying. But

I couldn't get Dean's breath on my face out of my mind. It was sweet and inoffensive. I'd like to feel it again, hot against my skin. I replayed our tumble, recognising how intimate it had been despite taking enough dives with opposing teammates on the basketball court. I'd been in close quarters with other guys too many times but dropping to the dusty tiled floor with Dean had been almost erotic.

I hoped I hadn't hurt him. I was used to taking a tumble on the court or, worse, being lifted off my feet on the rugby field and dumped in the mud to eat grass. But Dean looked so skinny that bending down to tie his shoelaces might snap his spine. He'd been winded as he walked away from our fall, but he didn't look injured. I had seen enough sprained ankles to know the difference.

At lunchtime, filing into the changing room for practice and eating an energy bar before changing, knowing that normal kids were eating lasagne or stew in the cafeteria, I pulled on my yellow jersey and shorts, listened to Coach talk us through the practice plays, and followed my teammates into the gym.

It was raining outside, so it was packed with kids on their lunch break. I looked across the open space. The team was fanning out and warming up. Erin was down on the half-court line. She was always there. She came to my practice sessions as though they were important games, and she was in the seat beside me in more than half of my classes. At lunch, she was dripping ketchup on my chips and, in the evening, she was Facetiming me or sitting in my bedroom pretending to study.

It was always me and Erin. Never me and somebody else.

Never Ben and Dean.

But there he was, sitting with his friends on the baseline.

They weren't paying the team any attention, like most of the kids in the gym. When Coach blew his whistle, nobody cheered. It was just practice, not a game.

I dribbled across the court, warming up. I moved away from Dean, hoping he wouldn't look up. He wasn't wearing the rainbow pin and I didn't blame him. I'd been stupid to buy it. I'd handed over a little piece of my heart, a section of my inner being. It was like scraping out your stomach lining and handing it to someone, saying, "Here, this is for you. Take care of it."

Nobody wanted that in their hand.

As point guard, I got the team to huddle up. I called a play and we broke at the coach's whistle.

Coach Williams said, "I want some hustle out there. Effort is what separates the good from the great."

I rolled my eyes. Coach's pep talks were straight out of a playbook.

As we spread out across the court, half the team playing against the others, I bounced the ball over to Alex Janey. "Pick and roll," I said. Alex nodded, popping the ball back to me.

It was our favourite play. When the coach blew his whistle again, I dribbled the ball, eyes locked on the basket at the other end of the court. With a quick, practiced motion, I passed it to Alex who had positioned himself as a screen between me and the defending players.

I manoeuvred around him, my feet dodging our defenders. Alex, knowing the timing, passed off the ball again. With a burst of speed that left my teammates trailing behind, I drove towards the hoop. I leapt into the air, my arm extending towards the basket, and laid the ball up and into the net.

Coach Williams applauded the score as I ran back up the court after the ball.

I tried to keep my eyes off the baseline seats where Dean was but playing towards that basket made it difficult not to see him. I wished the gym was off-limits during practice, but it was lunchtime, and nobody gave a crap.

Erin hollered from the half-court line, clapping and whooping.

I shook my head, trying to stay focused. When I had possession of the ball again, I dribbled down the court, sidestepping defenders, eye on the basket, on Dean, on the basket.

Somebody said, "It's snowing."

I travelled with the ball. I shot too late and crashed over the out-of-bounds line. Dean was on his feet, jumping out of the way.

Nobody was paying attention. I spun around to stop from falling and locked eyes with Dean. I raised my hands to show it was an accident. Again.

"Oh my God," a girl said.

Everyone was racing to the windows.

Alex Janey tossed me the ball. "What the hell, man?"

"What?" I said, scowling.

Outside, the snow was coming down hard. Fat, white flakes were settling on the ground. It wouldn't be long before the world was hidden.

"Snow day," somebody said.

Coach blew his whistle, calling the end of practice. And I stood beside Dean as we watched the snow falling beyond the windows.

Dean zipped up the neck of his coat as if he was standing

in that freezing snowfall. And I felt hotter than I should have been. I used my upper arm to drag the sweat off my forehead.

Dean looked away from me.

And Coach said, "Hit the showers."

I obliged. It would have to be a cold one.

— CHAPTER 9 —

DEAN

I kept my eyes on the falling snow outside the windows as the basketball team drifted out of the gym. The flakes popped against the glass like miniature grenades. Now that the court-squeak of the team's shoes had stopped and everybody was watching the windows in awe, the silence that drew itself around me was wholesome. I'd successfully dodged another tackle from Ben Hunter, even if it had been an accident this time. Not that I was convinced the takedown in the hallway was on purpose.

Maybe Ben was just clumsy.

He'd held up his hands in an awkward apology before Alex Janey punched the ball towards his chest. I felt responsible for the foul, though I wasn't the one playing.

Ben and I stood beside each other after the coach's whistle, Ben staring at me like an iridescent starfish, and I refused to look at him. The snowfall was enticing and electrifying as it drifted to the ground in a cascade of frost-kissed dreams. It stopped lips from forming words that shouldn't be said.

The wind rattled the windows and fractured my thoughts. With the team gone and the teachers ushering everybody out of the gym and back to class, Tony said, "You know what this means, don't you?"

"Hot chocolate at Grainger's after school," Ashley said.

"You know it."

As we came out of the gym, I heard the team's chatter and laughter from the boys' changing room. Alex Janey's laugh was louder than the others, but I heard Ben's voice among the rowdy teammates.

"Are you in?" Tony asked.

"What?"

"Grainger's. We can go straight after enterprise."

"Are you trying to make me miss choir practice?"

"In favour of hot chocolate?" Tony said. "Hell yes."

"I can meet you guys there after practice."

Our enterprise and innovation class was a huge part of transition year at school. It was a chance for students to form mini-companies and gain greater work ethics and entrepreneurial skills. It was supposed to gear us up for adulthood.

While Ashley's group had created a recycled furniture company they called The Cheap Seats, the group that Tony and I were in struggled to come up with an idea at first. Teaming up with two others, we argued over establishing a healthy snack business (Tony said, "Oats and grains aren't snacks. Forget about it.") or a sustainable clothing line. But none of us could sew. In the end, continuing our discussions in a group chat outside school, we agreed on creating a tech help service, and we spent the rest of the weekend throwing around fun name ideas.

Byte Me. Tech Trippers. Code Cannibals.

By the following Monday, we still didn't have a name, so when pressed by the teacher, we reluctantly settled on

Techsperts. Officially the worst enterprise name in the history of the vocational class.

But despite the name, our company got off to a successful start. We were allowed to set up in a spare office with a phone line, and we'd printed flyers for a leaflet drop around town. My first call when we launched was from a guy who said he was seventy-six and couldn't remember his email password. Although I helped him click "Forgot Password" and restore access to his account, the old guy kept me on the phone for over an hour and a half talking about nothing and everything. I guessed he was lonely and I didn't have the heart to hang up.

As we left the spectacle of the snowfall outside the gym, Ashley tied a bandana over her hair to go and sand down some old furniture, and Tony and I went to our tiny office. Roisin and Bridget were already there.

A printed sign outside the door said, *Get Techspert Help Here*, and listed our opening hours. Kids could come by with their phones, tablets or laptops if they had any issues and, although there was no charge, Bridget had placed a tip jar on the desk closest to the door.

Manning the phone, I put the headset on and tried to ignore the chatter from the others who were discussing our holiday tech support arrangements. We would redirect the phone line to our mobiles over the Christmas break and we'd each agreed to work for two hours a day, except Christmas day. Roisin had said we'd get extra brownie points for working over the holiday, and we'd probably double our tips.

The phone rang. "Techsperts. This is Dean."

"Is Stu there?" a high-pitched voice asked.

"Stu who?" I could hear the giggles. This wasn't our first

prank call.

"Pidassol," the voice said.

I put the call on speaker so the others could hear and said, "I'm sorry, can you say that name again? Who are you looking for?"

More giggling. "Stu Piddasol." They hung up before I could respond.

Tony said, "That one was almost funny, but hardly original." He scratched another tally mark on the board. We'd been keeping score since we launched our phone service. "Dean, you're only three points behind Roisin."

Somebody had to overhear the prank call for it to count, but I had answered two of them in our first week before we settled on a scoring system. Haywood U. Fakhmi was my favourite. It still cracks me up.

Operating the phone line helped take my mind off everything else. Outside the frosted window of the tiny office, the snow had stopped falling but the wind was kicking up in gusts that battered the building. I wondered who would be the first one out of school, to leave their footprint in the fresh whiteness. As a kid, when it snowed, I'd open the front door at home, take one giant step forward, and then leap back into the warmth of the house so that there was only one footprint out there. An hour later, it would be gone, hidden beneath the postman's treads and Dad's great big shoes and cat paws. Footsteps, like all things, were transient.

Christmas these days wasn't the same. I missed the wonder, that childish, wide-eyed innocence. I'd come downstairs on Christmas morning wearing thick pyjamas. I'd eat chocolate for breakfast while tearing wrapping paper from presents in a gleeful frenzy, knowing that a fat man in a red suit had squeezed down the chimney just hours before. It was wondrous.

Now, I'd roll out of bed, brush my teeth, force myself into the Christmas sweater Mum had bought me, and suffer the phone calls with aunts and uncles who always asked the same questions, and I always gave them the same answers.

How's school? Great, thanks.

Got a girlfriend yet? No.

Do you like the T-shirt we sent you this year? Yes, it's lovely. The reindeer doesn't look terrified at all, as it happens.

I still had that T-shirt, hidden at the back of my wardrobe where I hoped it would be eaten by moths.

My parents had tried to tell me that the spirit of Santa was real, that they were Santa, but I'd been old enough to know better that year, and that was the end of my childlike wonder. And yet I still enjoyed getting a scientific calculator in my stocking. Go figure.

I didn't have a downer on Christmas, but it no longer held the magic it used to. Gifts were getting smaller, Santa wasn't real, and snowmen didn't come to life and whisk you off to the land of make-believe.

But Secret Santa, he was real.

I leaned into the chair where I'd draped my coat and felt the small pin at my back. Secret Santa was very real.

A teacher stopped by the office looking for help with his iPad. "You can't open Zoom because it isn't on your iPad, sir," Roisin told him. "You just press here, do a search, and then press 'Get', see?" Other than that, nobody came near us, and the phone only rang twice.

The second call had been genuine but was a simple DNS

fix. I preferred the more complex issues that required detailed thought.

Bridget shook the tip jar and some coins rattled at the bottom, among the banknotes that had been in there for weeks. "You know what that sound is? That's the sound of a bankrupt business."

"We'll make up for it in January when everyone gets new tech for Christmas," Tony said. Ever the optimist.

We still had to write up our end-of-term paper, an outline of how the business had performed since conception and evaluate each other's performance. But we agreed to hold off on that for as long as possible.

When the bell rang, the snow was falling again, softer this time, settling on top of the already white school field, and as Tony said, "See you at Grainger's; don't be long," I folded myself into my coat, checked to make sure the pin was still under the collar, and wished I didn't have choir practice. It was terrorising me. Having Mr Elliot say that I could conquer my nerves was one thing, but I could barely conquer my emotions, let alone my nerves or my voice. Maybe I should quit the choir and let Gemma Ademola take my solo.

I watched from the end of the corridor as Tony caught up with Ashley and they skidded through the fresh snow. It was already dark, but the floodlights whitewashed the world beyond the exit.

I turned my back on the snowball fights and caterwauling teenagers and shuffled down the corridor towards the music room. I was too depressed to even pick up my feet. Rainbow pins and Christmas carols made up my entire focus. I'd get the two confused and start singing about rainbows at the choir performance, coming out in front of the whole town. Away in a manger, no crib for a gay.

When I got to the music room, the door was open and Mr Elliot was standing on top of his desk. A water pipe above him had burst and the choir members were moving his papers and music books out of the way. Mr Elliot was holding his coat against the pipe, trying to stem the flow and getting soaked in the process.

"What happened?" I asked as if it wasn't obvious.

Water was spreading across the tiled floor.

Gemma Ademola rushed in, carrying an armful of towels from the girls' changing room down the corridor, and everyone helped to mop up the flood even as it continued to explode above Mr Elliot's head. I wasn't the tallest guy in the choir, but I got on the desk beside Mr Elliot and helped him tie a towel around the pipe just in time for the water to be shut off.

When the maintenance man came in covered in grease, Mr Elliot and I were soaked.

"Take your coat off, son. I'll run it through the dryer in the boiler room."

I shook my arms, water flailing. "I'm not that wet. It's okay."

The floor was a mess and a bunch of textbooks were ruined, but the instruments at the back of the room were unharmed except for a small puddle of water that spackled the skin of the snare drum. Gemma Ademola carefully tipped it so the water ran off and then draped a towel over it.

"Is there much damage?" The maintenance guy asked.

Mr Elliot surveyed his room. "This morning's second-year homework has been ruined, so that's a stroke of luck. At least I don't have to look at one more out-of-place F sharp note on their music sheets." He turned to the choir. "Sorry, guys. No practice today. You can head on home."

Although I joined in with the moans of disappointment, I was happy. A few more days of bad luck and maybe they'd call the whole thing off. I was kicking myself for ever signing up for the choir.

I left the room with higher spirits than I'd entered it.

Outside, there were still some kids throwing snowballs, but most of them had gone home. There seemed to be three factions of warring teens all gunning for each other, and my only way through the carnage was via the car park. The bright floodlights had white halos around them and the snowfall eddied and danced to the churned ground, adding a fresh layer of snow on top of a multitude of footprints that were already disappearing.

I pulled my collar up, waved when Gemma Ademola said goodnight, and then ducked out to the snow. I weaved down the slope towards the car park, and narrowly avoided a snowball in the face as I rounded the corner. My hands were already pinking towards reddened skin and I could see my breath solidifying on the air. The shouts of militant kids peppered the sky and snowballs flew in all directions. A couple of boys crouched behind a car in the car park and took shots at anyone passing by.

I jumped as one landed in front of my feet, and then I slipped on the compacted snow, losing my balance.

I put my hand against one of the cars to stop from falling, and then I kept walking. The bus stop was empty. I'd missed the school bus.

I skated across the half-empty car park with my arms out

for balance. And just as I thought I was far enough away from the reach of the glistening missiles another snowball smacked the ground beside me. I looked over my shoulder. Three more snowballs were coming my way.

And then something lurched into me. It took the breath from my chest with a whoosh and I tumbled to the ground. Somebody's arm was under me, and there was a head in my neck. We slid to a stop against a red Hyundai.

Ben Tackle-Me Hunter. Of course.

"Hey," I said when I'd sucked enough air back into my lungs. "Are you trying to make a habit of this?"

"I saved your life," Ben said, trying to right himself.

My head was against the cold car tire. "My life?"

"If that snowball had hit your face you'd be crying."

"I've been hit by snowballs before. I'm not soft."

"Yeah? What about yellow snowballs?" Ben pointed. The smushed stain of the exploded snowball was darker than the rest of the snow around it.

"Gross," I said.

"See? I saved your life." Ben was on his knees, peering over the rim of the car at our assailants. "We're at a tactical advantage," he said. "There are about four cars between us and them. If we sneak around that way, we can hit them from behind."

I looked up. "How old are you?"

"You're never too old for a snowball fight."

Ben's jacket was thin and his trousers were soaked where we'd fallen. They were blacker in the seat and hip than the legs. He crouched as another snowball flew overhead.

I pushed myself upright. At least my glasses hadn't skittered away from me in our fall. I tried not to look at Ben's ass.

"Are we trapped?"

"Never. Follow me."

He scooped up his backpack and kept low. We came around the back of a car and dashed towards the next, narrowly avoiding another volley of grenades.

Ben poked his head above the parapet and a fresh snowball smacked the side of his face. He fell back.

"We'll never make it." He held his head as if it was falling off.

"Don't you die on me," I said. It sounded weird and forced, but it felt natural to play along.

Ben reached up, feigning agony, and gripped my coat collar. He pulled me close. "Go. Save yourself. Tell my kids I love them."

I was aware of the rainbow pin under Ben's fist—the rainbow shape of it in all its rainbow colours, shining rainbow-like in the brilliant rainbow glow of the floodlights.

I gripped Ben's wrists, hoping he hadn't seen, and said, "I'm not leaving you behind, soldier. It's just a flesh wound." I touched Ben's cold ear. "It's still attached. We're going to make it. Do you hear me?"

"What's our exfil strategy?" Ben asked, struggling to his feet and crouching.

I pointed as another onslaught of grenades assaulted us. The school gate was less than one hundred feet from our position.

Ben shouted, "Go, go, go."

And as I ran, slipping on the icy ground, I wondered what the hell I was doing. Snowball fights were one thing but playing a game of soldiers with a boy you had barely spoken a dozen words to was something else. We weren't teenagers in that moment. We were little kids and we were warriors.

Boys and men.

Caught between worlds.

CHAPTER 10

BEN

I pushed Dean ahead of me, a bombardment of snowballs at our backs. One of the missiles smacked the top of my head and cascaded over me in a sparkling mess of glittering snow that rained across Dean's back. And even as we ran, I was smiling.

Dean O'Donnell was wearing the rainbow pin. It was tucked under the collar of his coat, but I saw the glint of it when I was play-acting. I'd felt it under my thumb.

We ducked behind a car as a snowball exploded against the wing mirror.

Dean looked at me, his glasses at an odd angle, and there was something about his frost-reddened nose and flushed cheeks that made me want to cup his face. His hand on the rear bumper of the car was close to mine. I pulled my fingers away like a nervous tic.

Another snowball zipped overhead. If it had hit the car, there was enough power behind it to break the windscreen.

I chanced a look over the car. I didn't know who was targeting us, but it didn't matter. You never know who the enemy is in war.

But we weren't playing anymore. Dean said, "The bus is

coming."

We could hear the chugging sound of its diesel engine as it struggled up the hill behind us.

"We can get the next one," I said. I flexed my fingers and gathered a ball of snow, patting it into a perfect sphere. I held it out to him.

Dean stared at the snowball like it would explode in his face, and then he took it from me, careful fingers holding it loose. He hefted it to check its weight and I swear when he smiled my mouth mirrored his.

I formed another ball. "On three?"

He nodded and adjusted his glasses with a knuckle.

I didn't count it out. I shouted, "Three," and we lobbed our missiles over the top of the car. The enemy camp retaliated and we couldn't make our snowballs fast enough. When the ground between us was scraped clean of snow, we had no choice but to move.

"This way," Dean said.

But I pulled on his coat sleeve to stop him. "We can't leave mid-battle." I stared across No Man's Land. I had pinpointed which car the enemy was hiding behind. If we could get around behind them, we could take them out with one throw.

My knees were wet and one of my shoes was letting in water. My toes were cold and my fingers were turning blue. But I felt good. My cheeks were sore from grinning.

Dean scooped up a few fresh snowballs and laid them in his arms. "You go that way. I'll double back around here. Take them from both sides?"

"Got it," I said. I made a couple of snowballs and crept around the car as Dean went in the opposite direction. I lobbed one as a distraction and then darted between two cars. I saw Dean crouch into place at the far side of our target. He nodded.

I jumped.

I had scooped a few more snowballs in my hiding spot, and when I leapt out from behind the car, I attacked, volley after volley at the crouching enemy. Dean hit them from the far side, his aim accurate and firm. The two boys covered their heads with their arms and ran.

I reached my hand up for a high-five and then lowered it before Dean saw. I was conscious of my frozen fingers and I tucked them into my jacket pockets. I really need a new coat, something thick for the winter.

"Good aim," I said. "The way you smacked that one guy right on the forehead."

Dean shrugged. "It's just maths."

"I could use a bit of that for basketball."

Dean smiled and I looked at my shoes. I could feel my right sock was soaked.

"Oh shit," Dean said. "There's the four thirty-five."

Another bus had chugged up the hill and drove right past the bus stop. We were too far away to flag it down.

My fingers were thawing in my pockets. "There'll be another one in ten minutes."

But Dean shook his head and knuckled his glasses again. "After the four thirty-five, there aren't any more this far up Crest Hill for forty minutes."

"How're your feet?" I asked.

"My feet?"

I bopped him on the chest with the back of my hand. "Looks like we're walking."

I turned away from him towards the gate. I didn't look back over my shoulder. I just hoped he was behind me.

"You coming?"

There was a moment of silence before I heard his soft footfalls in the crunching snow and I let out a long breath. When he caught up, he shrugged his backpack over his shoulder and looked at me. I couldn't hold his gaze and I studied my feet as we turned out of the gate and down the hill towards town.

He kept pace with me but he was silent and I didn't know how to start a conversation. In the end, I didn't have to.

Dean said, "Where's Erin?"

"She caught the first bus."

"Without you?"

"I know, right?"

We lapsed into silence again. I could almost feel the heat of his body beside me as we walked. Or maybe I was imagining it.

"How's your enterprise business going?" I asked, just to fill the void. "You're doing a call centre thing or something, right?"

"Tech support. If you get a virus, I'm your guy."

"When I catch the flu, I'll let you know."

"I'd probably have to put a new hard drive in you," Dean said. If that was a deliberate innuendo his face didn't show it.

The sock in my right shoe was cold and heavy.

"What kind of company did you form?" he asked.

"Sports therapy."

"Therapy? People tell you their darkest secrets and you prescribe them three weeks of football and a crash course in cross country?"

"Not that kind of therapy," I said, but I knew he was joking. "We offer nutritional advice, fitness training sessions and massage therapy."

"What would you recommend for me?"

"That depends on what you want to get out of it."

"I'm not very sporty," Dean said.

"You don't have to be an athlete to enjoy the benefits of sports activities."

"Now you sound like a pamphlet."

"I'm enthusiastic."

"I can tell," he said. "What name did you come up with?"

I'd seen Dean's tech support company posters around the school. Their name—Techsperts—wasn't original. Alex created our posters on one of the library computers but we only put them up around the gym and changing rooms. In truth, we didn't have very many clients.

"We're called MVP Wellness."

"That's cool," he said.

I wasn't sure if he meant it.

We'd slipped to the bottom of Crest Hill and crossed the busy road to Main Street. Christmas lights glinted off Dean's glasses when he said, "Is that what you want to be when you graduate?"

I shrugged but he wasn't watching so I said, "Maybe. I don't know yet. Something to do with fitness, probably. What about you?"

Dean had pulled his wallet from his pocket and was counting the cash in it. "Mum wants me to go into finance."

"Because you're a maths genius."

"I'm not a maths genius."

"Yeah, you are. I swear you understand it better than Mrs James half the time."

"Yeah," Dean said. It wasn't conceited, it was a matter of fact. "Chips?" he asked, pointing at a takeaway on the corner. "I'm freezing. It'll warm us up."

I didn't have any cash on me so I said, "I'm good. But you go ahead."

He ordered a large bag of chips and asked for a packet of ketchup which he squeezed onto the side of the polystyrene container, and before leaving the takeaway, he grabbed two wooden forks. He handed one to me.

"It's cool," I said, but the smell of them was making my stomach growl.

"I'll never eat them all."

I took the fork and stabbed a couple of fat chips onto it. "I'll buy the next ones."

We walked, our breath hot and white before us, the chips warming our stomachs. Christmas music warbled from shop-fronts and a net of bright lights lit the sky above us from building to building, reflecting off the slushing snow. The roads in town had enough traffic to keep the snow off them, but it had collected in mounds along the gutters and pavements like an army of sick snowmen.

We didn't speak while we ate and it felt comfortable. He held the container of chips between us and when it was empty, he dropped it into a street bin.

"I can catch a bus from here that stops at the end of my street," Dean said.

There was an elderly woman at the bus stop, sitting on the narrow bench under the shelter, shielded from the wind by a glowing advertising board.

I checked my phone for the time. "I can wait with you."

"You're not in a hurry?"

I was in no rush to get home to Dad's shouting or Mum's slurring. "You trying to get rid of me?" I asked.

The old lady shuffled up the bench to give us room and Dean patted the seat beside him. "Be my guest," he said.

I sat with my hands in my pockets and my elbow pressed against his. It was intimate and normal all at once. "You sound really formal sometimes," I said.

"Sorry."

"Don't be. It's cool. Is it posh where you're from?"

"Hardly."

"See?" I teased. "Nobody I know says 'hardly' like that. I guess your home is posher than a housing estate with a dozen cars up on blocks and a corner shop that has a security guard at the door and a metal detector."

"How much do you get for copper wire these days?"

I laughed. "Okay, it's not that bad." Although there was a gang of kids that were chased off the top of the shopping centre for trying to steal copper pipes to sell. I said, "Alex could tell you some horror stories. His brother was arrested twice last year."

"What'd he do?"

"I don't know. Drugs, I think."

Dean nodded and looked up the street in the direction of the oncoming traffic. "Why do you hang around with him?"

"Alex? He's okay."

"He's a dick."

"He thinks he's funny, that's all. He might come across like a dick, but he's actually a nice guy when you get to know him."

"Is he?" He looked at me with a disbelieving expression.

"When we were eleven, he helped me put up a homemade hoop and backboard in our local park. We played there most nights for years."

"Such a good guy," Dean said.

I swallowed my words as I tried to think of something witty to say. But all that came out was, "Is he giving you a hard time?"

Dean stood. "There's my bus."

The bus inched towards us in the slow traffic and we stood in silence until it settled in front of the stop and the doors opened. Dean stepped back to let the elderly woman on first, and he stood behind her on the steps in front of the driver.

"Hey," I called. Dean turned to face me. "We have a game against Millstreet on Friday. Are you going to be there?"

"Football's not really my thing."

"It's basketball."

"I know," he said. He was smiling.

"That's cool," I said. "I'll probably not be at your dumb choir performance, either. It's not really my thing."

And Dean laughed.

He sat in a window seat and, as the bus pulled away, he gave me a quick wave.

I pulled a funny face. He ran his coat sleeve across the condensation on the window and rolled his eyes.

And only when he was gone did I feel the cold. My fingers were tingling and red, and my feet were like blocks of ice.

I turned north towards home. If I walked, I could be there in twenty minutes. Thirty if the snow slowed me down. I didn't care. It's not like I had anything to rush home for. A pathetic little Christmas tree in a pathetic little house. The snow had started again and it fell around me in languid drifts. I held my tongue out to catch some flakes. They were cool in my mouth for a split second before they melted, one after another, disappearing like promises.

When I got home, Mum was in the living room. She was watching a reality show on TV and there was a half-empty wine glass beside her. "You're late."

"Yeah," I smiled.

There was a cloud of cigarette smoke above her head.

"Where's Dad?"

"He's not home yet. Erin's waiting in your room."

I went upstairs. If Mum was already drinking, I didn't want to be around when Dad got home.

"Where have you been?" Erin asked when I closed the door of my bedroom and dropped my book bag on the bed beside her.

"I missed the bus."

"You were throwing snowballs, weren't you?"

"Is the Pope Catholic?"

She rolled her eyes but it wasn't the same way Dean had done it. Her eye roll wasn't funny or ironic.

I slumped onto the bed, the pillows folding around my head. I couldn't take the grin off my face.

"What?" she asked.

"What?"

"Why are you grinning?"

"I'm not."

She threw a foam stress ball in my face and it bounced off my forehead before she poked my stomach, making me tense up.

When my dad got home, Erin said, "That's my queue. Are you getting a lift in the morning or are we grabbing the bus?"

I got up on one elbow. "I don't know. I'll text you."

I stood at my bedroom window and watched her run up the street to her house. Yellow streetlights were fogged with flurries of snow and the street was white. Erin disappeared into the blizzard before she even got home.

I wanted to go outside and make snow angels, but that would mean going downstairs and passing my parents.

Instead, I breathed on the window and drew a smiley face.

The condensation ran, making the face cry, and I wiped it away. My reflection was still grinning.

I rolled onto the bed and pulled the quilt over me even though it was early and I hadn't undressed. Downstairs, I heard Mum say something and Dad raise his voice.

But I must have fallen asleep because I didn't hear another sound until morning.

— CHAPTER 11 —

DEAN

I could smell bacon when I woke. Mum announced last night that she was taking a mental health day off work and she was going to use it for a day of Christmas shopping.

"Can I take a mental health day from school?"

"Not a chance," she said.

But I didn't mind. School was where my friends were. And Ben.

I hadn't realised before how down-to-earth he was. My ribs were still tender from where he bashed into me outside school, but I didn't blame him. I had fun throwing snowballs around like kids and playing war. And it was cool just to chill together on the way down the hill from school. He was easy to talk to.

When I showered and went downstairs, there was a bacon sandwich on the kitchen table along with a mug of milky tea. We were normally so rushed in the mornings that breakfast was toast or a bowl of cereal. Bacon was a welcome change.

Mum was standing on the back deck in her dressing gown and holding a warm mug in her hands. The snow hadn't disappeared overnight and I wondered if we'd get the snow day that everybody was hoping for.

But Mum broke that bubble when she came in and said, "Your principal emailed. School is open as normal. Eat your breakfast. Give me ten minutes and I'll drive you in."

"What about the bus?"

"Would you rather sit in a freezing bus or a warm car?" she asked.

I bit into my hot sandwich. "Car."

"Thought so."

I sent a text to the group chat and told Ashley and Tony that I'd see them at school. Tony replied, *I'm already at the bus stop. If the bus isn't here in five minutes I'm going back to bed.*

I should have asked Mum to drive them too but I didn't want to ruin her buzz. She didn't take time off work often and I figured a twelve-minute car ride would cover our mother-son time for the month.

Bacon is bliss. Just saying.

While I waited for Mum, I grabbed the car keys and started the engine to warm it up. I sat in the driver's seat with the door closed, the air blasting at the windscreen, watching the fog lift in pyramids. Dad had already left for work and when Mum came out to the car, she was wearing a velour sweater and a pair of jeans. She threw a coat in the backseat and I hopped over the central console into the passenger seat. I held my hands against the warm air from the vents.

The road out of our street was like an ice rink and Mum crawled along it at two miles per hour. The bus stop was empty when we passed it so I guess either the bus came on time or Tony had gone back to bed like he said.

Mum said, "I can pick you up after school if you like. We can stop for pizza on the way home."

"Wow, you really are taking a mental health day, aren't you? Pizza for dinner?"

"It's Christmas," she said. She wasn't exactly a health nut, but pizza wasn't on the menu very often. She liked to limit her carb intake.

"I think I have choir practice today if the music room is operational again. But I'll let you know."

She said, "You should serenade me."

I scoffed, but her attention was on the traffic lights and the lorry that pulled up alongside us. The roads around town weren't covered in snow but there were patches of black ice and Mum had tensed her fists on the steering wheel twice as we aquaplaned along the road.

She drove up Crest Hill in first gear and I felt like I could have gotten out and walked faster, but the car was warm and I half expected to be walking down the hill again this evening after practice.

When we got to the school, she nudged her way into the drop-off point and gave me some cash for the cafeteria. "Make sure you eat something hot. Have you got your scarf?"

"We're not in Victorian times," I said. "The school has heating, you know."

"If Principal Scrooge adds some coal to the boiler." The principal wasn't that bad, but he did have a reputation for withholding funds for the essentials.

She made me kiss her before I got out of the car, and when I stood on the snow-covered pavement, she pumped the horn and waved before edging back into the busy school traffic.

"Nice car," Ben said.

I turned. He was getting out of a silver car behind me and

I looked to see who was driving. The man—his dad—was already looking over his shoulder to push into the traffic. I bet Ben didn't have to wave and kiss him goodbye.

"All right?" I said.

He fell into step beside me without a word and my mind went blank. I didn't know what to say. Ben's hair was dishevelled and his school tie was crooked. I wanted to reach up and straighten it for him, my desire for neatness overwhelming, but I pushed my hands into my pockets instead.

That's when Erin came between us and put her arm around his waist. She didn't even acknowledge me. She said, "Did you do the geography homework? I need to copy it before class."

She led him away, quickening her pace towards the entrance.

Ben looked over his shoulder and gave me a smile that was as uneven as his tie.

Ashley and Tony were standing on the steps when I got there and I stood under the warm overhead heater inside the door. "What did he want?" Ashley asked.

"Who?"

"Hunter."

I looked for him. He was all the way down the corridor towards the stairs. "Nothing."

Tony and I went to Irish class, and Ashley was in advanced geography with Ben. I hoped she wouldn't talk to him. About anything.

Mrs Bannon, our Irish teacher, insisted we call her by her first name, Fiadh. "Fee-ah," she told us on the first day of term, stressing the opening syllable. She had a faint moustache that nobody acknowledged publicly, and her Limerick accent made her sound nasally when she spoke.

We suffered through double Irish, two hours of stilted conversations about the weather. She used the snow as an opportunity to talk about global warming and we conjugated the verb *cosnaím*, meaning "to protect" the environment.

I had double maths after a fifteen-minute break, and when I met up with Tony in the cafeteria at lunchtime, I didn't realise I was raising my head like a meerkat until Tony pointed it out.

"Who are you looking for?"

I pulled the sloppy lasagne apart with my fork. "No one."

I couldn't tell him I was looking for Ben Hunter. He wouldn't understand. But Ben wasn't in the cafeteria and neither was Alex Janey, their teammates, or Erin McNally. If they weren't at practice, I didn't know where they went at lunchtime.

Ashley joined us when we had fifteen minutes left, coming in for her later lunch break. She sat at our table with her lunchbox and said, "Gemma Ademola is helping to organise the Christmas party this year."

"So?" Tony asked.

"She's in transition year just like us. That's unheard of. Normally the committee is made up of Leaving Cert kids."

"You're not actually thinking of going, are you?"

"When is it?" I asked.

They both said, "The last Friday before we break up for Christmas."

Then Ashley said, "I mean, I'm not going to dance or anything lame like that, but it'll be fun, right?"

Tony winked at me. "She's got a lady boner for Gemma Ademola."

"I do not."

Tony backed away from the swing of her hand that was

104

aimed at his head. "The lady doth protest too much, methinks. What do you reckon, Dean?"

"I'm saying nothing. I saw how fierce that slap looked."

Ashley elbowed Tony and bit into her sandwich. "Anyway," she said. "Are we going or what?"

"I'm down," I said before Tony could object.

"Two against one," she told him.

"It's not fancy dress, is it?"

"It better not be," Ashley said.

We left her in the cafeteria before the bell went, and I told Tony I'd see him in the enterprise office in a minute. I turned down the west corridor towards the men's room and saw Ben coming in the opposite direction.

He was alone, with his head down and his bag over his shoulder.

He reached for the toilet door before I got there but stopped when he saw me. "Hey."

"Hey."

"How's your day?"

A kid came out of the toilet and we backed away from the door. "I just had double maths before lunch so, you know."

"Like Christmas came early for you, eh?"

"Something like that."

"You're so weird."

"Hey."

"In a good way," Ben said.

Our conversation hadn't been this awkward last night, I was certain. "You've got enterprise now?" I asked, already knowing the answer. The whole transition year class had enterprise and innovation class on Wednesday and Thursday afternoons.

"Yeah."

"Sports massage," I said, trying not to make it sound seedy. "If you've got knots in your shoulders, I'm your guy."

"I'll keep that in mind."

Ben turned to the men's room door. "Are you going in?"

"No, I"—shit. Play it cool. Say something clever—"I'm going that way."

My bladder screamed at me but I couldn't walk into such an intimate space with Ben Hunter.

"Hey," he said. "Don't forget my game on Friday."

"Didn't I already say that wasn't really my thing?"

"Yeah, but I thought maybe you'd change your mind."

I stared at him, forcing myself to maintain his gaze. "And why would I do that?"

He shrugged. A smile twitched at the commissure of his lips, that little depression in the corner where upper lip met lower. And he backed into the toilets. I watched the door swing closed behind him.

When I got to the office, Bridget was manning the phone line and Tony and Roisin were trying to reattach a broken joy con onto a Nintendo Switch for a first-year student.

"We should go to the basketball game tomorrow," I said, slipping into a seat and trying to say it in a casual manner.

"Why?" The pain in his voice was clear.

"For a laugh. We can take the mick out of their baggy uniforms."

Roisin said, "The team's not all that bad. They were twenty points up against Millstreet the last time they played."

I shrugged like it didn't matter. "It beats sitting in Grainger's all night."

"Cut your tongue out," Tony said. "Grainger's is life."

Bridget didn't get any prank calls today and when I went to the music room to see if choir practice was on, the room was empty. I walked out to the bus stop in time to catch the bus and, as I stood in the queue to board, I looked around to see if Ben was getting on. When I didn't see him, I almost got off to wait, but Ashley thumped at the window from inside the bus and Tony pulled a face at me from the seat beside her.

I got on and dropped into the seat behind them. I watched the school gates as we pulled away, but Ben didn't come out.

That night, after dinner—Mum was true to her word and ordered pizza—I sat in the living room as she showed Dad and I the presents she'd bought for various relatives. "My feet were killing me when I got home," she said. "Next year, I'm doing my Christmas shopping online."

Dad patted her ankle where she'd curled her legs up on the couch between them and I flipped through the apps on my phone. I kept the volume low on TikTok so as not to interrupt Mum's blow-by-blow account of her day, and I typed Ben Hunter's name into the search function. He had an account but no videos. Not that I expected to see him working out without a shirt on or anything.

I looked at the people he was following—mostly his teammates and some sports stars and a few musicians—and the people who were following him. Other than fellow classmates, there wasn't anybody I recognised.

Mum said, "I got this for Marcia but tell me if you think it's dumb." Marcia was her sister who had an unhealthy obsession with giraffes. Mum pulled something out of a shopping bag and held it up.

Dad laughed. It was a fluffy onesie in giraffe-brown and the hood had little giraffe antlers and ears.

"I would totally wear that," I said. I switched to Instagram where I had better luck. Ben had over two hundred posts.

I yawned and stretched and said, "I'm going to bed. Good night."

In my room, I undressed and settled under the quilt, propped against my pillows as I scrolled through his images. Ben and Erin in Grainger's. Ben and Erin in what I assumed was his bedroom, in front of a full-length mirror. A candid shot of Ben taken by somebody else—probably Erin. It must have been during the summer because he was wearing a thin T-shirt and the sun glinted behind his head. He was looking to the right as if something was way more important than the camera.

I shuffled down the bed a little more and continued scrolling.

And then my phone pinged.

Benhuntss07 wants to send you a message.

My phone slipped out of my hand.

When I picked it up, I could feel my chest splitting open, like my heart was breaking through my ribcage.

I clicked the notification.

Ben's tiny profile icon crouched beside his message.

Yo, was all it said.

And I didn't know how to respond.

CHAPTER 12

BEN

The silence that woke me felt different this morning. I didn't hear Dad rushing around downstairs or Mum talking on the phone to her colleagues from the salon with her happy voice. I never understood why they called each other an hour before work when they'd be in the same building for the rest of the day. There was no type of gossip that couldn't wait.

My phone was lost under the quilt and there was drool on my pillow. I didn't remember saying good night to Dean and when I kicked the quilt aside to find my phone, the battery was dead. I plugged it in, waiting for the screen to light up. But I got impatient and went for a shower instead.

My parents' bedroom door was closed, a thick silence seeping out from under it. It was Friday; they should have been pushing each other into a frenzy as they got ready for work.

When I'd showered, I flicked my hair into an effortless mess and sat on the edge of my bed. I scrolled through my DMs with Dean. I had debated sending him my opening gambit for almost thirty minutes last night before I typed it and pressed send. It was a real winner. *Yo.*

The first timestamp was 10:41:16.

Dean replied less than a minute later. *New phone. Who dis?* He followed it with the nerd face emoji and I would never see that icon again without picturing Dean's face complete with his thick, black-framed glasses and huge smile.

I didn't tell him I'd been staring at his profile picture for half an hour before messaging him. His account was private so I couldn't see any of his photos, and when I sent my awkward hello, I wasn't ready to send him a follow request as well.

He knew exactly who I was, but I played along.

benhuntss07
You don't know me, but I heard you're good in a snowball fight.

dean_odd_donnell
My days of active warfare are over. I'm afraid I've retired.

benhuntss07
What's it gonna take to pull you out of retirement?

dean_odd_donnell
Can you guarantee that my face is immortalised in the official Snowball Hall of Fame?

benhuntss07
I'm making a sculpture out of snow as we speak.

dean_odd_donnell
I probably shouldn't ask to see it, should I?

A second later, I got a new notification. *Dean_odd_donnell started following you.*

I followed back and waited for him to accept my request. And in between messaging him, I checked out his profile. He had sixty-four followers and only a handful of images. Most of them were landscapes or coffee art. I recognised the cups from Grainger's Coffee Stop. From last May there was a selfie of him with his friends, Ashley and Tony. Tony wore a giant *15 Today* badge on his shirt, Ashley looked like she was mid-word, her mouth formed into an exclamation point, and Dean was smiling at the camera. It was a self-conscious smile, a curl of the lips that said, "Just let me blend into the background."

I pinched the image to zoom in on that smile.

The rest of our conversation last night had been enthralling even though our words meant nothing. Dean asked me about my enterprise company and told me about the prank calls they'd been receiving. He made me laugh as we chatted, and the heavier my eyelids got, the bigger my smile was. It's weird having the top half of your head going to sleep but the bottom half still laughing.

I kept scrolling. It was after one in the morning when I fell asleep. We'd talked for two and a half hours. Dean was funnier than I thought, and he didn't once make me feel stupid, except when I mentioned my horrific failure at baking chocolate chip cookies last year. Erin had helped, but I didn't mention that part. He asked if I had to call the fire department or if the cookies had achieved a level of hardness that they could replace Captain America's Vibranium shield. His humour caught me off guard, and it was nice to be on the receiving end, even if it did mean admitting to my culinary disasters.

I scrolled back and read our entire conversation a second time. It'd be creepy if it wasn't cute, right?

I forced myself off the bed and into my school uniform. My sports bag was already packed; we had a game against Millstreet tonight. And as I tied my tie in front of the mirror, I kicked myself for not reminding Dean about it in our chat. I didn't really expect him to be there, but every time I mentioned it to him, I was giving him a little piece of me. A slice of Ben to fit into his otherwise normal life.

At the top of the stairs, I hesitated. I didn't like how quiet the house was. There was no smell of overcooked toast—the default morning scent in our house—and the TV wasn't on in the kitchen. I stood outside my parents' bedroom door and listened. I knocked but got no response.

When I cracked the door open, the room was in darkness, the curtains closed, and there was a dad-shaped lump under the blankets. The other side of the bed was empty.

"Dad?"

He didn't respond.

I took a step into the room.

"Are you awake?"

Dad grunted. As I came closer, I saw the outline of his face above the quilt, the bristle of his cheeks. His eyes were closed.

"Dad?"

His voice was flat. "Go to school."

"Are you okay?"

He rolled over in bed, turning away from me. He should have dropped me at school by now and been on his way to work.

"Where's Mum?" I asked.

He didn't answer.

I closed the door and the click of the catch in its hollow

seemed louder than it should have.

Downstairs, there was no sign of Mum and no note explaining where she was or why Dad was in bed. I took down the pasta jar from the top of the fridge that had coins in it instead of spaghetti and counted out enough Euros for the bus and for a small lunch. I could walk home after the game if I had to.

I checked the time. I'd missed the school bus but there was a bus to town in a few minutes. Before I left, I stood at the bottom of the stairs and listened. "I'm going now," I called.

But Dad didn't respond.

On the bus, I sent a text to Mum. *Did you leave early this morning? Dad's still in bed.*

I didn't expect a reply. When she got to the salon, she tended to leave her phone in her bag until lunchtime.

The bus laboured up Crest Hill, struggling against the black ice. If the snow continued to fall, public transport would stop running. And why weren't we given a snow day yet? Principals don't remember what it was like to be school kids. Snow over maths equals fun.

Classes had already started when I got to school and my name was put in the late register. Two more of those and they'd send a letter home to my parents. Whatever good that would do. It was their fault in the first place.

I slipped into geography class as quietly as I could but the teacher made a grumbling display of annoyance at the interruption.

Alex Janey whispered, "You look like shit. Are you good?"

"Thanks, man. You're awesome."

Erin gave me a concerned look but I lowered my eyes from her and pulled my books out. I spent the rest of the class drumming a pen against my notebook and staring into space. I faked a laugh when Alex said something to the teacher that I wasn't paying attention to and he backhanded my arm looking for solidarity. Erin rolled her eyes, so I knew whatever Alex said had been an innuendo.

At lunch, we had a thirty-minute drill session in the gym ahead of tonight's game. Coach Williams made us do suicide runs across the court, and then some box-out drills and a three-man weave where we ran down the court in threes, passing the ball between us.

After that, I went to the cafeteria with Alex Janey and could afford a slice of cottage pie and a Bakewell tart. Erin waved us over to her table where she sat with some of the girls from our year and, as I ate, I looked around for Dean, but he must have already left.

I checked my phone. There was no reply from Mum and no DM from Dean. I worried that when I got home this evening, Mum would be drunk and Dad would still be in bed. I sent her another message. *Got a game after school. Gonna be late.* And when Erin said, "I wish our last class on Friday wasn't maths," I put my phone away and agreed with her. Except Dean was in maths class so I had to force my face not to grin.

Erin said, "How come you were late this morning?"

With Alex Janey's attention elsewhere, I lowered my voice and said, "Guess."

She didn't have to. She said, "You should come over tomorrow and we can hit up the mall or something. It'll get you out from under their feet."

"Yeah, maybe. I'll let you know."

She took my hesitation at face value and didn't say anything else.

When maths class rolled around, I slumped into my seat at the back of the room between Alex and Erin and looked like I was trying to pay attention to the teacher even though my mind was elsewhere. I still hadn't heard from Mum and I didn't want to text Dad and make things worse.

I watched the back of Dean's head and tore my eyes away from him when he glanced back. When he looked again, I gave him a nod and an eye roll like the teacher was boring me or something. I slipped my phone out of my pocket and typed a quick message to him, clicking off the screen before Erin saw.

benhuntss07
If E=MC2, where do jelly babies come from?

I saw him touch his pocket where his phone was—he must have felt its vibration—but he didn't take it out. He was in the front row and the teacher was facing the class. When she turned her back to us, he checked his phone and I watched his shoulders chuckle. He shot me a pained look.

I pretended I had no idea what he was reacting to and lowered my head to my textbook, hiding a smile.

A jeer ran across the room when Millstreet's bus pulled into the car park outside. Alex Janey barked like a dog. We watched them file off the bus and across the snow towards the building.

When the final bell went, Erin said, "Good luck," and as everyone made a beeline for the door, I looked around for Dean. But he was already gone. In the changing room, I dumped my bag under the bench and checked my phone again.

Still nothing from Mum and I was getting worried now. But Dean had sent a new message.

dean_odd_donnell
When two gummy bears love each other very much, they squish their bits together and out pops a jelly baby. Break a leg out there.

I laughed and shut my phone off.

On the court, Millstreet's players looked huge and formidable. Their centre towered over all of us and the shadow on his cheeks was more than teenage fuzz. I kept my eye on their point guard and shooting guard as they warmed up, and when the ref blew his whistle and the centres went for the opening jump ball, I knew we were in for a tough game. We lost possession early and we were close to closing out the first quarter without any points before Alex Janey zipped in and stole possession, tripping out at the far end for a rebound. That's why Alex was the small forward.

I heard Erin whooping from the front row of the mid-court line and when I gave her a smile, I almost tripped over my feet. Dean was sitting two rows behind her, clapping along with everyone else. I blinked sweat from my eyes like he might have been a mirage, but he was still there when I looked again. I gave him a quick wave and Erin thought it was for her.

As the game progressed, the tension on the court grew. Millstreet's aggressive defence was intimidating, but our team, the Clannloch Falcons, were tenacious, matching each of their points. I felt like a whirlwind on the court, all sharp passes and quick moves as I helped keep Millstreet's defence on their toes.

The game was a flurry of steals, rebounds, and intense face-offs. We kept our lead after an abysmal first quarter, but the gap was narrow, a constant tussle that kept the spectators stomping their feet.

As the clock ticked down, the Falcons led by two points. Millstreet had possession, their point guard dribbling the ball up the court. I could see the steely determination in his eyes. He shot from beyond the arc, an attempt for a three-pointer. The ball traced through the air and I barked an order at Alex to pull him back.

The ball bounced off the rim. I reacted fast, launching myself towards it and securing the crucial rebound. I knew the clock was counting down.

With the ball in my control, I pushed through the court, my heart pounding in sync with the final countdown.

Alex shouted from his position near the basket and I spotted him as I dribbled. I tossed him a quick pass and he caught it, going up for the shot.

Someone in the crowd shouted, "Buzzer beater."

The ball left Alex's hand, the shrill sound of the buzzer echoing through the gym. I'd say time slowed down or stood still, but it didn't. It sped up. The ball swished through the net as the buzzer ended.

The crowd cheered. The Clannloch Falcons had won, and I couldn't help the victorious howl that came from deep inside me.

Sweat burned my eyes.

When I looked, Dean was on his feet, hollering just as loud as our other supporters.

I could barely catch my breath when Coach smacked me on

the back and Alex Janey jumped me from behind with a roar.

The crowd was already leaving. It wasn't a big game—half the seats had been empty—but it felt good to get one over on Millstreet. Their side was notorious. We heard their grumbles from the other changing room on the far side of our shower block.

When I'd showered and changed, I sat on the bench and switched my phone on. I still didn't have a message from Mum. There was a lump in my chest that I realised had been with me throughout the game and it wasn't because of Millstreet or Dean. Where the hell was she?

Most of the team had gone outside when I zipped my coat up and threw my bag over my shoulder. Coach said, "Good game. We need more sessions like that."

Outside, the floodlights made the school look like the only building for miles. The light stopped at the edges of the world.

And sitting on the low wall beside the steps, Dean had his hands in his pockets and was scuffing his shoe in the compacted snow.

He stood up as I got close.

"I didn't think football was your thing," I said.

"Is that what that was called?"

"I mean, we generally refer to it as basketball, but I can't blame you for not knowing the lingo."

He pointed at my empty hands. "Don't you get to keep the winning ball or something? Isn't that a sports thing?"

"No, Dean."

"It should be."

I tried not to smile. "Why are you still hanging around like a groupie? Did you miss the bus?"

He shrugged and scuffed his shoe in the snow again. "If you're walking down the hill, I can walk with you."

That's when Erin came up behind me. Like a stealth bomber.

"Oh my God, that layup," she said. "I was literally biting my nails in those final minutes." She looked at Dean before turning back to me. "Are you coming?"

I rolled my shoulders. There was a knot in my back. "We're going for pizza," I told Dean. "With the team."

"Oh," he said.

"Do you want to come?"

Erin said, "Yeah, come. The more the merrier." But her tone said otherwise.

"Nah, it's cool," he said. "There's a bus in a few minutes."

But I couldn't let that happen. He'd waited for me. The only reason he was here was because of me. "You should come. It's just pizza. Coach is paying."

Dean looked over his shoulder and said, "If I miss the bus, I'm screwed. But have fun. And well done. Or good game, or whatever you say to the star player."

I watched him walk away. He sat on the thin bench at the bus stop and Erin tugged my coat sleeve. Coach Williams had pulled the minibus around to the front gates and Alex Janey's face was pressed up against one of the windows.

And when we turned out of the school grounds and our dark blue minibus slouched down the hill, I gave Dean a wave as we passed the bus stop.

But he wasn't looking.

— CHAPTER 13 —

DEAN

Saturday morning filtered in through the thick curtains above my head. I could feel how frosty it was outside just from that sliver of cold air and I pulled the quilt around my face as I knuckled the sleep from my eyes. I still hadn't built a snowman. What was up with that?

I loved the sound of Saturday mornings. Mum and Dad were still in bed and the clock on my wall issued a calming swishing tick that lulled me back to sleep. In spring, I'd lie here and listen to the birds that nested in the tree above the lawn outside, and in winter the sound of the gurgling radiators made the room feel cosy and tranquil. Dad had helped me paint my room when we moved here last year. It was a pale mustard colour that dazzled in bright fluorescence when the sun flooded through the window in the afternoons.

I had come home last night feeling alone and sorry for myself. I'd skipped choir practice to go to Ben's basketball game, and watching him zip up and down the court in bright yellow shorts was totally worth it. The hair in his armpits when he double high-fived his teammates was dark and appealing. Watching him was much better than singing Christmas carols all evening, even if I would get it in the neck on Monday from Mr Elliot.

I'd waited around after the game, sitting near the steps outside as two buses drove by on the road and I could have caught either of them if I'd tried. When Ben came out my heart was racing. I was going to ask if he wanted to walk to town together like we did the other day. We could recreate that feeling of carelessness we shared, eating chips and talking about nothing and everything.

But Erin clung to his side and, anyway, he had a team pizza night. I should have known.

I pretended not to see the minibus pulling away from the school but I'd already spotted Ben and Erin in one of the seats together.

I wasn't jealous.

I wasn't.

I had to wait another twenty minutes for the next bus and the driver was wearing a Santa hat and had flimsy green tinsel wrapped around his steering wheel. I sat in the middle row and hugged my schoolbag as we laboured down the hill, the engine grumbling and vibrating my head against the window as the streetlights and bright shopfronts flashed by outside.

Mum was annoyingly cheerful when I got home. After dinner, she poured herself a Baileys over ice and forced me to watch a Christmas movie with her while Dad slept in the armchair opposite us. But I couldn't pull my mind away from Ben.

He wasn't the first straight boy I'd fallen in love with—show me a gay guy who hadn't. That had been Daniel MacNevin, back in Blarney where I grew up. Never mind the fact that he was fourteen and I was nine. I crushed on him harder than an apple press. I fell into the River Martin behind Station Road once where a bunch of us were playing. It wasn't deep, more like a stream than a river, but I still got drenched. Danny Mac helped me take off my dripping T-shirt and let me wear his leather jacket. The sleeves were too big and I held the jacket close to my damp skin. I had to give it back to him later and I didn't want to. But for twenty minutes, I felt closer to him than I'd ever felt to anyone.

Ben Hunter didn't make me feel that childlike awe. He just made me feel horny and embarrassed.

And tongue-tied.

I gave up on the movie and told Mum I was going to bed. I was halfway up the stairs when my phone buzzed.

benhuntss07
OMG I ATE SO MUCHHHHH.

I read it eight times before I replied.

dean_odd_donnell
Pizzaaaaaaa.

benhuntss07
You should have come with us. It wasn't really a formal team thing. Nobody would have minded you being there.

dean_odd_donnell
Am I that tiny I wouldn't have been spotted?

benhuntss07
What do you weigh? Like 8 and a 1/2 stone? One slice of pizza could feed you

for a week.

> **dean_odd_donnell**
> Small bites, chewed 32 times as per the
> government recommendations.

benhuntss07
Screw that. Down the hatch!

Have you been to the Christmas market
yet? I thought about going tomorrow. If
you're up for it?

> **dean_odd_donnell**
> Me?

benhuntss07
Nooo, the other Dean that's nowhere
near as funny as you are.

> **dean_odd_donnell**
> What time? Who's gonna be there?

benhuntss07
I hear Santa lets kids sit on his lap, if
that's what you're into.

> **dean_odd_donnell**
> Can I tug on his beard? Seriously,
> though. When and with who?

benhuntss07
If beard tugging is your thing, you get
your rocks off. What about 12? And I
wasn't thinking of inviting anyone else?

I'm only slightly embarrassed to admit that I did a little
dance around my room. And then I realised I hadn't replied.

> **dean_odd_donnell**
> Santa won't know what hit him. Meet
> you by the entrance?

He agreed and said he'd see me there, and he signed off with that cute blushing emoji. Whatever that meant.

I swished around my room like a Disney princess.

I didn't sleep much that night. But when I did wake, it was in a cosy chill with the quilt up around my face listening to the sound of the clock and the thrumming of the radiators.

Mum made me eat a bowl of oatmeal for breakfast—which is only marginally better than porridge—and I told her I was meeting the guys in town. I let her make her own assumptions.

I stopped myself from messaging Ben that morning and asking if we were still on for the afternoon. I didn't want to come across like a lovestruck kid. I was no longer a nine-year-old in an older boy's leather jacket.

I tried on a dozen different shirts and settled on a brown and orange plaid button-down and dark brown khakis. I was an autumn palette kind of guy when I wasn't forced to wear a navy school uniform.

I splashed on some of my dad's cologne and sat on the edge of my bed for the next hour, waiting until I could leave for the bus. Dad offered to give me a lift, but he said it in a way that made it sound like a chore. Mum gave me fifty Euros on the promise that I buy my friends a hot chocolate and buy my dad a Christmas gift. I think she was just happy I was going out and meeting people instead of sitting on my tablet all weekend. I know she used to worry about me in that way. I don't make friends easily, but it's not like I needed them. I enjoy my own company. I know people say that, but I meant it. Let me listen to music or blast my way through a sudoku puzzle book and I'm happy.

Although I guess if you put a book of puzzles in front of me as well as Ben Hunter and asked me to choose, I wouldn't be sharpening my pencil and eyeing up the puzzles.

I was at the bus stop fifteen minutes before I needed to be there. Just in case. And I was freezing by the time I got to town. The snow had been cleared off the roads but it was built up in the gutters and turned to ice on the pavements which meant I was walking like a penguin.

When I got to the entrance gate of the pop-up Christmas market, I expected to have to wait for Ben, but he was already there, leaning against the fence with his elbows on the top like an American rancher. He wore an oversized off-white wool sweater that looked warmer than my coat, and when he saw me, he smiled and nodded. "All right?"

"Hey."

Christmas music fell out of the speakers above the gate. An animatronic Santa said, "Ho, ho, ho," and he waved at anyone who passed. As I followed Ben through the gate, he gave Santa's plastic hand a high five.

"What do you want to do?" he asked.

"Um."

"Um?"

"You see how awesome I am at conversation? I'll be holding classes later. Don't worry."

The temporary market was made up of rows of wooden chalets with fake felt snow on the roofs and twinkling Christmas lights everywhere. Each mini shop had its own music, *Silent Night* competing against *Jingle Bell Rock*.

Ben pushed his fingers into his jeans pockets with his thumbs hooked out over the top and he drew his shoulders up to keep his neck warm against the frosty wind that barrelled down between the rows of gift shops. There was a Build-A-Bear and a Soap & Co that smelled of cinnamon, bergamot and gingerbread. And there was a shop that sold nothing but bags of broken Yellowman candy.

At the open shopfront of a toy store, Ben pushed the buttons on all the toys to make them light up or sing or dance, and when the woman behind the display gave us an exasperated smile, Ben elbowed me and said, "Stop fingering the dolls, Dean. Jeez, I can't take you anywhere."

I bought a singing Elvis Santa for Mum just to appease the shopkeeper and my conscience.

"I owe you some chips," Ben said as we passed a burger van. The smell of fried onions was entrenched in the air around us.

"You don't owe me anything," I said.

But he insisted.

The chips were fat and hot and soggy with too much vinegar, but they were the nicest I'd ever tasted. We straddled a bench beside a Lego store, facing each other, the bag of chips between us, picking at them with our fingers.

When it was empty, Ben scrunched the paper up and tossed it into a waste bin like a basketball.

At the far side of the park, there was a rank of claw machines and a carousel filled with little kids. Ben dropped a coin into one of the machines to try to win a teddy, but as the claw gripped it and the arm raised, the teddy slipped out of its weak vice. We took turns and we must have put ten or twelve Euros into it when Ben nudged the arm back, craning his neck around the side of the machine to see where it was going. The claw dug into the field of teddies and came up with one locked in its grip. It looked like it was going to fall but it made it over to the release tray and dropped into the opening below.

I cheered. "Oh my God, for me?"

"No way," he said, holding it to his chest. "I won it fair and square. Get your own." He carried it around with him for the rest of the afternoon.

We hopped on the carousel and sat on two wooden horses beside each other, and as we bobbed up and down, gripping the uprights, listening to children screaming and laughing, I watched as Ben closed his eyes and held his head back. He was lost in the moment. A child again.

The music was warbling and tinny.

I was giddy when we got off and slipped on a patch of ice on the path. Ben gripped my elbow. "Walk much?"

"This is my first time. How am I doing?"

"Six out of ten," he said. "Could do better."

I bought a scarf for Dad because I didn't think he'd appreciate another Christmas ornament like Mum, and I said, "My mum gave me some money for hot chocolate."

"I had to steal some money from the pasta jar," Ben said.

We stood under the green and white awning at a coffee hut and I ordered two hot chocolates with extra marshmallows. Ben drew my attention to a sprig of mistletoe that hung above us like a promise.

"Uh-oh," he said.

I elbowed him. "Come on, then. Pucker up and give us a kiss." I made smooching noises to mask my embarrassment and the man behind the counter chuckled.

"Piss off," Ben laughed, pushing me away.

There was a lump in my throat. I am the least funny person sometimes. I thought I'd ruined the day for a minute, but Ben lifted both paper cups and nodded at one of the small tables. I chewed on my tongue to stop myself from saying anything and we sat.

He pushed my cup towards me. "I'm going to need a job to pay you back if you keep buying me things."

The hot chocolate was dark and sweet. "I didn't buy it, my mum did."

"Thank you, Mrs O'Donnell."

A couple of snowflakes landed on the table and melted. Ben brushed his fingers through his hair. A team of Christmas carollers gathered around the carousel to serenade the children.

"I had fun today," I said. I wasn't sure what else to say.

Ben slurped the marshmallows off the top of his chocolate. It gave him a moustache. He licked it off. I hadn't noticed how dark his eyes looked until now.

"Are you okay?"

"Me? Yeah. Why?"

I shrugged.

He nodded.

And then he said, "I thought my mum had run away." I was going to say something but his words just tumbled out. "Dad didn't go to work yesterday and Mum was gone before I woke. She still wasn't home when I got in after pizza. And Dad was still in bed like he hadn't moved all day. I went to bed sometime after midnight and I couldn't sleep. But she finally came home at, like, four a.m. and they argued and screamed at each other for another two hours."

I could see how exhausted he was.

"Ben. You should have said something when you messaged me last night. Was she okay?"

"She was drunk, but nothing I hadn't seen before."

"Shit, man."

"Yeah. Sorry. I didn't mean to say all that."

"You can tell me anything," I said, wrapping my hands around my cup to stop from reaching out to him. "You must be tired."

"I'm juiced up on energy drinks and caffeine. I've got this life thing covered."

"But everything's all right now? Your parents, I mean."

"Yeah," he smiled. "Of course. It's all good." He tapped the screen on his phone to check the time. "I should probably get going, though. Before they go ballistic."

We walked through the market to the exit and I stood with him at his bus stop until the bus came. I was going in the opposite direction.

Before he got on, he said, "Thanks, Dean. I really needed this."

"I didn't do anything."

"You did everything."

He paused, his lips parted just a little and a whole universe trapped behind them. I wasn't anticipating a kiss, but I wanted it all the same. Kiss me, goddammit.

"Anyway." He didn't lean in. Why would he? He held up the teddy. "This is Fred."

"You Christened him without consulting me?"

"I figured I should get to name him if you're going to be raising him."

"Me?"

He handed Fred over. "Take care of him. I want progress reports." And he hopped on the bus before I could object.

He waved as the bus pulled away.

And I inhaled the scent of the bear that I was convinced smelled like Ben already. "Come on, Fred," I said. "Let's go home."

CHAPTER 14

BEN

Weekends used to be sacred. They were a time to decompress, recharge, and gear up for the looming school week. On Sunday afternoon, I'd take a scorching hot bath, the steam from the water clearing my sinuses. My muscles would ease out of their tension from a week of running around the basketball court where my thighs and knees took the brunt of play. But that's not how it worked anymore. I sat on the edge of my bed and every shout or crash from downstairs sucked the calm out of the air. Mum and Dad were at it again, locked in their daily ritual of slurred accusations and alcohol-fuelled anger.

Even with my earphones in, their raised voices filtered through the breaks in the music. The rich, malty scent of whiskey filled the house. It used to be a comforting smell when Dad would have the occasional drink. He let me sip it once. Never again.

Now, it was the smell of resentment and anger.

I was trapped in their prison. I couldn't escape the echoing argument beneath me, every word a reminder of the chaos that was my life. The photo of my team, the Clannloch Falcons, mocked me from the wall above my bed. The grinning players

131

were a stark contrast to my current reality. I was in the front row, basketball under my elbow, with Alex Janey's arm around my shoulders. We'd reached the Under 15s schools' league semi-finals last year. *Courtside Ireland* said I had a combination of quick decision-making, precise passes, and a tenacious defence. We flamed out in the semis because our centre tore a knee ligament in the fourth quarter and his substitute just couldn't match up.

Dad slapped my back and said, "Next year." He wasn't a nightmare back then.

And Mum wasn't drunk.

I scrolled through my conversation with Dean, concentrating on the words instead of the screaming downstairs. He'd sent me a photo yesterday about five minutes after I left. It was of him and Fred on the bus, staring out of the window together at the passing snow. The teddy was sitting on his shoulder.

He'd said, *Progress report: Fred's first bus ride.*

Way to go, Fred.

I was about to send him a new message when the arguing downstairs peaked. There was a shattering crash. A vase or a glass.

I pulled my earphones out. The tense silence that followed stretched into an abyss. My heart thumped hard and my throat was tight and dry. I remembered coming home last week and finding blood on the floor and Dad's nose busted. I listened to the silence. If Mum had smashed something against his head this time, he could be dead.

Or what if he was the one standing over her bleeding face? Shards of glass embedded in her eyes and her flesh.

I couldn't bear the silence.

I stood up.

My hands shook as I brought my phone up, ready to dial 112.

I couldn't breathe.

And then my dad said, "For fuck's sake."

And Mum slurred, "Why've you always got to ruin everything?"

Their arguing continued. And this was my life now. I'm either scared they're going to kill each other or scared they've already done it.

Erin tried to Facetime me but I wasn't feeling it. I shot her a quick text after rejecting her call to tell her I wasn't ignoring her, it's just that Mum and Dad were doing their thing.

She'd understand.

I felt bad that, outside of school, I hadn't seen much of her. We went from inseparable to separated. It was my parents' fault, I told her. But my mind was elsewhere.

By mid-afternoon, Dad went out, slamming the front door behind him. Mum stomped up and down the stairs a couple of times. When she knocked on my door, it was tentative and quiet.

I rolled onto my side on the bed and pretended to be asleep. She knocked again, and then opened it.

"Benny?"

I kept my eyes closed, faking deep, sleep-filled breaths.

"Benny, are you awake?" When I didn't answer, she got angry. "I know you're awake. I know how you breathe when you're sleeping."

I kept up the pretence. It was bad enough to lie, but being caught out in a lie was worse. I didn't try to snore or move my eyeballs around under their lids like I was dreaming. I just lay there, breathing, and willing her to close the door and walk away.

"I'm leaving him," she said. But I'd heard that before. "We're leaving him. Do you hear me, Benny? We're leaving."

I didn't need to look up to know she was swaying in the doorway, trying to hold herself upright. There'd be a cigarette burning between her fingers, hot ash dropping to the carpet to create another scorch mark. She was ugly when she'd had that much to drink. Most people were.

I slowed my breathing a little more.

"Why are you lying to me, Benny? You're just like your father."

She closed the door and for a minute I didn't know if she was in my room or on the other side. I didn't look.

But then I heard Adele screaming from the TV in the living room, intense piano chords on a loop. *Someone Like You.*

Her drunken sway on the living room floor would turn into a slow dance with herself.

And I wanted to cry—for her. For Dad.

For me.

She'd fall asleep soon. If Dad went out, the whiskey bottle must be empty. When the sad songs went on, sleep was never far behind.

I did some push-ups while I waited. No point in wasting my time. I usually did a lot of legwork, but that would create too much noise, and right now even my breathing had to be a whisper.

Two songs. Three.

I'd give her ten before I checked on her.

When I did go downstairs, she was lying on the couch, one foot on the floor and a cigarette burning in the ashtray on the coffee table. I stubbed it out and draped a throw across her body. I turned the volume down on the TV. If I turned it off, she'd wake.

There wasn't much in the fridge but we had enough ingredients to make Bolognese if I substituted spaghetti with penne. I wasn't taking food tech at school but I knew my way around the kitchen. I had to. And it's not like I couldn't get basic recipes on my phone if I needed it.

I browned a packet of minced beef and diced some carrots, onions and mushrooms that were due to expire tomorrow. I poured a can of chopped tomatoes into a saucepan. I minced two garlic cloves, then added a third. There was no such thing as too much garlic, vampires—and kissing partners—be damned.

I added some dried herbs.

While I stirred the sauce, my phone vibrated in my pocket. I took it out. The sauce had sparked my shirt.

And I smiled. Dean had sent a photo of Fred sitting on his bed, reading *Lord of the Flies*. I could see Dean's hand holding the teddy up.

He captioned it, *Kill the pig. Cut her throat. Bash her in.*

benhuntss07
Poor piggy.

dean_odd_donnell
She probably had it coming.

benhuntss07
How did Jack even know it was a girl
pig?

dean_odd_donnell
True dat. Could have been a boy. Come
to think of it, is Piglet from Winnie the
Pooh a boy or a girl?

benhuntss07
Why does it have to be either?

dean_odd_donnell
Fair point. Non-binary bacon tastes just
as good.

I laughed. We joked a bit more about *Lord of the Flies*. I
wasn't much of a reader, but only getting through twenty pages
every week meant it felt like we'd been reading this book for
years. We'd reached the part where Jack had moved his splinter
group to the other side of the island.

Dean asked me what I was up to and I stirred the sauce
before replying.

benhuntss07
Just trying my hand at making penne
Bolognese. Ran out of spaghetti. Today
feels like a MasterChef kinda day. I'm
killing it.

dean_odd_donnell
I'm sure you look great in an apron.

benhuntss07
WORLD'S BEST CHEF!

dean_odd_donnell
Wait. Did you win that apron or did you
just make an unsubstantiated claim?
The people need to know.

benhuntss07
I claim nothing. The people already
know.

My sauce was bubbling and spitting. Mum was whimpering in her sleep. I could hear her from here. Dean mentioned that Gemma Ademola was supposedly heading up the committee for the Christmas dance. He and his friends were going "under duress".

benhuntss07
Who's Duress and how do I get under
them?

I almost deleted the word *them* and put *him*, but I didn't want to scare Dean off. He was wearing the rainbow pin on the inside of his coat collar, but that didn't tell me anything and I still didn't know how he identified. I know his friend Tony was open about being asexual, but that didn't mean Dean was too. Although it kind of said that at least he wasn't freaked out by anything outside the hetero checkbox.

dean_odd_donnell
I'll pass your number along. I'm sure
they'll oblige.

I told him I was going to the Christmas dance with the basketball team. Erin would be there too, of course, but I didn't mention her to Dean and he didn't ask. But I could think of nothing worse. The team were notoriously macho. If they weren't grunting through training, they were belching the alphabet or trumpeting team chants with their armpits.

They were the kind of guys, Alex included, that would spike the punch, if punch was a thing at an Irish high school dance. Which it wasn't.

Shit. My Bolognese was bubbling over. I stirred it and I could feel the thick layer where it had stuck to the bottom of the saucepan. I poured it onto three plates. Mum might eat it when she woke up and Dad, if he wasn't too drunk when he came home, would devour it sometime during the night.

I'd forgotten to cook the pasta. I couldn't tell Dean or he'd revoke my World's Best Chef status. I just said, *Dinner's ready.*

I put enough penne on for Mum and Dad and as it boiled, I ate my pasta-free Bolognese. Dean said, *Bon appetit,* and I sat at the kitchen table, spreading the sauce around on my plate with my mind as much of a mess as the Bolognese.

I checked the time on my phone. Dad still wasn't home, which wasn't surprising. If he didn't pass out beforehand, they'd kick him out of the pub at closing time. Part of me hoped he'd remember our address to tell a taxi driver, and part of me wished he wouldn't remember. I still can't comprehend these opposing feelings. I wanted him home, but I wanted him to stay away. If he wasn't so angry all the time, Mum might not drink so much. I wasn't sure if her drinking fuelled his anger, or his anger made her drink more.

Either way, I wished they'd stop.

There were more messages on my phone, from Erin and Alex. At least Dean had gone quiet for now. It was easier not to think about him while my life was this chaotic. But that was like telling my heart not to thump or my lungs not to breathe. I frowned at my phone screen, chewing over the last of my dinner as well as the gnawing thoughts that came with it.

Relationships were ugly. Mum and Dad were proof of that. Their love story—what was left of it—was visible in an angry, daily spectacle. I couldn't look at them without feeling a burning knot in my stomach. Nobody should want that. The hurt. The risk.

The remains of my Bolognese clung to the plate like thick, coagulating blood.

Dean. Just thinking about him sent a different sensation through me. Excitement, maybe. Or fear. Probably both. My feelings for him had become more real and insistent every day. The scariest part wasn't that he was a guy. I'd come to terms with that a long time ago. What scared me was the idea of liking someone so much and having it blow up in my face. Because that's what relationships did. They blew up.

Always.

By nine o'clock, I was missing Dean, but if I messaged him now, I'd spill my feelings about him or about my parents. And I didn't want to do either.

Mum had woken and gone upstairs to bed. She didn't check on me. I heard her in the bathroom and then the gentle click of her bedroom door closing.

And when I decided I couldn't stand being a part of Sunday any longer and would turn in for the night, too, I went down to get a glass of water. I was running the tap when Dad came home. The muscles in my back and shoulders tensed.

"Where is she?" he said. I didn't turn around from the kitchen sink. I heard how thick his voice was. Whiskey-thick.

"She's in bed."

The kitchen had two strip-lights on the ceiling on independent switches. He turned one off. I doubt he'd go to work tomorrow.

"Wasting money," he muttered. He shuffled towards the fridge. There were no beers there, I'd already made sure.

I filled my glass, pushed the tap off and drank. "Good night," I said.

As I passed him, Dad turned and I flinched. I don't know why.

"You've no future in basketball. You know that don't you?" he said.

That came out of left field. Or mid-court. I don't think he meant I wasn't any good. Just that it wasn't a sport Ireland was known for. Kids—and their dads—don't aspire to playing for the national basketball team the way they do a football club.

"I know," I said. I couldn't look at him. In the doorway, I could see into the living room where the lopsided Christmas tree was dropping needles like a leper.

"And university isn't cheap."

"I know."

He was struggling to unbutton his coat, his fingers red from the cold outside. He staggered backwards and then righted himself. "You want my advice?"

No.

"Get a job."

Thanks, Dad. I said, "Okay."

As I went upstairs, I heard him muttering something about money and the price of electricity.

With no more alcohol in the house, he'd go to bed soon, too.

I closed my bedroom door.

And switched off the light.

CHAPTER 15

DEAN

It had snowed overnight again, and the weather forecast was for more of the same for the coming days. Snowmen had sprung up along the street in various states of completion. Some were just a couple of balls on top of each other, some had hats and scarves and carrot noses.

After I'd messaged Ben yesterday, Mum knocked on my bedroom door and threw a pair of gloves at me. "What's wrong with you, son?" she said. "It's been snowing for a week and we still haven't built a snowman."

You know those cute Christmas cards of a brightly lit cottage with a young family standing in the snow making a snowman as their dog chases after a red ball and the stars are twinkling overhead? Picture that, only on a suburban street, not a cottage, and minus the dog.

We had a dog when I was a kid. That's how we discovered Dad's allergies. We had Pedro—I got to name him—for almost a year before he had to go and live with Aunt Marcia in Glenville, which I know sounds like he was going to live on "a big farm in the country", but he actually went to Marcia's house. She would put him on the call when she Facetimed us.

Dad rolled a snowball along the fresh snow on the street until it grew into the bottom third of a body, and when we were done, our snowman was over six feet tall and wore Granddad's old flat cap that Mum had kept and a scarf that she'd crocheted a few years ago when she was going through one of her phases.

I don't care what anyone says, building snowmen is therapeutic no matter how old you are. I wanted to make one with Ben. A bunch of them. Snowmen and snow boys side by side.

Mum took photos of us with Chill Bill. Dad got to name him, and later, when my parents were in the living room, I took Fred out and positioned him on top of the snowman's cap for another photo. Mum spotted me outside without a coat on and called me in before I sent the photo to Ben, and I'd forgotten all about it until Monday.

I saw Ben in the hall before our first period but he was with Alex, Erin and some of the basketball team. He gave me a nod as I passed and it felt private, as if it was just between us. I tried to offer him a wink, but I was never any good at blinking with one eye. I pushed my glasses up and rubbed my eye like I'd gotten grit in it instead.

He was in the line at the cafeteria at lunch time. He was six or seven people ahead of me, queuing with Erin, and when I saw that he'd got the chicken curry, I asked for the same, passing over the baked potato that I'd been craving all day. I wish I hadn't, because it was more like chicken soup than chicken curry, and the baked potatoes had looked perfectly crisp.

I ate with Tony, and we sat there until Ashley joined us. She was quiet, more so than usual, but I chalked that up to Monday blues. We were so close to the Christmas holidays that everyone was in the wind-down stage, ready to give up at the drop of a hat but too far away to start taking our hats off.

We agreed to go to Grainger's together. Tony and Ashley would wait for me in the school library while I was at choir practice.

When the final school bell of the day thrilled everybody else, I pulled my coat on and slipped the strap of my bag over my head. Gemma Ademola was perky in the hallway.

I didn't see Ben.

Every time I went to choir practice, my chest hurt. I was always an anxious person, but preparing for a solo performance was giving me a full-blown case of the jitters. It's like I'd had four espressos and two cans of Red Bull before practice. My brain was a mess and my stomach was threatening to go on vacation. Outside my body.

I stood stage-right on the front row of the choir while Mr Elliot had us warm up with scales. We hummed the notes to get our vocal cords moving before he told us to sing the solfège syllables made famous by *The Sound of Music*.

"*Do, re, mi, fa, so, la, ti, do.*"

Stick me in some lederhosen and call me Dean von Trapp.

Mr Elliot performed a glissando on the piano, running his fingers from the high notes to the low ones and then said, "Front and centre, Dean. No time like the present."

I cleared my throat. He hadn't mentioned my absence on Friday. He was probably holding back until after practice.

I stepped off the dais and put a hand on my chest. The water pipe above us had been replaced. If I was this nervous in the classroom in front of the choir, I'd never make it through the performance on Christmas Eve.

"Do I get a pair of maracas?"

"You're not in a mariachi band, Mr O'Donnell." He turned back to the piano. We'd gone over the arrangement last week. The choir would start with a slow opener, dragging through the first verse of *O Holy Night* before Mr Elliot changed key and I'd come in on my own.

"One and two and—" He played the opening notes.

The choir sang their intro. And I opened my mouth. A croak came out but I worked through it, singing loud.

But I forgot to breathe, running out of air in the second line. And then I stammered over the words and forgot where I was.

Mr Elliot stopped playing and said, "Not to worry. Let's try again. Use your diaphragm and plan your breaths. If you need to, we can mark them out on your music sheet."

"It's okay," I said. "It's just nerves."

Mr Elliot smiled. "Remember what I told you. Shape your nerves, don't let them shape you. You've got this. Are you ready?"

We started again. And again.

By the end of practice, my lungs were tired and my head was sore, but we were sounding much better. I hadn't intended to drop an octave in the final third of the song, but I'd started too high and didn't have a choice. Mr Elliot liked it and said he'd adjust the arrangement before our next practice to reflect the lower range.

On the night, we'd be accompanied by a chamber orchestra, but because of space and time limitations in the run-up to Christmas Eve, we wouldn't get to practice with them until an hour before the performance. Way to cut it fine.

As we walked out of the music room, Mr Elliot slapped my

back and said, "You're doing well. Does it feel better yet?"

"No," I laughed. But it did feel easier.

In the hall outside, I saw Ben. He was reading the bulletin board opposite, a collection of after-school club flyers and regulation notices from the principal. Was he waiting for me?

"Are you waiting for me?"

He turned with a smile. "No. I was just—did you know the board of governors have a meeting once every three months?" he thumbed the notices on the wall behind him.

"Oh, really?"

"They must have a lot to talk about in a school like this."

He was totally waiting for me.

"How many pregnancies have we had this year? Two?" I asked.

"Twelve. Must be something in the water."

"Can I offer you a glass of water?"

He smiled. "Only if you drink from it first."

"How was your dinner yesterday?" I asked, changing the subject before it got too awkward. "Penne Bolognese, wasn't it?"

"Delicious. I told you, I'm the world's greatest chef."

I lowered my voice. "And that thing you mentioned the other day? Your Mum?"

"Forget about it, we're all back to normal. How was practice?"

I could tell he didn't want to talk about it. His shoulders slumped when I mentioned her and he drew his hand to the back of his neck. The knot of his school tie was loose and chunky and the V-neck on his jumper had been stretched. His left shoelace was undone. The hall had emptied out and we were alone. Mr Elliot was still in the music room but he'd closed the door.

I looked up at his face. He was easily six inches taller than me. "It was good. I guess. We were practising my solo, which is terrifying, but whatever."

"Will you remember us little people when you're famous?"

I held my hand up to my head and measured out in front of me. My fingers came to his nose. "Little people?"

"You know what I mean."

"I'll probably let you come and visit my Dublin penthouse suite one time. I'll have my people remind me what your name is so it looks effortless when I say hello."

"I can believe it," Ben laughed.

It felt like he was going to ask me something, like maybe this whole conversation had been building up to a question, but Tony and Ashley came around the corner at the end of the corridor and I instinctively took a step back from Ben like I'd been caught doing something I shouldn't.

"Anyway," Ben said. "I'd better run for the bus. See you."

"There you are," Ashley called as Ben walked in the opposite direction and they came near. "We thought you'd got lost."

Tony said, "The library's that way."

"I was on my way."

"What did Ben Hunter want?"

"Why do you always think he wants something?"

Ashley said, "Because he's a jock and you're not."

"I could be a jock," I said, bulking my arms out like I'd been pumping iron for twenty years straight.

"Not in a million years," Tony said.

As we walked down the corridor, Ashley said, "He's not

making you do his homework, is he?"

"God, Ashley, what do you think this is, a teenage girl's wet dream?"

"That literally makes no sense," Tony said, and the three of us laughed.

I didn't see Ben on the bus and when we got to Grainger's half the tables were empty. Most kids stop off for an hour after school before going home and we were late thanks to choir practice.

Ashley's sister was about to finish her shift but said she'd wait in the staff room out the back for thirty minutes so we could bum a ride home.

I stirred a sugar packet into my flat white. Why did I step away from Ben when Ashley and Tony approached? I should have stayed where I was. It's not like we were doing anything secretive. We weren't swapping spit (I wish) or touching each other inappropriately (if only). Ben's reaction to walk away might have been because my friends had come, but part of me thought he'd taken offence to me backing away from him like I was treating him as my guilty secret. I wanted to text him but didn't know what to say. Sorry being near you makes me so nervous my gut hurts?

Tony asked Ashley when she was leaving to go to her dad's house for Christmas and they talked about being separated for four days like it was the end of the world, which led Ashley to say, "Not that Dean would know what that feels like."

"What'd I do?"

"Hello? When was the last time we managed to get any time together?"

"A few days ago," I said. I'm sure we sat at this very table just before the weekend.

"Yeah, but even when you're with us, you're absent."

"I can't be here and not here. That's not mathematically possible."

"You know what I mean. You've been distracted."

She's right. But I couldn't tell her why. "I'm just freaking out over my performance. I've got less than three weeks to perfect a song and learn how to sing it in front of a packed auditorium at the city hall. And you know how crazy that sounds."

"It's not just that," Ashley said.

Tony said, "And here I thought he was just moonlighting as a superhero, saving the universe one falsetto at a time."

"With my red trunks on top of my tights?"

"Please. I called you a superhero, but you could never pull off a pair of Speedos."

"Note to self," I said, "take the Speedos off my Christmas list."

But Ashley wasn't appeased. "And why are you hanging around with Ben Hunter? If he's not bullying you, what enlightened conversation is he offering that's better than this?"

"I'm thinking about joining the basketball team."

"As if."

"Ben's not the moron you think he is. He's actually very intelligent."

"For a jock," Tony said.

"He can't be that intelligent," Ashley said, "if he's best friends with Alex Janey."

"All right," I agreed. "Janey's a prat. We can't deny that."

"The epitome of a Neanderthal in a jockstrap eating crab cakes with a rock," Ashley said. It was so out there that it took us a few seconds to register her words before we laughed.

Tony imitated a Neanderthal voice and pretended to crack a crab open. "Crab good. Cake better."

And that was enough. I didn't have to steer the conversation away from Ben. Ashley and Tony managed it themselves. I'll just have to mention Alex Janey the next time somebody wants to get the truth out of me. That'll distract them.

Ashley's sister called to us from behind the counter. She already had her coat on. "Are you guys coming or what?"

We finished our drinks and walked behind the counter to the back room and into the car park outside. The air was freezing. And the car was freezing. But my head was full and warm.

The falling snow sparkled in the headlights as we crawled down the narrow road towards home. Each flake was a fairy falling to its death, their bodies littering the streets in a blanket of glitter. Rest in peace, fairies. You will be snowmen tomorrow.

When I got home, a thick layer of snow had settled on Chill Bill's cap. I dusted it off and straightened his carrot nose.

Christmas lights danced around the windows and the wreath on the front door was rattling against the glass in the wind. I tightened the cord that held it in place before going inside.

Ashley's sister had dropped me off before continuing to Tony's, and I'd said good night to them like old times. I had been distracted. I knew it. But my brain didn't mind.

Ben was my first thought in the morning and my last one at night.

And I knew at that moment what the constant hum at the back of my mind was.

Its name was Ben.

CHAPTER 16

BEN

Get a job, Dad had said. So I got a job.

It was easier than I thought. The local cinema had a sign outside that said *Help Wanted* and when I went in, the bored girl at the ticket booth handed me an application form. I was filling it in with a pen whose ink wasn't flowing well when the manager came out and the girl jutted her chin towards me.

The man came over. "You got any experience?" He didn't introduce himself and he wasn't wearing a name tag like the girl at the booth.

"I've seen a lot of movies," I said, hoping my smile was professional and friendly. When he didn't respond, I added, "And I head up our transition year business at school."

"How old are you?"

"Sixteen."

"What's your favourite popcorn?"

I didn't hesitate. "Salted over buttered over caramel."

He nodded, holding his hand out for my application form. "You're one of those." He flipped to the second page, but I hadn't got that far yet. "I've got ten minutes if you want an interview now." He walked back towards the manager's office without waiting.

I gave the girl at the ticket window a quizzical look and she shrugged and made a walking motion with her fingers. I wasn't sure if she was telling me to follow him or leave.

I thought interviews were all pressed shirts and oversized suits. But I followed him into his cramped office. There was a window on the far wall above his desk and a large gunmetal safe in the corner. A shelving unit was filled with box-files, but I didn't see any film reels lying around like I'd expected.

He lifted some papers off a chair and indicated that I should sit as he got behind his desk. "It's only seasonal work, just over the Christmas period. Jenny left us three days ago to have a baby and we haven't had the overseas workers this year the way we used to. Are you a hard worker?"

"Yes, sir."

"Tell me your strengths."

The old questions are the best. I'd read up on these interview techniques when we were establishing MVP Wellness at school. "I'm resilient. I know I'm only sixteen, but life has thrown some lemons at me in the past. I always make sure to push through the grind. When I decide to do something, I go all in. Whether its basketball, which I play at school, or a job, I'm a total people person."

I knew what was coming. "And your weaknesses?" the manager asked.

I pretended to think about it but my brain had already come up with an answer. "I guess my obsession with the perfect pop-corn-to-salt ratio is a weakness. But seriously. I can sometimes spread myself too thin, maybe. I tend to take on a lot, and it can be too much at times. But I'm learning to manage it, setting priorities and all that. I've given myself a schedule now for splitting my day up and it's working well."

The manager smiled. I still didn't know his name.

He said, "Why you? Why should I give you the job and not some other Joe Schmoe who wanders in off the street?"

"Aside from the fact that I'm dedicated and hardworking, I'd say it's because I have a clear reason for wanting this job. I'm not just looking for pocket money or a way to kill time. I've got responsibilities that I'm trying to meet, and I understand the value of hard work."

"Got your girlfriend pregnant, have you?"

"No, sir. Nothing like that. I'm just trying to help my parents out. College isn't cheap."

He looked at my incomplete application form. I was expecting a "thanks but no thanks" or "I'll let you know."

He read my name off the form. "I have two questions for you, Ben Hunter. One: Do you have a PPS number? And two: Can you start tonight?"

"Wow. For real?"

"I'm short staffed and it'll be quiet enough tonight to get you trained up."

I grinned. "I'll have to run home first, but yeah, I can start tonight. No problem. Thank you, Mr—?"

"Carlin," he said. He shook my hand and turned to the locker beside his desk. "What are you, a medium?"

He handed me a plastic bag with a black polo shirt in it. It had maroon sleeves and the cinema logo on the breast.

"Wear dark trousers. Preferably black. Your school trousers will do for now. Can you be back here at seven?"

As I walked home through the snow, I texted Dean before

I messaged Erin. He said, *Man, that's awesome news. But can you even fit it into your busy schedule?* Erin said, *Yay, free movies.*

I wasn't worried what my parents would say. Dad had already told me to get a job and Mum would mutter something about not seeing me enough as it is, never mind with a job on top of basketball. But staying out of the house for longer would benefit us all.

I got home and Dad was out. Mum was in the yard, her coat zipped up, and she was using a shovel in a drunken attempt to clear the snow. I stood in the doorway and watched her. "Finally buried him, have you?"

"Don't joke about it," she said.

"I've got a job at Bates' Cinema. I start tonight."

She dug her trowel in the dirt. "What time will you be home?" She didn't give me any of the responses I was waiting for.

"Late."

I showered, put a pair of black trousers on, and the hideous polyester polo shirt. I took a selfie and sent it to Dean.

benhuntss07
I look presentable, right? Tell me I don't look like a dick.

dean_odd_donnell
Fred says you look hot. But I'm sure he'd say the same if you were wearing a paper bag.

For a second, I thought maybe Fred—or his owner—was trying to say I looked cute. But nobody looks good in polyester.

My first night went so well that Marty Carlin, the manager,

gave me a free scoop of popcorn at the end of the night and told me to come back tomorrow. I wasn't selling tickets. I had to sweep the floors when I first got there, which were sticky and disgusting from the early showings, and then I had to check the toilets for any disasters, jotting my name and the time on the inspection sheet on the back of the door. The ladies' room was a mess, toilet paper everywhere, a glob of God knows what in one of the sinks. I cleaned up and signed my name on the sheet, then Marty had me jump on the concession stand where I shadowed Linda and Jeff before they let me serve a young family on my own.

"Let me guess," I said to the dad who had his wallet in his hand. "You look like a salted popcorn kind of guy, but the lady here likes sweet. How about a half and half? And a small caramel for the little one?"

"Just two large Cokes," the guy said. "And a small Fanta Orange."

Okay. So I'm not a popcorn wizard. But it was worth a shot.

I messaged Dean on my breaks to give him updates and he seemed genuine in his interest. And it was a break from Erin's constant questioning about my parents and their evil deeds.

On Friday, I suffered through maths and made it to lunch without falling asleep. The snow was still everywhere outside, although it hadn't snowed more in almost two days. I couldn't remember such a white winter.

Coach had us run drills in the gym before we could go to the cafeteria, and when I got there, Erin was sitting with some girls from class, and Alex Janey and the boys were requisitioning a table near the windows, forcing a few students out of their seats. I grabbed a prepacked sandwich from the fridge, paid for it, then took it outside into the cold air. I hadn't been given a wage yet, but I used the tips that Linda and Jeff shared with me from my first shift.

I didn't have basketball practice this evening, and I would go straight to work from school. My answer to one of the manager's questions struck me while I was eating my sandwich. I sat on the wall by the steps, sheltered from the wind by a column that jutted out from the main building. He'd asked me what my weaknesses were and I said I could spread myself too thin. I told him I was working on it, but here I was doing exactly that.

I heard the crunch of shoes on compacted snow.

Dean was smiling when I looked up. He pulled his coat collar up around his chin to show how cold it was. "I guess this is one way to keep your sandwich chilled."

"Thought I'd match my lunch temperature to your icy demeanour."

"Ouch." He sat on the wall. Not beside me, but close.

I held out the cardboard wrapper. "Want the other half?"

"What is it?"

"Mexican chicken."

"That's too spicy for me. Are you trying to warm yourself up from the inside out?" He indicated that I had sandwich filling on my chin and I wiped it with the back of my hand because I couldn't ask him to use his tongue.

"What are you doing out here?" I asked.

"Shouldn't I be asking you that?"

I finished the first half of my sandwich before responding. "I guess I just needed to be alone, you know?"

"Oh. Sorry." He stood up.

I gripped his coat sleeve. "No, stay. I just mean—I don't know what I mean."

"You mean Alex Janey can be a bit much sometimes."

I snorted. "Yeah, I guess. And what about you? Where are your friends?"

"Ashley's on a later lunch break and Tony's in the library finishing a food tech report."

I looked around at the almost empty grounds. There were a few first or second year kids throwing snowballs at the edge of the car park where two weeks ago we'd done the same. And there was a boy and girl by the gate that looked like they were about to jump each other's bones.

"Sucks to be us, eh?" I said.

After school, I saw Dean walking down the corridor towards the music room and I said good luck. He gave me the universal "I'll text you" sign with his hands and I dashed outside for the bus to town.

I ran through my early chores as fast as I could before getting behind the concession stand. I was sweating popcorn salt within an hour.

The lobby was filling up in time for the nine p.m. showings and we were rushed off our feet. From the heat of the popcorn machines and the overhead lights, I could feel thick beads of sweat on my back as if I'd been playing an intense game of basketball. I accidentally short-changed a guy and had to get a supervisor over to correct my mistake, and because that flustered me, I didn't see Alex Janey and the boys from the team until they were standing at the counter in front of me.

"Dude. Are you working here now?"

"No, Janey, I'm just back here helping myself."

The boys laughed, but they were on Alex Janey's side—of the counter and his humour.

"Can you dribble some butter on my popcorn?" one of the guys laughed.

"Ben Hunter," Janey said, "switching out his hoop dreams for popcorn machines."

"Very funny, man. What do you want? There's a queue."

"I'd love a free popcorn and a Coke."

"So would I, but we've all got to pay."

Alex Janey made a show of peeling open the Velcro of his wallet. "At least I don't have to work for my money. I'll have a large popcorn. Extra butter—or is that just for your butterfingers during games?"

I scooped out the required amount and slid the bucket across the counter to him.

"I didn't say butter, I said salt."

"Come on, man. Give me a break, will you?"

Alex slapped a twenty on the counter. "Fine, give me the buttered stuff that I didn't even ask for. And I'll be counting my change."

I turned my back on them to ring it through the till and Linda whispered, "You're doing fine. Dickheads like that usually give up after a few minutes." I didn't tell her he was my best friend.

I gave him the change and served the others with Linda's help. She was in her twenties and had pink hair. I could tell she wasn't the kind of person to take any crap.

As Alex and the others filed through the foyer and into screen three where the movie that was showing had an 18s certificate, I nudged Linda. "I know those guys from school.

157

And I'm sixteen. So, you know. I'm just saying."

She unhooked the radio from the belt of her jeans. "Say no more."

A few minutes later, I watched as they were escorted out of the building.

I'll say one thing. Having a job can give you an unlimited amount of power. And it was even better when Marty Carlin handed me an envelope at the end of the night.

"It's not a lot. You've only worked two days. But it's better than a kick in the gonads, right?"

I didn't even count it. I stuffed the envelope in my pocket. Anything was better than a kick in the gonads.

CHAPTER 17

DEAN

The sun wasn't up and I was already awake. We were fast approaching the winter solstice when the days would start to grow longer and, normally, I'd be willing it to happen sooner. But this December, I was loving the darkness. There was something in it that wasn't threatening. Something warm, despite the blistering chill.

I went downstairs and put on some coffee, just enough for a cup; it would be stewed and bitter by the time Mum and Dad woke. I left the overhead lights off but switched on the Christmas tree lights and they twinkled as I stood by the window staring out at the empty street. I never get up this early at the weekends. I didn't realise how beautiful our street could be when it was sleeping. Plastic snowmen were lit up like sentries at the edges of gardens and although most people turned their outdoor Christmas lights off overnight, some of them burned a multicoloured landing strip for Santa Claus. There were enough little kids living on the street to make Christmas still feel magical.

I was restless. I knew what was keeping me awake. It was Ben's increased presence in my life, the way he got under my skin with his smiles and his generous charm. And it was the anxiety of singing in front of an audience of hundreds. Both things were balanced in my head, taking up equal amounts of space, just as Ben somehow balanced any anxiety I had about performing when he was near me. As I talked to him, I wasn't thinking about singing. But when I was singing, I wasn't stressing over this odd new friendship we had developed. They were yin and yang, pushing and pulling at each other until they found a comfortable headspace.

There was a light snow falling through the dim morning light. The sky was turning a dull grey behind the houses on the other side of the street and I rinsed my cup and put it in the dishwasher. I put on a thick sweater and a scarf, coupled with a winter coat that came down to my knees, and I pulled on the thickest gloves I could find and a beanie. I put my ear pods in under the hat and stepped outside with *O Holy Night* playing on a loop.

I was smiling as I walked. Like an early-morning lunatic. I kicked up the fresh snow and nodded at Chill Bill before going down the street in the direction of the local park, which was nothing more than a small wasteland that had been converted into a football pitch and had a pond at the far end. A kid drowned there a few years ago, Ashley told me. I can't look at the pond without imagining a red bobble hat floating on the still surface.

The quiet of pre-dawn was a stark contrast to the power of the song in my ears. I sang along under my breath, matching the pace of my feet to the rhythm of the song. I had to practice my breathing, and each sharp inhalation gave me a reminder of the winter chill as it filled my lungs. Breathing was like maths. Each intake had its own rhythm, a calculus of the body that needed to be measured. It was about fractions of moments, holding a note until the end of a line, drawing breath at the right pause, conserving oxygen for the lung-stretching highs and the rolling lows. It was as precise and patterned as solving equations, a song of numbers played out in the body. Because that's what songs were. Numbers. Patterns. You didn't just breathe anywhere. There was a time and place for it, and knowing it—understanding it—that was the key to the perfect performance.

I'd been nervous in practice. It's like I didn't forget *when* to breathe but *how*. I needed to get a handle on those nerves or I'd never be able to walk out on the stage on Christmas Eve.

I'd reached the park and the song had looped six times. The sky had turned from a bruised purple to dove-grey, broken in pockmarks of gold where the sun was too tired to break through the skin of clouds. I breathed, sang, and breathed, and I concentrated on the fog of my words. Seeing my breath helped me to visualise the necessary rests.

I was warm in my thick clothes, but I could tell my cheeks were reddened and my nose was running. Snow clung to my shoes in clumps around the edges.

A car passed, slow, careful of the ice, and I stepped off the path onto the empty playing field. The overnight snow had eradicated any footprints from yesterday, wiping out a day of play, and I walked into the middle of the football pitch. I tapped my phone to restart the song. Singing to the silent world, my voice was raw but determined, battling against the winter elements. I took in a lungful of crisp morning air and released it as I reached the bridge, timing my breaths so much that I didn't have to think about it.

I hit the high note. I don't know if it was the cold air in my lungs or my confidence in a silent world, my personal rehearsal stage that had been shaped by the snow, but it came out with perfect pitch.

When the music closed out, I stopped it from playing again. And in the silence, I looked around, embarrassed. But nobody was there.

On my way back, treading through my own footprints, I sent a message to Ben. I wasn't expecting a reply.

> **dean_odd_donnell**
> Sorry it's early, but Fred won't let up. He was expecting monthly visitations and he thinks you've forgotten about him.

benhuntss07
OMG he's such a needy baby.

> **dean_odd_donnell**
> What can I say? You gave birth to a brat.

benhuntss07
Or is it nurture over nature? Did you turn him into a brat by mollycoddling him?

> **dean_odd_donnell**
> I'm a model parent.

benhuntss07
Sure you are 😊 . He's probably right though, I've been an absent father. I've got work later but I'm not doing anything today if he wants to hang out.

dean_odd_donnell
I'm sure he'd be down for that. Where
and when? And why are you awake so
early?

benhuntss07
Damn alien abductions. They never
consider the time difference. At least
they didn't leave the nostril probe
in this time. I can come to yours? My
place is a bit chaotic.

My cheeks were red and it wasn't from the chill. And they
ached because my grin was massive. If I grin like this when he's
around, I'm going to get myself in trouble. Or sectioned.

I gave him my address and he said he could be here in an
hour if that wasn't too early. Of course it damn well wasn't.
But also it was. I had an hour to tidy my room. Not that I was
messy but yesterday's boxers were still on the floor.

Mum was awake when I got home and I told her I had a
friend coming over. She didn't ask who, though I could see she
wanted to. Until Ben got here, she'd assume it was probably
Ashley or Tony.

I picked a few things off the floor and straightened the items
on my shelves, then I put Fred on top of my pillows, relocated
him to the desk, and then put him back on the bed because
holy crap Ben Hunter was going to be in my bedroom very
soon and that wasn't scary at all. I took a shower, wore what
I believed was my cutest winter jumper, and used my mum's
hairdryer to fluff my hair out.

A little after nine-thirty, the doorbell chimed. "I'll get it," I
shouted, and I almost slipped down the stairs in my socks and

thumped against the front door before fumbling to open it.

"Hi. Hey. Sorry."

Ben grinned. "Nice sweater."

He stepped inside and we stood in the short hallway between the dining room and the living room. He unzipped his coat but didn't take it off.

"What should we do?" I asked.

He shrugged.

Every single pore in my body was blushing. I pointed over my shoulder. "Fred's upstairs. You can hang your coat here."

He toed his shoes off at the heels and sat them by the front door, then put his coat on the rack and I heard his soft footfalls as he followed me to my bedroom.

Letting him into my sanctuary felt weird. It was like letting him see me naked, the real me.

Ben laughed when he saw my collection of NECA figures, but then he stopped and cocked his head. He was looking at the chalkboard above my desk. There were a few doodles around the edges, but the faded equation across the middle of the board read:

$$\zeta(s) = 2^s \, \pi^{s-1} \sin(\pi s/2) \, \Gamma(1-s) \, \zeta(1-s)$$

"You didn't tell me the aliens have been leaving cryptic clues on your wall."

"It's maths."

"No shit." He was smiling. "All right, Mr Brainbox, what does it mean?"

I shrugged like it was no big deal. "It's part of the Riemann Hypothesis, one of the biggest unsolved problems in mathematics. I'm trying to figure out where the nontrivial zeros of this function fall on a complex plane. Solving it would be a huge leap forward for number theory. And net me a million US dollars."

"Are you, like, some kind of genius?"

"Well, Einstein and I both kissed the Blarney Stone, so you tell me."

"Is that true?" I could see in his eyes that he wasn't sure if he should believe me.

"I have no idea," I said, and I threw Fred at him. To be honest, I'd written the equation on the board over two years ago, when we were still living in Blarney, and I'd almost forgotten it was there.

Ben sat on the edge of my bed, holding Fred in his lap. "Apart from sharing custody of Fred, you don't have any other children or siblings?"

I could have sat on the bed near him but that felt too intimate, so I pulled the desk chair out and turned it to face him. "That's a big fat zero. What about you?"

"Do you mean kids or siblings?"

"If you have so many of them that you have to differentiate, I'm going to be freaked out."

He gave a short laugh from his nose. "Fortunately no kids. Unfortunately no siblings. I've always wanted a little brother. These days, I'm glad it's just me."

"How come?"

He shrugged. His face was open but his body language was closed.

I changed the subject. "Favourite movie. Go."

He didn't hesitate. "*Spider-Man: No Way Home*."

"And you call me a geek?" I laughed.

"What?"

"Superheroes. Do you go to comic con and dress up as Spidey?"

Ben tossed Fred at my face and I ducked. "All right, genius, what's your favourite movie? A documentary about Einstein?"

"Oh, have you seen that one, too? It's on Netflix." He didn't bite, so I said, "*Jojo Rabbit* is probably up there. It's a pretty funny satire despite being about the Hitler youth."

"I've actually seen that one. I get it."

"So you don't just want to Hulk-smash everything?"

"I only Hulk-smash when I'm on the basketball court."

Our conversation meandered through movies and childhood memories. He asked me about Blarney and what my school was like before we moved here. It was an all-boys school which, you know, might annoy other boys but I was cool with it. I didn't tell Ben that. I've always had friends, but never many. Too many people can freak me out, which is probably why I'm terrified of standing out there on Christmas Eve in front of a zillion people.

At noon, I grabbed some snacks from the kitchen, and we shared a large bag of Tayto crisps and Ben ate almost half a packet of chocolate-coated Hobnobs, sucking melted chocolate from his fingers every so often. And when we ran out of things to talk about and we lapsed into a silence, we watched *Jojo Rabbit* on my laptop. I'd positioned it on the desk so we could see it from the bed and we sat with our backs against the wall and an array of snacks between us like a moat that separated him from me.

We stopped paying attention halfway through the film

when Ben asked, "What do you think it means to be a good person?" His eyes didn't leave the screen but I could tell he had something on his mind.

"That's a bit deep for a Saturday afternoon."

"Humour me."

I thought about it, forcing my eyes back to the movie to avoid staring at him. "I guess it's about treating other people the way you'd want to be treated. But also it's about having empathy and understanding."

"And if someone screws up? Can they still be a good person?"

"Everyone screws up. That doesn't make us bad. We just have to learn not to do it again. It's about trying to do better the next time around."

He looked at me then. I could see the smile that kicked up the corner of his mouth. "That's pretty wise."

"Well, I am a genius, remember?"

He laughed, and whatever tension had been building in his voice was gone. "Stop interrupting the movie," he said.

"Hey, it was your fault."

"Was not."

He stretched over my legs to pick Fred up from the floor and I almost kneed him in the chin when I flinched at his closeness. But he sat Fred on top of the mound of snacks between us, flipped a wine gum into his own mouth, and turned his attention back to the screen.

When it was time for him to leave, Mum accosted us at the bottom of the stairs. I introduced him and she shook his hand.

"You're more than welcome to stay for dinner, Ben."

"That would have been awesome, but I've got work tonight.

Thanks, Mrs O'Donnell."

"I'm going to walk him to the bus stop," I said, putting my coat on.

"Ben," Mum said, and I braced for whatever witty thing she was going to say and embarrass me. "You should take him into town sometime. Help him find a girl."

"Mum!"

"What? Tony's a darling, but he's not really helping you meet new people, is he?"

"Oh my God, will you stop?"

Mum shrugged at Ben. "I don't know what I said wrong. Nice to meet you, Ben."

Outside, I pulled my collar up pretending I was cold, but I was trying to hide my embarrassment from him.

"She's funny," he said.

"Yeah, she's hilarious."

"Why don't you go out and meet more people? I mean, you're smart. And funny."

I kept my gaze on the ground as we walked. "People scare me."

"Do I scare you?"

"You used to."

He stopped walking. "Really?"

"Look at you, and then look at me," I said. "You're the popular kid that's into sports and has an attractive girlfriend and I'm a maths nerd with glasses."

"I like your glasses."

"I appreciate the sympathy vote."

"That's not what I meant."

We started walking again, our pace slow. I didn't want to

reach the bus stop. I didn't want to move.

Ben said, "I'm not hanging out with you because you're a geek."

"Good, because I'm not doing your homework."

He laughed. "I wish you would."

And there was the bus stop. And the bus was coming around the corner.

He pulled some change from his pocket. "Anyway," he said. "Erin's not my girlfriend. She never has been."

"I thought she was."

"Everyone does. But she's not my type."

The bus pulled up and the door hissed open for him.

"What is your type?" I asked, dreading the answer.

Ben smiled, bought his ticket, and then turned back to me. "See you, Dean."

As the bus pulled away, the vision of his smile lingered.

CHAPTER 18

BEN

You're my type. That's what I wanted to say, but I couldn't tell him. I rode the bus into town, paying attention to the new landmarks I wasn't familiar with on this side of the city. The houses were bigger here, detached or semi-detached. Not like the rows of bland terraced housing on the north side of the River Lee where everything was creeping in on itself. Dean's bedroom was as big as our living room.

I couldn't begin to comprehend the maths equation on his wall, scrawled on the board like alien graffiti. His room had subtle notes of laundry detergent mixed with blueberry muffins, with a slight undertone of freshly sharpened pencils. That's the only way I can describe it. I liked it. It had a sense of regimented organisation, books where they belonged, drawers closed—their contents probably folded with meticulous care—and I bet the space under his bed was empty and vacuumed often. Unlike mine, which was a mountain range of busted basketball shoes that I could no longer wear.

I got to town in ten minutes, and when I walked into Bates' Cinema, Bowls & Arcade, I changed into my polo shirt in the staff room. I adjusted the collar in the mirror and then joined

Linda and Jeff at the concession counter. I still wasn't sick of the smell of popcorn, but Jeff said it wouldn't be long. An army of screaming kids erupted out of the late afternoon showing of a Universal movie, and the adults that followed them were trying to herd them towards the food court. It was like watching a group of cats trying to organise a fireworks display.

"Heads up," Linda said. She turned to the popcorn machine and Jeff spun towards the shelf of snacks, pretending to count them.

"We'll need another box of Peanut M&Ms and we're running low on Twirl Bites."

Marty Carlin had come out of his office. As he locked the door, he didn't look over his shoulder. "Ben, why are you standing there with two arms the one length?"

I picked up a sack of popcorn kernels like I was already busy. "I'm not."

"Who's on sweep up? Whenever we get a busload of kids in one of the screens, you can be sure there's piss, puke or shit on at least three seats."

"Ben is," Jeff and Linda said at once.

"Good night," Marty said, putting his coat on.

The lights were up in screen two and Marty wasn't wrong. I had to clean up the worst mess I'd ever seen—or smelled—and I felt sick when I was done. A new bunch of teens and adults were already filtering in for the next show.

I hid in the back and checked my phone. Erin had been trying to reach me all day but I'd had my phone on silent. I really should pay more attention to her. Her last message, over an hour ago, was just a bunch of question marks. I sent her a quick text telling her I had to get out of the house for the day and I'd be home after work if she wanted to stop by. It would be late, but she needed me as much as I needed her.

I was such a bad friend.

When I got back to the counter, the queues were twelve deep. "About time," Jeff said.

I jumped on another till and was swallowed by the rhythm of the popcorn machine, the scent of hot butter and the occasional shout or laugh from the lobby.

I was knee-deep in popcorn kernels and cola syrup for an hour as the staggered movie times drew closer and the lobby emptied out, but after the last of the blockbuster crowd had shuffled into their respective screens, I needed the respite it granted us. There was sweat in my hair and my shirt stuck to my back. When all the movies were playing except the ten o'clock arthouse film that was still an hour away, the quiet that swept through the empty space was welcome.

I rested my hands on the countertop, my fingers slick from the oil that clung to the popcorn scoop. I realised, now that my mind was free to delve into its darker itches, that I hadn't thought about my parents all day. Not since I'd rang Dean's doorbell and he opened the door in that gorgeous sweater that made him look smaller than he was.

Jeff helped himself to a cup of tangy Fanta Lemon from the dispenser and Linda said she'd do the toilet check.

I heard the buzz and whir of the arcade machines in the next room even though the automatic doors were closed, and I took a second to check my phone. Dean had messaged me ten minutes before. *How's work?* It was a simple question but coming from Dean it felt sincere, like he really wanted to know.

I was tapping out my reply when Linda said, "That's the

rush over. One of you can probably go home. We won't need the three of us here for the rest of the night."

"I'll go," Jeff said.

But Linda stopped him. "Let the newbie go. He deserves it."

I undid the top two buttons of my polo shirt. "This newbie doesn't have to be told twice." But I had a better idea.

benhuntss07
I've just been given the rest of the night off. Can you get here before 10? There's an arthouse movie on which I bet is right up your street.

dean_odd_donnell
OMG you're going to watch something that's NOT a superhero movie?

benhuntss07
You're right. We can call it off if you prefer.

dean_odd_donnell
Nope, I'm on my way.

benhuntss07
Meet me by the side door in twenty minutes?

I should have invited Erin instead. But she wouldn't be into a low-budget movie about a drug addict trying to make it in London's West End while her little sister dies of Ondine's Curse. Whatever that was.

What am I saying? I wasn't into it either.

But I'd only spend the movie staring at Dean from the corner of my eye and revelling in how close his leg would be to mine, so I guess it didn't matter what was on the screen.

Jesus, Ben, pull it together.

Twenty minutes later, I pushed open the side door. Dean was wearing a fur-lined coat with the hood up, pink cheeks shiny from the overhead lights above the entrance. I ushered him in and when he said thanks it sounded breathy and shy.

I took my small work-issued Maglite out of my pocket, clicked it on, and flashed it across his face. "This way, sir. Allow me to escort you to your seat."

I led him to Screen Five but before going through the door, he said, "What about a ticket?"

"It's covered," I said. "One of my perks."

"For real?"

"Would I lie to you?"

He smiled. I wish I had his willing acceptance. Sneaking him in the side door should have been a giveaway.

We went inside and I showed him to a seat near the back. Screen Five was our smallest room, with only forty-six seats, but it was the most luxurious. The red velvet executive seats were larger and reclined independently of their neighbours. "Sit here. I'll be right back."

The screen was reminding patrons to turn their phones off and that recording equipment was prohibited. When I came back, a local firm of solicitors was advertising their ambulance-chasing services.

"What the hell?" Dean laughed.

I was carrying an extra-large popcorn and two Cokes. The popcorn tub was as big as a bath. "I didn't know what you liked so I got half and half."

He took the Cokes off me so I could sit down beside him.

"What do I owe you?"

"Shut up," I said.

"But I've got to pay you something."

I took a fistful of popcorn and passed the tub over. "You're not going to keep interrupting the movie like you did earlier, are you?"

"That wasn't me, remember?"

"Shut up and watch the movie, Mr O'Donnell."

"It hasn't started yet."

But the lights dimmed and he turned his head to face the screen. Arthouse movies always skipped the previews and the movie opened on a sprawling, black-and-white aerial view of London before cutting to the protagonist crawling out of the gutter in a narrow side street where the camera pans down to reveal a spoon, a needle, and a lighter.

"That's a bit intense to start a movie with," I whispered.

"Shush."

"You shush."

I could see his smile in the ethereal glow from the screen.

The entire movie was in black and white except for the main character's little sister. She was about seven. It was weird that she was the one dying from Ondine's Curse and yet she was the only thing in colour. I knew that had to mean something, but I didn't know what. I don't understand arthouse movies.

Ondine's Curse meant that her body would forget to breathe during sleep.

I settled into the chair and reclined it a little so that I could see the side of Dean's face without having to turn my head too far. He was intent on the film. Every time the little girl came on screen, I could see his smile return. He reached for the popcorn between us and I put my hand in the tub with his.

"Sorry," he said.

I wasn't.

The movie's soundtrack was an odd mix of violins and tambourines. It was sharp and cacophonous. And Dean's knee was just there, in my space. He was wearing a pair of tan khakis. I moved my leg closer, not daring to touch him.

And in the soft glow of the movie screen, my eyes were dragging closed. The seat was comfortable. And so was the company. I realised how little sleep I'd had lately and how much energy I'd been expelling on the court and at work. I was out of the house for longer in the evenings, which was excellent, but when I was there my parents were still fighting. I can't remember the last time I got more than four hours sleep. If their violent screams weren't waking me, their silences were waking me harder.

The little girl was back on screen. None of the characters had names. The colour of her dress stood out in stark contrast to the black and white tears on the older girl's face.

I closed my eyes. The drug addict said something dark and depressing but her little sister came back at her with a joke. I felt Dean's laughter through the chair.

And then Dean was leaning over me, his face a blur, eyes sparkling.

"You fell asleep?"

"No," I said, straightening up in my seat. The credits were rolling and the popcorn bucket was only half empty.

"You totally fell asleep."

I looked around. I'd wanted to spend time with him, not invite him over and then fall asleep. The lights were up and people were leaving.

"Shit. What happened? Did the little girl die?"

He nodded. I could see he'd been crying.

"I'm not sure if I even understood it."

"That's because you didn't see the whole movie. It was about the fight for dreams. But also just a fight for breath. Literally breathing. The little one couldn't breathe in her sleep and the older girl couldn't breathe in her life."

We stood up and he pulled his coat on. The glaze in his eyes made me want to hold him. But I couldn't jinx this.

As we came out of the screening room into the lobby, the lights above the concession stand were off and I couldn't see Linda or Jeff.

"I can't believe you get free movie tickets," Dean said. "That's awesome."

"Yeah."

The automatic doors swished open and Dean zipped his coat up further. It was almost midnight.

"Hang on," I said, "I need to grab my jacket." I went behind the concession stand and into the staff room, and on my way out I stopped at the till, rang it open and saw that the drawer was empty. I took the envelope Marty had handed to me yesterday out of my pocket and put enough money into the empty drawer to cover Dean's ticket and the popcorn. I'd been feeling guilty since I let him in through the side door. And I wasn't a thief.

Dean was leaning against a bollard at the bottom of the steps outside. The snow had been cleared from the carpark but a fresh dusting had settled across the tarmac and made it glisten like diamonds.

"I've ordered an Uber. We can share."

"But I'm going in the other direction."

"Perfect. I was hoping to take the scenic route home. It'll be like a low-budget road trip."

I didn't want him to see where I lived. What if my parents were screaming in the garden when we pulled up?

We sat in the back seat together, separated by a broad armrest that came down from the seat between us. I kept my eyes on the clock on the dashboard, hoping Mum and Dad would have worn each other out by now and gone to sleep.

"That movie was so good," Dean said.

"What was up with that whole colour thing anyway? Why was the little girl the only thing in colour?"

Dean frowned. "The whole movie was in colour once she died."

"What was that all about?"

"Life," was all he said.

I still didn't understand it. Maybe my brain just doesn't work the same way as Dean's.

The car came down my street and I knew my heartrate had quickened. I handed the driver the fare from my envelope, covering the rest of Dean's journey, but Dean said to give half of it back.

"It's only fair. Thanks for the movie. I loved it."

I didn't argue. I needed to get out of the car and let them drive away before one of my parents let out a scream or smashed something.

"See you at school," I said, and I stood on the pavement watching as the car went down the street, turned and drove back up. Dean waved on the way past.

When the car was out of sight, I went into the house. Dad was lying on the couch, staring at the TV. It wasn't switched on.

"Where's Mum?"

He didn't answer.

I went upstairs. My parents' bedroom door was closed so Mum must have already gone to bed.

In my room, Erin was sitting on the bed. I'd forgotten that I'd told her to come round after work. "Who was in the taxi with you?"

"No one."

"I saw you talking to somebody."

I kicked my shoes off. "Just someone I caught a ride home from work with. It was cheaper to share."

"I thought it was Dean O'Donnell," Erin said.

"Why would it be Dean?" I pulled my polo shirt off and sprayed my armpits with fresh deodorant, refusing to look at her.

"You're spending a lot of time with him."

"Am I?" I pulled on a clean T-shirt and spent my time picking invisible lint from it instead of turning to her.

"Unless there's another short, geeky, maths-loving kid in a bobble hat you've been hiding."

"There's nothing wrong with him."

"Where have you been all day, anyway? With him?"

"Maybe."

Erin said, "Are you gay for him or something?"

"I'm not gay for anyone, Erin. I'm just gay. There's a difference."

Her words were poison on barbed wire. But she was right. I

was happy being gay so long as Alex Janey and the boys never found out.

I'd be the butt of the changing room. And not in a good way.

"I'm just saying," Erin said. "People might start talking."

"You make it sound like they already are."

"All I'm saying is that whispers can get pretty loud."

I dropped onto the bed beside her. As if I didn't have enough shouting in my life.

CHAPTER 19

DEAN

"Come on, guys, this isn't a game," Mr Elliot said, and his words reminded me of Coach Williams at one of Ben's practices.

We have less than two weeks until Christmas Eve's performance and today we sound worse than ever. Or at least I do. I can't pull my voice up from my diaphragm and all I seem to do is squeak and groan. Gemma Ademola said I should drink some hot lemon.

"Let's try again," Mr Elliot said. "Dean, I need you to dig deep, okay? I know you have it in you."

I shook my limbs as if loosening my body would free up my vocals. We had other songs to practice, not just my solo, and when we were going over *Ave Maria*, I was only mouthing the words, trying to save my voice from the fires of whatever hell it had decided to throw itself into.

I wasn't sick. I didn't have a sore throat or a fever. My voice just wasn't pulling its act together today.

At home, I messaged Ben, then Tony and Ashley. Ben suggested I walk around with a clipboard for the next two weeks so I could write instead of talk. Tony said I should totally follow Gemma Ademola's advice, and Ashley said it was just nerves or stress and it would probably be better in the morning.

I drank a cup of disgusting hot lemon, its viscous pulp threads swimming in the brew, and I hoped Ashley was right.

We were having daily practice sessions now that we were getting closer to the performance. Mr Elliot was on my case all the time. Even at lunch on Tuesday he accosted me. I'd been sitting on the wall opposite the car park with Ben, which had become our unofficial meeting spot. He was eating a home-made sandwich and I could see the collar of his work top under his school shirt. His gym sack was at his feet.

"When do you ever get a chance to sit down?" I asked.

"I'm sitting now."

"You know what I mean. School, basketball, rugby, work. Do you ever sleep?"

"Do I look like I sleep?" he laughed. And he really didn't. His eyes were puffy and his hair was a permanent mess. It was cute bedhead, but taken up a notch.

From behind us, Mr Elliot said, "I certainly hope Dean O'Donnell is getting enough sleep."

"You should give him some sleeping pills, sir," Ben said, sliding an inch further away from me. "Maybe it'll help to knock him out at night and kill off his solo fear."

"I've seen you on the basketball team, haven't I?"

"Yes, sir."

Mr Elliot pointed at Ben as he looked at me and said, "Maybe this one ought to give you some breathing lessons. You can't run around the court for an hour and not figure out how to breathe, right?"

I never noticed before, but Mr Elliot had a plastic lunch-box, like something you'd see a little kid with. He must have been carrying it in from his car.

"I've been breathing all my life," Ben said, "and I'm still alive."

Mr Elliot nodded. "Maybe give him some lessons so he doesn't pass out before Christmas Eve."

"Yes, sir."

Mr Elliot went inside and Ben looked at me with a side-eye. "What?"

"You know he was literally telling me to breathe for you."

"I do just fine. I've got two lungs and as far as I can tell, they're both in working order."

Ben put his sandwich on top of the foil it had been wrapped in and sat it on the wall. "Stand up."

"Piss off."

"Stand up."

We stood up. He reached out and unzipped my coat—which was not erotic in the slightest, okay? He put his hand on my chest, his fingers on the school crest of my jumper. "Breathe."

I couldn't breathe.

"Are you breathing?"

"No."

"Why not?"

"Because you're freaking me out."

"Shut up and breathe."

I breathed. Once. Twice. He wasn't looking at me. He was watching his hand. It gave me the chance to study his face. If I'd leaned in, I could have kissed him.

He unzipped my coat further and pressed his hand against the top of my stomach. "Now use your diaphragm."

"I thought I was."

183

"Breathe. Use your belly."

I let my stomach swell as I took a deep breath and he grinned. "See?" I said. "Breathing's not my problem."

"Then I'm afraid there's nothing more I can do. You have exactly"—he raised his arm like he was checking a watch—"seventeen seconds left to live."

"I haven't even written a will."

"Should have thought of that before joining the choir."

I held my chest as though I was in pain. I remembered his award-winning death scene during our epic snowball fight a few weeks ago. "Is it getting dark? It's getting dark." I held a hand out. "I can't see. Why can't I see?"

He gripped my hand in both of his. "Go to the light, Dean. And remember, the password for Heaven's Wi-Fi is BananaLoafers."

"Can I haunt you?" I asked, wilting on the wall like a dying lettuce leaf.

He checked his imaginary watch. "And three, two, one—are you dead?"

I patted my body to make sure I was still there. "I—don't think so?"

Ben sat down and picked up his sandwich. "Well. That clears one thing up."

"What?"

"I wouldn't make a very good doctor."

On Wednesday, Mr Elliot gathered us in the gym where the basketball team were warming up. Coach Williams let us use the bottom corner while Ben and the team were running suicides across the court width, using a set of coloured agility cones. Mr Elliot made us sing scales and he stood at the far side of the gym, beyond the basketball team, with his hand cupping his ear.

"I can't hear you."

We sang louder. Ben gave me a discreet wave and Gemma Ademola waved back.

"*God Rest Ye Merry Gentlemen*," Mr Elliot shouted at us.

The basketball team moved on to free-throw shots inside the arc. I'd spent Sunday looking up some basketball terminology, not that much of it made sense.

Alex Janey said, "Coach, they're putting us off our game."

It was weird seeing my history teacher in a pair of shorts. He said, "If a little singing puts you off, what are you going to do come game day when you have a crowd chanting rhymes and stomping their feet? Don't blame a couple of lousy Christmas carols for your bad dribbling, Janey."

Mr Elliot said he objected to the word lousy, but honestly, they were putting us off our singing more than we were interfering with their dribbling.

I was doing my own dribbling over Ben.

Mr Elliot called, "*O Holy Night*," and my throat closed up. I wasn't prepared to sing my solo in front of anyone other than the choir.

We opened on the first verse, a choir collective performance. I had to keep time in my head because Mr Elliot didn't bring anything to play the music on. I tried not to look at Ben but when I did he pointed at his diaphragm. And then he turned and launched himself towards the hoop with the ball in his hand. There was an elegance to the soft arc that his body made before he slammed the ball through the net. He hung from the hoop for a second before dropping to his feet and I tried not to smile as I opened my throat to sing.

Show off.

The words came out. But I have no idea if they came out well. Or in the correct order. I watched Ben as he watched me. And before the end of the song, the basketball team had stopped playing and were listening to our performance.

When I let go of the final note, Alex Janey sneered and bounced the ball between him and Coach Williams. "Are they done now?"

I spent the rest of the evening at Grainger's with Tony and Ashley, and on Thursday we weren't allowed into the gym. The basketball team were playing their final pre-Christmas league game before the break. I'd wanted to skip practice and watch Ben play but Mr Elliot was adamant we would perfect our full repertoire before next week. I couldn't get out of it.

In the music room, Mr Elliot sat at the piano with his age-worn, yellowing keys, and he made me stand beside him, facing the choir. We practised until my throat was dry.

When I got home, Tony and Ashley had arranged to come over after dinner. They came with a suitcase full of clothes because Tony said we had to coordinate for tomorrow night at the school dance.

"I was just going to wear a shirt," I told them yesterday.

"Yeah, but what shirt?"

"I don't know. A white one?"

"Boring," Tony said. "You wear a white shirt to school every day."

"I still don't know why we're even going."

"Hey. You two are the ones who forced me into this. So we're going to get our wardrobes sorted and you're going to enjoy it."

"And for God's sake," Ashley said, "wear that dumb rainbow pin. Whoever bought it for you deserves to see you wearing it at least once."

"Sure, and strut my stuff through the school gym saying, 'I'm here and I'm queer'?"

Tony said, "You could at least say something original."

"Anyway," I told them. "I've been wearing it. On the inside of my coat."

"Where no one can see it."

"That's exactly how I like my homosexuality while I'm still in school."

Tony was filtering through the shirts in my wardrobe, crinkling his nose up at my salmon-coloured long-sleeved paisley. "If you wear this, you won't have any need for the rainbow pin."

"You're just jealous of my style."

"What style? If I wanted to dress like a colourblind magician, I'd raid my little brother's dress-up box."

Ashley, who had no qualms about undressing in front of an asexual and a closeted gay boy, slipped into five different outfits before Tony gave his seal of approval on a pair of white, tailored, high-waisted trousers with a fitted, white blouse. Tony called it monochromatic chic. Ashley was not the kind of girl to wear dresses. "If I wanted my legs to be exposed to every breeze and prying eye, I'd have become a lifeguard at a nudist beach."

"In Ireland? Everything would be cold and shrivelled," Tony said.

"I thought that was just a natural state for all boys."

I had a few more qualms than Ashley, so when I was trying

on the selection of trousers Tony picked out for me, I turned my back to them.

"The grey ones really cup your butt," Tony said.

"They do raise the bar in terms of posterior presentation," Ashley agreed. "They've just turned your 'no comment' bum into a full press release."

I turned, fumbling with the button on the trousers. "Can we stop talking about my bum like it's a newly discovered planet?"

"Pluto ain't got a look in."

I looked at my ass in the mirror. "Remind me why we thought this was a good idea. I can't dance, modern music sucks, and I don't even remember the last time I stayed awake past midnight. It's boys on one side of the dancefloor and girls on the other, right? Do we still do that at high school dances?"

Ashley said, "We've gone beyond gender norms now, Dean. You can stand at whichever side of the dancefloor divide you want to."

"Yay for modern society. Now I can feel awkward everywhere instead of just designated areas."

Tony handed me a shirt. "Try this. And unless you've got weird nipples, you really don't need to turn away from us in order to change."

I turned away regardless.

"Just as I thought. Three nipples," he said.

When I'd buttoned the shirt up, I realised Tony was better at dressing me than I would ever be able to manage. I gave myself a playful point in the mirror and Tony and Ashley laughed.

But I was nervous. I didn't do well at school functions, whether it was a science fair or a dance. I once shattered a test tube when demonstrating the intricacies of a chemical reaction between vinegar and baking soda. The pressure build-up was more than I'd anticipated.

And if Ben asked me to dance with him tomorrow night, there'd be another pressure build-up that I wouldn't be able to contain. I don't have big dreams, just impossible ones.

I'd wanted to kiss him on Saturday evening when he invited me to the cinema. He fell asleep during the movie and although I knew I needed to nudge him awake, part of me was prepared to pucker up and plant one on his lips. But I did neither. He looked like he needed the sleep, so I pressed the side of my knee against his leg and watched the movie, content just to be in his company.

When Tony and Ashley had gone home, I hung the shirt and trousers back in my wardrobe for tomorrow night, and I sent Ben a message.

dean_odd_donnell
Did you win?

benhuntss07
Of course. 57-54. Did you boss your
rehearsal?

dean_odd_donnell
Of course. 50-50.

benhuntss07
Lol. Catch you at school tomorrow?

I took his question as a way to put a quick end to our conversation.

dean_odd_donnell
Sure. See you then.

I put my phone on charge. I need these constant reminders that I'm not his entire life. He's got other friends, other things to do.

And I need to be okay with that.

CHAPTER 20

BEN

Dad was shouting. Again. Mum was crying. And I was sitting on the floor of my bedroom with my back pressed against the door. No amount of death metal would block out the noise of them.

I woke up on Monday in hell, and by Friday morning I was knee-deep in fire and brimstone.

Dad was in bed when I left for school on Monday, and still in bed when I got home. The only thing that helped me through the day was Dean. I can't even say Erin helped. She reminded me as we sat at the back of maths class that some people might be worried—her words—about me hanging out with Dean O'Donnell.

"Why?" I whispered, leaning over to take a pencil sharpener from her desk.

"Because it's not natural."

I sharpened my pencil even though the point was already lethal. "How's it different from me hanging out with Alex or you spending time with Gemma Ademola?"

"Because I don't want to put my dick in her," she said.

I slammed the metal sharpener on her desk, butterfly shards

191

skittering to the floor. "Everybody wants to put their dick in Gemma Ademola," I hissed.

On Tuesday I almost sat with Erin and Gemma in the cafeteria but they were whispering conspiracies to each other so I went outside. Dean was already there and I lowered my head as I sat on the wall beside him so that he didn't see how wide my smile was. The music teacher said something to us about breathing and I honestly can't remember what I said next but that's when I had my hand pressed against Dean's warm chest. His school jumper was giving off enough heat that my cold fingers were tingling, and he was breathing, and I was reciting recipes in my head to keep my mind off how damn close I was to him.

At home that evening, my parents were laughing.

Both of them.

They were sitting at the kitchen table with whiskey tumblers filled with something on the rocks and a pack of cards spread out between them.

"Buddy," Dad said, kicking the leg of an empty chair for me.

"What's going on?"

"Nothing's going on," Mum said, and she giggled like a naughty child. I dropped my schoolbag on the floor and she said, "Don't leave your bag there. Put it in your room."

"And then come back down," Dad said.

I stood there for a second, staring at them, stunned by this complete change in mood. I could tell they'd had sex for the first time in months. Gross. They'd been screaming at each other when I left for school this morning. And the day before. And for weeks before that.

I put my bag in my room and sent a text to Erin. *They're laughing. I think they've descended into hysteria.*

And I realised that was the first time I'd gone straight to Erin with my problems instead of Dean. But Dean didn't know the history. Erin would just get it.

In the kitchen, Dad pushed the chair out further while Mum poured more drinks. I didn't see the label to know what they were drinking, but if it was happy juice, I wanted some.

A sliver of grey smoke spiralled towards the ceiling from the cigarette that burned in the ashtray by her elbow.

Dad dealt three hands. "The game's Texas Holdem. The aim is to make the best five-card hand using your dealt cards and the ones I put on the table."

"What are we playing for?" I asked. I was confused not by the game but by this shift in personalities.

Mum shot back her drink and slapped the empty glass on the tabletop. The ice didn't have a chance to melt. "Loser has to drink."

"I'm sixteen."

She rolled her eyes like I was a party pooper. She went to the fridge and came back with a carton of milk. "Have a milk slammer," she said. "You'll need salt and a lemon wedge."

I couldn't imagine Dean's parents playing Holdem or making up fake cocktails with pasteurised cow's milk.

Dad put three cards face up in the centre of the table and Mum peeked at her hand. I had a pair of nines and nothing else.

"Two fingers," Mum bet.

"You going to raise?" Dad asked me.

"I can do three fingers of milk."

He put another card on the table.

And Mum was beaming.

Dad nudged me. "Find yourself a woman who doesn't have a good poker face and you'll never be worried what she's up to behind your back."

I couldn't tell if Mum's poker face was terrible or if it was a double bluff. And I chose to ignore the reference to finding a woman. Because that would never happen.

When Dad put the final face-up card into play and Mum called, she slapped her hand down to reveal a pair of threes.

Dad almost fell off his chair he was laughing so hard.

"What're you laughing at?"

"You," Dad said.

She poured more drinks. "Why?"

"That's a pathetic hand."

Mum glared at him, her eyelids drooping. She was at the flashpoint of slurred oblivion. "Fuck off," she said.

Dad's laughter stopped. And Mum's face twisted into an ugly caricature.

The party was over. I lifted the milk carton out of the way just as Dad swept his hand across the table, sending the cards and their drinks spinning. I jumped out of my seat.

"What the fuck?" Mum yelled.

Dad stood up. His fists were clenched.

"Dad."

He stared at Mum.

"Dad."

He grabbed his car keys from the kitchen counter. When he was gone, I couldn't bring myself to look at Mum.

"You and me," she said. "We're leaving. Tonight."

I slammed the milk on the table. "Grow up," I said. And I hated myself even as I dashed upstairs and threw myself onto the bed.

She called up behind me. "The next time he raises his voice, we're leaving."

She didn't see that she was the one who'd soured the mood. Because Dad was laughing at her instead of with her, she took offence. I didn't know which of them needed more help. Dad needed a doctor, but Mum needed AA.

Wednesday morning, they were shouting at each other again and I slipped through the front door into the slush of morning rain and went for the bus. I rested my head on Erin's shoulder and she said, "After the dance on Friday you can stay at mine. Bring your toothbrush. We can do something fun on Saturday."

"With my toothbrush?"

"Is it electric?" She tried to give me a purple nurple.

At practice after school, the choir filed into the gym and it felt like I hadn't seen Dean in months, not just a day. I slam dunked a ball into the basket and hung from the rim, timing myself, making sure he saw.

I don't know why I did that.

I got to work late because of practice and I reminded Marty that I couldn't work on Thursday because I had a game against St Paul's RC Wanderers, and I had the school party on Friday.

I was so tired I didn't want to attend either.

Wednesday evenings wasn't a big deal for cinema goers and I spent most of the night slumped against the counter, listening to the thrum of the popcorn machine and the clink and clatter of electronic games in the arcade room. I wished the arthouse movie from Saturday was still showing so I could find out what happened to the little girl or if the drug addict turned her life around. It would give me something else to talk about with Dean, anything to keep our conversations going.

Do arthouse movies ever make it to Netflix?

When a guy came out of Screen Two and asked for two medium, buttered popcorns, I accidentally gave him salted. I yawned, put them aside and scooped out two large buckets to make up for my mistake. I'd cover the cost. It was my own fault.

Linda picked a handful from one of the buckets and said, "Don't let Marty catch you yawning on the job. Aren't you getting enough sleep?"

I shrugged.

"Come on," she said, "Let's get some air while it's quiet."

She led me through the side door, and into the cold night. The snow was turning to slush but the weather forecast said there was more on the way. It was a week until the twenty-fifth and it looked as though we might have a white Christmas after all.

She propped a wedge under the door so we weren't locked out. "What gives?"

"What do you mean?"

"You're a young lad. You should be full of energy."

I yawned.

"See?" she said. "Come on, spill."

I shook my head. "It's nothing." But then I said, "My parents are about to murder each other if I don't do it first. And I've been practising flat out for basketball every day and then working in the evenings. And there's this person at school that

I sort of like but have no idea how to tell them. I can just about afford the bus fare home this evening, and if my parents are still awake, I'm not going to get any more sleep until the weekend."

"That's a lot," Linda said. She leaned against a bollard and folded her arms. "First things first. Are your parents really in danger of killing each other?"

I had to think about my answer before I spoke. Maybe they were. "I don't know," I admitted. "But all they do is argue and fight."

"Most couples fight. Doesn't mean they're going to stab each other forty-seven times and freeze their livers for supper. Second," she said, "who's the boy at school? Is it the guy you snuck into the movie with at the weekend?"

I looked at her.

"Don't give me that look," she laughed. "We recognise our own."

I snorted. "Is everybody queer in this pokey little town?"

"Everybody except the boy you're into, eh?"

"Seems like."

"For what it's worth, I couldn't get a read on him. But he's cute. For a lad."

"Aren't you old enough to be his mother?" I joked.

She punched me square in the chest. "I'm six years older than you, but you're not too big to be put over my knee and spanked."

I wriggled my eyebrows in the most salacious way I could manage. And then I rubbed my chest where she'd thumped me. "I swear you've cracked a couple of ribs."

"Suck it up, buttercup. You'll live."

It felt good unloading on her like that. And it was nice to

come out to someone new, somebody that wasn't going to judge me. When I got to university, I knew things would get better. Something happens to other guys between high school and campus life. There's a line to be crossed between homophobia and acceptance. The summer after high school and before your first semester at university, all boys—or most of them—finally grow up. Maybe their balls descend. I don't know. But the kids that call you names in school are the ones that are sharing beers with you in the student bar. The idiots that call you gay boy end up joining you for a round of karaoke, singing Lady Gaga at the top of their lungs. Unironically.

I yawned my way through the rest of the shift and Linda gave me a ride home when we were done. We sat in the car outside my house and she said, "Want me to come in with you?"

"I'll be all right."

"You sure? Maybe hide all the sharp knives and tequila bottles."

"Don't tempt me."

I told her I'd see her on Saturday and she gave me her number. "Just in case."

"See you."

"Knock 'em dead tomorrow. The basketball game, not your parents."

Inside, Dad was on the couch and Mum was in the kitchen.

"I have a game tomorrow," I said, standing in the doorway between them. They didn't acknowledge me. "We still have our exhibition game next week, but this is the last league game before Christmas." All the other kids' parents are going to be there, I wanted to say. But it'd be better if they didn't turn up.

"Okay," Mum said. It was a reflex word, not a promise to

be there.

"Dad?"

"I heard you," he said.

I went to bed. Don't ask me how either of them was holding down a job. I expected an eviction notice Sellotaped to the front door in time for Christmas Eve, and we don't have a rich benefactor to Scrooge our way out of it. In December, Mum usually disappeared. She was so busy at work with pre-Christmas up-styles and balayage transformations that we never saw her. But her drinking was getting out of hand. If I called the salon tomorrow, would they tell me she'd been sacked three months ago? I wouldn't be surprised.

And Dad's inability to get out of bed in the morning was a massive liability. His job was on the line and we all knew it.

I woke on Thursday morning to the sound of Dad shouting and Mum crying, and I punched my fist against my headboard and grazed my knuckles.

When your day starts with a bang, you know it's going out in a whimper.

I struggled to get through the school day. I almost fell asleep at the back of maths class even though Dean was sitting in the front row and I tried to keep my eyes open long enough to study the back of his head. I could run my fingers through his hair, blindfolded, and know it was him.

At the end of the day, I caught up with him at the bottom of the corridor after our last class.

"Choir?"

He nodded. "Big game?"

"Just a game. Not a big one."

We walked along the hall together. "Isn't it the end of the

season or something?"

"No. It's our last game before Christmas, but the season still has another couple of months left."

"Who are you playing against?"

"St Paul's."

"Are they good?"

"They're no pushover. They're fourth in the league. But we're third. So it's close."

We'd reached the music room. "Good luck," he said.

"You, too."

When the shrill whistle sounded and the game between the Clannloch Falcons and St Paul's RC Wanderers got underway, the court became a whirl of colours—our plain yellow uniforms contrasted against their navy and red. Coach Williams paced the sidelines, his gaze alternating between the game and the play clock.

For the first three quarters, we were toe-to-toe. We'd score a layup, and they'd respond with a three-pointer. Alex Janey was on a streak, scoring basket after basket, but the Wanderers matched us at every turn.

I dribbled, passed, shot. But I was a few beats slow, missing shots I should have made with my eyes closed. I couldn't get my dad's voice out of my head. "Go to hell," he'd told Mum this morning.

"After you," Mum had screamed back at him.

I could tell Coach Williams was on edge. His face folded into a scowl every time I missed a shot or stumbled over my feet. Twice I looked down to make sure my laces were still tied.

We were sitting on 36 to 34.

As the third quarter neared its end, I sprinted down the

court with the ball when one of the Wanderers' players rammed his shoulder into my chest. I smacked my back on the polished floor. Pain shot up my spine from my coccyx. A heat surged in my chest and I rolled onto my feet, tired anger replacing the pain. I lunged at him with my fists balled.

I couldn't stop myself. I hit him. Even as my knuckles connected with his face, I knew I was in trouble. But I punched him again.

It was Dad I was punching. And Mum. And every other bastard that was down on me.

The guy had to be six foot five. He shielded his face with his fists like a boxer, and then he jabbed back at me. Jab, cross. Jab, cross. He was relentless.

I ducked, twisted, and sprawled him out with an uppercut. But I wasn't done. I dropped on top of him. All the anger I'd ever felt—everything I knew I shouldn't do—it all came out of me at that moment. I hit him. And I hit him again.

The court was in chaos. The referee blew his whistle and Coach Williams was on the floor, pulling me away from the St Paul's giant.

"You're out," the referee shouted, pointing at the bench, his face red with anger.

I didn't argue. The fight had left me. I trudged off the court, holding my throbbing eye.

Alex Janey sucked his teeth and scowled. He didn't have to say anything. I knew what he was thinking.

I watched the final quarter from the sidelines. I'd never been ejected from a game before. I should have just gone home. My teammates rallied around my substitution. Alex Janey took charge of the court, weaving through the Wanderers' defence like a man on a mission.

The minutes were ticking down. Each shot was on point. Alex was showing off. He performed a reverse dunk, pulling up from one side of the basket before slamming it in from the other.

I watched the clock.

With seconds to go, we were tied 54-54. The Falcons had possession. Alex blasted up the court, reaching the half-court line. The buzzer sang, but the ball had already left his hands. It iced through the air, spinning, until it swooshed through the net. Backboard be damned.

A buzzer-beater.

The crowd were on their feet. I whooped. And I was grateful my parents weren't there.

As my teammates cheered and celebrated, I was left to nurse my black eye—which didn't hurt half as much as my pride.

At our pizza debrief later, Coach Williams said, "Get a handle on your issues before I kick you off my team."

"It's my team," I muttered. But I only said it after he'd walked away. I wasn't brave enough.

Erin said, "If hanging out with geeks, freaks and weirdos is getting you so angry, I already told you that you should stop."

My eye was swollen. I'd checked it in the changing room mirrors after the game and it was red and puffy. It'd be a rich purple by tomorrow, just in time for the Christmas dance.

Dean messaged me a few seconds after Erin reminded me—again—that my friendship with him would destroy my reputation. And although all I wanted to do was pull him into my arms and hold him until the ice caps melted (or until next Tuesday, whichever came first), he wasn't here and I knew I couldn't. I messaged him back. *Catch you at school tomorrow?*

I felt like the worst friend in the world. I knew I was being abrupt. But, tonight, I needed a break.

From everyone.

— CHAPTER 21 —

DEAN

When Ben walked into English class, I forgot all about Mr Dobbins who'd been standing at the front in a red Santa hat with his arms wide, looking for praise. "What happened?" I asked. Ben's left eye was swollen and purple from a bruise that ran across his cheekbone like wet mascara.

Erin McNally glared at me as though I had no business speaking. And maybe I didn't.

But Ben's smile was big. He crouched down, arms folded on my desk with his chin resting on top of them. "Another alien probe. Only this time, they missed my nostril when they were trying to put it in."

"I think you need to erect an early warning system around your bedroom."

Ben lowered his voice. "You make it sound as though I'm not supposed to like being abducted in the middle of the night and probed until the sun comes up."

He winked and went to his desk between Erin and Alex Janey. And my cheeks were burning. The heat was melting my corneas.

"Is everybody here?" Mr Dobbins asked. He put the large

Christmas box on his desk and tried a jolly Santa laugh that made most of the class groan. "It's the moment you've all been waiting for. Never mind yesterday's basketball game—am I right, Mr Hunter?" Ben shook his head in disgrace. "And never mind Christmas Day, today is far more important. It's Secret Santa Day."

I didn't really care anymore. The rainbow pin that had been slipped into my pocket a month ago had been all the Secret Santa I needed, even if I didn't know who gave it to me. I had my suspicions, and I knew who I wanted it to be, but without proof, the mystery wore on. Whatever gift I received today wouldn't be as special.

Mr Dobbins held up a badly-wrapped gift from the box and squinted at the name on the tag. "Tony Rowles. Looks like you're up first." Tony did jazz-hands before getting out of his seat. He took the present and turned to sit down again, but Mr Dobbins said, "Front and centre, Mr Rowles. We all want to see it."

He tore the paper open as Mr Dobbins shook out a bin bag for the discarded gift wrap. His present was a pair of pink, fluffy earmuffs. Alex Janey wolf-whistled when he put them on.

"Miss Grant, you're up," Mr Dobbins said, pulling another gift from the box. He called a few more names before saying, "Mr Hunter, let's be having you."

When Ben stood at the side of Mr Dobbins' desk, the teacher withheld the present at first. "Do you deserve a gift from Santa? It doesn't look like you've been a very good boy, young man."

Ben poked the edge of his black eye. "If it's a cold compress or an ice pack, I definitely deserve it, Santa."

"Well, seeing as we won the game, I'll strike you off the naughty list just this once."

Ben tore his present open. It was a book called *Basketball for Dummies*. "Very funny guys," he said, slouching back to his seat.

When Alex Janey ripped open the gift I'd bought him, I lowered my gaze to my desk and waited for the snarky comments. He put the Cork City FC sweatband on his head and the two wristbands on his arms.

Mr Dobbins said, "Now you can keep the sweat out of your eyes when you're boogying on the dancefloor tonight."

Alex bucked his hips. "Or when I'm—"

"You don't need to finish that sentence, Mr Janey. Get back to your seat, please."

"I don't even like Cork City," Alex said.

By the time Mr Dobbins had called my name, my palms were sweaty. As each new gift was opened, I convinced myself that I was about to receive another rainbow pin. And with nowhere to hide while I opened it, the whole class would see. Which meant either I was gay, or somebody else was. And the only person seen hanging out with me recently, other than Ashley and Tony, was Ben Hunter. And I had no intention of ruining his reputation.

"Come on, Mr O'Donnell. Don't dawdle."

I stood by his desk. The present was small and square. I couldn't lift my eyes to meet Mr Dobbins' smile. He held it out, but I didn't take it.

"It's not going to explode, Mr O'Donnell. At least, I hope not."

I took the box. I was careful with the Sellotape along the edges, peeling it off and rolling it into a sticky ball. Inside, a small piece of clasped metal was about to shine its rainbow light around the classroom like a beacon. I knew it.

I pulled the paper off. The small cardboard box was red and there was a label on the top in thin, scratchy letters. It said, *To Dean. From Santa.* It was the same handwriting from the note that accompanied the rainbow pin.

"Open it," somebody said.

I eased the lid off, holding the box high enough that nobody could see it other than Mr Dobbins who was standing beside me.

"What is it?" Ashley asked.

I looked in the box. I knew what *used* to be in it. The note that came with the rainbow pin last month—*Because I'm too chicken to be your Secret Santa*—was all the evidence I needed. But whoever gave me the pin still had to give me something today or Mr Dobbins would get suspicious. Inside, there was a teddy bear keyring.

I smiled. I think I might have laughed. "A keyring." I held it up so they could see. "Just a keyring." I clenched the smile on my face to disguise the relief that it wasn't another gay emblem. But the shape of the velvet cutout inside the box screamed at me.

Alex Janey said, "So lame." Some of the boys laughed.

Ben smiled, his black eye a permanent wink, and I returned to my seat.

There was a heaviness in my chest that put a catch in my breath for the rest of the class.

Our Christmas party was this evening, and nobody wanted

to do any work, but we still had three days of next week to get through before we broke up for Christmas.

"Your homework," Mr Dobbins said, and everyone groaned, "is to read the next chapter of *Lord of the Flies* and answer the following questions." He wrote on the board.

When the bell sounded, I dropped the keyring into my bag and got out of there before Alex Janey could make another snide remark, or before my Secret Santa could make themselves known.

We went through the rest of the day in a cloud of boredom. Classrooms were filled with chatter about this evening's party, who was wearing what, who'd be sneaking alcohol in, or who was going to make out in the stationery cupboard.

At home, Mum forced me to eat dinner with her and Dad before Ashley and Tony could stop by to get dressed, and while we were eating, Mum said, "We know what happens at school proms."

"It's not a prom, it's just a Christmas party."

"Same thing," she said. "But we know there's a lot of peer pressure at these things. And we don't want you getting into any trouble."

"What kind of trouble can I get into at the school gym?"

"You know exactly what kind of trouble we're talking about," Mum said.

I really didn't. "It's not like I'm going to get pregnant. That's not physically possible."

"What your mother means is stay away from alcohol."

I put my fork down. "It's a school party full of kids, not a kegger."

"There's always alcohol at these things," Dad said. "Just be good."

Mum said, "And no parties while we're in Dublin this weekend." They did that every year, on the last Saturday before Christmas.

I jumped up from the table when the doorbell sounded. Rescued by Ashley and Tony.

Mum brought us some hot chocolate before we got changed and then I locked my bedroom door so we couldn't be disturbed. Ashley slipped into her monochrome number and Tony had a last-minute wardrobe wobble. He brought three new outfits to try on and Ashley said, "Purple is not your colour."

"I like the green shirt, though. It's very Christmassy," I said.

Tony slumped on the edge of the bed, shirtless. His nipples were small and dark and you could see his ribs under his skin. I didn't realise how painfully skinny he was because his personality was so big.

"I might as well just go home," he said.

"Stop being so dramatic," Ashley told him. "What was wrong with the first shirt?"

He tried all three shirts on again before settling on the purple one that Ashley said didn't suit him. He wore an olive-green jacket over it, which sounds terrible, but the two colours contrasted instead of clashed. He really did know what he was doing with fashion.

When Dad drove us to the school, up Crest Hill in the thick snow, we didn't think the car would make it, but he pulled in through the gate and we cheered.

Inside, the hall that led to the gym was decorated with balloons and streamers, and we could hear pop music tumbling down the corridor. "Yay," Tony said, and there was no way we could confuse his word for one of joy.

All the benches and bleachers had been taken out of the gym and a disco ball that hadn't been there yesterday was casting sparkles across the floor. Nobody was dancing. Tables had been placed around the edges but most of the kids were standing in clumps, conspiring against other groups. Teachers always thought these things would bring school kids together, but instead, they put cliques under the spotlight, showing the world that jocks really do stick together, and mean girls were the heart of every scandal.

A DJ was dropping tunes at the far end and two rows of catering tables had been crammed along the edges of the gym. Balloons floated from chairbacks and teachers were dressed as elves or draped in tinsel.

"If Mr Dobbins comes out dressed like Santa, you can be the first to sit on his knee," Tony said.

"You're disgusting," I muttered.

I looked around. Alex Janey and the boys from the basketball team were lurking in a darkened corner, away from the strobing spotlights, but I couldn't see Ben. If I'd come home from school with a black eye, my parents might have grounded me. But if Ben was grounded, I had no interest in staying here. Ashley and Tony would have fun without me. I wasn't looking to dance with a hot boy in front of our entire school, but just being able to talk to him in public would have felt nice. Between basketball, his job, and my daily choir practice, I'd not seen much of him all week. Not to mention the fact that he was a popular kid with a bunch of friends who couldn't spend all his time with me anyway.

Tony walked away and came back with his fingers wrapped

around three paper cups of Coke like a Mobius strip.

Ashley said, "Nobody is dancing."

"And we should keep it that way," I said.

Whatever the DJ screamed into his microphone was too muffled to understand.

I couldn't keep my eyes still. A couple being separated by a teacher for looking far too cozy in the corner; a group of boys were pitching coins at the wall to see who could get closest; half a dozen girls were whispering secrets and pointing across the gym at another group of girls; and Ben had just come through the door with Erin.

I brought my cup to my lips to stop smiling. Ben wore a white shirt with a black skinny tie and a navy jacket over a pair of dark khakis. The strobe lights flashed over his face and the blemish across his eye and cheek gleamed hot and black.

Erin was in a red, floor-length number, looking like she was on her way to prom. I felt underdressed. Ben waved at the basketball team and Erin tagged along behind him before spotting her friends.

Tony said, "Lift your jaw off the floor before people start slipping in your drool."

"Does that shiner make him sexier?" I whispered.

"Not to me," Tony said.

And Ashley slapped the back of our heads. "You, stop preening your feathers. And you, stop egging him on. It's bad enough having to listen to him moon over a jock without you making it worse."

"What'd I do?" Tony asked.

She took his hand. "We're dancing. Come on."

"But nobody else is."

"Exactly."

She dragged him onto the empty floor, right on the mid-court line, and the DJ dropped a fresh tune that had Ashley pumping her arms in the air. People were watching.

Tony shuffled a little at first, but then as the beat picked up, so did his rhythm. I didn't have the guts to get out there and join them. I never danced alone in my bedroom, never mind in front of others. But Ashley and Tony, self-professed misfits, were giving it their all. They strobed around the dancefloor. All dancing was just erratic movement, and I couldn't do that. Maybe three hundred years ago when people were doing the waltz, I could have performed those manoeuvres because they were planned, timed and calculated. This step followed that. But moving to pop music was way beyond my skill set. My body wasn't loose enough to throw my arms around and bop my head and kick my feet all at once. I'd fall over.

Ben was chatting to Alex Janey and the others and even though Erin was standing beside him, she was deep in conversation with Gemma Ademola. They looked good together, Erin and Ben. I knew she wasn't his girlfriend because he told me so, but I wondered why not. They'd been friends forever.

The music made the gym vibrate. Tony waved me onto the dancefloor but I shook my head. I was embarrassed for them, but they didn't care. I was expecting laughter and finger-pointing from the mean girls. But a couple of younger girls joined them on the floor and, a minute later, more were coming out.

It takes two people to change the course of an evening.

My paper cup was empty and I looked around for a wastebin. The gym was filling up and it was getting warm. Everybody was pairing up or chilling in groups. Gemma Ademola was leading a conga line around the gym and even the teachers in their fancy dress were joining in.

I wasn't having fun anymore.

I counted the multicoloured spotlights just to give my brain something to focus on. Counting calmed me down. Lights, tables, balloons. When I was younger, I used to count my fingers. Repeatedly. Until I heard my mum asking Dad if they should get me tested. I knew what that meant, so I stopped the physical action of twitching my fingers as I counted them and did it internally instead.

I dropped my cup into a bin, grabbed another one from the drinks table and gulped it until it was empty.

When I turned around, Erin McNally was behind me.

"Hi," she said, all sweet and high-pitched.

I nodded at her and tried to sidestep her.

But she said, "How needy are you?"

"What?"

"Ben's got too much going on in his life that he doesn't need your social-climbing drama, too."

I looked at her, then over her shoulder to find Ben. I couldn't see him. "What are you talking about?" I asked. Had he put her up to this? His cool *catch you at school* text flipped through my head.

"I'm not one to talk," Erin said, "but people have mentioned how much of a cling-on you are. I told them they were being silly, Dean's a nice guy, but I just wanted to warn you. Nobody hates gossip more than me, so maybe just leave him alone once in a while, yeah?"

I had no words. So I got the hell out of there.

Outside the gym, the corridor was busy. A couple of boys

were sitting on the floor with their backs against the wall looking far from sober, and some of the dancing had spilled out from the gym. A line of people stood outside the toilets further down the hall and I could feel a breeze slipping up from the foyer. I followed it, undoing the top button of my shirt.

The vice principal, wearing a Mrs Claus costume, was talking to a few younger pupils and she nodded at me as I passed. I pushed through the front door onto the icy steps and I looked up to count the stars. But there were none. Thick grey clouds threatened more snow. What the hell was Erin talking about?

I went down the steps, away from the building, and I stood under the cover of an oak tree that had probably been on the grounds since before the school was built. Its branches were wrapped in fairy lights. The thin grass at its base was free from snow and frost. Its thick limbs were naked, but they gave me enough cover from the wind that pushed against me, begging me to leave.

I was going to get my phone out and ask my dad to pick me up when Ben said, "What're you doing?"

"Jeez, you nearly gave me a heart attack."

"Sorry." He leaned against the tree trunk. "What're you up to?"

"Apparently, I'm social climbing."

"Huh?"

Did he put her up to it? I didn't think so. I pressed my back against the other side of the tree.

Ben said, "You're doing that thing where you go quiet."

"I don't do that."

"Yes, you do."

214

I shrugged against the tree. "I don't have something witty to say all the time."

"You should work on that."

I didn't respond. Instead, I said, "What really happened to your eye?"

Ben came around the tree and stood beside me. "I got into it on the court with one of the boys from the other team."

"Does it hurt?"

"Nah. I have a skull made of iron."

"You didn't get suspended?" I asked.

"From school? No. From the game? Yeah."

The bark of the tree was pulling the hair on the back of my head like it was trying to keep me there. I said, "Why aren't you inside with everyone else?"

"I saw you leave."

I looked at him. His face was unreadable, but I knew Erin's words hadn't come from him. "So you came after me? People will talk," I said, keeping my voice airy.

"And what would they say?"

I didn't have an answer.

Ben said, "I'm sick of people talking behind everyone's back. We should just be open about everything."

"Some things should never be said."

"Why not?"

I stepped out of his shadow. I was feeling uncomfortable. "Because sometimes the truth is terrible."

He came closer. "How can it be terrible if it's the truth?"

I shrugged. My mouth wouldn't open anymore.

Ben said, "Did you like your Secret Santa gift?"

"A keyring?"

"I mean the real gift. I put it in your bag last month. The one that you wear on the inside of your coat."

Ben reached up, touched the collar of my jacket. I'd put the pin there before getting in the car. It was still on the inside, but Ben eased the collar back and touched the rainbow.

He didn't let go of me.

"Ben," I said. It was the only word I could think of.

His lips parted and I could see his tongue moisten them. His hand was still on my collar. "I like you," he said. "I don't know if you feel the same. But I just have to tell you, okay? Whatever the consequences. Because I'm tired of hiding now. Life's too short."

I reached behind me for the comfort of the tree. The lights from the school were behind me and Ben was in the shadow of the branches.

"I like you, too," I said. And my throat was tight. My voice was a harsh whisper.

Ben put his free hand up and gripped the other side of my collar. He stepped closer and pulled me towards him at the same time.

He kissed me, his lips warm and damp against mine. And my chest was on fire.

When his tongue eased forward, I let him in.

And then he stepped back, my face cold in the sudden wind.

I tried to study his good eye, but he was buried in the shadows again. I didn't know what to say. "We should probably go back inside. Or something."

Ben pointed above him. I looked up. There was a sprig of mistletoe tied to one of the naked branches over our heads at the end of a string of lights. He whispered, "I've been wanting

216

to do that since the Christmas market." He straightened my jacket collar and patted it flat. "See you later?" He walked back towards the school with his hands in his trouser pockets.

He didn't look back.

I couldn't move. My feet weren't working.

I stood there for another ten minutes, staring at the mistletoe above me. Did Ben Hunter really just kiss me?

CHAPTER 22

BEN

There is a moment of suspension when you're flying for a dunk. When both of your feet are off the ground and you feel the rush of air on your face and the world below you has faded away. There's nothing left but you and the hoop. That was my space-walk, the brief second on the court when I was soaring before slamming the ball home and returning to Earth.

I felt the same way as I walked back into the school gym. No exaggeration.

I left Dean by the tree and I couldn't look back in case he wasn't there. In case I'd made the whole thing up. I heard the spill of the music from the gym even as I navigated the icy steps outside and felt the blast of warm air from the overhead heater as I went inside. I shook the chill off my shoulders and stamped snow from my shoes. I didn't think my heart was ever going to slow down. This wasn't that buzzer-beater feeling when the ball leaves your hands and the clock flashes all zeros and your heart squeezes itself until the ball swooshes through the net or jars off the hoop and away from the point. This was a far greater rush.

"Where did you go?" Erin asked.

"Toilet," I lied.

I'd seen Dean dashing out of the gym in a hurry and something in his walk made me follow him. I had no idea what made him leave like that, but my legs ran after him because his face had gone dark. I'd slipped away from Alex and the others without being noticed. It made me wonder if I hadn't come back in, how long it would take for anyone to realise I was missing and come looking for me.

Erin clung to my arm. "Gemma's parents have put a stop to her after-party, so she and the girls are coming to mine. You don't mind, do you? You can bring the boys."

I didn't answer her. I was watching the entrance, waiting for Dean to come in. He was taking his time.

"Ben?"

"Yeah?"

"Is that all right? I've already told Alex."

"Yeah. Cool." I was supposed to be staying at Erin's tonight so we could spend time together tomorrow and now she'd turned the evening into a party, not the quiet conversation I was anticipating.

Alex slapped my back and pressed his mouth to my ear, shouting above the music. "When we get to Erin's you've got to get Louise Quinn to follow me upstairs. I'm counting on you, bro."

"Can't you ask her yourself?"

"Not with Jenny hanging around her like a bad smell. I can't have her blocking me."

"I got you," I said, though I had no intention of helping him take advantage of anyone.

When Dean came into the gym at last, his head was low,

his gaze on the polished floor, and he stood in the corner, alone, watching his friends on the dancefloor. I wanted to go to him. It was too dark to see if he was looking at me or carefully avoiding my eye, but when Tony and Ashley bounced towards him, he smiled and turned his back away from me.

Erin was at my side again, tugging on my arm. "We have to dance."

"No, we don't."

She took my hand. "We absolutely do." She dragged me onto the floor, right into the centre where the cool kids had pushed Dean's friends out. I stood there, rolling my shoulders a little, pretending like I gave a crap what any of them thought. Dean had stepped up to the edge of the dancefloor with his friends. Tony and Ashley were giving it their all and Dean was just shuffling his feet. I knew how he felt.

Erin threw herself against me, twisting her body with the music. Then she turned with her arms in the air, her hair twirling behind her.

Alex and my teammates had turned the dancefloor into a mosh pit, holding on to each other as they jumped around. He was moving more than he ever did on the court.

And between Erin's arms as they floated in front of my face, I watched Dean. When the strobe lights lit him up, I could tell he was staring back at me. He was bobbing his head and moving his feet and I inclined my chin in acknowledgement of our pathetic dance moves.

I span around, tried to pop and lock my arms, and then shrugged in his direction. Dean laughed.

He wasn't mad at me.

Erin's hair swished across my face and I had to duck as her

arms followed.

The basketball team brought their Rage Against the Machine aggression closer and as Erin moved out of the way, I was swallowed by their pogo mosh.

Alex chanted, "Throw a fist, shoot the twist, Ben Hunter's top of our Christmas list." The others joined in and I was jostled among them, pushed and shoved until I was almost knocked off my feet.

"Throw a fist, shoot the twist, Ben Hunter's top of our Christmas list."

I couldn't see Dean. But by now the whole school had heard about my ejection from yesterday's game. The mosh pit grew as other's joined, and the chant continued.

Somebody shouldered me.

And I jumped. Not to join in their elated dance, but to find Dean among the crowd. I jumped again. I was shoved. And I bounced, using my calves and my thighs to get more air. I found him at the edge of the gym with his friends. The mosh pit was growing, but it hadn't reached the outer rim yet.

I jumped again.

"Throw a fist, shoot the twist, Ben Hunter's top of our Christmas list."

The DJ killed the music and all you could hear was the screaming chant and the thump of feet on the floor.

And when I jumped again, Dean had joined in. His hands were in the air and he was bouncing on his feet. He was the first one to start moshing that far out, but soon the entire school was jumping. The dancefloor was alive. And I tried not to think about the reason for it. I might have thrown a punch on the court, pretty much where I was standing right now, but the teachers wouldn't want anyone glorifying that. And neither did I. I wasn't proud of what I'd done.

I jumped ahead of the curve and I saw Dean. He was smiling.

But then the vice principal had stepped up to the DJ booth and took the mic. She said, "All right, children, you've had your fun." When we didn't stop, she said, "That's enough."

The DJ dropped another track and teachers shouldered through the crowd to break us up. Alex Janey gave me a bro hug and rubbed the back of my head. "Keep that temper in check next time, yeah?"

"You bet."

When the party was kicking out, I looked for Dean but couldn't see him.

Erin said, "You coming? Our taxi's outside already."

The kiss had felt so long ago that I could have sworn I made it up. I licked my lips. Had Dean really been pressed against them just a couple of hours ago?

Erin lifted her clutch bag off the table, kissed Gemma Ademola's cheek, and said, "See you there." Then she took my wrist and dragged me after her.

Alex Janey jumped into the taxi with us and when we got to Erin's house, her mum had left a note on the kitchen counter. *We'll be back by 2 a.m. No alcohol. If you need to use the bathroom, stay out of our room. Much love to Ben too.*

They'd gone out to give Erin and me some space and had no idea that she'd turned the evening into a free-for-all.

She kicked her heels off by the front door and threw some snacks into bowls. She brought one of her dad's bottles of vodka in from the garage and filled another bowl with ice. She cranked up Spotify on the sound system and opened the door with a smile when Gemma Ademola and a few of the girls arrived.

Alex Janey was flipping through the shelves of CDs in the living room that belonged to Erin's mum. When Louise Quinn and her friend Jenny arrived, he gave me the nod and I pretended I didn't notice. I asked James from the team about our MVP Wellness programme's Christmas report. He shrugged like he didn't know or didn't care what I was talking about.

Nobody wanted to think about school at midnight on a Friday.

Erin slumped onto the couch beside me. She said, "Three more days and then we're off for two full weeks."

"Thank Christ," Alex said.

Erin leaned her head on my shoulder. "Your parents know you're here?"

"Yeah."

"Are they okay?"

I shrugged against her temple. It said, *Probably not but please shut up in front of the others.* Out loud, I said, "What happens when your parents get home and everybody's still here?"

"You can sweet talk them," she said. "They like you better than me."

James said, "I bet you get all the girls 'cause their mums love you."

"And half the mums, too," Alex said.

I stretched out on the couch like getting all the girls and half of the mums was no big deal.

Erin said, "As if." But she didn't lift her head off my shoulder.

And because I'd just kissed Dean not too long ago, I let her keep her head there, and I let the boys assume she was my girlfriend. Because that's what you do when you're in the closet. You spend your teenage years figuring out who you are while you're hiding it, and then you spend the rest of your life undoing all the angst and pain. I hadn't gone that far in my journey yet.

When Erin got up to open the front door for somebody new, I pulled my phone out of my pocket. My parents, at the end of the block, would be either arguing or drunk. Or both. And I really didn't want to go home, but Erin's house had turned into an after-party for forty people and Alex Janey no longer needed my help getting to Louise Quinn. He was sitting on the living room floor with her, snogging her face off while Jenny sat on the other side of Louise looking disgusted.

I pulled up the messages on my phone. Dean hadn't been in touch. He probably had his own after-party to go to, with his own friends and his own life. Did he really want to kiss me, or did I force it on him? I remembered pulling him towards me, planting my lips against his in the shadows under the tree. I never should have done it. Not there.

I should have kissed him at the Christmas market when we first stood under the mistletoe. It would have saved weeks of aggravation.

I scrolled through our recent DMs. The last thing I said to him was, *Catch you at school tomorrow?* I typed a new message. *Was it real? Did we do that?* But I deleted it. Then I typed, *I saw you moshing. How many people do you think got elbowed in the eye tonight?* But I deleted that, too.

I didn't know what to say. Acknowledging the kiss felt

wrong, like it was staged, but ignoring it seemed worse.

I put my phone away and grinned at Jenny. I patted the seat beside me.

When she sat there, far enough away from me that she couldn't be considered close, I said, "It's okay. I won't bite." I pointed at Alex and Louise on the floor who were oblivious to everyone around them as they ate each other's faces. "Does that happen often?"

Jenny said, "More than she'd ever let on."

"Why do you stick around while she's getting it on with somebody? That can't be fun."

"It's not. But she's my best friend. I'm going to look out for her."

"You're a good friend."

"Are you?" she asked.

"What?"

"Are you a good friend?"

I looked at Alex, but I couldn't keep my eyes on him as he pawed at Louise Quinn in front of everyone. "I try to be," I said.

Jenny looked at her watch. "Do you think they've had their seven minutes in heaven by now?"

Alex's hand was slipping under Louise's crop top.

"I think so, yeah."

I jumped on top of them, pulling Alex away from her. "Dog pile," I shouted, and a few of the lads fell on top of us.

Somebody tried chanting, "Hunter's top of our Christmas list," but Alex wormed out from under us and swore he'd kill us all.

When we stood up, Louise and Jenny were gone.

"What the hell, man?" he said.

I went in search of Erin. She wasn't on the stairs where someone looked like he was about to be sick, and I didn't see her in the kitchen where a group of girls were whispering together. But the back door was open and when I looked outside, Erin was out there with Gemma Ademola, sitting on the patio chairs.

"I wouldn't go out there if I were you," someone said. "They're talking about boys or something."

I didn't want to stick around any longer. Erin was safe. It was after one in the morning and her parents would be home in an hour. How she was going to get rid of everyone I didn't know.

I called out to her. "Erin?"

She waved at me.

"Erin, I'm going to go home, all right?"

Gemma Ademola looked like she was crying.

Erin said, "Yeah. Sure. See you."

"Are you guys okay?" I asked.

"We're fine. See you."

I hovered for a second, wondering if I should even mention Gemma's tears or ask if they needed anything. Instead, I closed the back door to give them some privacy and I walked back through the house. I grabbed my coat from a hook in the hallway.

Alex said, "Have you seen Louise Quinn?"

I shrugged. I went through the front door and pulled it behind me.

It had started to snow again. I could still feel Dean's top lip between mine, like it had a permanency there that wasn't my doing.

I went home, walking up the block through the fat flakes of snow that seemed to drive out of my way as I moved. They swirled around me like hummingbirds.

Two things were pushing through my brain. My fingers gripping Dean's collar as his lips were pressed against mine, and his smiling face as he moshed along with everyone else on the dancefloor.

When I got to the top of the street, blue lights swirled across the snow. An unmarked police car was parked outside our house. The front door was open and a guard—what we call a police officer in Ireland—stood outside.

"What's happened?" I said. I pictured Mum in pieces on the floor.

"Move along," the guard said.

"I live here," I told him, trying to push past him. "Mum? Mum?"

He let me through. Inside, Mum was sitting on the couch, a female guard standing over her.

"What's wrong?" I asked.

Mum was smoking. Her hand was shaking. "Nothing, sweetheart. It's okay."

"Where's Dad?"

I looked. He was sitting at the kitchen table with another guard.

I couldn't see any blood.

The vase that lived on the counter near the fridge was shattered across the floor. There hadn't been any flowers in it for six months.

The cops got up to leave. "If there're any more complaints,

we'll be back. Do you hear?"

Mum and Dad, now standing beside each other at the front door, nodded and looked chastened.

"What's going on?" I asked again.

Dad closed the door. "Nothing." He went to bed.

"Mum?"

She touched my blackened eye. "Did you have a good night?"

"What the hell, Mum? What happened?"

"Nothing," she said. And that was that.

I stood in the kitchen. The ceramic vase had shattered and skittered across the linoleum and I swept it up, making sure I got it all.

I went upstairs. I undressed, brushed my teeth, and went to bed. Erin was handling her situation. I couldn't be blamed for leaving early.

In bed, I checked my messages again. My last text to Dean scowled at me. *Catch you at school tomorrow?*

Since I sent that message, I'd seen him at school, followed him outside, kissed him, and danced in a mosh pit. And my parents had probably almost killed each other.

My life was a mess. So what else could I do?

So I sent him a message.

benhuntss07
Hi.

— CHAPTER 23 —

DEAN

I was still awake, listening to *O Holy Night* on repeat. I had one week to learn the words and now I couldn't even remember what the song was called without looking at it. Ben was swimming through the darkness of my brain, his hot breath on my face, his lips against mine. I remembered his hands gripping my coat, revealing the rainbow pin that he admitted to giving me. Ben Hunter was my Secret Santa. And he was gay—or bi or pan. Something. But he kissed me. He pulled me into him and pressed his face against mine, his tongue easing between my lips as my pulse took the bullet train through Tokyo Station at rush hour, frantic yet perfect in its intensity.

That was my Holy Night.

I'd jumped along with everyone else when the dancefloor had been turned into a scene from Glastonbury, but I wasn't enjoying the music or the chanting. I was jumping for joy. If you can believe it.

Ashley's sister had picked us up when the vice principal turned the overhead lights on after the DJ's final song, a slow number that was meant to pair everyone off with some other lonely soul. I watched Ben dance with Erin and felt an uncomfortable hollowness in my stomach. But he was watching me over her shoulder.

In her sister's car, Ashley said, "Well, that was boring."

Tony said, "I can't believe you dragged me up to dance when no one else was on the floor."

I hadn't told anyone what happened. I didn't have the words for it. Maybe I never would.

When I got home, my parents were waiting for me.

"Did you have a good time?"

What they meant was: did you have any alcohol?

I stood close enough to them so they could smell my breath and I shrugged with noncommittal angst. "It was all right." I put my hands in my pockets because they were shaking, as though my body had too much energy that couldn't escape.

Mum said, "Don't forget we're going to Dublin tomorrow. We've already warned you: no parties while we're away."

I rolled my eyes. Who was I going to have a party with?

When I went to bed, I put my ear pods in and used *O Holy Night* as a calming device, something to focus on other than Ben's face. Those lips.

I was wide awake.

And then Ben messaged me.

benhuntss07
Hi.

dean_odd_donnell
Hey 😁

benhuntss07
Wasn't sure if you'd be awake.

230

dean_odd_donnell
I'm counting sheep but it's
not working.

benhuntss07
You could count my failed free throws.
You'd be asleep in no time.

dean_odd_donnell
Maybe I should count black eyes
instead. Suits you, though. Gives you
that rugged bad-boy look.

benhuntss07
Just trying to make an eye-conic
statement. I think I nailed it.

dean_odd_donnell
Is THAT how you got your black eye?
Making terrible puns?

benhuntss07
Busted. Don't tell anyone, OK?

Our conversation went everywhere from basketball to
maths. Ben asked me if I'd solved the *Ryman Hypothesis* yet,
and even though he spelled it wrong, I congratulated him on
remembering it.

dean_odd_donnell
Solved it. Won the Fields Medal
(which is basically the Nobel Prize for
Mathematics) and now I'm ready for
world domination.

benhuntss07
Do you need a general to help with
your global plans?

dean_odd_donnell
What would a general do?

benhuntss07
Lead the troops and help raise morale.
And . . . maybe . . . provide kisses. Or
something.

I sat up and reread his message. When I didn't reply at once,
Ben followed it with a zip-mouthed emoji. I double-tapped his
message.

dean_odd_donnell
I think I almost definitely need a
general. You know, to raise morale. For
the troops. And maybe do the kissing
thing too.

benhuntss07
Kissing an entire army? Sounds
exhausting. But for morale's sake I
suppose I could prioritise and start at
the top.

dean_odd_donnell
That's a battle plan I could get behind.
Um, you probably have other things to
do but my parents are going to Dublin
tomorrow. Do you want to hang out?

benhuntss07
For kissing?

dean_odd_donnell
Is that an option?

benhuntss07
Let me consult my Magic 8 Ball. It says:
"Signs point to yes".

In the morning, I tried to look as casual as I could, standing in the living room in my fleece pyjamas with my hair a mess, not caring about my milk moustache as Dad hovered by the front door and Mum was hunting for her purse.

Dad said, "What's wrong with the green bag?"

"It's not big enough."

"Are you planning on putting the kitchen sink in it?"

It was eight a.m. and Dad was desperate to beat the Saturday morning rush on the last weekend before Christmas. They did this every year. Until I turned fourteen, I'd gone with them, but last year they let me stay at home alone. The neighbour kept an eye on me and gave me a key to her house in case I needed anything during the night. This year, I'd convinced them I was old enough not to need the neighbourhood watch looking out for me.

"If we hit the M8 and get stuck in traffic," Dad said, but he didn't finish the sentence. Mum was upstairs. Dad looked at me and I scratched an armpit. "What are you going to do all day?"

I shrugged. "Nothing."

"Why don't you get dressed and come with us?"

"I've got plans."

"Doing what?"

"Nothing."

When Mum came down with an enormous bag in her hand, she said, "Have you got change for the toll?" She kissed my cheek and Dad ushered her out as she listed a dozen warnings about emergency phone numbers, cash in an envelope on the kitchen table, don't leave the fridge open, and turn off the lights when they're not in use.

I stood at the door and waved as they drove away.

And then I hurried to the bathroom for a shower. I brushed my teeth—twice—and got dressed, sitting on the edge of my bed so as not to disturb anything. I checked the time. It was just after nine.

The next three hours took seven hours to pass. And when Ben rang the doorbell, I'd seen him walking down the street and was already standing behind the door.

"All right?" he said.

I nodded. I forgot what words were for.

He came in and I closed the door. And then we stared at each other.

"What do you want to do?"

I squinted. Didn't he know what we were supposed to be doing? "I don't know about you, but that kissing thing is probably top of my to-do list."

He smiled. The confident Ben from last night was gone and in his place was this blushing boy with shining eyes. "I think that's definitely in my top three."

I didn't know how to move forward with this. We were standing in the hall looking awkward.

Ben said, "Your parents?"

"They left this morning. They'll be back tomorrow."

Ben stepped into my space. He was so close that I had to look up to see his face. I didn't know what to do with my hands. Or my body. He was trying not to smile. When he leaned into me, my legs almost gave way.

Ben said, "Take a deep breath."

"Why?" My voice was tiny.

"Because when I kiss you, I might not stop."

And he kissed me.

I closed my eyes and my chest was thumping. I felt my pulse in my ears. Ben slipped his hands onto my lower back. If he didn't, I might have fallen. He held me and I touched his hips and I was on my toes as I stretched up to him.

I don't know how long the kiss lasted—seconds or days—but when he pulled back from me, I couldn't open my eyes. I didn't want it to be over.

His breath was fogging up my glasses. He said, "Say something."

"I can't."

"Is that a good thing?"

I opened my eyes. "Yes."

He took my hand and led me into the living room, and we kissed on the couch for an hour. His hand was under my sweater, warm fingers touching the skin of my hip. When we stopped, I was dizzy.

Mum phoned and I tried to sound natural and bored. They were stuck in traffic. Of course. She asked me what I was doing. I looked at Ben on the other side of the couch and I said, "Just testing the springs on the sofa. Do you know the middle seat is bouncier than the others?"

"If you damage the furniture, I'll take it out of your hide," she laughed.

When I hung up, I said, "Are you hungry?"

Ben got to his feet. "Good idea. Better build up our energy for later."

"What's happening later?"

"More kissing."

"Oh," I said. "Okay." In the kitchen, I opened the pantry

and asked, "What do you like to eat?"

"Cake is good."

"We could probably make a cake. I think we've got all the ingredients."

"Do you even know how to bake a cake?"

I said, "Hey Google, how do I bake a chocolate cake?"

We lined the ingredients up on the counter. By the time we'd stirred everything together, the kitchen was a disaster. Cake gloop—you couldn't even call it batter—was smeared on the countertop and the floor, and Ben had flour dust on his chin.

He took the spatula and scooped up some of the brown mess, holding it out to me with his hand under it as if now was a good time to stop anything dripping on the floor. "You first."

"You're the general. Aren't you supposed to taste-test all my food in case it's poisoned?"

"So you're willing to let me die for you?"

"The cake was your idea. It's only fair."

Ben eyed the spatula with suspicion, but he brought it to his lips. He screwed his face up. "It'll taste better once it's baked. I hope."

We poured it into a cake tin, put it in the oven and set the timer.

"Now what?" I asked.

"Didn't somebody say something about more kissing?"

We were still kissing when the timer buzzed. The cake was burnt around the outside and still soggy in the middle. Where's Tony when you need him?

"Pizza?" I said.

In the late afternoon, when the sun was going down and

the snow outside was piling up thicker than it had been in days, we settled on the couch and spent almost an hour scrolling through Netflix until we found a movie that we both agreed on. Ben had said, "We can watch one of your arty Einstein documentaries if you want."

I said, "You do look sleepy. We can watch the Sir Andrew Wiles lecture on Fermat's Last Theorem if you want. It's on YouTube. That'll knock you out in no time."

"You're such a geek," he said.

We chose a disaster movie that neither of us had seen before and when I sat on the sofa, Ben shuffled closer. His hand took mine and he held it between us, his long fingers linked between mine. The Christmas tree lights twinkled like a galaxy in the corner and I leaned into Ben's shoulder. He squeezed my hand.

My lips were sore from kissing all day, but kissing was the best thing in the world.

I jumped when an explosion happened on screen and Ben laughed. He was still holding my hand and even though my fingers were going numb, I didn't want him to stop.

I was sitting on the sofa with a boy, outing myself to the walls around us. I leaned my head against his shoulder again and forgot about the movie. I was staring at the Christmas lights and the lyrics to *O Holy Night* were swarming around my head. I wanted to say, "If I wrap you up and put you under the tree, can I keep you?"

But I didn't.

Ben's leg was pressed against mine. And I was awkwardly comfortable.

When the movie was over, I turned off the TV and we sat in the dim glow of the tree lights as they chased around inside his eyes.

He said, "I have to go to work soon."

I nodded. I hadn't thought about this moment. Part of me expected him to sleep over—on the couch or in my room, it didn't matter. I just needed him to be close.

He said, "I don't want to go."

"I don't want you to, either."

He kissed me. When we stood up, I felt so small beside him. Even with his shoes off, he was at least five inches taller than me. I stood behind him in the hallway while he crouched to put his shoes on and then he zipped his coat up. We kissed again.

When he opened the door, the world outside was white. The snow was drifting in fat flakes. I couldn't see the house across the street.

"Jeez," Ben said.

"You didn't bring a scarf?"

"I was coming over to kiss you. I wasn't really thinking about winterwear."

I took my scarf off the rack, the brown and green wool fraying at the edges, and Ben ducked as I wrapped it around his neck.

"You can give it back to me whenever."

"Tomorrow?" Ben twisted the ends of the scarf to protect his neck from the cold.

"Okay," I said.

He stood in front of me, toes to mine, and he smiled. "I'll text you."

I closed my eyes. I was done waiting for him to kiss me again. I gripped the scarf and pulled him towards me as the snow and wind from the open door flustered around us. His body was a barricade against the chill.

"I'll miss the bus," he said. But he was grinning.

I let him go, and when he was gone, the house was empty.

And the snow was melting on the carpet.

CHAPTER 24

BEN

The smell of him lingered on the scarf he'd given me, and I pulled it up to cover my mouth and nose as I rode the bus to work, breathing him in. When I got home later that night, I could still smell him on it. The soft wool was warm around my neck. Dad was on the couch, crumpled blankets beside him, a smeared look of exhaustion on his face. I knew how he felt.

In the morning, he was still there. I don't think he and Mum had said one word to each other since the police left.

I stood in the kitchen, staring out at the snow as the kettle came to the boil, and I made a strong cup of tea. I'm not sure Dad had slept, and Mum was struggling to pop open a blister pack of ibuprofen. Her dressing gown hung from her thin body like an oversized rag on a mannequin. She'd pulled her hair back so tight that her face was taut, and I'd never seen it before but there were silver streaks at her temples.

She muttered something, and I took the blister pack from her, popping two capsules into her hand. I filled a glass with water and handed it to her. She didn't say thanks.

I listened to the sound of her slippers as she stomped upstairs and heard the quiet hush of her door over the carpet pile. I heard Dad breathing in the living room.

The paperwork left behind by the officers was still on the kitchen table. I couldn't bring myself to read it.

The house was mired in something dark that I didn't want to understand. The silence between them was different now. I could feel the aggression even as they ignored it. They were heading for divorce this time, I was certain. If it wasn't that, it'd be murder.

In my room, I wrapped Dean's scarf around my neck. Like that arthouse movie we watched, it was the only thing of colour in my life. I needed to get out of there, so I sent him a message.

benhuntss07
Do you know the park behind Chard
Lane? Can you get to it? I'll be there in
twenty minutes. I'll wait for you.

I didn't hang around for a reply. I showered and got dressed and slipped down the street towards the park with my gym bag over my shoulder. The pavement was covered in compacted snow and the roads were icy.

I dusted frost from the wooden seat of a rope swing that had hung from a giant oak tree since I was a kid, and I dangled from it, my fingers red as they gripped the thick rope. I leaned back and watched the strong branch above me, the rope twisting as I turned, knots chafing where they'd chafed for years without relinquishing their hold on the tree.

When Dean said, "Need a push?" I looked up. I hadn't heard him approach. He was wearing a thick beanie with red tinsel wrapped around the rim and I laughed. I didn't get off the swing when he came near. I lifted my feet and let the rope unwind and when I came to a stop, I was dizzy. Dean's face swam as he put his hands on my shoulders.

I stiffened. I looked around to make sure we were alone.

Dean said, "Sorry," and he pulled his hands away.

I stood up, clinging to the swing, and I leaned in. "Don't be," I said, and I kissed him. His face was cold.

I felt his mouth grinning against my lips. "Why are we here?"

I picked up my gym bag and pulled out a basketball. The hoop I'd hung on the handball wall as a child was lopsided and covered in snow. I held the ball out to him. "We've done your weird movies. It's time to see how good you are with a ball."

"I'm not."

"You will be by the time we're done."

"Not likely."

I tried to scrape some of the snow away from the handball court but most of it was frozen. Then I jumped, knocking my fist against the pallet backboard to clear it of ice. There was no net. The hoop had been naked for years.

I bounced the ball and it skittered away on the ice, but I chased after it and then scraped some more free snow away from the ground. I popped the ball towards Dean and he caught it just as it smacked against his chest. The tinsel had slipped around his forehead like a twisted halo.

"One-on-one," I said. "You try to score and I try to stop you. Then we switch."

Dean looked at the wonky basket. "It's kind of high."

"It's regulation height. Sort of." I took a defensive stance in front of him.

He said, "I don't know what I'm doing."

"Put the ball in the hoop."

"Oh, we're playing *that* version of basketball. I thought we were doing the other kind."

"What other kind?"

"The one where you serenade the ball with a song and hope it rolls closer to the hoop out of sheer musical appreciation."

"Shut up and throw the ball," I said. I watched him study the hoop. "It's just maths. Trigonometry. You can do it."

Dean pulled his gloves off, sucked a finger and held it up against the wind. He made a show of calculating angles, and then he hunkered, raised the ball, and he jumped. As the ball left his hands, I reached and slapped it away. It thumped into a mound of snow.

"Hey. I could have made that shot."

"But I wasn't going to let you. That's the point of one-on-one."

He grabbed the ball, dusting snow from it, and threw it to me. "Your turn."

We swapped sides and I dribbled the ball as best I could on the icy ground. Dean spread his arms and waved them around as I sidestepped him. His hand thwacked my chest when I took a leap, and the ball hit the backboard before rolling off the rim and into the snow.

"Nil-nil," Dean said.

I laughed. I let him keep his football terminology.

When I passed him the ball, he said, "You won't stop me this time. This one's going in."

"If you make it, I'll kiss you."

"It's totally going in, but just in case, what do I get if I miss?"

I shrugged. "A consolation kiss?"

He bounced the ball on the ice. "I like these rules."

I spread my arms like a peacock but I kept back from him and let him think he was going to make it this time. When he jumped and threw the ball, I leapt towards him and wrapped my arms around his waist. I twisted, knowing we were going down, and I saw the ball hit the rim, roll, and slip off the outside.

We crashed onto the snow and I put my hand under his head to protect him. He was laughing.

"Did it go in?"

"Does it matter?" I asked. I brushed the snow out of his hair. His breath was in my eyes. I watched his jawline, and the roll of his lips as he laughed. I could tell he was looking at my mouth.

"Kiss me," he said.

The park was empty. It had to be. I kissed him.

Then he said, "But did it go in?"

"I can't lie. It was so close. You'll get the next one."

Dean picked up some snow and blew it in my face. The wind was kicking up and his nose was red.

"You look like Rudolph," I said.

"And you look like Jack Frost."

I sat up and shook my head, snowflakes cascading like dandruff. It was cold, but I was warm.

Dean stood. He looked around as though he was trying to find something and then he went to the corner of the handball wall where it was protected from the wind. A snowdrift had piled up there.

He crouched and started scooping the snow with his hands.

"Come on," he said.

"What are you doing?"

"You'll see."

I joined him. "That's not how you make a snowman, Dean."

He was patting the snow into a circular perimeter from the wall, stacking it up.

"An igloo," I said.

"A home for the day," he said.

I found his gloves on the court and shook them off before handing them to him. "I don't want to be answering to your mum if your fingers freeze and fall off."

I got on my knees—my jeans were already wet from our tumble—and started compacting snow into place against the other wall, turning our igloo into a lean-to. We met in the middle, leaving a two-foot gap for the entrance.

I scooped more snow and packed it on top of our frame.

I watched him work. He was diligent, stopping to analyse the thickness of the walls and the amount of snow we had to work with. He skimmed out a line with his shoe and when the snow wall was three feet tall, I could see the gears in his head turning as he patted the snow into an arc, forcing it to slope into a roof.

"Will it stay up?" I asked.

"If we pack it tight."

"I'm trusting you that we won't get buried alive."

He threw the handful of snow that he'd been holding at me and I ducked out of the way. "I promise you," he said, "that you won't be buried in two inches of snow."

"I heard about this woman who drowned in an inch of bathwater."

"It won't collapse. And if it does, I promise to protect you."

"Thanks," I said. He was teasing me, and I liked it.

The walls of our igloo rose towards the corner of the concrete wall at its back. Dean got inside to finish the top of the roof and I gathered fresh snow through the entrance for him.

When his fingers disappeared and he packed in the final piece of the roof, I stepped back and admired our work. It had taken over an hour to build. At its peak, it was about five feet tall.

"Knock, knock," I said.

"Who's there?"

"Icy."

"Icy who?"

"Icy you in there. Let me in."

"Hang on," he said. I heard him shuffling around inside. "Come in," he called.

The entrance was big enough to crawl through. As I went in, he was grinning. He'd taken his coat off and spread it on the ground for us to sit on. The walls glowed from the bright daylight outside.

"You'll freeze," I said.

"It's actually quite warm in here."

I settled on his coat beside him. I loved how cute he looked in his huge glasses and thick winter jumper. The tinsel on his beanie had come undone and was hanging around his ears. It was warmer than I'd thought. We were out of the wind and the snow walls around us were sweating.

"We forgot to put in a window. We'll never get a good price for it on the property market."

"It's a seller's market," Dean said. "We'll make a cool

fortune. Get it?"

I hung my head in shame. "That was terrible."

"I know."

When I looked at him again, he had pulled the tinsel from his hat and was packing it into the ceiling above his head.

"Very Christmassy," I said.

"We can pretend it's mistletoe."

I laughed. "I thought we were past the need for a physical reminder to snog."

"But it adds to the festive ambience." When he'd finished packing it into place, he smiled, puckered up, and made smooching noises.

I didn't need a second invitation. I hadn't kissed many people over the years, but kissing Dean was my new favourite pastime. I put my hand on his shoulder and leaned into the kiss. The flavour of his mouth was distinct. Like fruit salad. He shuffled his butt and lay back on his coat and I slid down beside him, my hand on his warm chest. His fingers curled into the back of my hair.

My body was pressed against his side and I knew that if I shifted, even slightly, he'd feel me, and he'd know what he was doing to me.

His free hand pushed under my side and he gripped the back of my sweater as we kissed. I slid my fingers under his jumper, pulling his T-shirt out of his jeans. I needed to feel his skin on my fingertips. I craved the warmth of him. His stomach was boiling and taut as my thumb found the rim of his shallow navel.

He moaned into my mouth.

We kissed for hours.

When we took a break, Dean pressed his head against my chest and I stroked my fingers through his hair. His beanie was discarded in the corner of our igloo.

He said, "I'm nervous about singing on Friday."

I was nervous just having him pressed against me. I said, "You'll be great."

"Will you come?"

He had no idea how close I was. "I told you before, it's not really my thing."

"Oh," he said.

I kissed the top of his head. "I'm joking. I'll be there."

I felt him sigh and his hand curled around my side in a hug. "This is nice."

"Yeah." It was too nice. I didn't want to leave our makeshift home.

"My parents will be back from Dublin soon, I guess," Dean said. "But maybe later I can come to yours? If you're not doing anything."

"You don't want to come to mine."

"Why not?"

"Because my parents are a nightmare."

He kissed my chest. "Is it that bad?"

I was glad he wasn't looking at me. "If they could ever love anybody other than themselves, I know they'd love you. But Mum's a drunk and Dad—I don't know. He's just angry all the damn time."

"I'm sorry."

"It's not your fault," I said. "Mum's drinking isn't helping, though."

Dean sat up and I joined him, our knees pressed against

248

one another. He took my hand. His fingers were warm. He said, "I can't say anything you haven't already considered. But if you ever need a break from them, you know where I live."

I lifted some snow from beneath me and formed it into a ball. Then I wrote on the concrete wall, *1 Igloo Lane, Cork.* The letters were fat and wet.

"Most people don't own their first home until their thirties."

"Most people don't have a mathematical genius for a boyfriend," I said.

He didn't say anything, and I wanted the igloo to collapse and bury me alive. I was rushing things. We'd been making out for two days and I'd read more into it than I should have.

But he grinned. And he kissed me.

And then I said, "For God's sake, I nearly had a heart attack just now."

"I've never been a boyfriend before," he told me.

"You're doing fine."

"Just fine?"

"For a first-timer," I said, and he pulled me into a headlock. I could have overturned him, but I didn't. The warmth of his body would be the last thing I recalled before falling asleep that night.

"When we get to school tomorrow," I said.

He nodded. "You don't know me. I'll keep my distance. We can keep it a secret."

"I was going to say we should have lunch together. Is that what you think of me? That I'd ignore you?"

He shrugged.

I said, "We can tell a few people. The ones we know won't get weird about it. We don't have to rush. I don't think I'm ready to, you know, come out or anything. Not fully."

"Me either."

"Is there anyone you want to tell?"

"Ashley and Tony, I guess. But they already know I have a thing for you."

"Is that why my ears are burning every night? Because you're talking about me?"

"It's not like that. Anyway, are you going to tell Erin? Or Alex?"

"Definitely not Alex. And I'm not sure about Erin. I came out to her a year ago but I don't know if she believed me. I'll play it by ear."

"We don't have to come out," Dean said. "I don't even know what I am."

"You're Dean. Why label it?"

He laughed. "Now you're sounding like Ashley."

I took his hands. "I won't ignore you at school as long as you don't ignore me. But we can play it cool. Just for now."

"Secret high fives in the corridors, then?" Dean flipped up the collar of his coat where it was scrunched beneath us, covered in frost and snow. He dusted off the rainbow pin. "I won't put this on the outside just yet, but you'll know it's there."

"Maybe one day," I said.

Outside the igloo, the sun was going down.

I watched him walk across the park and when he got to the gate, he turned and waved at me.

If I didn't think I'd freeze to death, I'd have stayed in the igloo all night.

Anything would be better than going home.

— CHAPTER 25 —

DEAN

I'd gone to bed on Sunday with the taste of Ben's skin on my tongue and I'd tossed and turned through the night, unable to get to sleep as thoughts of him shivered around inside me. I felt the memory of his fingers on my stomach, the scrape of his fingernails at the waistband of my jeans.

I messaged him when I went to bed, and I messaged him when I woke.

And Ben Hunter sent me a kissing-face emoji.

benhuntss07
Three days of school then two whole weeks of freedom. We can spend all day together on Thursday.

dean_odd_donnell
I've got rehearsals. But you should come to school and we can make out in the cafeteria when no one else is around.

benhuntss07
Woah. Making out AND school food? Dream date!

dean_odd_donnell
I know how to treat you right.

benhuntss07
I'm going for a cold shower before I get
all hot and bothered.

dean_odd_donnell
See you in maths class.

Mum drove me to school and the radio was playing Christmas songs. We sang along.

When she pulled up to the school gate, she said, "You're in a good mood."

"I'm always in a good mood."

"Not on a Monday morning. What's got into you?"

I beamed at her. "First-period maths."

She used to quiz me every time we drove to school when I was a kid. "What's twelve times thirty-two?" or "If a train travels sixty kilometres in an hour, how far does it go in forty-four minutes?" When I told her the answers, she wouldn't say well done. She'd ask another question. A few times, I caught her using the calculator on her phone when we stopped at traffic lights.

I once said, "If you use a calculator at the speed of light, how fast would you be travelling?"

She said, "Really fast."

I'd folded my arms and huffed for the rest of the car journey, and when she opened the back door to let me out, I said, "Three hundred thousand kilometres per second."

She said, "I knew that."

Now, she shook her head. "Maths might be your one true

love, but nothing gets you this happy." She nudged my shoulder. "Did you meet someone?"

"No."

"You can tell me."

"Mum."

"Who is she?"

"It's no one," I said, and I got out of the car. But I couldn't stop smiling.

When the automatic doors of the main school building slid open, a buzz of chatter hit me like a runaway train. Monday mornings were usually filled with weekend stories and laughter, but I felt a heaviness as I stood in the foyer.

Hushed whispers crawled down the hallway like a clutter of spiders, scuttling in all directions.

Phones were pinging and groups of kids huddled together.

I caught fragments of hushed conversations, punctuated by brief flashes of screens as phones were passed around.

"No way," somebody said. "I always thought he was straight."

I couldn't walk anymore. The neck of my shirt was too tight and my feet were cemented in place. Kids were laughing. Somebody ran past me and I had to press up against the wall to avoid being knocked over.

"There you are," Tony said.

I looked up. "What?"

"Where've you been all weekend?"

"Nowhere."

"Have you seen it yet?"

"Seen what?" I didn't want to see it. I'd never want to see it. Tony pulled his phone out.

"Stop," I said.

"You have to see this."

"Please, Tony."

"It's all over the school." He pressed play on a video and held it out to me.

I didn't want to look. I heard rustling and muffled voices, distant music.

I looked.

The screen was blurry, the camera zooming in and settling on a tree covered in fairy lights. I knew what was coming.

"Tony," I said.

"Just watch."

I watched as Ben Hunter leaned in and kissed me. Except my face was hidden from the camera in the shadows. A voice on the video said, "Young love. Big respect. Times are good."

Another voice said, "Give them their privacy, for God's sake."

The video stopped, then looped, zooming in on us again. Tony shut it off. My throat was full of stones. When I looked at him, his teeth were grinding at his lower lip. He pushed me into the empty classroom behind us.

"Keep calm," he said.

"How?"

"It's not you. Nobody can tell."

"But that's Ben."

"Why didn't you tell me?" Tony asked.

I shrugged. "I was going to."

Tony looked out at the corridor. The chatter was louder now. Kids were streaming into the room we'd invaded. He took my arm. "Nobody knows who the other boy is. It might not even be a boy."

One of the kids said, "It's definitely a boy."

Tony dragged me back into the hallway. The bell rang. "What do we do?"

"Nothing," Tony whispered. "Unless you want to out yourself, you keep quiet."

He pushed me along the hall towards Mrs James' maths class. I needed to let Ben know. He'd been outed before the whole school and when I spoke to him this morning, he had no clue. I was terrified. What if somebody recognised me?

"Such a waste," a girl said. "I always thought he was fit."

"Who's the other boy, though?" her friend said. "That's what I want to know."

I lowered my head and shuffled into maths class.

"Was it you?" Alex Janey asked as soon as we entered. He pointed his finger in my face. Then he turned to Tony. "It was probably both of you, taking turns."

"Piss off," Tony said, "before I break your finger."

"Was it you?" Alex asked another boy as he entered.

Ben wasn't in the classroom. Mrs James said, "All right, settle down." She closed the door. "I know it's your last few days, but we're still here to learn, not gossip."

"Have you heard, Miss?" somebody asked.

"I don't subscribe to school rumours," she said. "And if I see one more phone, I'll confiscate all the phones in the room. No exceptions."

She wrote a problem on the board. When the door opened, Ashley came in, looking flustered. "Sorry, Miss. My mum's car wouldn't start and I missed the bus."

"Sit down," Mrs James said.

Ashley took her seat behind Tony, pulled out her notebook, and wrote something on the back page. She closed the book and passed it to Tony. He read the note, then slipped the notebook across to me.

I opened the back cover. Under a series of notes that Ashley and Tony had been passing between them last week about the school party, Ashley's new words were in capital letters.

B'S IN THE PRINCIPAL'S OFFICE.

I coughed, pushing the book back to Tony, and I raised my hand. "May I go to the toilet, please, Miss?"

"Is it urgent?"

"Yes, Miss."

"Go on, then. You have three minutes."

"Can I go to the toilet, Miss?" Alex Janey asked from the back of the room.

"Not until Mr O'Donnell is back. Wait your turn."

I slipped out of class. The corridor was empty and I walked to the foyer as though I needed to be there. The principal's office was behind the secretary's desk, a glass wall broken into strips by a row of blinds.

"Classes are that way, Mr O'Donnell," the secretary said. "What are you doing down here?"

I leaned against the tall desk, staring over her shoulder. Ben was in the office, his back to me, and the principal was leaning forward, talking with animated hands.

"My phone's dead and my Mum's expecting me to call her at lunch time," I said. "Have you got a charger?"

"You're not supposed to be using your phone during the day, Dean. Come back at lunchtime and you can charge it then."

I pointed at the principal's office. "Is he in trouble?"

"Did you get him in trouble?" she asked, though she wasn't accusing me. Her voice was dismissive.

"No, Miss."

"Then it's none of your business, is it? You can go back to class now."

Twenty minutes later, when Mrs James was discussing the concept of probability, somebody knocked on the door and when she opened it, she stepped aside to let the principal in. Ben stood behind him with his head down and his schoolbag clutched in his hands in front of him.

"Take your seat," Mr McLaughlin said. "Sorry for Ben's tardiness, Mrs James. It won't happen again."

Ben slouched past me. Everyone was staring at him, but he kept his gaze on his feet. When he slumped into his seat, Alex Janey shunted his desk in the other direction.

"Settle down," Mr McLaughlin said. "Not a word out of any of you. If Mrs James, or any of your teachers, tells me otherwise, I'll be handing out suspensions like they're Christmas gifts."

He stood by the door, tall, in a tweed suit jacket and corduroy trousers, and he folded his arms. He watched as Mrs James went back to her lesson, and then he flattened his thinning hair and closed the door behind him.

I couldn't concentrate. Mrs James asked the class what the probability was of drawing a face card from a standard deck of fifty-two playing cards and when nobody answered her, she turned to me. "Dean?"

She always called on me when nobody else knew the answer. Teacher's pet.

I shrugged. I couldn't even remember the question.

She wrote on the board. "Twelve over fifty-two can be simplified down to what?" The room was silent. "Come on, people. This is an easy one."

The bell rang. Everyone stood up.

"Not so fast," she said. "No one leaves until I get an answer. I don't care how late you are for your next class."

Alex Janey said, "Come on, O'Donnell, give her the answer."

"If you're so eager," Mrs James said, "you can do it." She held out the chalk for him.

When he went to the front of the class with his bag already over his shoulder, he took the chalk, poised it against the board, and glared at me. He wasn't going to write a thing until I told him the answer.

"Three over thirteen," I said. I might not remember the question, but I knew how to reduce a fraction.

Alex scratched the numbers on the board, slapped the chalk onto Mrs James' desk, and left the room.

"Quietly," she said as everybody got up to leave.

I stood in the corridor with Ashley and Tony and Ashley had her hand on my forearm.

When Ben came out of the classroom, I wanted to step forward, but Ashley stopped me.

The bruise on Ben's face was blurring at the edges and the purple was leaking into green. He gave me an imperceptible shake of his head as he walked away.

"Leave it," Ashley whispered.

"I can't," I said. I wanted to hold him. I wanted to tell him it'd be all right.

But it wouldn't.

He'd told me yesterday, as we held each other in our igloo, that he wasn't ready to come out. And now the whole school knew.

Erin McNally was unusually quiet. She tailed down the corridor after Ben and Alex Janey stood in front of me.

"Which one of you lads turned him gay?"

Ashley said, "How do we know it wasn't you?"

"Because I'm not a fag."

"Neither are we," Tony said. "I'm aro-ace."

"The fuck does that even mean?"

"It means I'm not into anyone. Least of all a jock like Ben."

Ashley's grip tightened on my arm as she stepped up to me.

Alex said, "So it must be you, then."

I had no words. I could smell whatever he'd had for breakfast on his breath and it wasn't nice. My chest hurt.

"It wasn't me," I said. And once the words were out, I couldn't take them back. I'd probably say it again, twice more before the cock crowed.

Ashley said, "Sixty percent of the kids in this school are boys. Go pick on somebody else."

Alex Janey tutted, snorted like he was going to spit, and then walked away.

The bell rang for the next period. Tony said, "What the hell's his problem?"

"Isn't it obvious?" Ashley said. "He's threatened by his own self-awareness."

I waded through the rest of the day in a swamp of gossip and whispered conversations. At lunch time, I slipped outside to the front steps where I'd normally meet Ben, but he wasn't there. I could see the offending tree from the top of the steps where we'd kissed. From the angle of the video that was circulating around school, whoever filmed it had probably been standing right here.

The fairy lights around the tree had been switched off like a derelict electric chair.

We didn't have any classes together on Monday afternoons and as I struggled to concentrate during after-school rehearsal in the music room, everybody was talking about the video.

"Your only concern," Mr Elliot said, "is Friday's performance. We have less than a week, people, and we still sound like a choir of tone-deaf frogs with pennies in their mouths. Dean, get your head in order and your voice in check."

When I got to town after rehearsal, I took the bus to Chard Lane. In the park, the basketball hoop on the wall was coated in fresh snow, and our igloo had a hole kicked in the side of it.

I crawled inside. Ben wasn't there. An animal had been in and scratched at the snow, thinning the wall out where it had been kicked by a kid who couldn't leave somebody's house well enough alone.

I pulled my phone out. I hadn't checked Instagram all day, but when I looked, the video was all I could see. I watched as it zoomed in on us, and I squinted to see if I was recognisable. I traced the video back to its source through a series of stories, but the owner was anonymous, a throwaway account.

I switched to my messages with Ben, but I didn't know what to say. Sorry you kissed me and the world found out? Sorry I didn't come to your defence?

Fresh snow was seeping in through the hole in the wall.

dean_odd_donnell
Are you OK?

He left me on read.

CHAPTER 26

BEN

I'd come out before; I could do it again. That's what I'd thought on Sunday night after leaving Dean. On Monday morning, that right had been taken from me. But my first concern, when I walked through the school gate and heard somebody say, "Faggot," and somebody else say, "Way to go, man," was for Dean. I hadn't known the extent of the damage at that point, but I'd hoped he wasn't suffering.

I looked for him as I entered the warm foyer, smacking fresh snow off my shoes, and Mr McLaughlin pointed at me from behind the secretary's desk. "Can I have a word, please, Mr Hunter?"

I knew the word was out, but I didn't know how. Not until I'd sat in the hard, leather chair opposite Mr McLaughlin and he leaned across the desk, told me what was going on, and then held his phone out to me.

He'd shut the door. He never shut his door unless it was serious. Even when he was shouting at someone, the door was always open.

I watched the video. Twice. Then I handed the phone back to him and said, "Thanks," like it was a privilege to be outed by an anonymous source.

"Are you okay?" Mr McLaughlin asked.

I looked at his long face, the sagging jowls, and his hooded eyes. He was unnaturally tall, even when sitting down.

I shrugged. I didn't know how I should be feeling.

He talked and I wasn't listening. My brain was fogging over as an avalanche of worry threatened to bury me. I heard him say, "We'll get to the bottom of this," and, "Let's talk to your parents." And when he asked me a question and I didn't answer him, he leaned forward, softening his features into a weird, scowling semblance of friendship. "Ben? Do you?"

"Sorry?"

"It's a lot. I get it. Would you like to take the rest of the day? Go home and put some distance between you and this—malicious rumour."

"But it's not, is it?"

"I don't follow."

"It's malicious, but it's not a rumour," I said. There was a hard edge to my words. We both heard it.

"We will get to the bottom of it, I promise you. But for now, perhaps it's best to go home. Come back fresh tomorrow."

"No."

"I'm sorry?" Mr McLaughlin said. I don't suppose anybody said no to him often.

I straightened up in the chair, faking an air of confidence. "There's only three days left before the end of term. May I go to class now?"

We stood up. Mr McLaughlin said, "The other boy."

"I won't say."

"You don't have to do this alone, Benjamin."

263

"What good does it do anyone to out somebody else?" I said. I could feel the hot bite of tears behind my eyes, but I wasn't going to let them out.

"If you tell me, I can protect him."

"I won't take that chance."

Mr McLaughlin had walked me to Mrs James' maths class and when he gave his warning to the students about keeping in line, I forced myself into my seat and Alex sneered. He gripped his desk and shuffled a few inches away from me.

I couldn't even look at Dean for fear of somebody noticing. I smelled him as I walked past his desk and I wanted to hold him.

I'm not sure if I'd ever get to do that again.

Erin leaned in and whispered, "Are you all right?"

I nodded and kept my head down for the rest of the class.

When Mrs James let us go, five minutes after the bell rang, I slipped out of the room and walked straight down the corridor to the foyer. I needed some air. The last thing I expected was for Erin to follow me.

"Butts against the wall, lads," somebody laughed. "Don't drop a pencil or he'll bum you."

I clenched my fist.

Behind me, Erin said, "Piss off, Grimes. Get a life."

"Fighting the girly-boy's battles now, are you?"

I turned to Jim Grimes. He was a sixth-year lad on the Under 18s rugby team.

"What'd you say?"

"You heard me."

Erin took my arm and pulled me away from him. She pushed me through the doors to the cold air outside.

She hugged me. I felt the sting inside my head again and I kept my arms loose at my sides. If I hugged her back, the tears would come.

"I tried calling you all day Sunday."

"I turned my phone off."

"It's him, isn't it?" She lowered her voice. "Dean."

I sat on the wall where I'd normally spend lunchtimes with him. "Does everyone know?"

"About him? No." She sat on the wall, further away from me than usual. "Why didn't you tell me?"

"I tried. Half a dozen times. You wouldn't listen."

"I thought you were joking about being gay or—"

"Confused? Going through a phase?"

"That's not what I meant," Erin said.

"It's what my parents will think. Again. Just waiting for the right girl to come along. If I can get them to stop fighting long enough to listen."

"You don't have to tell them."

I balled my fists and pushed them into my coat pockets. I couldn't look at the oak tree where Dean and I had shared our first kiss. And our first public performance.

Erin said, "Was it worth it?"

"Was what worth it?"

"Kissing him. Outing yourself at school."

"I didn't out myself. I never got the opportunity to do that. Somebody stole that from me. And if I find out who it is, I'll kick his head in."

"Anger isn't going to get you anywhere, Ben."

"Anger's all I have left." She had no clue. She didn't know what I was feeling. She never could. "Don't pretend to understand my life, Erin."

"I'm the only one who *does* understand you."

"Are you?" I looked at her, dragging my gaze off the slush of snow at my feet to meet her icy glare.

"I tried to warn you," she said. "And I told him to back off and give you some space."

"You did what?"

"I was just looking out for you, Ben. I'm your best friend."

I stood up. "Some best friend."

I went inside, smacking my shoulder on the automatic door even as it was opening. I went to my next class amid a storm of whispers and sneers, and when Erin came in a few minutes later, she sat at another desk.

I'd bricked my first shot of the day. Well done, Ben.

I saw Dean once more before lunch. Tony and Ashley were with him. My one consolation at not being able to hold him was knowing that he hadn't been identified in the video. My ugly face had blocked him from view.

I could still taste his breath, still feel the press of his thigh between my legs as we'd stretched out on his coat in the igloo. Yesterday was so long ago. And tomorrow wasn't coming.

Ashley touched his shoulder a few times and when Tony said something, Dean smiled, but his face was turned to the floor, hiding those eyes I wanted to get lost in. I didn't go near him. Anybody in a two-metre radius of me now would be under suspicion.

Which proved true at lunchtime's basketball practice. The whole team had crowded against the far wall to get changed and when I said, "All right?" to one of the boys on the way into the gym, Alex Janey put his arm over his shoulder and said,

"So, about my party in three weeks. You're totally down for it, right?" He dragged him away from me.

Although we'd played our final pre-Christmas league game, we still had a non-league exhibition game against Millstreet on Wednesday after our final lesson. It was called a friendly game, but everybody knew it would be anything but. At least it was somewhere to direct my aggression.

We ran suicides. Coach had us do ten minutes of box jumps and then verticals. When he told us to do some mirror drills, where one player moves in a random direction and another mirrors him as fast as possible, nobody volunteered to reflect me.

On the way back to the changing room, Alex shoved past me, his shoulder smacking against me hard enough to make me stumble. Then he swiped his hand across his shoulder as if I'd left some contagious disease there and he wiped his palm on somebody else's shirt like he was eight years old.

"What the fuck, Alex?"

"What?" he said, squaring up.

"Hit the showers," Coach Williams said. "Ben, my office."

He closed the door behind me. What was it with people closing doors today?

"I don't know what's going on," he said.

"How could you not know?"

"What I mean is, I don't want to know. Is this going to affect your game on Wednesday?"

"No, Coach."

"Is it going to affect my team?"

"Ask them."

"Do you really want me to?"

"No."

He nodded. "Okay, then. Sort it out. You can go. Maybe skip the showers for today. At least until they calm down."

"Yes, sir."

As I was leaving, he stopped me. "And Ben?" I looked at him. "I don't know what to say in these kinds of situations. But good luck out there. Don't let the dickheads get you down."

I nodded. In the changing room, somebody had tipped the contents of my bag all over the wet floor.

I was still drying my school trousers under the hand dryer when everyone else had gone. There was only fifteen minutes left of lunch, not that I could face sitting at an empty table in the cafeteria, being stared at like a book everybody had read but nobody understood.

So I left.

I went home, riding the cold, empty bus towards Mount Doom. I had work tonight, which might be a blessed relief from all the attention, but until seven o'clock, I would just have to hide in my bedroom and suffer my strained family life.

I swear neither of my parents had been to work for almost a week. Were they even making money anymore?

I opened the front door just as Mum shouted, "Every single fucking time."

"For Christ's sake," Dad said.

I didn't stick around. I hung my coat up on the hook and darted into the kitchen to grab a packet of crisps, not because I was hungry, but because I didn't want to face going back downstairs later. They must have heard me because they lowered their voices, a quiet, simmering argument that was worse than the screaming ones. Every hushed word between them was loaded. Shots fired.

The muted tension followed me upstairs. I shut my bedroom door, trying to drown out their voices, but the muffled sounds of their argument seeped under the door like water in a sinking ship.

I collapsed on the bed and buried my face in the pillows. I was beginning to forget what silence sounded like. The longer I lay there, the louder my parents became. Something shattered—another vase or a lamp or a skull.

"Go to hell," Mum screamed. It was her stock phrase.

I pulled up Instagram on my phone. But I shouldn't have.

Aaronandrewss
Who's the fag?

FlowerPower22
Just saw this! I know that boy!

JoxLife
Bro, seriously? With another dude?

SparkleShineee
Honestly, who even films this stuff?
Invasion of privacy much?

HoopMaster008
I played against his team this season.
Dude, that's disgusting

GoldenGal07
#loveislove

PartyMike_
Always knew he was a bit off. This
proves it.

TechVizDamo
If anyone has the uncut vid, DM me.

PennyPiperr
Dribbling needs to remain on the court!

VeggieLover
Anyone else wondering who the other guy is?

LoudMouthLucy
If his basketball skills were as good as his kissing, maybe they'd have won more games!

I threw my phone on the desk and it slipped off the edge onto the floor. I heard it vibrate as more messages came in.

I couldn't face them.

Dad was crying. Again.

I used to well up when I heard him cry, hurting for his pain, but now the sound of his tears embarrassed me.

Mum screamed, "Fuck you."

And Dad said, "Get off my fucking case already."

I fell into an uneasy sleep. I'd been spending most nights awake, listening to their battles, trying to study but failing, tired from work. Tired from living.

When I woke, it was dark outside. I hunted for my phone under the desk. I had less than thirty minutes to get to work.

Dean had sent me a message.

dean_odd_donnell
Are you OK?

I was too upset to reply. I wanted to but couldn't.

When I got to work, I was already wearing my polo shirt and Linda said, "Shit's going down. Marty's on the warpath."

"What's going on?"

"You tell me," she said. "Are you doing okay?"

"Why wouldn't I be?"

"My cousin's at Clannloch. I heard about the video."

I shook my head. "I'm handling it. What's up with Marty?"

"God knows. But he's been in a mood since I got here."

The popcorn machines were glowing and hissing. Jeff came out of the back room with a few tubs of butter and I helped him lift them onto the counter.

Linda said, "Butter is so gay."

"What the hell does that mean?" Jeff asked.

Linda said, "Straight boys are so boring until you cover them in a little butter."

Jeff said, "What the fuck?" and I'm glad he did. Because I probably would have said something worse.

We laughed.

Marty Carlin came out of his office. He said, "Team meeting. Now."

He disappeared back inside and Jeff said, "One of you is getting fired. I didn't do anything wrong."

We crowded into Marty's tiny office and he looked at us, seven staff members pulled away from whatever duties we'd been on. The girl from the ticket booth hadn't come in.

Marty picked up a TV remote and pressed play. The screen in the corner of his room lit up. It showed a CCTV camera that was pointing at the side door of the cinema. The footage was in black and white, but it was bright. You could see the swirls on the patterned carpet.

A kid, no older than five or six, came into frame and her mother followed, dragging her away. Marty pushed a button on the remote and the tape ran forward. The timestamp sped up.

He stopped running it forward and pressed play as the counter ticked over on 21:42:46.

Somebody walked into view, skulking across the carpet towards the emergency door. It took me a second to realise who it was.

Me.

There was no sound. I opened the door, stepped outside, and a few seconds later, I came back in with Dean behind me. His grin was bigger than I remembered.

The camera switched to another angle and we watched as I led Dean to one of the cinema screens and went inside.

Marty said, "It gets better." He forwarded the tape and, in quick time, I came back out of the screen and returned a few minutes later with popcorn and drinks.

"Shit," I said.

Marty paused the tape. "Yeah. Shit."

"I can explain."

"I really hope you can, because that looks like theft to me."

"Theft?" Linda said.

Marty said, "He snuck somebody in through the side door instead of paying for a ticket."

"I paid," I said. "I put the money in the till."

Linda said, "I rang it through the next day. He'd left it in the empty till drawer. Where's the footage from the tills?"

Marty turned the TV off. Nobody said anything.

My chest was heavy, like an SUV had screeched to a stop on top of me.

Marty looked at me. "Hand your polo shirt in. You're

dismissed."

How many baskets was I going to brick today?

"I paid for his ticket," I said. "Please, Marty, I need this. You can't fire me."

"It doesn't matter what your conscience made you do after the fact. You stole from Bates' Cinema."

Linda said, "It was one ticket and he paid for it."

"I'll pay you up to this shift," Marty said. "But you're done here."

I scanned the room, at the faces that were unwilling to look at me. Marty shook his head.

"Mr Carlin, please. Let me explain."

"I can't have staff members that I don't trust. Theft is theft whichever way you dress it up. Get out."

He escorted me into the staff room to get my jacket and then he followed me outside. Fresh snow was falling.

That fucking snow. I was sick of it now.

"Mr Carlin, please."

"Rules are rules," he said. "Good night."

I walked home. Each step was heavy, weighed down with the burdens of the day. By the time I stood outside my front door, I was ancient, a haggard elephant at the gates of his graveyard. The silence inside my head was matched by the whispers that had echoed through the day.

When I went to bed, I wanted a reprieve from the spiralling chaos that the rest of the world called Ben.

Me? I called it Anarchy.

— CHAPTER 27 —

DEAN

I didn't message him again. I'd been ghosted by friends before, so I knew the drill. The last thing I should be doing is bombarding him with texts, even though that's all I wanted to do. Meet me. Talk to me. I don't want to be alone.

Because Mum was already on annual leave from work, she drove me to school on Tuesday. The principal was standing at the gate, talking to a couple of parents, and he waved as Mum joined the row of unloading cars.

"See you tonight," I said, and I opened the door. I needed to get out of there before she decided to stick around and speak to Mr McLaughlin.

"Choir practice?" Mum asked.

I nodded. "I'll be home by six."

"Got money for the bus?"

"You could give me some more, just in case."

"Nice try," she said. We hadn't sung along to Christmas tunes this morning, but she didn't point out the change in my demeanour. "Love you," she said, before driving away.

The school was still a murky hell of rumours. A list of boys' names started circulating yesterday afternoon and by two p.m.

the same list came around again, this time with betting odds scribbled beside each name. Half of the basketball team were on it, and Alex Janey was listed as a 40/1 outsider. His reputation as a ladies' man was well known.

Somebody had put Tony's names on the list at 2/1, and my name was beneath his. But most of the names were 2/1 and Tony said we shouldn't worry.

But worry was all I could do. Listening to the language of the kids at school showed how homophobic a lot of them were. It didn't matter that Ireland was supposed to be a progressive country, at an individual level, people were entrenched in prejudice. *Gay* was still a slur. And that terrified me.

We had a free period before lunch on Tuesday and Ashley and Tony dragged me into the science block. I leaned against one of the islands where a rack of beakers had been stacked up, and Ashley said, "I know it's not right that he has to go through this on his own, but if you speak up, you know what's going to happen."

"Everyone's playing detective," Tony said, "like a bunch of old cops brought back from retirement for one final case."

Ashley said, "It'll blow over before you know it. It was one stupid kiss."

"It's not the kiss that counts," I said. "It's the fact that he's been outed against his will."

"Outing yourself isn't going to help him."

I kicked one of the heavy stools and we stopped talking when we heard footsteps outside the door. Whoever it was— wearing high heels; probably Miss Ashton—walked by and Tony shook his hands loose like he'd been ready to fight and needed to release the built-up energy.

He said, "Who was that kid two years ago who got outed? The little one with the red hair."

"Sean," Ashley said. "Before you came here," she told me. "The bullying got so bad he had to move schools."

When I looked horrified, Tony said, "But he was only thirteen. Ben can handle himself. He'll probably punch a few faces before we break up for Christmas and that'll be that."

"He's not like that."

Ashley leaned on the counter, studying one of the glass beakers. "We should culture some botulism or whatever. Poison a few kids. Get people talking about something else for once."

Tony and I looked at each other with mock fear. "She's a dark one, is Ashley."

"Step away from the beakers," I said. "Anyway, Ben's not going to punch people—but if he does, they deserve it."

"You like him, don't you?"

I lowered my voice. "I'm hardly going to kiss somebody I don't like."

"He leaned into you in that video. We could claim it was force."

"He didn't force me."

"It was just a suggestion."

Tony said, "Look, man. Whatever you decide, we've got your back. You just have to make sure it's what you want. Are you ready to come out to a school that evidently doesn't like queer kids?"

"No," I said. "But if it helps Ben, then maybe."

"It won't help Ben."

"But it'll take half the weight off him."

"And put the fallout at your feet."

Later, I stood in the shadows of the foyer opposite the secretary's desk. Mr McLaughlin's door was open. I could walk right inside and confess. Tell him I was the other boy in the video. But Ashley's words turned over in my head. Outing myself wasn't going to help Ben.

The secretary looked up from her computer but before she could focus on me, I hurried back to class.

I'd hoped Ben hadn't come to school today—it's not like we were learning anything anyway as teachers wound down for the impending break. But I saw him a few times in the halls, gripping both straps of his backpack and walking with his head down and the hood of his coat up. Even from behind, I'd recognise him. It was funny. He'd been the one sitting behind me all year, but I knew I could pick him out in the dark. And if his head hadn't blocked my face from view in the video, how many other people could have recognised me, even among the shadows? Luck had come to my rescue but she'd forgotten about Ben.

He looked lonely as he walked down the hall. Erin McNally wasn't at his side. And Alex Janey had been seen mouthing off about gay boys in straight toilets and how it wasn't right.

Dickhead.

If Ben was going to punch someone, I hoped he'd start with him.

Ben walked past me. "Hi," I said. But he kept walking. I tried to tell myself that he was just preoccupied with his public shaming and didn't hear me. But as I watched him turn into a classroom and disappear, I knew I was being ignored. I didn't know if he was angry with me or sparing me from scrutiny, but either way, I felt guilty as hell.

I shouldn't have gone to the school party. If I'd stayed home, none of this would have happened. And yet I wanted him to kiss me again.

Somebody bumped into me and said, "Watch it, dumbass."

I scuttled away. Drawing attention to myself would make things worse, and pining after Ben wasn't doing me any favours.

I just wished he was okay. I couldn't imagine having anyone other than Ashley or Tony knowing I was gay, never mind the whole school. He didn't need this, not this close to Christmas. As he held me in the igloo, he told me about his parents. I wondered if they knew. Or even cared.

If I could get him in my arms, somewhere where we could be alone, I knew it'd be okay. If I could talk to him, I'd share his pain.

But he wasn't talking to me.

And that was my fault for not coming out beside him.

I suffered through choir practice that afternoon, singing songs that held no meaning to me anymore. Joy to the world, my ass. And it was definitely not the most wonderful time of the year.

When I got home, Chill Bill on the front lawn was just a disgruntled blob of refrozen slush. Mum had taken the flat cap and scarf he'd been wearing into the house last weekend. The snow wasn't soft underfoot anymore. It was hard and crunching as I came up the gravel drive where both my parents' cars were parked. Mum always drove on and reversed off. Dad would reverse on. They were weird like that.

Lights twinkled around the window frames and across the guttering, and the three-foot ornament of Santa's sleigh in the garden was wheel-clamped in ice. The dwarf conifers at either side of the front door—Mum's prized possessions that stood over five feet tall—were wrapped in more lights and the needles sparkled in the early evening frost.

I wasn't looking forward to Christmas anymore. There was nothing to look forward to. When I slept, variations of Ben kissing me rolled through my dreams, followed by paparazzi-style videos from people lurking in the bushes. Accusations and name-calling came after.

When I went inside, the living room TV wasn't on. Four effigies of Santa's joyful face greeted me in the hall and I hung my scarf and coat on the hook. "Mum? Dad?"

"In here," Dad said. I knew from the tone of his voice that something was up.

I kicked my shoes off and went to the kitchen. They were sitting at the table, but the table hadn't been set. We didn't do takeaway often, but when we did it was usually a Friday. So the lack of dinner on a Tuesday meant something terrible had happened.

"What's wrong?"

Dad nodded to the seat opposite them. I didn't want to sit down. Mum's phone sat on the tabletop in front of her like she'd just been on a call to somebody.

Or watching videos.

I gripped the back of the chair but didn't pull it out.

"How was school?" Dad asked.

I shrugged, noncommittal. Why hadn't Mum said anything yet?

I sat down just in case whatever came next would give me away if my legs buckled from underneath me.

He said, "Got any homework?"

"No. Tomorrow's our last day."

"And choir. How was choir?"

I stared at the phone, its blank screen scowling between them. This was the moment in a horror movie when it would ring and make everybody jump.

"What's going on?" I asked.

Mum pinned a strand of hair behind her ear.

Dad said, "That new friend of yours. What was his name?"

"Ben," Mum said, and her voice was so hoarse she had to say it twice to get the word out. It sounded like she hadn't spoken in weeks.

"Did you speak to Mr McLaughlin?" I asked, accusing her. I thought she'd driven away when I got out of the car this morning but I hadn't been paying attention. I was too busy looking for Ben.

Mum said, "I got a text from the school. All the parents did."

I counted to the tenth number in the Fibonacci sequence—thirty-four—just to keep my cool and give myself time to come up with a suitable answer when they asked me the inevitable questions.

"What did it say?"

She unlocked the phone and slid it across the table. If I looked, I would betray myself.

I looked.

Clannloch Community School (+353 821 518 681)

Parents/guardians, be advised. A video involving two students from our school is being circulated online. We are

concerned about the emotional well-
being of the students affected. We
kindly request that you discuss this
with your child and reinforce the value
of empathy, discretion and inclusion.

I read it three times. Ben's name wasn't mentioned. I looked at them. "So?"

"Tony's Mum sent me the video," Mum said.

"It has thousands of views," Dad told me.

I didn't know how Tony's mum got hold of it. But I hoped they weren't about to show it to me.

Dad said, "It shows two boys. Kissing. And one of them is Ben."

I didn't speak. The words to combat this hadn't been invented yet.

"Do you know anything about it?" Mum asked.

I studied the woodgrain on the tabletop. There was a coffee cup ring where Dad always had his morning coffee. "I've seen it," I said. It wasn't a lie.

"Is the other boy you?"

"Me?" I think my voice reached the *O Holy Night* octaves I'd been struggling against all week. "Why would it be me?"

"He's your friend," Dad said.

"He has plenty of friends."

I stood up. Then I sat down again. My tongue was fat and my throat was closing over.

"It's too dark to see the other boy," Mum said. "And Ben's head protects him."

"Protects him?"

"From view. Dean, we just need to understand. Is it you in the video?"

I cleared the lies out of my chest and one of them escaped my mouth.

"No."

"Have you spoken to Ben? Do you know who the boy is?"

"He's not talking to anybody," I said. "His life is ruined."

Dad said, "He shouldn't have been kissing a boy on the school grounds."

"So this is his fault?" I asked. I felt the lies settling back down inside me. Mum put a hand on Dad's arm.

Dad said, "It's a public place. I'm surprised there aren't more videos floating around. Your generation never have your phones out of your hands."

I pushed Mum's phone across the table to them. I never wanted to touch another phone in my life.

"We're just trying to understand," Mum said. "He should be getting help, not harbouring these secrets on his own."

She made it sound like conversion therapy was the only answer.

"Are we done here?" I asked.

Mum looked at the glowing clock on the stove. "I'll put dinner on. Then we can watch a movie." She picked up her phone.

Dad said, "Keep away from him, Dean. At least until everything settles down."

I stood up again. "He's doing a good job of hiding from everybody already."

In my room, I closed the door and saw Fred on top of my pillows where Mum had put him after making my bed. I'd lied

282

to them. It was becoming a habit lately.

I turned my phone off. I didn't want any more reminders about the video or the text message from school.

The world needs to label everything. I sounded more like Ashley by the minute, but she was right. People shouldn't need to know. They shouldn't care. It doesn't matter what I do with my life or who I want to kiss.

Mum and Dad should have known that. Society should respect that. But they didn't. Why should the idea of coming out make me feel so weak and pathetic? I was just one little cog in a very big machine. I wasn't big enough to make a difference. I knew that. Ben did, too.

And my parents were demanding answers to questions I didn't know.

I should have told them the truth.

But I was chicken.

CHAPTER 28

BEN

Here we go again. All I had to do was get through the next two days and then I could hide for the Christmas break. I was tempted to skip school—who would even know? It's not like my parents were in any position to care. But if I did that, I wouldn't see Dean. And despite not wanting to be near him right now in case his association with me proved detrimental, I needed to know he was safe. I was accepting my position as the black sheep, the outcast. Clannloch Community School's answer to *The Lion King's* Scar. But I'd do everything I could to protect Dean from the backlash of rumours.

I saw the list of names that had been passed around yesterday. Tearing it up wasn't an option; somebody would just recreate it. So I added Alex Janey's name to it just to piss him off.

This morning, I sat in business studies, surrounded by an emptiness as people kept their distance, and I remembered our first kiss. I'd been brave then. I gripped his coat and pulled him in. I thought we were alone. And when my lips met his, we were, if only for that instant. The branches of the tree above us were lit up with fairy lights that flickered in his eyes, but I'd thought we were shaded from the main school building. When I brought my face to his, nothing else existed. He became my world, my breath. Dean O'Donnell was my pulse.

I had floated into the gym after the kiss like a balloon freed from a kid's hand, zigzagging through the sky. I didn't know where I'd pop and fall to the ground.

I guess that happened on Monday morning.

Today, I kept my hood up and my head down. The less chance of catching somebody's eye the better.

Halfway through the morning, when classes broke for fifteen minutes, a couple of girls from the year below stopped me in the hall.

"I think it's very brave," one of them said. "We love you."

"It's so sweet," her friend said. "If you need us to pass notes to the other boy, we can do it."

I tried to push past them. "I'm good, thanks."

"If you tell us who it is, we can get him to meet you somewhere."

"No, thanks."

"We won't tell anybody," they called after me as I kept going. When did fourteen-year-olds get so good at lying? I knew they were trying to sound me out for his name.

They weren't the only ones. At lunchtime, somebody shouted across the cafeteria, "Where's your butt bandit? Who is he?"

Erin sat with Gemma Ademola, who looked like she was consoling her. And Alex was consoling the team at another table. Everybody was being consoled except me.

I bought a sandwich with the last of my wage from Bates' Cinema and I was going to sit on the wall outside before I realised that Dean might try to find me there. I went to the library instead and found a corner desk to eat my lunch among the self-help books, tucked between *How to Win Friends and Influence People* and *The 7 Habits of Highly Effective Teens*.

I should have apologised to Erin yesterday, but now I felt it was too late. I didn't need to say sorry for being gay, but I should have told her the truth. Her reaction when I came out last year made me wonder how she'd take the news this time. I hadn't been kissing boys back then. Was I wrong about her?

Some guy I didn't recognise came and sat at my table in the library. He was older, probably in his final year.

"Yes," I said, "I'm the kid in the video. You can leave me alone now."

"I'm not here to hassle you, Ben." He knew my name. I guess everybody did. "I just wanted to say sorry. You shouldn't have to go through this shit in a school full of dickheads and sad-sacks. If I can do anything, let me know."

"Can you turn back time?"

He put his fingers to his temples and squinted like he was concentrating. "Did it work?" he looked around. "Sorry, man. Time travel clearly isn't my thing."

"Thanks for trying," I said, and I chewed my sandwich.

"I only came over to let you know it gets better. I know that sounds like a cliché, but it's true. Gay, bi, pan, demi—it doesn't matter. One of these days, nobody's going to care. But until then, you're welcome to sit with me and my friends over there. No one will bother you. They look like a rough bunch of yobs, but they're good people."

"And what are you? My knight in shining armour?"

He tapped the desk. "I'm hoping the other boy in that video is your knight. If he's not, you're kissing the wrong people."

"I appreciate your concern," I said, trying to put an end to this awkward conversation, "but I've got everything covered, thanks."

He stood up and pushed his chair in. "I know you do. I just wanted to let you know that not everyone at school is a shithead."

He walked away. I didn't even get his name.

In English class after lunch, Mr Dobbins made us read from *Lord of the Flies* like the world was turning the way it always had. People carry on with their lives while other lives are crashing into oblivion around them. We were reading chapter eleven. Piggy's final scenes.

Books didn't interest me. Why should I care what happened to some kids on an island? It was just a story. A useless allegory for human nature. Kids don't kill each other. Not with boulders. They do it with words and with silence.

Mr Dobbins closed his copy of the book. "How does Golding create tension here? How does he put across the emotional impact of Piggy's death?"

Alex and Erin had swapped seats with two other kids and Dean, in the front row, kept his head down.

"Mr Hunter," Dobbins said.

I looked up. He was standing in front of me.

"You're not paying attention."

"Sir."

He lowered his voice. "Stay behind after class, please."

He asked another question about *Lord of the Flies* and I stared out the window at the white world beyond. The magic of Christmas was gone. It doesn't slip away with a gradual dulling of the emotions. It just disappears. One year, you're waiting up for Santa with a desperate desire to catch a glimpse of the wonders of Christmas, listening for the jingle of his sleigh bells and the sound of hooves on the rooftops. The next year, it's over. You know the truth, and the truth is worse than any lie. It was four days to Christmas and I longed to have that childish wonder again. Little kids don't have to worry about anything except how weighty their stocking would be when they come downstairs on Christmas morning.

I looked at the back of Dean's head and wondered if he was still wearing the pride pin. I hoped he wasn't. I didn't want anyone to discover his secrets.

If I could ask him, he'd be able to tell me how many hours it was until Christmas Day, and he wouldn't have to think about it. I loved that his mind was as powerful as a calculator. I flipped my notebook over and tried to calculate it myself. Twenty-four hours a day. Three days, plus what was left of today.

About eighty-two and a half hours. But I was probably wrong.

The bell rang. I stayed in my seat. I knew what was coming. Mr Dobbins would mention the video and tell me all the teachers are here for me if only I would open up to them.

Instead, when the room was empty, he leaned against his desk at the front of the room and folded his arms. He said, "Where's your head, Ben?"

I didn't answer. I was waiting for the sympathy.

Mr Dobbins sighed and waited. I refused to look at him. He checked the time on his watch. The silence ticked between us like an itch.

"I don't know what you've got going on, but if you need extra help, I want you to tell me. You're all over the place. You haven't been participating in class—and I don't just mean since yesterday. You haven't been paying attention for weeks. Long before this business with the video." When I looked up, he said, "I haven't seen it. But there's no avoiding the rumours. I just don't believe that's where your problems started." He unfolded his arms and leaned back against the desk like he was trying to be casual. "Do you want to talk about it?"

I shrugged. Whatever. "I'm good," I said.

"I don't think you are, Ben. Is it home? Family? Your friends? Something's in your head and it isn't William Golding. And I know what it's like for you kids. I used to hate my teachers too. But whatever's going on outside this classroom is affecting your performance inside. You don't have to talk to me—maybe try talking to your friends."

"Haven't you heard, sir? I don't have any left."

"I'm sure that's not true, despite how it might feel."

"People hate me," I said.

"I don't. Your true friends won't, either. Everyone needs a proper friend. The question is, Ben, who is yours? And if you think you've lost that person, maybe it's worth the effort to find them again—or find a new one." He went to the door, signalling an end to our conversation. "Maybe when you come back in January, your personal circumstances will be better. I certainly hope so. I don't want you failing my class because that'll reflect badly on me. And I'm not in the habit of losing students. Have a good Christmas, Mr Hunter," he said.

I tried to pay more attention in French class that afternoon, but when Alex Janey asked the teacher, "How do you say 'gay bar' in French, Miss?" I zoned out. He was acting like an angry child. And I knew he had a chip on his shoulder, picking on other kids to hide his own lack of self-worth, but I didn't think he'd be like this.

We didn't have practice the night before an exhibition game, so when the final bell rang on Tuesday, I stood at the far side of the car park, out of view, and waited for him. I saw Dean waving goodbye to his friends before going back inside. He'd be off to choir practice. I couldn't believe his solo performance was in just a few days. I hoped this thing with the video wasn't affecting his confidence.

Alex came out of the building with a couple of the boys from the team and as they went through the front gate, I caught up with them. "Janey."

He glanced at me, then said to his friends, "Do you smell something, boys?"

"Jesus Christ, Janey, you're not eight years old. I just want to talk."

He turned to me. The others kept walking. "What?"

"I'm still your point guard," I said. "You can't shut me out of tomorrow's game."

"You should do yourself a favour and sprain your ankle. Keep the bench warm, yeah?"

"Why are you acting like this?"

"Like what?"

"Like a homophobic jerk."

"Why are you acting like a gay boy?"

I didn't have an answer beyond the truth. "Because I am one," I said.

"We've been showering together after practice for years. I bet you've been checking me out all that time. It's sick."

"Piss off. I wouldn't touch any of you. This is stupid, Janey.

We've been friends since we were eleven."

"Were you gay back then, too?" he asked.

I shrugged. "I guess so, yeah. But it shouldn't change anything."

"Yeah? Well, it does." He turned away.

"I don't hate you," I said.

"I fucking hate you, gay boy."

"You're just going to walk away?" I called after him. He didn't respond.

Fuck this.

I met Alex on our first day at Clannloch. We stood on the edge of the school gym at lunchtime as Coach Williams refereed a casual basketball exchange. Anybody could jump in for a few minutes of play on Coach's whistle. We just had to wait in line.

One of the kids ahead of us ran onto the court, chased after the ball, and when he got possession of it, he legged it towards the basket. He didn't dribble. He gripped it like a rugby ball under his arm and ran up the court even after Williams blew his whistle.

And Alex, who was in the queue behind me, nudged my arm and said, "Think he's in the wrong sport?" He shouted, "Rugby try-outs are next week, mate." Then he looked me up and down, a deliberate evaluation of my height and physique. "Do you play?"

"Shooting guard or point guard," I told him. "You?"

"Small forward."

"Not tall enough to be a guard or fast enough to be a centre, then?"

"Piss off," Alex laughed. "I'm the Swiss army knife that

everybody forgets about until they need a bottle opened."

As I watched him walk to the bus stop now, I decided not to chase him. It wasn't my responsibility to change him.

I was no activist. I just wanted to be loved.

— CHAPTER 29 —

DEAN

It was the last day of school and I still hadn't spoken to Ben. The wall between us was getting higher and I hated it. Last night, I'd scrolled through our messages, all the way back to his very first *Yo*. It felt like a thousand years ago. I laughed when I got to the images I'd sent him of Fred on the bus, sitting on my shoulder. I'd felt like a kid back then.

Now, I didn't.

My parents avoided me after our conversation at the table. Mum made dinner and we ate in silence. Then I loaded the dishwasher without being asked and they watched TV in the living room while I locked myself away inside Ben's messages. He'd amended his profile so that it just said *B-Ball is all*, and he'd deleted some of his photos, the ones that weren't from the court. It was like he was erasing his life. Ben Hunter had gone into hiding and I couldn't blame him.

It was my fault. If he didn't kiss me—if I hadn't kissed him back—he'd still have a life.

I tried to sleep that night but couldn't. I pictured him in his black polo shirt for work, smelling like buttered popcorn and serving excited kids that had come in with their parents to watch Christmas movies, grinning like he does with that wide expression on his face, his cheeks bunching up under his eyes. I wanted to pull him into my arms and kiss that black eye that would probably be faded yellow by Christmas Day. I'd been planning to buy him a gift, something better than our five-Euro Secret Santa exchange. I couldn't even remember what he'd received. I'd have offered to meet him on Christmas morning, maybe at our igloo if it had survived the week. But other kids or animals would have destroyed it by now.

And he wasn't speaking to me anyway.

On Wednesday morning, Dad drove me to school instead of Mum and at the gate, he said, "Have you got money for lunch?"

"Yeah."

"Take some more." He handed me ten Euros. Then he said, "It's your last day. Stay out of trouble, okay?"

I said, "I was thinking about spray-painting a giant Christmas tree on the side of the principal's car."

"Don't," he said, and his voice was stern. But that's not the kind of trouble he was talking about. He meant keep away from gays, queers and reprobates.

Ashley and Tony met me at the entrance. "Let's do this," Tony said, pumping his arms like a WWE star.

Ashley said, "That's far too much testosterone for a Wednesday."

As we walked inside, Tony bumped his shoulder against me. "Sorry. I had no idea my mum saw the video. I only found out after she'd sent it to your mum."

"It's okay," I said. "I deflected."

"Were they okay about it?"

I shrugged. "They don't know it was me. Or that's the story they're sticking to."

Tony said, "The only thing worse than being blind is having sight with no vision. Helen Keller. 1880 to 1968."

"How much useless information is trapped in that head of yours?"

"I'm not the one who can recite pi to the two-millionth place."

"That's virtually impossible," I said. It didn't matter how depressed I was, Tony could always make me smile. I never gave him or Ashley enough credit for my happiness.

I didn't see Ben most of Wednesday morning, except during history, right before lunch. History, with Mr Williams— Coach Williams—where Ben and Alex Janey sat in the front row, either side of me.

Ben took his seat, slouched low, and buried his neck in his shoulders. He folded his arms. He hadn't even pulled his textbook out. Mr Williams was reading a biography of a footballer, his feet up on the corner of his desk, and when we came in, he folded down the end of the page and slapped the book closed.

He dug out the class textbook from the mess on his desk and said, "Page two-hundred and—Dean?"

"Two twenty-nine," I said. Not that it mattered. They'd be talking about basketball before Mr Williams could find the correct page.

Alex Janey, coming in late, dropped his book bag at his feet and fell into his chair like he knew it would catch him, playing the trust game with furniture. "Have you changed the starting line-up, Coach?" he asked.

I heard Ben make a dismissive noise with his tongue, low

enough that I don't think Mr Williams heard.

Their coach said, "We start as we always start, Janey. You know that."

The school wouldn't let anybody forget about the non-league friendly game against Millstreet, Clannloch's rival team. There were posters taped to every corridor wall, advising us to *Come See the Falcons Charge! Clannloch's Pride is Flying Large!*

Pride. Yeah.

Ben slipped further into his seat.

I wanted to pass him a note. Or ask to borrow a pencil. Anything to have an interaction with him. But with Alex Janey at my other side, I knew better than to give rise to suspicion. I'd punch myself in the face and bust my nose open if I thought it'd give the school something else to talk about.

I looked over my shoulder, as if I wanted to see something at the far side of the room, my eyes lingering on Ben's bruised eye. The swelling was going down, but I still wanted to make it better. He was hurting. And there was nothing I could do about it.

Alex Janey said, "Who's on the bench, Coach? Just in case somebody has an accident."

Ben put his head back and studied the ceiling. I heard the threat in Janey's words as much as Mr Williams must have, but their coach said, "Larkin, Simkins, White and Robinson."

I couldn't believe he missed it. Everybody could see the tension between them since Monday. It was in direct opposition to the joyful chanting that Janey had started on the dancefloor on Friday night. Best friends ripped apart because Ben kissed a boy.

Come to think of it, I hadn't seen much of Erin this week,

either. She wasn't glued to Ben's side the way she used to be.

I took a pencil out of my case and flipped open my notebook. I couldn't stand the awkwardness anymore. I copied down a line from our history textbook and pressed with overwhelming force against the page, enough to break the pencil lead.

"Shit," I said, and I fumbled around inside the case, looking for a sharpener. I had a small metal sharpener at the bottom of the case, as well as another three or four pencils, but I slapped the case on the desk and said, "Anyone got a spare pencil?" I looked at Ben.

He met my gaze.

"Got a pencil?" I said again. I held mine up to show him, the lead hanging at an awkward angle, like a broken finger.

He stared at me and I couldn't tell what he was thinking. Then he grabbed his bag, dug into it, and held out a mechanical pencil.

I gripped the end of it and, for a second, he didn't let go. I thought he was going to say something.

But he didn't.

I said, "Thanks. I'll give it back after class."

"Keep it," he said.

If he was going to be like that, I damn well would keep it.

I sat with Ashley and Tony at lunch and I don't think I said more than three words. Anger was building at the back of my head, swelling between the memories of kisses and snow-coated basketball in the park. I know he was hurt, but so was I. He'd been avoiding me all week and now I wouldn't see him for two weeks. When we came back to school in January, it would be like the kiss never happened. He'd go back to sitting at the back of the class and I'd be a nobody to him.

Was it me he kissed on Friday, or was it just a boy?

Whatever. I wasn't going to pine after him.

Not anymore.

Afternoon classes were a chaotic mess of celebration as kids and teachers were looking forward to getting away from each other for a while. Maybe we all needed to take a break.

I didn't even look for him at the end of the day. I had no need to say good luck for his game against Millstreet. I told myself I didn't give a damn how they performed. I didn't care two months ago, so why should I care about it now?

At the final bell, kids erupted through the exit like elves clocking out on Christmas Eve.

I hugged Ashley and Tony and said I'd see them soon. If I didn't meet up with them before Friday due to my choir practices, they'd be at the performance in the city hall.

Then I pushed against the grain of excited kids as they left school and I went to the music room. But even there I couldn't escape the drama.

They were still talking about that damn video.

"It has to be a boy in the same year as him," somebody said.

Gemma Ademola, aloof as always, refused to be engaged, and in between running scales, one of the girls nudged me and said, "Ben's in your year, isn't he? Do you know who it is?"

"No."

"But what's your best guess? Who does he hang around with?"

I shrugged, do-re-mi-ing myself into silence.

Gemma Ademola cleared her throat and the girl went back to singing.

Mr Elliot rippled his fingers over the piano keys and one of the girls behind me whispered, "I bet it's somebody on the basketball team. All that sweat and aggression." I heard the lust in her voice and I had to admit, if it wasn't the geeky maths kid he'd been snogging, the likelihood of it being a team member was high. I couldn't shower with a bunch of guys three times a week without developing a crush on at least twelve of them.

Mr Elliot whipped into a short rendition of *Flight of the Bumblebee*, his fingers a blur over the keys, and then he crashed the lid down hard.

The scales and the gossip stopped.

"Are we quite finished?" he said.

Gemma Ademola cleared her throat again, and this time the cough said I told you so.

She was eloquent, I'll give her that.

"We get up on stage in two days. Two days. And instead of paying attention, what are we doing?" Mr Elliot stood up and closed his music book. He held it out to us. "Would any one of you rather take over? Because there's only so much I can take of who kissed who or why or where or when. Listen up, people. Some boys kiss boys. It's not a big deal. Does it have to interrupt our training?"

Nobody answered him.

"Please," he said. "I'd really like to know. Why is some mindless gossip far more important to you than doing your best in this choir?" He opened the classroom door. "In a little over forty-eight hours, you will get up onstage—or you won't. It's up to you. Because, honestly, I'm just about beyond caring anymore."

I wasn't going to say anything. Speaking out wasn't my thing. But I, too, was sick of hearing about the video. I stepped forward, looked at the choir behind me, then said, "We care. The gossip needs to stop. Can we just get back to singing?"

Gemma Ademola clapped her hands but nobody joined in. We got through practice without any more incidents.

Mr Elliot said, "Do you think you're ready?"

And the mumble that passed between us was a positive one. We'd meet tomorrow at noon for three hours, in an empty, quiet school where we'd belt out our tunes until we were perfect. And the day after that, we'd meet at the city hall at five o'clock with a chance to practice on stage before our live performance.

And then? It'd be over. And despite having fun, shaky as it was, I didn't think I'd miss these guys. I joined the choir while I was unsure of myself. And although I loved singing, I still wasn't overjoyed about singing alone. I wanted to be a part of something, not the head of it.

I said as much to Mr Elliot after practice, while he was collecting our songbooks and straightening up the room.

I waited for the others to leave before saying, "I know you think I'm good enough for this solo, but are you sure it's not too late to give it to Gemma Ademola?"

Mr Elliot took the songbook off me and said, "Why does everybody call her by her full name? Why is she never just 'Gemma'?"

I shrugged. "Because she's Gemma Ademola. She could never just be Gemma." I didn't understand it either. Perhaps it was her fame. It was the same for Alex Janey. Even Ben— my Ben; Ben Hunter—was known by both names. Me? I was just Dean. Or O'Donnell. Never both. "Maybe there's another Gemma in her class?" I offered.

"And what makes you think either of the Gemmas could do a better job at this than you?"

"I don't," I said. "I'm just nervous." He opened his mouth to say something but I interrupted him. "I know. Shape my nerves, don't let them shape me. But I'm still not the kind of person to stand up in front of strangers and give it my all."

"You're an introvert. I get it. I was the same at your age. Put me at the back of the choir or the orchestra. I never wanted to be first chair. But sometimes you've got to break out of your mould or you'll never grow. You can't be a little boy forever, Dean."

"Growing up sucks," I said.

He nodded. "And how. But also, it's not so sucky as an adult. If you're lucky, you get to be what you want to be. Musician, singer, or construction worker. But only you and your experiences can make that happen. Nobody else can decide that for you. Be the backing singer or the solo artist. If you don't try, you won't know what's right for you."

I nodded. I said, "Sir?"

He turned away from me. "He's a good friend of yours, isn't he? The boy in the video."

"Sir."

"I've seen you eating lunch together."

I felt my Adam's apple fighting against the skin of my throat.

Mr Elliot said, "It doesn't matter who the other boy is, does it?" He turned back to me, and he was playing with the wedding band on his finger. "What matters is who's going to rally behind Ben Hunter now that he's on his own. When you get up on that stage on Friday night, it's called a solo performance, but you still have the backing of the choir. They're all there for you, every single one of them. They've got your back. Who's got his?"

I couldn't answer him. I don't think I was supposed to.

He said, "Coming out is hard. Being forced out is worse. And whoever that other boy is, he doesn't have to rush to come out. Nobody does. Coming out is a personal thing that needs to be done in their own time. But right now, Ben needs his friends. Even if those friends have to be quiet about it. Do you know what I'm saying?"

I did. And I didn't.

He slipped his wedding ring over his knuckle and back again. "Singing is a lot like being a member of the LGBTQ community. Sometimes you've got to hide it. Sometimes you can let it sparkle. Life sucks, Dean. But it doesn't have to."

"Yes, sir," I said, because I didn't know what else to say.

"So, you'll give it a try?" he asked. When I narrowed my eyes, unsure what he was referring to, he added, "Your solo performance. Remember, it's three minutes out of your entire life. What's the worst that could happen?"

"I'm the boy," I said. The words were already in my throat before I could stop them.

Mr Elliot smiled. I didn't need to clarify what I meant. He said, "Good night, Dean. I'll see you tomorrow."

I reached for the door handle and looked back at him. "Mr Elliot?" I indicated the ring he was still playing with. "Your partner. They're lucky to have you."

"Yes. He is."

When I left, I think he was grinning more than I was.

When I checked the time, I realised Ben's game was starting

soon. The car park was filling up with parents and supporters. I slipped into the gym among the crowd and grabbed a seat near the centre-court line.

When Millstreet's team came out, two thirds of the audience booed. A minute later, Ben led the charge from the Clannloch Falcons. Alex Janey came behind him like somebody had stolen his thunder. Ben Hunter kept his eyes ahead of himself.

And as everybody cheered, I tried to clap the loudest.

— CHAPTER 30 —

BEN

I ran onto the court as the crowd cheered. I kept my gaze on the far wall and as I stretched and loosened my limbs, I ignored Alex Janey's loud huffing beside me.

He said, "Last chance to fake an injury and get off my team."

I crab-stepped away from him like I was practising manoeuvres and turned my back. When I got to the changing room earlier, I heard the rowdy noise of Millstreet in their room at the far side of the showers, and their point guard, my counterpart, was standing in the corridor, holding two bottles of water.

I lowered my head, hoping he hadn't seen me, but he shouted, "Hunter. Think fast." He threw one of the bottles to me and I caught it. Suffering sneering looks and uncomfortable questions from my classmates was one thing. I didn't need it from Millstreet. But he said, "We're going to take you down, out there. I'm betting sixty-six to twenty."

"In your dreams, Barr."

He came down the corridor to me. Donal Barr wasn't the tallest player in the league but he was up there. He was at least four inches taller than me. He opened his water bottle and sipped before saying, "You still putting up with the fallout from that video?"

"Piss off, Barr," I said, turning from him.

"I'm not having a go. I think it's shit what happened. Nobody should give a crap who you're into. This isn't the Dark Ages. Queer shouldn't be a slur. You got to own that shit. So, you know, I'm sorry. That's all I'm saying. You got a raw deal." He tapped the butt of his water bottle against my chest. "We're still taking you down, though. Your love life might be a tear-jerker, but on the court, it's going to be a horror show."

I smiled. Donal Barr was a dickhead, but at least he was an equal opportunities dickhead.

In the changing room, I was greeted by a very different atmosphere. I took up my usual spot in the corner, and as soon as I did, the team chatter dropped to a whisper.

I pulled my school shirt off—left shoulder before right because that was my ritual. I unsnapped the clasp of my trousers, and only then kicked my shoes off. I pulled my shorts and jersey on and said, "I think we should be running a pick-and-roll in the second quarter. I've been looking at Millstreet's defence and I think we could pick up some easy baskets."

Alex Janey cleared his throat as though he had twelve different frogs in it. Nobody said a word.

"Come on, guys."

Nothing.

"What about a zone defence then? They've got some decent shooters, but if we crowd the paint, we could force some bad shots."

Even the whispers had stopped.

I stood up. "Guys." They were ghosting me. In person.

"Janey. This isn't funny."

He bent down to tie his laces and said, "We should run a fast break, guys. Their transition defence is useless. It's easy points."

The boys nodded and grunted their agreement and their animated chatter resumed as they discussed his strategy. I was worse than a black sheep. I was dead to them.

"Hunter, Janey. Get your no-good asses in here now," Coach Williams said. I hadn't seen him standing in the doorway of his office at the head of the room.

I had rolled my left sock down. I had way too many pregame rituals. When I went into Coach Williams' office, Alex Janey behind me, Coach closed the door and went to his desk. He stared at us.

Janey said, "This better not be where you tell us to kiss and make up, because he'd enjoy it too much."

"Piss off," I said.

"That's enough," Coach said. "You've been at each other's throats all week and it's messing with my team. Do you want to play basketball?"

I shrugged. "Yes."

"Do you?" he asked Janey.

"Not with a—"

Coach Williams picked up his ball pump and slammed it on the desk. "Not another word. From either of you. Do you hear? I will not tolerate dissention among my players, whatever the reason. When you're on that court, you're a team. Kill each other on your own time, but this is my time. They don't pay me enough to put up with your shit. So you either get out there and play nice or get the hell off my team. It's an exhibition game.

Don't think I won't forfeit and go to the pub instead. This game is eating into my holiday time as much as it is yours."

He draped his whistle around his neck.

"What's it going to be?" He pointed at me. "Will you play?"

"Yes, sir."

"Janey?"

Janey's fists were clenched at his sides.

"I need an answer, Janey."

"Yes, sir," he said. And on our way out of Coach Williams' office, he pushed past me and cursed under his breath.

On the court, when he told me to fake an injury and I walked away from him, I knew he wasn't going to make this an easy game.

I tried not to listen to the chanting from the audience. Basketball fans weren't as cruel as football supporters, but they were always quick to come up with topical slogans. What rhymes with gay?

As I warmed up, I kept my head down, but I glanced at the benches where Erin would usually sit. She wasn't there. I'm not sure who was hurting more—me or her.

I'd call her after the game. I wouldn't be welcome at the traditional post-game pizza night, but maybe I could convince her that a movie night was just what we needed.

And then I saw Dean. He was two rows back, right above the mid-court line, halfway between the home benches and the away team. Tony and Ashley weren't with him, and he was clapping and grinning along with everyone else.

Coach indicated that we should huddle up, and as we did, I tried not to look back into the bleachers.

"We've had a good season," Coach said. "After tonight, you

get a well-earned rest. Whatever Santa brings you, it had better be good manners and an extra helping of skill as we come back fresh in the new year. Hunter, it's your play. Call it."

The weight of his expectation—and his faith—settled on me. I looked at my teammates, even at Alex Janey who couldn't meet my eyes.

"Let's start with the Falcon Sweep," I said. I could feel the tension in the air.

"Good," Coach said, clapping his hands to break the huddle.

The first quarter started with chaotic energy as our team and Millstreet's players fought for every inch on the court. As the whistle blew, Alex Janey took off like a rocket, elbowing his way to the basket for an easy layup. But his aggression wasn't just aimed at Millstreet.

Any time I called for the ball, he pretended not to hear or outright ignored me, taking difficult shots himself or passing to anyone but me. When I did manage to get the ball, his passes were hurried and poorly timed, setting me up for failure. I saw Coach Williams' face scowling.

By the end of the first quarter, we were down by six points. As the second quarter opened, Alex escalated his efforts to thrash me. He was talking trash to the Millstreet players and getting physical, pushing and shoving his way around the court, but during a defensive play, he undercut me just enough to throw off my timing, but not enough to draw a foul.

We were down by ten points as the second quarter drew to a close. Alex smirked as he walked off the court for halftime, ignoring Coach's rant about team spirit.

I looked at the bleachers. There was worry on Dean's face. I bet the whole audience could see what game Janey was playing, and it wasn't basketball.

When the whistle blew for the start of the third quarter, I checked the scoreboard. We were already down by ten. The Millstreet players looked cocky, and they had every right to. We were a mess.

Right out of the gate, they scored a three-pointer. Our defence was falling apart, and it wasn't for lack of skill. Alex Janey was more interested in working against me than our opponents. He missed key passes, hesitated at crucial moments, and the whole team felt it.

When I was setting up for a defensive play, my eyes locked on Donal Barr's enormous height. Alex Janey was supposed to cover the strip. As I sidestepped to intercept a pass, Janey crashed into me, full-bodied, and I skidded across the polished court on my ass.

The ref blew the whistle and gave Janey a warning. "Unsportsmanlike conduct, number seven. Another one and you're out."

Alex muttered something unintelligible as he hustled down the court, and threw me a look, his face defiant.

Coach was livid, pacing the sidelines, his fists tight. "Get it together, Falcons. You're not playing against each other; you're playing against them."

We hit the fourth quarter. We were down by more than twenty points. Coach Williams looked like he was about to erupt. The Falcons were a mess. It was like we'd already accepted defeat. Millstreet capitalised on our disorganisation, scoring while our attempts at the basket seemed more desperate than strategic.

As the final whistle blew, I covered my face. Our misery

was over. Millstreet had trounced us, and when we shuffled off the court, it was clear this was more than just a lost game. This was a team torn apart, a fact underscored by the silence that followed us into the changing room.

We sat on the hard wooden benches that lined the changing room. Alex Janey threw a ball at the far wall and it bounced and rolled towards the showers. "Fucking mess," he said.

"Because of you," I said.

Coach Williams came in behind us. He blew his whistle and we looked at him. And although his voice was calm, his words weren't. "What the hell was that? I thought we had an understanding. I thought I had a team that knows how to play together."

Janey said, "It's not my fault we lost."

Coach Williams blew his whistle right in his face. He let it fall from his lips on its chain around his neck. "My office. Now." As Alex Janey stormed into the office, Coach said, "Pizza night is off. Go home. Cool off. And do whatever the hell you need to before coming back in January to sort your shit out." He went into his office after Janey and closed the door.

We saw him pointing and screaming through the window, and Janey arguing back.

I looked at the broken team. "Come on, guys. I'm over this. Give me a break, will you? I'm still the Hunter."

"Fuck this," Pete Wilson said. He hadn't showered or changed. He put his coat on, threw his bag over his shoulder, and looked at me. "Sorry, man. Janey's a loudmouth prick. Have a good break."

He left.

And the others followed suit. A few of them gave me fist

bumps, some ignored me. But anything was better than Alex Janey's aggression.

He was still in Coach's office, but he wasn't arguing anymore. His face was red as Coach towered over him, his arms folded and his thick beard glistening with spit. Janey was leaning away from his tirade.

When he came out, everyone else had gone. He threw his things into his kit bag, glared at me, and left.

Coach switched his office light off. "You okay?"

I nodded.

"Go home, Ben. Don't let this be your last memory of the year."

"Yes, sir," I said, and I pulled my sweaty shirt off. When he was gone, I sat down again. Home or school—it didn't matter where I was anymore, I was surrounded by anger and aggression.

I looked up when I saw somebody standing in the doorway.

"All right?" Dean asked.

I shook my head. "You shouldn't be here."

I couldn't look at him. My chest ached every time I did. Seeing him in class or the corridors, watching him in the cafeteria. I was mourning him even though he wasn't dead.

"How's your eye?" he asked.

I didn't need to touch the bruise to know it was healing. "Better than my ass right now."

"Is Alex Janey off the team? I saw what he did. That was deliberate."

"He got a warning," I said. I dropped my shirt into my bag and pulled out a hoodie with our Falcon crest on it. The sweat on my back was drying in the chill of the empty changing

311

room.

Dean took a step into the room, his school shoes loud on the damp tiles.

I said, "You should leave before anyone sees you and it makes things worse. Don't you know? I'm a pariah."

"I don't care," he said.

"I do."

"Ben."

I turned away from him. "Don't," I said.

"Don't what?"

"Don't say my name. Because when you do, I just want to kiss you."

"Ben," Dean said.

I took my shorts off with my back to him, and I pulled my jeans on over my compression shorts. Then I stabbed my feet into my shoes.

"You should go, Dean."

"I don't want to."

"I'm not asking you." I refused to look at him. I'd crumble if I did. "Go home. I don't want you around me. It won't end well."

"Ben. Look at me."

I shook my head. "Go. Forget about everything. Worry about your choir performance, not me. Your reputation's still intact. You should keep it that way."

"Ben, please."

"Leave me alone. It's not worth the risk."

He was silent. I kicked the bench. And when I turned, he was gone.

— CHAPTER 31 —

DEAN

I didn't want to get out of bed. It was the first day of the school break and I should have felt free. Instead, there was a weight on my chest that stifled my energy. I burrowed under the duvet and clenched my eyes against the sting of morning.

"I don't want you around me," Ben had said. Like I was an annoyance, a single warrior at the drawbridge of his fortress, small enough to be swatted away.

It took me over an hour to walk home from school and I let the sleet dampen my face and hair. Car headlights dazzled in my wet glasses as I inched between puddles of softer snow, fresh drifts that muted the grim earth. When I looked behind me, my footprints were disappearing. I made no lasting impression.

I was freezing by the time I got home. I stood under the hot shower in the bathroom and cried. I held my face under the fierce bite of the water for as long as I could. And then I towelled off my skinny body, wiping condensation from the bathroom mirror and hardly recognising the dissolving face that stared at me. My skin was red from the heat.

I crawled into bed and stared at the wall. Mum came to my

door and said dinner was ready, but I told her I didn't feel well.

She sat on the edge of my bed, the back of her fingers judging the temperature at the side of my neck, and she said, "Are you nervous about Friday?"

I nodded and wiped away the tear that dripped over the bridge of my nose, hoping she hadn't seen.

"We'll be right there supporting you," she said. "I'll put your plate in the microwave. You can eat it later." She kissed my temple and closed the door behind her.

This morning, buried under the duvet, I tried not to think about Ben but he was the only thing turning circles in my head.

I had choir practice at twelve o'clock. While all the other kids were still in bed or meeting up with friends, I was pulling on a pair of khakis and a thick sweater and sitting in the passenger seat of Dad's car, waiting for him to drive me to school. When I came downstairs, yesterday's dinner plate was still in the microwave. I emptied it into the food-waste bin and stacked the plate in the dishwasher.

Mum said good luck and Dad said, "Go start the car, I'll be right out."

Before I left, Mum reminded me it was Christmas Eve Eve. I nodded. I couldn't match the energy of her enthusiasm. I'd started Dad's car, flipped on the heaters, and got in the passenger seat.

We said nothing of worth on the way to school. When he pulled in through the open gate, there were only a few cars in the car park. Most of the classroom windows were dark and lifeless.

Dad killed the engine. "Is that the tree?"

"What?"

"Is that the infamous tree?"

"Don't know," I lied. Was that my third time denying it, or my fifth? I'd lost count.

I got out of the car when I saw Gemma Ademola slip into the foyer from a black Audi. I said, "I'll get the bus home."

Dad touched the horn as he pulled away. A gentleman's goodbye.

I went inside. The overhead door heater wasn't on and the foyer was cold. Mr McLaughlin's office door was shut.

Being at school when it's closed felt weird. Empty halls and classrooms. The echo of pipes whose gurgle had been a constant unknown companion for months, now loud enough to interrupt your thoughts.

The sound of my footsteps rattled down the corridor ahead of me.

"We're this way," Mr Elliot's voice said. To my right, they were setting up in the gym. I hoped to God Ben's team wasn't in there.

With fourteen students, one teacher, and an upright piano that had been pushed into the corner under the scoreboard, the gym felt hollow, as though a thief had stolen all the other kids and teachers. We were in an end-of-the-world disaster movie. The only ones alive in an otherwise desolate land.

Mr Elliot clapped his hands. "I know it's a drag being here when you should be enjoying your time off, but I want to thank you all for coming. You're giving up your valuable time ahead of tomorrow night's performance, and for that I'm grateful. After today, we'll meet two hours before the performance at the city hall. Please, whatever you do, don't arrive at school tomorrow. Nobody will be here and you'll be missed from the performance."

Gemma Ademola held out a box of bananas wrapped in red and green ribbons, and a parcel of homemade ginger cookies that she said were to encourage energy and soothe our throats. As Mr Elliot warmed his fingers on the piano, I ate one of the green bananas, finding it difficult to swallow. None of its energy-boosting properties were going to open my lungs today.

Nobody referenced Ben or the viral video. I think Mr Elliot had scared us into silence yesterday, and I was glad of the reprieve.

The gym was huge with nobody else in it. The empty bleachers were pushed back against the wall, and the high ceiling absorbed the notes we sang, allowing their echo to fall back on us.

"All right. *O Holy Night*. From the top. And Dean, remember to breathe," Mr Elliot said from under the scoreboard. We'd assembled on the mid-court line, far enough from him that if he struggled to hear us, we'd know about it.

I dropped my hands to my sides and made fists, hoping the pressure would help me concentrate.

Ben. My parents. Tomorrow night's performance in front of hundreds of people. I forced them out of my head. I needed to focus. The gym was choir space now, not Ben's. Any sweat stains on the polished floor today would belong to us.

Mr Elliot nodded and his fingers glided over the keys.

"Breathe," I said and flushed for saying it out loud.

As the first chords filled the empty gym, the choir ran through the opening verse. And as Mr Elliot's key changed, I opened my mouth to sing.

The notes flowed, every word enunciated, each breath

measured and rehearsed. I could feel Mr Elliot's gaze on me. *O Holy Night* was my sanctuary, and within its embrace, I was worthy.

With every verse, I fed in my emotions—my frustrations and fears—letting them ride on the melody. We were cohesive. We weren't just a collection of students; we were a choir.

I stretched, reached, and hit the high note. I felt the words slide out of my throat like they were meant to be there.

As the final notes faded into the gym's high ceiling, Mr Elliot let his hands fall away from the keys. For a moment, he said nothing, just looked at us, as if gauging our spirits.

"That was excellent, everybody. Dean, you were perfect. If you sing like that tomorrow, you'll have nothing to worry about."

I wish he hadn't said that. We ran through the song again, and this time his words rattled in my head. Excellent. Perfect. Everything I never was.

I fluffed my lines. I missed my entry. And I buried my face in my hands when, in the third verse, my voice bottomed out and croaked. I was fine a minute ago. How can two little words—*excellent; perfect*—mess with my head so much?

And the more I messed up, the angrier I got.

Mr Elliot stopped playing. He shook his head. "It's okay. From the top." He started playing again.

By the fourth rendition, I was sick of it. Ben was back in my head, telling me to leave him alone. And my mum was there, saying Ben needed help. And Dad was asking me about the tree. And my grandmother was saying all sorts of homophobic things, scratching at the back of my mind like an itch I couldn't reach.

All the choir and Gemma Ademola were laughing at me, but when I looked, she was singing with her eyes closed.

I stopped. The backing vocals continued for a few bars before they stopped too. And then Mr Elliot stepped away from the piano. He waved me over.

I dropped my shoulders and slouched towards him, away from the others.

"What happened?" he asked, his voice quiet.

I shrugged. "Nerves, I guess."

"What've I said about owning your nerves, Dean?"

"I know."

"It's okay to be nervous. That means you care. It's a good thing. But don't let them control you. What's in your head?"

"I'll get it next time," I said.

He leaned closer. "Look at them." I glanced over my shoulder. "Do you know what they say about you when you're not in the room?" I felt the panic rise in my chest as though I was about to hear some confessions. But Mr Elliot said, "Nothing. Do you know what that means? It means they respect you. If they didn't, they'd be fighting over each other to replace you. They believe in you. And I believe in you. Your voice has the power to touch people. It's time to believe in yourself."

I nodded.

Mr Elliot tapped his temple. "Clear your head. Whatever negativity is going on in there, get rid of it. Your voice isn't holding you back, Dean. Your thoughts are. Whatever—or whoever—is getting in your way, you need to let them go. You're better than you think you are, here," he said, touching his heart, "and here." He put a finger to his lips. His gold wedding ring flashed under the overhead lights and I remembered his words to me yesterday, his revelation that he was married to a man. How much of the faculty knew that? How many students? He trusted me with that information. Teachers don't have family photos on their desks, but if they did, would he have a picture of his husband?

Mr Elliot put his hand on my shoulder. "Harmony in music, just like in life, comes when every note, every part of you, is in the right place. Singing is just another form of speaking the truth. You need to be heard. So take those fears and face them. And then open your voice, Dean. Sing."

I returned to the choir.

"One more time," Mr Elliot said as he sat at the piano.

He riffled the keys.

And I sang.

I closed my eyes and let out my voice and my emotions. And with every word, I felt the fetters of my lies and my life unhook from me.

At three p.m. we hugged each other. Mr Elliot ate one of Gemma Ademola's ginger cookies and we heard him humming to himself as he pushed his piano back to the music room.

Outside, it was snowing again. Mum's car was in the car park. I opened the passenger door as she started the engine.

"I thought I was getting the bus."

"I can leave and let you stand at the freezing bus stop if you prefer."

I got into the warmth, dusting fresh snow from my hair.

"How was it?" she asked.

"Good," I smiled.

She looked in the rearview mirror before pulling away from the kerb, but as she pressed her foot on the pedal, I put my hand on her arm.

"Mum?"

She looked at me.

"Can we sit here for a minute?"

She took her foot off the pedal and the engine idled. "What's up?"

I looked at the infamous tree, as Dad had called it. The fairy lights were off and the tree was dead, its branches a crooked filigree against the darkening sky.

"I need to tell you something," I said.

"Okay."

"But you can't get angry."

She shut off the engine. "Why would I get angry?"

I couldn't look at her. I counted the buttons on the stereo and then calculated the aspect ratio of the windscreen. 1.6:1. The dead tree outside was framed by it.

I breathed.

"Sweetheart," she said.

And when she said it, I felt the tears prickle behind my eyes. I said, "I've messed up."

"What do you mean?"

"I'm a failure, Mum." My voice was shattered, pitching against itself. I let the tears out.

"No," she said. She pulled me into her arms. "It's just a performance. Tomorrow night, it'll all be over. You'll do brilliantly."

I cried into her hair.

"Baby," she soothed, stroking my back. She hadn't held me like this since I was a child.

I clung to her.

"What's the matter?" she asked.

I couldn't catch my words. I pulled my arms tighter around her neck and I cried harder than I did the day I found out Granddad was gone.

Mum kissed my head and held me. She made soothing sounds against my ear.

When my sobs subsided, she released me. She cupped my face. "Sweetheart. Why are you like this? This isn't nerves. What's going on?" She ran her thumbs under my eyes to wipe away my tears.

My face was numb. And when my words came out, they weren't coherent.

"The boy. Is me. In the video. I'm him. With Ben."

Mum took my hands in hers. She didn't say anything.

I said, "He hates me. And I don't know what to do."

She pulled me into her arms again. "I'm sure he doesn't hate you, Nee Nee." She hadn't called me Nee Nee since I was a kid when I couldn't say my own name.

"Mum," I said, feeling the pathetic nature of my voice, needing her comfort more than I needed air.

"Shush," she whispered against my skin. "It's okay, Nee Nee. I'm here. You're safe."

I let it out. All my fears and anxieties, all my truths.

And as we sat in the car park on Christmas Eve Eve, my mother held my sorrows in her hands.

CHAPTER 32

BEN

He pushed me against the wall of the changing room, the tiles cold at my back. He slipped his hands under my basketball jersey, and I felt his fingers touching my skin which was slick with perspiration. He pressed his warm lips against my neck, his teeth grazing the flesh. "Kiss me," I whispered, my breath ragged and full of heat.

And then I woke up.

The sheets were damp with emotion.

Leave me alone, I'd told him. And now I couldn't get him out of my head. When I'd turned around in the changing room last night and he was gone, I cursed, sat with heavy anger on the bench, and punched my knuckles against it until they stung. I went home, fury dogging my steps, and when I went inside, Dad was sitting on the couch, staring at the lopsided Christmas tree. The lights weren't switched on. Mum was painting her nails at the kitchen table, a large mug beside her with a reusable straw poking out of it. The sink was full of dishes and her face was uneven. She was drunk. The state of her painted nails told me that, without having to see the red wine in her mug.

I went to my room.

I was done with school until January, but I never wanted to go back. There should have been another scandal by now. There was always something new to detract from the drama of the day before. But I was this season's MVP. Most Vilified Person.

I was sixteen. I could drop out of school and get work, something full-time. Maybe I'd go back to Bates' Cinema and beg for my old job back. I know I'd broken the rules, but I did pay for Dean's ticket later that night. Marty had overreacted.

Everybody was overreacting lately. Even Erin.

But that was my fault, too.

So, on Thursday morning, with no school and nothing to lose, I dug out last year's ugly Christmas sweater, took twenty Euros from the pasta jar in the kitchen—I hadn't expected to find any money in it—and ran to the corner shop. I bought a bottle of sparkling Shloer and a box of dark chocolates, and I stood on Erin's doorstep, looking like a fool.

Her Mum, who'd always insisted I call her Maggie instead of Mrs McNally, laughed when she saw Rudolph's lit-up nose on my sweater, and she hugged me before letting me in.

"I haven't seen you in ages," she said.

"I've been a bit AWOL."

"Don't let it happen again. Erin's in her room. Keep the door open," she called after me as I kicked my shoes off in the hall and went upstairs.

I composed myself outside her door before knocking.

"Go away, Mum."

I said, "It's me."

I couldn't tell if her silence was shock or dismay.

She opened her door. "What do you want?"

"I come bearing gifts."

She looked at the chocolates. "Have you poisoned them?"

"I was going to, but my apology is going to be hard enough to swallow without you choking on these, too."

"Shloer?" she said, taking the chocolates but not the bottle.

I followed her into her room. It was purple and dark. The poster of Freud above her bed depicted him with bright pink hair under a prism of colour. The caption said *Pink Freud*.

I unscrewed the bottle cap and took a swig. "Apparently, kids in Christmas jumpers aren't old enough to buy the hard stuff."

I held the bottle out but she didn't take it.

"Go on then," she said. "Let's get this apology out of the way."

I said, "Hold on, I've got to set the scene." I pushed Rudolph's nose on my sweater and a warbling, tinny version of *Rudolph the Red-Nosed Reindeer* played. The battery was running low and the music was drunk.

"You're not going to rap, are you?"

"Would that make you forgive me quicker? Because I can."

She sat on her bed and tore open the box of chocolates. Why do they have just one piece that's wrapped in foil like it's better than all the others? It's the first one Erin always eats.

"Please don't," she said.

"My name's Ben Hunter and I—" I couldn't think of anything to finish the rap.

Erin said, "And you are a munter."

"Right in the feels."

"You deserve it."

"I know I do. I should have told you about Dean. I'm sorry."

"Why him? Of all the people in all the world, you had to choose the geekiest."

"He's not geeky, he's just smart. Anyway, it's over now."

"Good," she said. She held the chocolates out to me and I took the praline that I knew she didn't like. Heathen.

I sat beside her.

"So you're actually gay, then."

"I told you that last year. I don't know why you didn't believe me."

"Because you're not camp," she said.

I held up my fingers to count. "Wentworth Miller. Zachary Quinto. Neil Patrick Harris."

"Elton John. RuPaul. Alan Carr," she countered.

"Are we just listing out celebrities now or are we making a point?"

"The point is you should have told me. And you absolutely wouldn't suit big hair and spandex."

"Are you annoyed?"

"I'm annoyed that the whole school found out about your first gay kiss before I did."

"Who said it was my first?"

"Oh my God, you whore. How long have you been dating him?"

"We're not dating. That was my first kiss with him, but not my first kiss. But it's over now. Not that it ever really began."

"He's not out, is he?"

"Neither was I—until now."

"Do your mum and dad know about the video yet?"

I fell back onto her bed, forgiven, and pulled one of her pillows into a hug. "They're too out of it to notice I even exist."

"Keep it that way. You don't need the added aggravation."

She put the chocolates aside and lay down beside me. I put my arm around her and I couldn't help thinking that Dean slotted into that space better than she did. But I didn't say that. "I've missed this."

Erin said, "I'm sorry, too. For having a go at Dean about leaving you alone. But I didn't know you two were a thing."

"We weren't."

"Next time you decide to kiss a boy—don't. At least not in public."

"Noted."

She snuggled into me as we spooned. "Is he a good kisser?"

"Yes."

"Better than me?"

"We were ten when we kissed. And I don't think it did anything for either of us."

"Speak for yourself," she said. "I was naming our children and looking at wedding dresses online. And we weren't ten, we were nine."

"And you hated me even then when I said I didn't want to be married."

"Did you know?"

"That I was gay? Maybe not at nine. At least not with words. I guess I think I always knew. I can't explain it."

"I'm sorry," she said.

"What for?"

She turned on the bed to face me, her nose an inch from mine. She said, "You go through life thinking you know somebody. Then you realise it's all a lie."

"I didn't lie," I said.

"That's not what I meant." She stroked my hair, pushing it off my forehead. And then she leaned in to kiss me.

I let her. For a second.

When she pulled back, she said, "That's a page we'll never turn again, isn't it?"

"I didn't know you wanted to turn that page. Not since we were nine."

"You're a piece of shit, Ben Hunter."

"I mean, I am a munter, after all," I said.

She slapped my shoulder, but it was playful, not firm. She turned back into our spoon. "Dean, though?"

"What? He's cute."

"Cute like a novelty mug. You'd put it on your shelf but you wouldn't drink out of it."

"I would."

"Sounds like you already have."

"I might be inexpensive, but I'm not cheap." I remembered the dream that woke me this morning. And I wanted it to come true.

But I'd been forced out of the closet against my will. Before I was ready. And I wouldn't wish that on Dean.

When the sky outside was dark and threatening, she stood with me by her front door as I pulled my shoes on. I heard the electric hum of the fake fire in the living room where her mum was.

"You leaving already?" her mum called.

I'd been there for over five hours already. "Sorry, Maggie, I have to sweep the snow off the lawn."

"Oh, it's the lawn, is it?" She stood in the doorway of the living room as Erin opened the front door for me. Outside, three feet of pavement separated the house from the road. The only lawn around here was the local football pitch. "You ought to call in the groundskeeper or you'll be there all night."

"I would, but we gave him the evening off. And wouldn't you know it, Jeeves is late picking me up. I suppose I'd better walk home instead."

"You can't get the staff these days," Maggie McNally said. She hugged me. "Will we see you on Christmas Day?"

"I live seven houses up. I'm pretty sure you'll see me."

When I got home and shook the sleet off my Rudolph jumper, I pushed his nose, but it didn't play the tune. It looked like Rudolph was finally dead.

My parents were arguing. As if that was something new. One of these days, I'd come home and they'd be making love on the couch. It was gross, but it would have been better than this.

"For Christ's sake, Liam, that's not what I said."

"You just accused me of stealing twenty Euros from the tin."

"Fuck off."

"You fuck off."

I didn't dare interrupt their shouting to tell them I'd taken it. I was full of chocolate and Shloer. I didn't need dinner, so I went to my room. My one good deed for the year was fixing my friendship with Erin. Her kiss was—I didn't know what it was. It was weird. But it was done now. I didn't know if she was trying to prove something to me or to herself, but she'd done it and it meant nothing.

It wasn't even late, but I undressed and got into bed. I was exhausted. I turned on my side to face the wall, watching the blur of car headlights as they splayed across the magnolia paint, streaks of white light that I counted like sheep.

Then I turned onto my back, staring at the stains of the dead stars on the ceiling, a universe that no longer worked. Just like my own.

When I turned again, facing my room, I saw Dean's scarf lying on the floor, the brown and green wool coiled like a snake. I reached out of bed and picked it up. I smelled it.

It was Dean.

His solo performance was tomorrow night. If I went, would it give him away? I couldn't go anywhere without the threat of outing somebody else. I could be in a coffeeshop and whoever was in line behind me would be outed as my boyfriend.

This was my life. Once you're outed by somebody other than yourself, you can't contain it. You are no longer your own person. I belonged to the world now. Wherever I went, gossip followed.

I wrapped his scarf around my face and I looked at the stick-on stars on the ceiling that had no life in them, and I knew how they felt.

I closed my eyes. Just for a second.

And when I opened them, I was disoriented. I heard a noise downstairs. Something had shattered. Was this really going to be my life now? I turned over in bed. I heard the rattle of something metallic and then Dad's quiet swear words.

I waited for Mum's reaction, but it didn't come.

Dean's scarf had slipped to the floor.

Whatever Dad's words were, it sounded like, "Get in, you bastard."

I put my hands over my face and waited. Mum would

yell something and he'd retaliate or leave, slamming the door behind him.

Were the pubs even open? I reached for my phone.

It was four a.m.

Downstairs, Dad said something but I didn't catch it. I heard more rattling.

And then silence.

I listened.

There was nothing.

And nothing is terrifying.

I got out of bed, waiting for my mother's voice or her screams. Anything. But nothing came. I opened the bedroom door and stood at the top of the stairs, my hand on the pommel of the banister, praying for somebody or something to make a sound.

Nothing did.

"Dad?" I whispered. "Mum?"

I crept downstairs. When I was younger, my toes would sink into the pile of the carpet. Now, it was threadbare and my toes were cold.

I stood outside the kitchen. "Dad?"

I opened the door.

He was in front of the oven with his back to me.

"Dad? Where's Mum?"

He didn't turn, didn't react.

"Dad?"

The kitchen was a mess. The ceiling lights were off, but I could see a small turkey sitting in a foil tray on the counter with half-peeled potatoes and carrots around it.

Shards of potato peel had slipped to the floor.

"Dad?"

No reaction.

"Dad," I said, my voice firm, like I was talking to a child.

He turned.

He was wearing his *No. 1 Chef* apron. And his hands were black.

"Christmas dinner," he said.

"It's barely Christmas Eve," I told him.

He nodded.

I switched on the overhead lights, and the black of his hands turned red. The counter was red. His apron was red. The floor at his feet was painted crimson.

"Jesus, Dad, what have you done?"

"Christmas dinner," Dad said.

I saw the knife in his hand. Blood dripped from his fingers.

"What have you done?"

He looked at me.

I couldn't see the wounds. There was too much blood.

I went to him. Turned from him. Gripped his hands. "Mum," I shouted. "Jesus, Mum."

Dad looked at me. His lips quivered. "Christmas dinner."

I turned the tap on. Held his hands under the cold stream. The pressure of the water moved the skin of his wrists. I saw something white. Like bone.

I grabbed a tea towel and wrapped his hands together. Tight.

And Dad looked at me.

I nodded. "It's okay. Sit down. I need to get my phone."

I pushed him into a chair, making sure the tea towel hadn't come loose. And I ran upstairs. I grabbed my phone and called the emergency services number as I pushed my way into my parents' bedroom. Mum was in bed, one arm splayed out from under the duvet. Her alcohol snores were loud.

I shook her.

Shook her again.

"Which service?" a voice on the phone said.

"Ambulance. My dad's cut his wrists."

Mum said, "What's wrong?" Her eyes weren't even open.

"Get up," I told her, and I went downstairs. And Dad had slipped out of the chair onto the worn linoleum.

The tea towel was thick with blood. Mum came in behind me as I spoke to the ambulance service.

"Jesus Christ," she said.

I gave them our address. And then I dropped my phone into his blood on the floor. I pulled my dad's arms together, tightening the tea towel around his wrists. His eyes were closed. I lifted his head onto my knees.

"It's okay," I said. "I'm here."

And Mum said, "My fucking turkey."

CHAPTER 33

DEAN

When I woke on Friday morning, my first thought wasn't of Ben or tonight's performance. It was of my dad's face yesterday when Mum drove me home from school and we sat together at the kitchen table, just as we'd done on Tuesday when they'd seen the video.

Mum made hot chocolate and said, "Dean has something to say."

But I couldn't say it. I'd worn myself out in the car as we'd sat in the car park outside school, staring across at that damn tree.

"It's okay," Mum urged, patting her fingers on my hand.

I couldn't look at Dad. He cleared his throat, waiting.

Mum said, "Go on, love."

There was a basketball in my chest and somebody was inflating it bigger than it should have been.

"What's going on?" Dad asked.

And as he spoke, I slipped my confession in between his words. "I'm gay."

I didn't look at his face, but I could tell from his body language that he'd turned to face Mum. The frog was back in his throat.

Mum whispered, "Say something."

I slouched in the chair, melting into this new hell.

Dad said, "The video?"

I nodded.

"Can we have it taken down? Get it deleted?"

"Forget the video," Mum said. "Say something to your son."

Dad held his hand across the table. I didn't take it at first, but he reached further. I slipped my fingers into his.

He said, "Are you happy?"

I looked at him at last. And my face crumbled. "No," I said. My tears burned my cheeks like acid. I felt them leak onto my shirt.

Dad came around the table and hugged me. He pressed my head against his shoulder and my glasses dug into the bridge of my nose. I struggled to pull them off.

And Mum's hand was on my back. They held me that way for ages.

When he released me, Dad said, "I hope somebody's got me a new shirt for Christmas. This one's covered in snot and tears."

I cried again and Dad put his large hand against my flushed cheek.

"Hey. I'm joking."

"Good," I said, my laughter coming in wet gulps. "Because I only got you a scarf."

I went to bed soon after, and Mum brought dinner to me. My body was drained and as I sat up in bed, taking small bites, she sat on the edge of the mattress and said, "Why did you think you couldn't tell us?"

I shrugged and swallowed. "When you asked me about the video, you said Ben needs help. Like it was wrong."

"God, no. I meant he should be getting help from the school and his friends."

"And you kept asking me about girls."

"I was projecting," she said. "Making assumptions. Most teenage boys are into girls."

"I'm not most teenage boys."

"No," she said, patting my leg. "You're my teenage boy. Leave the plate outside your door when you're finished. I'll bring up a slice of apple pie in a little while."

When I woke on Friday morning, the dinner plate was gone and the slice of pie had cooled on the nightstand beside me.

I put my glasses on and looked at the faded chalk on the board above my desk. Today I could do anything. Even solve the Riemann Hypothesis.

When I went downstairs, everything was different. Mum said, "Good morning," like she always did. And Dad grunted at me from the living room, his customary greeting. But there was a thread between us that wasn't there yesterday.

I ate warm porridge with a dollop of honey in it, and Mum kissed the top of my head like I was six again. She said, "Are you okay?" and it didn't have the same meaning as it did the day before. Today, it meant, "You're still mine. And I love you."

I nodded and said, "Are you?" and she knew what I meant. I'm still yours. And I love you too.

I said, "I have to be at the city hall at five o'clock. Doors open at six-fifteen."

"Parents can't get in early to watch you rehearse?" When I said no, she said, "We'll drop you off and go for coffee. Are you ready for it? What with everything."

"I'll never be ready."

"Don't sell yourself short. Will Ben be there?"

"He's not speaking to me," I said, shovelling more porridge into my mouth to save me from talking.

"Then he's a fool," Mum told me.

But I didn't blame him. He was outed because of our kiss. He'd never want to speak to me again.

We joined Dad in the living room where he'd lit the fire. The crackle and spit of the logs was soothing and the warmth as we sat around the coffee table to play our usual game of Christmas Eve Monopoly was perfect.

"Dad can be the old boot, as usual," Mum said.

"Careful who you're calling an old boot," Dad said, "before I break out the rope and the candlestick from Cluedo and spend the rest of my days in a nice quiet prison cell as a childless and wifeless bachelor."

Youngest played first. As a kid, I understood that it was Mum's way of giving me an advantage. But once the game began, I was given no more perks. Dad was ruthless in his rent collection if somebody landed on one of his squares. And Mum, the banker, who counted fake banknotes with more acuity than I had for numbers, was never tempted to cheat. Or at least she was never caught.

Mum played Christmas carols on her phone, and when *O Holy Night* came on, we sang along. It was pathetic and funny and healthy.

I picked up a Community Chest card and read aloud, "Advance to Go. Collect two hundred." I tapped my top hat across the squares on the board and as I did, I had a flash of

Ben dribbling down the court in one of his games, his cheeks flushed and his smile wide.

I tried to push him out of my head, but he was staring at me.

Mum said, "Where are you going?"

I looked at the board. I'd travelled beyond Go.

"That's cheating," Dad said, and I moved my piece back, letting Ben evaporate from my mind.

Dad won, as he always did. He ran a victory lap around the coffee table like he was playing Duck, Duck, Goose.

Mum said, "I let you win." They were both terrible losers.

When I packed the pieces into the box, I sent a message to Ashley and Tony and asked them to meet me at Grainger's. When I got there, they were already at a table. The coffee shop was packed with last-minute Christmas shoppers resting their feet before moving on to more stores, and I didn't envy anyone who had to traipse across town on Christmas Eve.

"What are you grinning about?" Ashley asked as I joined them. They'd already ordered my coffee.

I gripped the warm cup. "Nothing."

Tony said, "That's definitely a guilty look."

"No, it's not." I lowered my voice. "I came out."

Ashley screamed. "What? At school?"

"No, to my parents."

They hugged me.

When Tony pulled back, grinning, he said, "That's huge. How did it go?"

"Better than expected. I mean, they were shocked, I think, but understanding."

Ashley said, "We should celebrate. Marcee," she called to

her sister who was behind the counter. "More hot chocolate."

"Get in the queue like everyone else," her sister said.

I grinned.

Tony said, "Did your mum already know? Mums always know these things."

"I don't think so. She didn't say. You know what my mum's like, though. But it totally feels like a weight has been lifted."

Ashley took a sip of her drink. "Oh shit, do they know it's you in the video?"

I nodded.

"Poor Ben," Tony said.

We moved on to other topics—Ashley's plans to go to her father's on Christmas afternoon for four days, Tony's plans to binge on Chocolate until Ashley came back—but their eyes would meet mine as we talked and they'd smile, sharing in the warmth.

"What did your parents say?" Tony asked, coming back to it like the question had been bugging him.

"There was a lot of hugging. I thought they'd be angry, but they said they want me to be happy."

"My mum cried when I told her I was aro-ace."

Ashley said, "She was probably happy you were never going to have sex."

Tony looked hurt but he grinned. "Now your parents know you're going to have gay sex."

"Can we change the subject?" I was embarrassed.

Ashley hugged me again. Even they were acting different now. I wasn't the only one who had changed by coming out. Mum and Dad had changed, and my friends—even though they already knew—were also changed because of it. Life is a kaleidoscope of change.

Marcee came over with a fresh round of drinks. "What are we celebrating?" she asked.

Tony said, "Only the biggest confession since Darth Vader said, 'I am your father.'"

Ashley put her hand on my shoulder. "Our little Deano has come out."

"Of the house?"

"Of the closet," I said.

Marcee winked. "Congratulations, I guess."

"Does that mean this round's on you?" Ashley asked her sister.

"No chance. Cough up."

We pooled our change on the table.

When we'd covered the cost of the drinks, Ashley said, "Have you told Ben yet?"

"Why would I?" He didn't want to see me. He'd said as much on Wednesday when I tried to talk to him after his game. Maybe in January, when things had calmed down, we could go back to being friends. But that's not what I wanted. And I don't think I could be in the same class as him, knowing I couldn't touch him or kiss him.

"Why wouldn't you?" Tony said. "This changes everything."

"It changes nothing. I've come out to my parents but I'm not ready to tell anyone at school yet."

"You don't have to. Just tell Ben."

"So he can tell me he doesn't care all over again? No, thanks."

Tony rolled his eyes in that way he does. He said, "Are you really that thick? He was trying to spare your feelings. That much is obvious."

"Why would he do that?"

Ashley said, "He was forced out of the closet. He wasn't going to out you too. Which would happen by association."

"Yeah, but he told me to leave him alone."

"Exactly," they said together. Tony said, "Give me your phone."

"No way."

"Then you text him."

"And say what?"

"Start with hello," Ashley said.

So I did.

CHAPTER 34

BEN

White sunlight smacked me in the face and I squinted against the glare. The large window that overlooked the hospital car park faced east and the sun had burned through the clouds enough to dazzle the frost on the outside of the window. My back was sore from sitting in a hard plastic chair for six hours. I couldn't remember falling asleep but I knew I had. My dreams were dark and full of blood.

When the ambulance arrived, during the night, Dad was strapped into a stretcher. "Has he taken anything?" the paramedic asked me.

"I don't know. Probably just booze," I said. "Is he going to be all right?"

"There's room for one of you in the ambulance," he said, looking between me and Mum. She'd pulled some clothes on before they arrived, but now her sleeves were covered in blood from where she'd been trying to clean up.

"I don't want them seeing a mess," she'd said. The slip in her voice told me she was still drunk, even though her step was sober.

Mum said, "Ben, go with him. I'll drive and meet you

there."

"You're in no state to drive," I said.

The paramedic said, "It's now or never."

"I'll stay with Mum. We'll get a taxi. Which hospital?"

"Mercy," the paramedic said. He slammed the rear door of the ambulance shut.

By the time we got to the hospital, Mum had convinced herself that Dad was dead. A nurse told her to calm down, which made her worse. Eventually, they gave her something to settle her nerves. A drink would have done the trick quicker.

For two hours she paced the waiting area. The TV on the wall was tuned to a news channel but the sound was off and music from a local radio station filled the space, the DJ's voice melodic between tracks, the advertising jingles nonsensical.

There was a drunk man in the corner, holding a wad of gauze over his eye and he was shouting at anyone who went near him. I hoped Mum was paying attention.

A kid and his mother sat along the far wall. He had his arm propped on a pillow and it was twisted at an unnatural angle. I wondered what he'd been doing at four in the morning to break it.

"Sit down," I told Mum. "You'll wear a hole in the floor." I pulled up a quiz on my phone. I hadn't put it on charge last night and my battery was on thirty-four percent. "What's the smallest planet in our solar system?" I asked her.

"I know that one," Mum said as she slumped into the seat beside me. "Mercury. You were mad about space when you were little. Your dad helped you put that glow-in-the-dark universe on your ceiling."

"They don't glow anymore," I said. She looked sad, so I

asked the next question on the list. "Which small people make up the largest population on earth?"

"Small people? Like pygmies?"

I shook my head. "Think smaller."

"What's smaller than a pygmy?"

"Lego figures," I said. "There are more Lego mini-figures in existence than there are people in China."

An ambulance crew came through with a man on a gurney. The man groaned, his face soaked with sweat or rain.

"Male, late 30s, gunshot to the abdomen," a paramedic said. "BP's dropping. He's on IV but he's drifting."

"Prep for laparotomy," a doctor in a white coat said.

How does somebody get shot in Ireland? You can't pick up a handgun from Dunnes Stores.

Mum covered her mouth with her hand. "That poor man."

"Mrs Hunter?" a nurse said. We turned to her. "Your husband's being prepped for surgery. You can come with me to the family room."

The family room was just another waiting area, but it was quieter, and away from the busy Accident & Emergency room. But the chairs were just as uncomfortable.

I sent a message to Erin, telling her my dad had gone batshit crazy and tried to top himself, and she said she'd say a prayer for everyone.

When the sunlight woke me in the morning, Mum was still asleep in her chair. I'd taken my coat off and draped it over her. I left her there and walked down the corridor to the nurses' station, stretching a kink out of my neck.

"Can you tell me what's happening with Liam Hunter, please?"

The nurse tapped on her computer. "Are you the next of kin?"

"I'm his son."

"Where's your mum, sweetheart?"

"Family room," I pointed.

"They haven't updated his notes yet, but I'm sure he's fine."

"He can't still be in surgery, can he? I thought they'd just stitch him up and let him go."

"I'm sorry, son. When his doctor's available, I'll send him down to talk to your mum, okay?"

I walked away from her. What use was it being somebody's son if they weren't going to tell you anything?

On my way back to the family room, my phone vibrated in my pocket. It was Dean.

> **dean_odd_donnell**
> Hello. I'm probably the last person you
> want to hear from, but I just wanted
> to see how you're doing. I'm sorry for
> everything. The video I mean. Not the
> kiss. I'll never be sorry for that. Anyway.
> I've kind of told my parents I'm gay. So
> there's that. I just... I miss talking to
> you. So anyway. Merry Christmas. Dean
> x

I smiled. I didn't want to, but I couldn't help it. I sank into a chair in the family room, opposite my mum, and I replied to him.

> **benhuntss07**
> You told them? How was that?

344

dean_odd_donnell
I didn't think you'd reply. Figured you'd
hate me. And I guess it went ok. Better
than I'd hoped.

benhuntss07
I don't hate you. I just have shit going
on. I'm glad you felt ready to tell them.
At least it went well.

dean_odd_donnell
I'm at Grainger's with Ashley and Tony
but we can meet up? Not for kissing
(lol) but just to say hi?

I looked at Mum. She was still sleeping. If she woke now she'd probably have a grumpy head on.

benhuntss07
Can I call?

It took a minute before he replied.

dean_odd_donnell
I'll go outside. Just give me a sec.

I stepped out of the family room and went down the corridor. I pressed the call button on the lift and then the call button on my phone.

It rang. Once.

"Hi."

Dean's voice was high and light. I heard the sound of traffic around him and the wind against the mic.

"Hey."

"Are you okay?"

I didn't know what to say. "I guess." Then I said, "I'm sorry for, you know, telling you to leave me alone."

"It's okay."

"It's far from okay. Tell me about your parents. What happened?"

I heard him take a breath. Then he said, "I just couldn't keep it in any longer."

"And they're fine with it?"

"I mean, they seem to be. They know about the video."

"About me?" I pushed the call button on the lift again. When the doors opened, I got inside. A woman and a kid were in it.

"What floor?" she asked.

"Ground, please." Then I said to Dean, "Hold on, I'm in a lift. I might lose you."

"Don't lose me," he said.

When I got to the ground floor, I went outside. "You still there?"

"Yeah."

"So they know about the video?" It was cold outside, the wind cutting into me like a razor. My coat was upstairs, draped over Mum. "Do they hate me?"

"Of course not," Dean said. "If anything, they hate that it's such a big deal at school. Because it shouldn't be." I had no answer to that. Then he said, "Where are you? I'm pretty sure you don't have a lift at home and school is closed."

I turned my back to the wind. "I'm at Mercy."

"The church or the hospital?"

"Hospital."

"Shit. Why? What happened?"

I turned into the wind again, letting it eat my face. The harsh punch of it brought tears to my eyes. "My dad had an accident. He hurt himself."

"Is he okay?" Dean asked.

"Not really. But he will be."

"Are you okay?"

I brushed the tears from my eyes with the back of my hand.

"Not really. But I will be."

Dean said, "I'll come over."

"No. Don't. It's okay."

"Ben, you can't be alone."

"I'm not alone. Mum's here. It's boring. We're just waiting around for news."

"How long have you been there?"

"Since, like, four a.m."

"Jesus."

"Yeah." I went around the side of the building where it was quieter, away from the harsh wind. I walked under the sky-bridge that connected one building to another, and I stood at the wall that overlooked the curve of the River Lee. The stone buildings along the river's edge looked ancient and crumbling. There was a discarded shopping trolley in the water.

Dean said, "I'm coming."

"Dean, please."

"You can say no, but I'm still coming."

I smiled. The crosswind took my voice from me. "Okay."

"I'll text you when I'm there," he said.

I ended the call and looked at the brown water of the river.

It was shallow and uninviting. When I got back upstairs, Mum was still asleep. My coat had slipped from her onto the floor and I picked it up, draping it over her.

She roused and opened her eyes. "Where is he?"

"He's been in surgery," I said. "Stitching his wrists up. He's okay."

"Can we see him?"

"We're just waiting to hear from his doctor. Are you okay?"

She smacked her lips. "I'm parched."

"I'll get you some water."

She gripped my hand. "See if they have something stronger."

"Mum. You need to stop now."

"Stop what?"

I sat in the chair beside her, keeping her hand in mine. I stroked it, meeting her gaze. "You drink because Dad's angry all the time. Or he's angry because you drink. I don't know. But it has to stop."

"What are you saying, Ben?"

There was nobody else in the room now. I said, "I'm saying you have a problem. But it's okay. We can fix it."

"I don't have a problem."

She tried to pull her hand away from me, but I gripped it harder. I said, "Do you remember back in July, before I went back to school, when you bought my school blazer?"

"What about it?"

"You didn't get the Clannloch crest. Remember?"

"Of course I did."

"Mum. You got Carmichael Academy. I had to take it back the next day and change it."

"Don't be stupid," she said. "I'd know if I got the wrong

348

blazer."

"Would you? You'd been in the pub most of the day."

"What are you saying?" she asked again.

I was getting nowhere. Accusing her wasn't working. So instead, I said, "When's the last time we did something fun together? Just you and me."

She thought about it. "We baked a cake."

"When?"

"Recently. For your father's birthday."

"Mum, it's Christmas Eve. Dad's birthday was March."

She said, "We don't have to do fun things every day."

"No, but more than once a year would be nice, right?"

She closed her eyes. "Things change."

"I know they do. But they don't have to change this much. We're miserable. You still have time to be that mum again— the one who doesn't mix up school crests, who was there for all the important stuff."

"I'm there for your important stuff, Ben."

"You haven't been here for months. Dad knows it too, and he's in there fighting for his life. We should all be fighting, Mum. Together." I let that sink in before I added, "It starts with little things."

She said, "I don't have a problem with drink."

I said, "Mum."

She looked away from me. "It's not like I need it to get through the day."

"Mum."

She looked at me and I saw the woman I used to know. "It's not like that," she said. Then she added, "I like a drink. And your dad doesn't help."

"It's not too late to change."

She squeezed my hand. "Maybe," she said, and in that word, I heard the possibility.

I heard the future.

"I'll get you that water," I said. I kissed her cheek. "I'll be right back."

As I walked down the corridor in search of a water cooler, I yawned. My feet scraped the floor. I looked at the people sitting in the corridor. Old men with their grey chests covered in ECG pads. Little girls with broken limbs and kidney-shaped sick bowls.

The boy from the A&E waiting area with a broken arm sat with his mother. His arm was set and cast in plaster. He waved at me as I passed.

I found a cooler and poured some water into a paper cup.

I didn't know if I could go on any longer without screaming. My world was broken.

And I didn't know what could fix it.

— CHAPTER 35 —

DEAN

I got off the bus outside the hospital and pulled the scarf tight around my neck against the chill of Christmas Eve. It was almost one o'clock and I had to be at the city hall in four hours. I looked up at the stark building and felt sorry for anyone who was trapped here at this time of year.

I sent a text to Ben, letting him know I was here, and I stood in the foyer waiting for him. I hated that astringent smell that hospitals have, even in the non-clinical areas. An old man coughed. A couple of passing nurses laughed. A large lift clattered open and a porter wheeled an empty bed out of it and down a rear corridor.

The admissions desk had a queue of people and the signs on the walls pointed to A&E, obstetrics, oncology, and outpatient services. I wasn't sure if Ben's dad would still be in the emergency department or if he'd been moved to a ward already.

I checked my phone. Ben hadn't replied. I sent him another message. He was probably just busy with his mum or finding out about his dad's condition.

I stood in the admissions queue and when I got to the window, I said, "I'm looking for Mr Hunter. He was admitted last night."

"What's the first name?" the girl asked, tapping on her computer.

"I'm not sure. It's my friend's dad."

She looked at me. "I'm sorry, I can't give out patient details to anyone who's not family. Is your friend in the building?"

"He'll be with his mum and dad. But I think his phone's dead." I showed her the unread messages on my phone. Like she'd care.

"I'm sorry. It's policy."

"Please, Miss," I said, pushing my glasses up my nose in an innocent childlike way that I'd perfected years before. It had earned me a bike for my seventh birthday from my parents. "I'm just trying to find my best friend."

I thought I'd laid it on too thick when she hesitated. But she said, "You could check the waiting rooms, down the hall or on the second floor. If he's not in either of those, I'm afraid you're on your own."

"Thank you, you're a lifesaver." I ran down the hall in the direction she'd indicated. A&E's waiting room was packed and there was blood on the floor that a porter was mopping up. "Ben?" I shouted, looking at the pale faces of the people in the room. "Ben?"

He wasn't there. I took the stairs to the second floor, went past a couple of closed doors, and saw a sign for the Family Room. I pushed through the door. There was a young man in the corner with a toddler asleep in his arms, but nobody else was there.

As I turned to leave, pushing the call button on my phone and listening as Ben's phone went straight to voicemail, I saw a coat on the floor between two chairs and picked it up. It was Ben's. I held it up and said to the man, "Do you know where my friend went?"

The guy shrugged. "A doctor called them to the ward about twenty minutes ago."

I ran into the ward and looked through the glass panels on closed doors. Old men in beds, a young boy with a broken arm sitting with his mum in the corridor.

I said, "Have you seen a boy about my age? This tall?"

He pointed with his good hand.

I ran, checking rooms. A nurse came out of room 212 and I tried not to make it look obvious that I was lost. Before the door closed behind her, I saw Ben inside.

"Ben."

He looked. Smiled. There was a sleeping man in the bed and a woman sitting at the other side. She was Ben's mum, I knew; they shared a face, even if hers was gaunt and sagging.

Ben stood up and I jammed myself in the doorway. I held up his coat. "You left this in the waiting room."

He came to me. "Hi."

It was awkward. "Sorry," I said. "I sent you a text but you didn't reply."

He checked his phone. "It's dead."

I felt his mum staring at me.

"Sorry. I should have waited downstairs."

Ben pointed to the corridor and I gave him his jacket. He pulled it on as he stepped out of the room. When the door closed behind him, he stared at the floor.

"How is he?"

He shrugged.

"I tried calling you."

Ben said, "It's okay."

"Are you all right?"

He looked at me. And I could tell by his face that he wasn't. I came forward and wrapped my arms around him. I had to stand on my toes to reach him. He was stiff, ungiving, but the longer I held him, the softer he got. I felt his hands on my back.

"Are you all right?" I said again.

He nodded against the side of my face.

"Do you want to go grab a coffee? Or lunch?"

"I didn't bring any money," Ben said.

"I'm buying."

"You don't have to do that."

"Shush. I'm buying."

We went to the ground floor and found the café. We sat at a square table with our coffees and a couple of brownies, and I asked him again how he was doing. I didn't know what else to say.

He said, "They stitched him up, but they're keeping him in for tests."

"What happened?"

Ben turned the cup a full rotation on its saucer before answering. "He said he was making Christmas dinner. In the middle of the night. On the wrong night. But he cut himself." He lowered his voice. "His wrists."

"Shit."

"Both of them," Ben said.

"Shit."

He didn't look at me. He pushed the plate with his brownie away from him and pulled his coffee cup closer.

I said, "Is he going to be okay?"

"He lost a lot of blood but I think, physically, he'll be all right. He'll have scars. They're saying maybe it's depression. Or bipolar. I don't know. They're doing evaluations and they want to interview me and Mum."

"How's she doing?"

He put his head back, blinking at the ceiling. "She's sober. For the first time in God knows how long."

"Shit," I said.

He laughed. "You're beginning to sound like a broken record."

"Sorry."

He looked at me. "Don't be. I'm glad you came."

I shrugged like it was no big deal. "I love coming to visit the boys I kiss while they're in hospital. Gives me the warm fuzzies."

He looked at the tables either side of us, then said, "Boys?"

"Okay, fine. Boy. Singular."

"And you, a mathematician. I thought you could count."

"Hey, we're not in school anymore. I took off my maths cap yesterday."

He leaned forward, putting his elbows on the table. "I can't believe you told your parents. About the thing."

"The video? Tony's mum sent it to mine. I guess everybody's seen it. I denied it at first. I shouldn't have but I did. I told them the truth yesterday after choir practice."

"And they're really okay with it?"

"They seem to be. Apart from the initial shock. I feel better for telling them. But your shit is bigger than mine."

"Don't lessen the importance of your coming out, Dean. It's

355

a huge deal."

"I should have done it years ago."

"Oh, man, what time is it?" he said. "You have your show today."

"It starts at seven, but we're not the first school to go on stage. I'm supposed to be there for final rehearsals at five."

Ben tapped the screen of his phone to check the time but it didn't light up.

I put my phone into battery-sharing mode and sat his phone on top.

"You should be getting ready for your performance. Do you have to wear one of those silly robes with the big ruffles at the neck?"

"Just our school uniform," I said, and I saw the disappointment on his face. "I've got some time before I have to go."

It was weird, sitting with him again after the week we'd had. Never mind what he'd had going on at home. I wanted to reach across the table to take his hand, but I didn't dare.

He yawned without covering his mouth and when he was done, I said, "Dude, you nearly swallowed me whole."

He laughed, harder than he needed to. I guess that's what exhaustion does to you.

"Do you want another coffee?" I asked.

He pushed his empty cup away. "No, thanks. I should get back to my dad soon. I don't want to leave Mum alone for too long. She'd drink surgical spirits if she thought there was alcohol in it."

"Is she really that bad?"

He shrugged. "She said she'd go sober, but I'll believe it when I see it. When she's clean for a year, I'll still be worried."

I didn't know what to say to that. I'd be worried too. Instead, I said, "Is there anything I can do to help?"

He shook his head, then took a bite of his brownie. "Actually, yeah. There is."

"What?"

"You can help me find some mistletoe."

"What for?"

"Maybe it's time we had our second first kiss. If you want to."

I grinned. "Yeah?"

"Yeah."

I stood up and held my hand out. "What are we waiting for?"

Ben looked at me, hesitation toying at his limbs. And then he took my hand.

We ran out of the café, through the lobby where a giant Christmas tree hulked in the corner. There was tinsel and a string of Christmas cards on the wall. Ben circled the tree before taking off in the opposite direction. I followed him. He was fast. And I was half his size. He sidestepped an elderly man, yelled an apology as he went, and by the time I'd caught up with him, he was at the lifts, pushing the call button repeatedly.

"We'll check upstairs."

"Is the mistletoe absolutely essential?" I asked.

He nodded and I didn't argue. We rode the lift upstairs, standing against opposite walls, quiet and staring at each other. I steadied my breathing, laughed when he winked at me, and I felt the lift bounce to a halt. When it stopped on the next floor, Ben stood in front of the door, waiting for it to open.

He ran, turned, walking backwards as he looked at me. "Keep up," he said.

"Slow down," I told him.

"Mistletoe," he said at the nurses' station.

"What?"

"Have you got any mistletoe?"

The redheaded nurse squinted. "Are you supposed to be on this floor?"

Ben nudged me back the way we'd come. He pushed through the door to the stairwell and went down them two at a time.

"Where are we going?" I shouted.

"Downstairs."

"We've already been down there."

"Hurry up," he told me. I chased after him.

In the lobby, he took my hand and dragged me outside. I waved at the girl behind the admissions window as we went.

The snow on the pavements had turned to slush. A bus breezed by. The town's Christmas lights were lit up but faint against the afternoon glare.

"Where are we going?"

Ben looked both ways. He was still holding my hand. We went in one direction, then doubled back the way we'd come.

"Ben, we're not going to find any mistletoe on the street."

But he pointed. He dragged me to the bus stop. On the side of it, an advertising board was lit up from behind as it rotated through two different ads.

Ben said, "Look."

As the second ad came up from the bottom of the roller, I saw it. A photo of Santa drinking a Coke. There was mistletoe above the slogan.

I laughed.

Ben said, "It'll do?"

I nodded. "It'll do."

He pushed me against the glowing advertisement.

And he kissed me.

CHAPTER 36

BEN

We sat at the bus stop, holding hands. His fingers were warm as they laced between mine, and he squeezed. He leaned his head against my shoulder. We were at ease, for the first time since that damn video circulated. And even though my dad was lying in a hospital bed upstairs in what looked like an accident but felt premeditated, there was a smile at the back of my throat that threatened to reveal itself if only I would let it. Mum was half-sober for once. And Dad was in the best place he could be. He'd get help here. We all would.

Dean sighed.

"What's up?" I asked.

"Nothing. I just—I have to go soon."

"Don't go," I said.

"You'd let me suffer Mr Elliot's wrath if I don't turn up at the city hall?"

"I'll protect you."

"Against an army of choirboys? They'd defeat you with their a cappella artillery."

He walked me back to the hospital entrance, and when we stood in the foyer among the bustling crowd of pre-Christmas outpatients, I pulled him into a hug and held him. He slipped his arms around my waist and pressed his cheek to my chest. "I'm sorry," I said.

"What for?"

"For telling you to leave me alone. For kissing you at school."

"You were trying to protect me. And never apologise for kissing me."

"Never?"

He looked up at me and I kissed him again.

"Will your dad be all right?" he asked.

I nodded. I didn't want to say it out loud and jinx it. "I'd be at your performance if I could. You know that, right?"

"I know. But my mum will probably record it so you'll still get to see me making a fool of myself."

"Hey. Glow up, don't throw up."

"Yes, boss."

"Merry Christmas," I said. He offered to swing by the hospital on Christmas Day, just for a visit, but I told him I wasn't sure when Dad would be getting out. I know they were running a psych evaluation, but I had no idea how long that would take. He offered to buy me a charging cable for my phone but I said, "I'll ask at the nurses' station. Someone will charge it for me. Good luck tonight. Knock 'em dead."

We hugged again and I watched him walk back to the bus stop across the street.

"Who was he?" Mum said from behind me. When I turned, she looked haggard and dishevelled. She had an unlit cigarette in her mouth and her hair was pulled back into a tight tail, her roots showing.

I followed her outside and waited as she lit the cigarette.

She breathed thick grey smoke into the air and then coughed.

"How's Dad?"

"Still asleep. Who was the boy?"

I puffed up my chest. "His name is Dean. And he's my boyfriend."

When she finished her cigarette, she lit another one. Then she said, "We should go into the little chapel and say a prayer to Our Lady of Knock. For your father." She stubbed the half-smoked cigarette against the grill on the wall.

The non-denominational chapel was small and warm. There was a wooden Cross on a table at the head of the room which faced four rows of chairs. It was empty. Mum genuflect-ed, like she knew what she was doing, and then sat. I took the chair beside her, linking my hands together as though I was in prayer.

I knew neither of us were.

There were no other religious artefacts or statues, no candles or bibles. I closed my eyes because, despite my inability to feel anything akin to spiritual bliss, the room was calming. The underlying hum of an invisible heater perpetuated the chapel's soothing qualities, like the hush of a womb.

"Mum?"

"Shush," she said. And then she made a sign of the Cross. She kept her eyes on the little altar at the head of the chapel. Her silence was making me nervous. She rubbed her jeans with the palms of her hands. "They'll be wanting to talk to us soon. The doctors."

"What will you tell them?"

She shook her head. "I have no idea."

"The truth," I encouraged.

"I guess."

"Mum?"

"Not now, Ben. One thing at a time."

"It has to be now, Mum."

"Why does it have to be now?"

I shuffled in my seat to face her. "Because I just told you Dean was my boyfriend and you haven't said anything yet."

"I don't know what you want me to say."

"The truth," I said again. "Are you angry?"

"I'm hurting. But not because of you. And I—" she lowered her voice. "I want a fucking drink. Is that bad?"

"Yes," I said. I couldn't answer any other way.

We were silent for a minute. I turned back to the Cross on the table. Mum patted my thigh and then removed her hand. She said, "I always pictured myself with grandchildren. A whole brood of them. And you'd come round at Easter and Christmas for dinner like a proper family. And you'd drop them off on a Friday night for Grandma to babysit them while you went out on the town with your wife." I didn't interrupt her. "And your dad, he'd spoil them rotten. You know he would. Before—this. He'd buy them sweets and slip them ten Euros when he thought nobody was looking. Maybe grandkids would help to heal him."

"You can still have grandchildren. Being gay doesn't stop that."

"It makes it harder, though," she said.

"Not these days. There's surrogacy or adoption. I'm not ruling kids out of my future. But I'm sixteen. It's too soon to be thinking about children."

She stood up. "Let's get back to your father before the

doctors think we've run off."

"Mum. Is that all you have to say? 'What about grandkids'?"

She turned from me. "Are you looking for my blessing?"

"I don't need your blessing. I just want to know that you're okay with it."

"Jesus, I need a drink," she said.

"Dammit, Mum."

When she turned back to me, her eyelashes were wet and her sallow cheeks were flushed. "I knew you were gay from the time you were six. Maybe I've always known."

"How?"

She shrugged. "How does any mother know anything? I just did. I saw it in your face. I saw it every time I dropped you off at primary school and you chased around with the boys on the playground. It was in your smile when you talked about your friends and in your hips when you danced in front of the TV."

"I never did that."

She laughed. The tears had spilled onto her cheeks. "You always did that. Don't you remember? I'd put on MTV 90s and we'd dance around the living room like lunatics."

"When?"

"When you were three or four."

"I don't remember."

"I'll never forget. So when you ask me if I'm angry, the answer is yes. I'm angry at a world that made you feel the need to hide who you are. One that made me question the sexuality of my four-year-old. I'm angry that I want grandchildren and I'm furious that I want a drink, more than I've ever wanted anything in my life."

I hugged her. She was so thin that I could feel her spine beneath my hands. Her body was trembling as she clung to me in a tiny hospital chapel. I let her cry.

And when she was done, I said, "Thank you."

"For what?"

"For your blessing."

We went back to Dad's room, riding the lift in silence, and as we walked down the corridor, I took her hand and she leaned into me.

Dad was still asleep. We sat at his side and I stared at the bandages on his wrists. I don't think he'd ever tried to hurt himself before. But his wounds were not accidental.

When a woman in a trouser suit came in, she said she was a psychiatric liaison nurse and would like to speak to us individually. She took me to a small office and we sat in chairs, facing each other over a narrow coffee table. She asked me about my dad's mental state in the run-up to the incident and about his relationship with myself and Mum. I told her what I could without dropping the blame at anyone's feet. I only hoped Mum would tell her the truth when she came to sit here.

When the nurse was finished with me and called Mum in, I went to the top floor and walked through the corridors, winding my way back downstairs. I passed sick kids and old people. I couldn't get into the maternity ward to see the little babies, and at the end of the corridor an old man in a tartan dressing gown got out of the lift with a drip on a pole attached to the back of his hand. He slapped his forehead and got back in the lift.

On the first floor, there was a small room with its door open. A circle of chairs ringed the centre of the floor and a sign on the wall listed times throughout the week for AA and NA meetings.

There was one at five o'clock.

When we were back at Dad's side, I said, "What did you tell the nurse?"

Her leg was jittering with nerves or alcohol withdrawals. "Enough," she said.

"I found an AA meeting," I told her. "Downstairs."

She shook her head. "I don't have time."

"All we have is time."

"Leave it, Ben."

I pulled my chair closer to the bed and leaned against it. I was forcing myself into her line of sight. "It's right downstairs. You don't even have to leave the building."

"I can't afford it."

"It's free."

"Leave it, Ben."

"How bad do you want a drink right now?"

Her leg was getting more agitated. "I'll find a meeting closer to home. Your dad could wake up any minute."

"He's not going anywhere."

"Ben."

"Mum. None of this is your fault. They can help. Let them."

"Look at me, I'm a mess. My hair. My makeup."

"They won't care."

She looked at my dad, and then the door.

"If you don't do it now, you never will," I said.

She nodded. I took her downstairs and showed her to the room. It was almost five. There were people inside, cupcakes on a table, and the smell of weak coffee and strong tea. She turned away from the door and I put my hand on her back.

I said, "Do you want me to come in with you?"

"Wait here," she said. And she went inside.

I sat on a chair further down the corridor and waited. I expected her to come out in less than five minutes, leave the hospital and go straight to a bar. But she didn't.

The short charge that Dean's phone had provided me was back down to two percent. He'd be at the city hall by now. I sent him a message. *Good luck, Pavarotti.*

I didn't expect a reply. He'd be too busy panicking about his performance. And then my phone died. I walked down to the nurses' station and asked if they wouldn't mind charging it for me while my mum was in AA and my dad was getting a psych eval. Yeah—I used my situation to my advantage. Sometimes you have to.

I went back to my seat before Mum came out of her meeting and when she did, her hair was untied, falling over her face as she kept her head low. It was after six o'clock. She sat beside me without a word. The others who left the room didn't acknowledge each other as they went.

When we were alone, Mum held her hand out to me. It was balled in a fist. I thought she wanted a fist-bump, but she dropped something into my hand. It was a white token. *To Thine Own Self Be True*, it read. There was a circle with a triangle inside, and it said, *One Day.*

Had she been sober for twenty-four hours? Near enough. I wasn't going to argue.

"Congratulations," I said.

"Don't. I don't feel like I'm in recovery. I'm not worthy of that chip. That's why I'm giving it to you."

"But you earned it."

"Hold on to it. Give it back to me when I deserve it."

"You deserve it now. You went to your first meeting. That's a massive step."

I could tell she'd been crying. She said, "I sat in a circle and told them my name. But I still want a drink." She looked at me. "I'm going to try. Honest to God I am. But I'm telling you, Ben, when I fail it will be my own fault. Not yours or your father's. I'm going to fall off the wagon. I know I am. And you're going to be disappointed when I do. That's what I deserve. Your disappointment."

"I'm going to help you," I said. "And we're both going to help Dad with whatever he's got going on. Okay? Like a family."

Her smile was brief. I held the chip out to her but she closed my fingers over it. "Give it back to me later. You should go and see your fella. What was his name?"

"Dean. And he's got a performance tonight at the city hall."

"Doing what?"

"Singing."

She smiled. "Then go and dance for him the way we used to dance."

"I can't leave you."

"I'm hardly going to find alcohol in a hospital, Benny. Go. Come back here when you're done. I promise I'll still be sober when you get back. I can give you that much."

I pulled her into a hug. And then I picked up my phone from the nurses' station, went downstairs and into the night.

— CHAPTER 37 —

DEAN

I couldn't do it. I had to walk inside that squat grey building, get on stage, and open my mouth, but I was having issues making my feet work. Ben wasn't with me. And my parents had just dropped me off. Ashley and Tony sent me a message in the group chat earlier, telling me to break a leg. They had seats in row F, they said, and I'd probably be able to hear them cheering when I went on stage.

That just made it worse.

I didn't know how many seats the hall had, or how many would be occupied, but even if the room was empty, I didn't think I'd be able to sing.

It was raining and the snow was melting into pockmarked slush. The Christmas tree outside City Hall was over thirty feet tall, with baubles bigger than my face and lights that bled into the needles. Behind it, the sign above the entrance said, *Carols for Cork: Festive Favourites from the Schools Symphony.*

I saw kids in a multitude of school uniforms dashing around the side of the building and I followed them, dragging my feet on the wet pavement. The rain on my glasses turned the headlights of passing cars into shooting stars. I had the hood of my coat up, but my fringe was wet and stuck to my forehead.

The kids ahead of me ducked in through a door where a teacher or somebody was directing them. I stood on the path.

"You with the choirs?" the man asked me.

"Clannloch," I said.

"Are you coming in or are you going to sing for your supper on the street?"

My phone vibrated. I pulled it out, shielding it from the rain.

benhuntss07
Good luck, Pavarotti.

"Well?" the man in the doorway said.

I went inside, shaking rainwater off my coat and nerves off my skin.

I followed the other kids into a large open space where more than two hundred people from twelve different schools were grouped together in a storm of uniform colours. Gemma Ademola waved me over to our little ragtag band of outlaws and Mr Elliot was going over the setlist. Again. We'd been over it so often I could have made a mnemonic out of the titles.

We harmonised, ran through the scales two dozen times, and Mr Elliot had us shaking our limbs and running on the spot to wake our bodies. We were shown onto the stage and given ten minutes for sound checks. Mics dangled from the rigging above our heads and the empty auditorium was huge and cavernous. Mr Elliot told me where to stand for my solo—a spotlight marked the floor like a halo, and then we ran over some more scales before a technician ushered us off the stage for the next school's sound checks.

We would be the sixth school to go on, which was better than being first or last.

Mr Elliot took me aside. "Are you good?"

"Nervous."

"Don't look so panicked. You know what you're doing up there."

"But there'll be so many people. What if I mess up?"

"You won't. And once that spotlight is on you, you'll not even see the audience. Just pretend they're not there."

"Aren't you supposed to tell me to imagine them in their underwear?"

"I'm your teacher. How inappropriate would that be?"

I sat on the edge of a stack of tables and listened to the other schools rehearsing. A group of school kids that looked like they were eight weaved through the crowd as they played tag or kiss chase.

"I thought this was a secondary school performance," I said.

"It is. They're first years from St Finbar's Academy," somebody said.

"Are first years getting smaller or did we look so tiny back then too?"

"I think St Finbar's is letting hobbits in this year."

I sent a message to Ben, saying I hoped his dad was getting better already, and when Mr Elliot saw me with it, he reminded us all to turn our phones off.

We heard the audience taking their seats before the show and, at seven o'clock, we huddled up like Ben and his teammates in a time-out, and Mr Elliot said, "This is your moment. It all comes down to this. You've practised hard and you know you're amazing. When we go out there, we're going to show those other schools what Clannloch is made of, right? And listen, if you hit a bum note, you'll have Christmas Day detention." He grinned. "I'm kidding. We're a team, right? And teams carry each other. Your voices work because you all work together. Clannloch on three?"

He stuck his hand out. We stared at him like he was insane. We weren't a sports team about to destroy our rivals. We were a dozen teenagers about to sing Christmas carols.

"Don't leave me hanging," he said.

We piled our hands on and when he counted to three we said, "Clannloch."

Mr Elliot said, "You'd better be going on stage with more enthusiasm than that. Try again."

We didn't get a chance. The first school was going on and we rushed to the wings to watch.

The curtains lifted and St Peter's Boys School opened with a rap version of *God Rest Ye Merry Gentlemen*. By their third song, a modern twist on *Joy to the World*, their vocals were sounding lazy and cold.

From my vantage point, I looked at the audience. It was too dark to see anyone, but I counted back six rows to see if I could spot the silhouettes of Ashley and Tony. My parents would be somewhere in the third row.

The applause that followed St Peter's choir off the stage was enough to make me realise how many people there were in the audience.

When the third school had gone on, we went back to the waiting room for a last-minute practice. "They're good," one of the girls said.

Mr Elliot said, "It's not a competition, it's a recital."

"If it was, we'd win," I said. The others agreed.

"Five minutes," a technician told us later.

My nerves came back. I wanted to call Ben and ask him for a pep-talk, something positive and upbeat like Mr Williams would do for the team. But my phone was off and he was at the hospital. He'd be too busy with his parents.

A few minutes later, the technician directed us to the side of the stage and we waited as the previous school wrapped up their final song. The curtain closed to the audience's applause, and the choir left the stage.

The technician said, "Lights are dimmed. Watch your step." He said something into his headset mic and we took to the stage.

We got in our rows and Mr Elliot unhooked the button of his suit jacket. He faced us. "Eyes on me, guys," he whispered. "Just forget that anyone else is here."

But we couldn't do that. Somebody was wheeling a harp onto the stage. We'd rehearsed for so long without an orchestra, using piped music from Mr Elliot's computer, complimented by his piano, that listening to the sound of the orchestra during the other performances made me wonder if our voices would be heard.

Some of the instruments were retuning. And then the curtain opened.

Mr Elliot nodded. The orchestra began to play, but the harp on the stage remained unmanned.

Spotlights blinded us. And we sang.

We started with *Carol of the Bells* before breaking into a medley of *Silent Night*, *Mary's Boy Child* and *Joy to the World*.

We were singing all the same songs other choirs had already performed. I was just thankful our arrangements were different. By our fifth carol, my heart was banging its own rhythm against my ribs.

We were coming to the end of the song and my solo was next. I fluffed a line as I worried about it, but because the whole choir was singing, I don't think anyone noticed.

And then I saw a light at the top of the aisle, behind the audience. Somebody had opened the door. They came in, and I would recognise his silhouette anywhere.

Ben Hunter.

He waved.

I wanted to wave back but I was a little busy. We sang our final verse as he took a seat near the back of the auditorium. I saw where he went, so I kept my eyes on him. And I breathed. This was it. My three minutes of fame.

Mr Elliot nodded at me and I stepped forward. I heard Tony whooping from the crowd and somebody laughed.

The lights over the choir dimmed just enough to make them shift into the background, and two new spotlights were lit— one on me and one on the harp. A woman in a long sequined dress came on stage and sat behind the harp. She positioned her arms and looked at me.

Mr Elliot said, "In your own time, Dean. When you're ready."

I nodded. The harpist played her opening notes, and when the orchestra joined in, the choir sang the opening lines.

I stared at the outline of Ben in his seat. And when the choir sang, "*a new and glorious morn*," I took a deep breath and I sang the bridge.

"*Fall on your knees, O hear the angel voices.*" The words came from my diaphragm and I released them into the auditorium. I watched them leave me like orbs of light that drifted over the audience.

When I finished the bridge, I counted the beat and the orchestra faded out, leaving only the harpist. I repeated the bridge. But this time, I sang it in Irish.

Titim ar do ghlúine
Éist le guthanna na n-aingeal
Don oíche úd
Ón oíche ar rugadh Críost
Ó oíche Dhiaga
Ó oíche Dhiaga.

I thought my voice was weak, but Mr Elliot gave me the thumbs up before the choir came to my rescue to sing backing vocals on the next verse.

I want to say I sang loud and proud. Because Ben was there. Because my friends were in row F, and my parents loved me, and my world was peachy. But to be honest, I thought I sounded flat and uninspired. And I know I was shaky as hell. But I hit the notes that I needed to. And I knew it didn't matter how good or bad I was because Ben *was* here. And my friends and parents loved me. And my world was peachy.

For the final verse, the orchestra dropped down to a minimum and the harpist plucked her strings. The choir backed me up by singing in Irish as I continued in English, competing against their words, juxtaposing history with tradition. This was what Mr Elliot meant when he'd said, "Everybody knows the song. But let's show them how the Irish can take anything and make it better."

We closed the song with long, high notes, and as we fell silent, the audience erupted into applause.

The curtains closed. And Mr Elliot came to me. He slapped my back. "That was beautiful," he said.

I didn't believe him. But it was over.

We were pushed off the stage to make room for the next school. In the back room, he said, "See? I told you three minutes wasn't going to last forever."

My cheeks were burning and Gemma Ademola handed me a bottle of water. It was room temperature, but it was the most refreshing drink I'd ever had.

We weren't allowed to leave yet, so I sat on the floor with my back to the wall, drinking lukewarm water, and feeling the fizz of energy draining out of me like I had a leak.

When the final choir left the stage at nine-forty, all the choirs assembled for bows as an invisible announcer called out school names. The curtains closed for the final time and we hugged each other. I said Merry Christmas to everyone and Mr Elliot gave us each a keyring with a musical note on it. We thanked him, said we'd see each other in two weeks, and I think I was the first one off the stage to grab my coat and dash out to the lobby, hoping Ben hadn't left.

The foyer was packed as parents waited for their kids, and Mum and Dad were there with flowers. They hugged me.

"For me?" I asked, indicating the flowers in Mum's hands.

"Your dad bought them for me," she said. "You're a fifteen-year-old boy, what do you want with flowers? Where are Ashley and Tony?"

"I haven't seen them yet. But I'm looking for somebody else."

"Who?"

Somebody tapped my shoulder. I turned. Ben's smile was huge.

I think I managed to say the first letter of his name before he dragged me into a hug, his arms tight around my neck.

"Oh my God, you were awesome."

"Thanks. Why are you here?"

"I came to see you."

"What about your parents?"

"Mum knows where I am. She told me to come." I felt Ben's body stiffen against me. He was staring over my shoulder at my parents. "Oh. Shit."

He released me.

Mum said, "You must be Ben."

He chewed his lip like he wanted to say, "Must I?" or, "I'd rather be anybody else right now."

I stood beside him, facing my parents, the backing singer to his chorus. I said, "Mum, Dad, this is Ben Hunter." Ben leaned into me and whispered a word in my ear. I looked at him. "Really?"

He nodded.

I took his hand. "Mum, Dad, this is Ben Hunter. My boyfriend."

Mum hugged us both. "It's so lovely to meet you, Ben Hunter, Dean's boyfriend."

And Dad said, "Nice to meet you, Ben. I like your shirt. Is that boyfriend material?"

"Dad," I said, and Mum groaned.

But Ben smoothed out his collar and said, "I think it's a blend. Part cotton, part irresistible charm."

Mum laughed. "And comes with a thick layer of dad-joke repellent."

Ben put his arm around me and grinned.

And then Ashley and Tony descended on us like a four-armed octopus trying to hug everything in sight. Including Ben.

I have never been more uncomfortable in my life. But I guess we got the meet-and-greet out of the way in one go. Ashley whispered something to Ben and he nodded, his lips clamped.

Mum said, "Chinese? Ben, you're more than welcome to join us."

"I'd love to," Ben said, "but I have to get back. I have some family things."

"Are you sure?"

"Mum."

"Yes, I'm sure. Thank you. I'm already going to be late."

Dad said, "Do you need a lift?"

Ben checked his phone. "I'll grab the last bus."

"You're not getting a bus. We're parked outside. We'll give you a ride."

"Dad," I said. I knew Ben would be going back to the hospital and I didn't want that to be common knowledge.

Ben said, "We're probably going in opposite directions. It's fine."

"Nonsense. I haven't seen Dean crack a smile in weeks until now. If I let you get a bus, I'd never forgive myself." He pushed Ben's shoulder to turn him towards the door. Outside, Dad said, "Where to?"

"Actually, I'm going to Mercy Hospital. I'm meeting my parents there."

"Say no more," Dad said, and I wondered if he thought Ben's parents were doctors there, or patients. He didn't say. Instead, he said, "It's going to be cramped, though."

Tony said, "Dean's tiny. He can sit on Ben's knee."

Ashley agreed. "He's so small, you could basically put him in your pocket for keeps."

I rode the car with my head pressed against the roof and I felt Ben's body beneath me. His hands gripped my hips as Mum asked him questions about his interests and what he was going to do over Christmas. I felt his thumb slip under my shirt.

Ben's fingers curled tighter into my sides as he said, "I'm hoping to be able to relax for a while. It's been a tough year."

Dad pulled into the hospital car park and I got out with Ben.

We stepped away from the car.

Ben said, "You were so amazing tonight."

"I didn't think you were coming."

"Mum told me to."

"I'm glad."

"Me too."

"What did Ashely say to you back at City Hall?" I'd remembered her face pressed against his ear as she said something.

"Nothing," Ben said. "Just that if I messed you up, she'd mess me up."

"That's Ashley," I laughed. I took his hand. "So, um, boyfriends?"

"Boyfriends," Ben said.

We hugged. And Tony leaned out of the car window and made kissing noises.

I laughed. And Ben kissed me.

It was chaste, in front of my parents and friends. But it was long.

I watched him go into the hospital. He stopped as the doors swished open and he waved at me. I waved back and got in the car.

Dad said, "So, then. Chinese?"

And Tony said, "No, he's Irish."

And we laughed.

CHAPTER 38

BEN

When I got back to Dad's room, he was awake but doped up on pain medication. His voice was a bit spacey. Mum was chewing a thumbnail and her leg bounced with nervous energy. Her eyes were red. I hoped they'd been talking, not arguing.

"Ben," Dad said, stretching the word out like it meant more than it was supposed to.

"You're awake?"

"Barely," Mum said.

I ignored the pain in her voice; it was probably alcohol withdrawal. "How are you?" I asked him.

He looked like he was trying to shrug. And then his face contorted into a hideous wash of tears that I never wanted to see again as long as I lived. "I'm sorry," he said, his words slurred and high-pitched but understandable.

I went to his side and pulled him into a hug. His arms draped across his body, the thick wrist bandages fresh and clean. And I stared over the top of his head at Mum as he sobbed like a child against my chest.

"What have I done?" he cried.

And I made soothing noises the way Mum used to do to

me when I was little. I reached out to her. She watched me as I cradled my father.

Then she took my hand. And she gripped my dad's shoulder.

And when she connected with us, we were whole. A family. Something we hadn't been in a long time.

We stayed there, even though visiting hours were over, until Dad fell asleep. And we got a taxi home. Mum sat at the kitchen table and I made her a cup of strong, milky tea with two sugars. We didn't acknowledge Dad's blood that was splashed across the countertop and the floor.

I took the empty bottles of booze and put them in a cardboard box to take to the public recycling bins tomorrow. Mum pointed to the cupboard under the sink. There was a half-empty bottle of cheap vodka behind the washing-up liquid.

"Do you want to empty it?" I asked, thinking the symbolism might help.

She shook her head. "Don't let me touch it."

I poured it down the sink. I had to trust her that there was no more alcohol in the house.

I sat opposite her at the table while she chain-smoked, and when the clock on the oven blinked 00:14 I said, "Happy Christmas."

She looked at the clock. "It's twenty minutes fast."

"Oh."

She stood up, straightening her shirt, and she patted my hand. "Merry Christmas, Benny. Lock up before going to bed. Good night."

She went to her room and I heard the door close behind her. I hoped she'd still be there in the morning.

I wiped the countertops clean and mopped the floor. There

were shoeprints of blood on the hallway rug. I put the rug in a bin bag. I'd figure out what to do with it tomorrow.

When I crashed into bed, I was going to text Dean to wish him Happy Christmas, but my phone was dead again. I plugged it in to charge and when I put my head on the pillows, sleep gripped my eyelids and dragged me under her spell.

Mum woke me in the morning. She knelt at the side of my bed. She'd showered and dressed, but she didn't look as though she'd slept much.

I sat up.

"Merry Christmas," she said. Her voice was raw. She put a gift on the bed beside me. It was round and wrapped in newspaper with Sellotape patches all over it.

I tore the paper off. It was a basketball—my basketball. The one that had been sitting behind my bedroom door since I played one-on-one with Dean in the snow.

Mum said, "I'll get you a proper gift when I have some money. When your dad's better. What do you want? Anything at all."

I just wanted my family. I said, "Merry Christmas, Mum."

In the living room, the bald, lopsided Christmas tree was lit up like Vegas and I had to admit, it didn't look so bad after all.

Mum attempted to make pancakes for breakfast but when the smoke alarm went off, we opened the back door to let the air circulate, and we had buttered toast instead.

I checked my phone. I had a string of messages from Erin asking about my dad, and there was a text from Dean.

dean_odd_donnell
Merry Christmas, boyfriend.

Boyfriend. Is it weird that that sounds
odd?

benhuntss07
Merry Christmas, boyfriend. And it's
not weird, it's wonderful.

dean_odd_donnell
How's your dad?

benhuntss07
We're going to see him soon. He's OK I
guess. I hope.
And Mum's still sober.

dean_odd_donnell
Awesome news! You should come visit
later. When you're free.

benhuntss07
OK, boyfriend. After 4?

We drove to the hospital. With Mum in her second day of recovery, her driving was slow and considered. She asked me three times if I was wearing my seatbelt.

When we got there, we shared the lift with a fat Santa Claus and two elves. They got off at the children's ward and we went up to Dad's room. His hands were too weak to dress himself and as we went in, an orderly was buttoning up his pyjama shirt.

"How are you?" I asked.

Dad nodded.

The orderly said, "They're serving Christmas dinner in the cafeteria from noon."

When he left, Mum said, "We should go."

"Their turkey will definitely be better than Dad's," I said, trying to break the tension in the room.

Mum scolded me, but Dad laughed. "Too soon," he said. And then his face went back to the unnatural calmness it had when we entered.

He reached out for Mum's hand. She took it.

I helped him into a wheelchair at noon, even though he said he could walk, but he was unsteady on his feet from the pain meds. I pushed him down the corridor, standing on the bracket at the back like a little kid. And we got to the cafeteria ahead of the crowd.

A man in a loose-fitting suit crouched by Dad's chair and asked how he was doing. His voice was soft. He said he'd be along to see him at two.

When he smiled at us and left, I said, "Who was that?"

Dad tried to pick up his fork but his fingers weren't working.

Mum said, "There'll be so many doctors, it must be hard to keep track." She cut Dad's turkey and ham into bite-sized pieces, and she helped to feed him. It could be months before the damage he'd caused to tendons and nerves was repaired enough to allow his hands to function properly.

He held his wrists to his chest, crossed like he was deceased. And in a way, I think he was. We all were. We'd have to suffer through this awkward rebirth and figure out what our new lives would be as we came through the other side of the darkness.

I didn't mention Dad's quiet tears as he ate. But I put my hand on his shoulder and he smiled.

Mum made ridges in her mashed potato with the tines of her fork. She said, "I think I'll go to a meeting. When we're done."

The orange juice was weak and watery. It was a poor

substitute for schnapps.

I helped Dad back into bed in time for his appointment at two, and he pawed at me, unable to take my hand. "I'm sorry," he said.

"Me too," I told him.

Mum went to a meeting and I called Erin while Dad had his appointment. She was having an off day with her parents, she said. "But isn't that what Christmas is all about?"

We'd get together during the week, I told her.

She said, "You're coming to my New Year's Eve party, right?"

"Can I bring someone?"

"Who?"

"Who do you think?"

"You've patched things up with the prodigy, have you?"

"Do you mind?"

"I'll have to vet him. If he's no good for you, I'm going to tell him so."

I laughed. "If he's no good for me, we can set him up with Alex Janey."

"Don't be cruel," she said. "He could be a mass murderer and he still wouldn't deserve to be hooked up with Janey."

When Dad's appointment was over and Mum was back from her meeting, she held a cup of lukewarm tea under Dad's chin while he drank it with a straw, and I said, "I promised Dean I'd go and see him today."

"We should spend some time together," Mum said. "As a family."

"Who?" Dad asked.

"Dean."

Mum put the cup on the nightstand. "His boyfriend."

"Ah," he said. And I think I was hurt by how little he reacted.

When I got to Dean's house, I stood on the wide driveway and saw them through the window. His mum and dad were dancing. Was I the only one with broken parents?

Dean spotted me and waved. He opened the door two seconds later.

"You came."

"Hi."

His smile was huge. He was wearing a Christmas sweater and a pair of enormous fluffy slippers. I laughed. And I stood in his hallway feeling awkward while his parents said hello and asked how I was.

Dean took my hand and pulled me upstairs. When he closed the door, he leapt at me, wrapping his arms around my neck.

I kissed him.

And we fell on the bed together. There was a moment of awkward shifting, like our bodies didn't belong together, but his head settled into the crook of my neck and our arms and legs found their form in a shapeless void. I touched his chin, tilting his head, and I kissed him again. His hand slipped under the fabric of my shirt.

He kissed my chin. My jaw. The hot flesh of my exposed neck.

And I rolled on top of him, grinning. When he looked up at me with a shy smile, I gave him a small peck on the lips. His head lifted off the pillow as I pulled away, following me. His eyes were closed.

"Kiss me," he said.

"When did you get so demanding?" I laughed.

"Kiss me."

"What's in it for me?"

"Kiss me."

"Okay."

I pushed my fingers through his. And he moaned against my mouth. His phone vibrated and he ignored it. He put his hands on my back and pulled me closer, and he tried to push me off him and onto the bed so that he was on top. He didn't succeed so he resorted to tickling me. I collapsed in a red-cheeked mess beside him, laughing so hard it hurt.

"Shush," he said, clamping his hand over my mouth.

When we'd calmed down, I said, "I bet your parents think we're doing it."

"They tried to give me The Talk earlier."

I shuddered. "Gross. Didn't they do that when you were younger?"

"Yeah, but this was a modified version that didn't include— you know—girls."

"Ouch."

He smiled, touched my cheek, and buried his face in my chest. We lay there, holding each other, listening to the silence of his room, and I felt at ease. Life was a defensive basketball play, with everything trying to stop you from scoring a basket. But sometimes you dunked the ball regardless.

I pushed my fingers through his thick hair and said, "I should probably go soon. I don't want to leave Mum alone too long. Just in case."

"Will I see you again before school starts?"

"No, I was going to disappear and never come back."

He slapped my arm and I laughed.

"Of course, you will."

"Tomorrow."

"And the day after."

"And the one after that," he said. I kissed him again.

Downstairs, I said good night to his parents and his mum gave me a hug. His dad offered to drive me, but I said I'd just order a taxi.

"And pay Christmas Day rates? I won't hear of it. It'd be cheaper to fly to New York."

Dean said he'd come for the ride, and while his dad went to get his coat and car keys, Dean hugged me. We stood in the living room and I got my phone out. We posed in front of the Christmas tree as I took a selfie and Dean said, "Let me see."

He looked adorable in it, an arc of reindeer across his sweater.

"Post it," he said.

"Seriously?"

He looked at me and nodded. "If you want."

While we were alone in the living room, I kissed him. And I put the photo online.

I typed a caption and hit the share button just as Dean's dad said, "Everyone ready?"

We got in the car.

The caption said, *Doing it on our own terms now* 🖤.

CHAPTER 39

DEAN

He was waiting for me outside Erin's house, standing there in a light jacket like it was April. He smiled and when he did, I melted. Just a little.

Okay, a lot.

He came down the drive towards me, his hands in his pockets. "All right?"

I nodded. I was afraid that if I opened my mouth, my voice would crack.

Ben pushed his foot forward and tapped the toe of my shoe, a private greeting. Erin's front door was open and a couple of kids were smoking a reefer by the wall. Preppy pop music billowed out from inside. "You ready?"

I looked over his shoulder. I wasn't ready at all. Lying on top of the bed in my room or sitting in Grainger's Coffee Stop, holding hands under the table, was easy. He made it easy, just being with him. But walking into Erin's New Year's Eve party as a couple required a new level of bravery that I wasn't comfortable with.

"It'll be fine," he'd said at the start of the week, his fingers stroking my arm as we spooned on my bed. Mum had made me keep the bedroom door open, but they were downstairs and we'd hear them coming up. They were making a point of talking or stomping on the stairs to let us know they were coming. I think they were more afraid of seeing anything than we were of being caught.

"How will it be fine?" I asked. "All your friends, your teammates."

"Everybody knows now. Nobody's going to say anything."

They'd been saying it all week. He didn't think I saw the negative comments on the photo he posted of us on Christmas night—he did a good job of deleting them when they happened—but I'd spent the week refreshing the comments, smiling every time somebody said something nice (*Aww guys, so cute*), and feeling a horrible weight in my chest when they said something terrible.

"Will Alex Janey be there?" I asked.

"I didn't invite him."

"But he'll know about it and turn up anyway."

"So what if he does?" Ben asked. He kissed the corner of my nose and then pulled my glasses off. When he did that, I knew we were about to get passionate. "He won't say anything. There are too many people behind us for him to even try."

Later, after we'd almost been caught by my mum twice, I put my glasses on and ran my finger in a spiral pattern on his chest. I felt the definition of his muscles even when he wasn't tensed. I said, "I won't know anyone."

"You know me. And Erin. And the guys from school." Then he said, "Invite your friends."

"I'm not sure it's their scene."

"It's just a party."

I nodded. When I mentioned it to them the next day, they said they'd come because it was our first official public appearance. "We're not famous," I said.

Ashley said, "When you walk into the party, we'll take photos like we're paparazzi. People will be so blinded by flashes that they won't see you snogging him in the corner."

I wasn't going to kiss him in front of everyone. That would be too much.

And yet, looking at him as he faced me outside Erin's house with his hands in his pockets and his foot touching mine, kissing him was all I could think about.

"Don't be nervous," he said.

"I'm not nervous."

"Do you want to tell your face?"

I smiled. It came easy because it was for him.

I knew he was nervous too, even though he wouldn't say it. He had more to lose than me. Other than Ben, Ashley and Tony were all I had and all I needed. I never had enough energy in my body for more than a few close friends. But Ben was popular—or he had been. Before.

We hadn't heard from Alex Janey all week, and only half of Ben's teammates had left encouraging comments on our first official photo as a couple. We didn't know what the others thought or how they'd react when they saw us together. Part of me worried that they wouldn't even show up. We'd go through Erin's front door and it'd be just her, Ashley and Tony, sitting beside each other on the couch, strobe lights set up in the corners, flashing on an otherwise empty room.

But I heard the chatter of voices above the music and Ben was looking at me with that hopeful expression he does when he wants to know I'm okay.

I said, "Let's do this."

Ben held out his hand.

Somebody whooped from inside the house and I thought maybe it was aimed at us. But the whooping continued and fell away into the background behind the music.

Ben smiled.

And I took his hand.

When we went through the front door, we were met by a crowd of teenagers in the hallway, paper cups in hand. They said, "S'up?" and, "Yo," and, "Hey, Hunter." And Ben pulled me along behind him, into the kitchen. If they spotted his hand in mine, they didn't mention it.

"Oh, thank God," Ashley said, pulling me into a hug.

Tony said, "We literally just said we'd give you another two minutes and if you didn't show up, we were leaving."

Ben said, "Hey, guys." Then he said, "I'm going to find Erin. You'll be okay?"

I nodded and watched as he walked away.

Ashley hugged me again. "Check out his ass on your own time, this is ours."

I'd met up with them twice during the week, while Ben was at the hospital visiting his dad. They kept him in for four days before releasing him with medication and support from the crisis team.

His mum had locked herself away in her bedroom, he told me. I hadn't been over to his house yet and I wasn't going to press it. They had a lot of shit to work through and I would only get in the way. "She looks like hell," Ben said. "Like somebody took half the stuffing out of her."

She was going to AA meetings twice a day and she'd found a sponsor, which basically meant she could call him up at three in the morning, screaming about the need for a drink, and he'd crack a joke and make her feel better. Pretty much the same thing Ben did for me when I got in a panic about tonight's party.

Ben would text me every morning and report, *Still sober.*

And although it felt like a ritual, I think it was helping him. Every daily message about her sobriety was another twenty-four hours under the belt. He showed me the one-day chip she'd given him. He drilled a hole in it and threaded it on a chain.

"When will you give it back to her?"

He shrugged. "On her birthday. If she makes it that far."

"When's that?"

"June." If she lasted six months, I was certain the worst of it would be over, but Ben said, "She'll always be a drunk. That's what she says. The cravings get you and they throttle you. But she's willing to be a drunk that isn't drunk."

Ashley took my arm and said, "How does it feel to be out in public with your boyfriend?"

I smiled. "Nice."

"Nobody has said anything bad?"

"Nobody's saying anything. Is that weird? I feel like that's weird."

"It's normal," Tony said. "Nobody else has changed, only your perception." He looked around the kitchen full of teenagers and said, "So, this is how modern homo sapiens spend their time, is it? Deep in the wilderness of questionable life choices and dubious fashion trends."

Ashley said, "He means booze and miniskirts."

When Ben came back, Erin was behind him. She looked stunning, wearing a tight red dress and with her hair brushed over one shoulder. "Here she is," Ben said as though we'd all been searching for her.

We said hey.

Ben put his arm over my shoulder and pulled me closer. His cologne clung to him the way I wanted to.

Erin said, "Thanks for coming."

"No sweat," Ashley said.

"Your parents don't mind you having a party?" I asked.

"They're in Dublin for the new year so, you know," she sucked from the straw in her glass, "they're trusting me and all. And if I don't break that trust by throwing an epic New Year's Eve party, how am I ever going to learn those valuable life lessons?"

"She has a point," Ben laughed. I could see why he liked her. When you cut through the superficial gloss, there was a layer of fun underneath.

When the music faded out between songs, I heard a group of guys laughing, and in the middle of it, I recognised Alex Janey's voice. I think Ben felt me tensing beside him because he dropped his arm off my shoulder and took my hand.

And Alex was in the kitchen doorway with his goons. He had a bottle of cider in his hand. "All right, ladies?"

I saw Tony clench his jaw.

Ashley said, "What do you want?"

Janey slapped his mate on his chest. "Hey. What do you call a gay dentist?"

"I'm warning you," Ashley said.

Tony stepped in front of me like a shield. Ben tightened his grip on my hand.

"Give it up, Janey," he said. "We're just trying to have a good time."

"What do you call a gay dentist?" Janey said again.

Ashley took a step towards him and Alex came forward. She said, "Get out of here before I bust your teeth out of your face and shove them up your ass one at a time."

"It's not your party."

Erin stood beside Ashley. "No," she said, "but it is *my* party. And I agree with her. It's time for you to leave."

Alex Janey held his hands up. "We're just having a laugh."

"Some laugh," I said, freaked out by the fact that my voice was working better than I'd expected it to.

"Benny," Alex said. "Come on, man. It was just a joke. You know we're buddies."

"Do I?" Ben said.

"We're all good."

"I don't think so," Ben said. His fingers were getting tighter on my hand. Somebody had turned the music off. "I can't be friends with a homophobic jerk. I think it's time you left."

"Dude."

"Go," Erin said. "Clear off."

He muttered something under his breath as he turned and left. Ben looked at me. "You okay?"

I nodded. "You might have broken my fingers."

"Shit."

I grinned. "I'll survive."

One of the basketball guys slapped Ben on the back. "Good riddance," he said. "No offence, but I kind of want to know what a gay dentist is called."

In the silence that followed, Tony said, "Tooth fairy."

And Ben was the first to laugh.

The music was turned back on and Erin's party got back to being fun. We drank and ate pizza and danced. Ben pulled me close to him as we danced in the living room and I felt his warm hand against my back. "You okay?"

"Stop asking me that."

"But are you?"

I nodded. I actually was.

At eleven-forty, Gemma Ademola came in and said sorry for being late. She hugged Erin and then pulled me and Ben into her arms. She reached for somebody and brought her into view. "This is Tina."

We shook hands.

When they'd walked away, Tony said, "I knew it," and Ashley punched his arm.

Later, Erin switched the music off and put a YouTube live streamer on the TV. We were minutes away from midnight and Ben pushed through the crowd to get to me.

He said, "I'm going to kiss you."

"Now?"

"No. At midnight. I'm just warning you."

"Sure," I said, and a single butterfly stroked the inside of my stomach.

"Is that okay?"

I nodded.

"Ten," Erin shouted, "Nine."

We joined the countdown. And when we got to the end, and the first thump of fireworks outside sent a shockwave through me, Ben put his hands on my shoulders.

"Happy New Year," he said.

He kissed me.

And when we went outside to watch the neighbourhood fireworks, his warm fingers laced with mine, I looked at the remnants of snow in the gutter across the street, and I smiled.

The fireworks were big and pretty. And Ben's eyes were alight with colour.

I touched the rainbow pin on the outside of my jacket.

And I let him put his arm around me. Where it belonged.

Printed in Great Britain
by Amazon

45074687R00233